I0731309

All I Ever Wanted

Jessie

Copyright © 2018 by Athina Paris.

ISBN: Hardcover   978-1-945286-25-4
        Softcover   978-1-945286-52-0
        EBooks   978-1-945286-23-0
                       978-1-945286-24-7

All rights reserved. No part of this book may be reproduced or transmitted in any form or by any means, electronic or mechanical, including photocopying, recording, or by any information storage and retrieval system, without permission in writing from the copyright owner.

This is a work of fiction. Names, characters, places and incidents either are the product of the author's imagination or are used fictitiously, and any resemblance to any actual persons, living or dead, events, or locales is entirely coincidental.
Date 6/26/2020

Published By

RockHill Publishing LLC

PO Box 62241
Virginia Beach, VA 23466-2241
www.rockhillpublishing.com

All I Ever Wanted

Jessie

Athina Paris

To my Son and my Daughter

Who gave me focus,
Love that strengthened me,
And uplifting courage.

XXX   Thank you   XXX

CHAPTER ONE

2002

It was to be a grand celebration in a most impressive mansion, but she couldn't be there. Opening a file, Jessie did the next best thing; flipped through a hidden glossy magazine and gazed at the picture where said festivities were to take place.

Three storeys high, it dominated the eastern part of the estate with a magnificence that was hard to find anywhere else in South Africa. Built in the 1800's when Sir Julius Barrymore had travelled to Africa to oversee his investments, it was a dazzling reminder of a British Empire that had promoted splendour and opulence. In Africa, Sir Julius fell in love with the land, made a fortune in the burgeoning textile industry, found a bride, decided to stay, and adapting quickly to the new world, did away with the title.

Jessie sighed and traced the house's outline with a finger. Ever since she could remember, she had wanted to visit this majestic place, to see the furniture and ornaments, the fabulous treasures she knew existed in every hall and boudoir. She had seen them from time to time in magazines, but that was hardly the same as having them up close, to even touch a few.

Closing the file, she started doodling, and somewhere in the background, she heard the word assignment. She wondered if John had already left.

The occasion was his parents' thirtieth wedding anniversary and if she recalled correctly from her own parents' celebration two years earlier, the gifts were to be pearls. She smiled as she imagined a Sultan bowing before Grace Barrymore with a treasure chest full of jewels; rings, chokers, bracelets, necklaces, earrings…

"Am I boring you, Miss Stevens?"

Jessie returned her attention to the lecturer. "Sorry, sir."

He pointed to the note in front of her. "That's the assignment. Thank you, class."

Grabbing the note and books, she tucked them under one arm, flicked her long black hair away from her face, and stepped outside. "John," she greeted surprised. "I thought you had already left."

"Was still hoping you wanted to tag along."

She rolled her eyes. "Can't imagine a better way for a Barrymore to die than of apoplexy when you said, '*and let me introduce you to Jessica Stevens. Yes, those Stevens.*'"

"We don't have to tell them who you are."

She smacked her forehead. "Ah, yes, good ol' reliable lies. Why didn't I think of that? Lies snowball, and when they catch up—"

"Okay, I admit, this weekend is risky, as there will be tons of people we both know. But another weekend when we're alone shouldn't be a problem."

"You do know that you are courting trouble. And as much as I do want to see it all, no."

Pushing the blond hair out of his blue eyes, he leaned over and kissed her cheek. "See you Monday then. But we'll discuss this visit."

"Whatever." She waved him away.

Gazing over the well-trimmed lawns extending over the hill, a smile spread on her lips. A visit to the Barrymore estate? Her dream, but also pure foolhardiness! Yet, he never stopped asking; as if the past didn't exist, and for them, it was irrelevant.

The story went something like this.

There was a time when Barrymores and Stevenses were close friends, in fact, somehow distantly related. But decades ago, the two families were torn apart and the fallout was still being felt in the present generation. Then, fate traipsed casually in, by making certain two of them went to the same learning institute, followed similar fields of study, and crossed their paths once more. Two things happened simultaneously; first, Jessie moved into college residence. Second, John changed two subjects, and the reshuffling of his schedule landed him in one of her classes.

Both arrived late, and realising all other students were standing in pairs, they stood together at the only available workstation.

"Hi," John whispered loudly, smiled, and asked. "Why are you late?"

"I just moved in and lost track of time, I had to run," she took a deep breath, as if to prove her statement. "You?"

"Was on the phone with my brother. Wants me to babysit his apartment while he travels."

"Nice." She offered a hand. "I'm Jessica Stevens."

Something flicked in his eyes. "John—"

"Are you two taking class today?" The lecturer queried.

Grinning, they said no more.

Over the next few weeks, they went to class, shared a couple of snippets about themselves, and waved when they ran into each other across campus.

One afternoon, while having lunch with another classmate, Jessie became aware of someone standing beside her at one of the local coffee shops. Looking up, she saw him. "John!"

"Hi," he greeted. "May I sit with you?"

"Of course," Jessie placed a hand on the other girl's arm. "This is Meghan."

He nodded. "We share a class. Which I seriously doubt I should be taking, but hey, textiles." He said cryptically then grabbing a chair, sat down, fixed his gaze on Jessie, and began. "I have a confession to make."

She regarded him, whatever he was about to impart was making him nervous. She shifted in the seat, wondering if he were about to make a fool of himself, because although he was cute; blond hair, blue eyes, nice smile, and mega-friendly, she was unsure how to handle a public romantic declaration.

"Do you know who I am?" He continued.

The girls exchanged a glance. Perhaps he was silly, had grandiose delusions, or was an incognito celebrity.

"Obviously not," he said matter-of-fact. "Which is what I wanted anyway, but since I like you guys, I'm introducing myself. John Barrymore."

Meghan choked, started coughing, then said in a strangled voice. "As of… Barrymore Textiles?"

He nodded and turned to Jessie. "I've heard many things about your family, but most sound ridiculous. And now that I have met you, I know I'm right. Tell me you don't care, because I sure don't that your surname is Stevens. And whatever mess is in the past, can we leave it there?"

Jessie, recovering from shock, shrugged. "That's fine by me."

"Huh, people," Meghan interrupted. "Even I know this is crazy. Okay, ignore me, but I hope the two of you know what you're doing, which you don't."

Arriving home, Jessie found it deserted of family members, except for her grandmother, who couldn't leave her apartments because of a mishap at a friend's house earlier in the week.

Samuel, their butler, stood chatting for a few minutes. He always checked on eating schedules, sleeping patterns, if her clothes were being looked after as they should be… Did he expect five-star service at college?

She smiled, it was good to be home and feel pampered, but that was what she liked about residence, everything was crazy and unplanned. Then, excusing herself, she walked briskly across the hall, ran up the marble staircase, sauntered down the long-carpeted passage, took a few turns, stopped outside a door, knocked, and waited for the enter.

"Hello, grandma."

The old lady's eyes brightened instantly as she took a step with the aid of a cane. "Hello, my darling! Did I have to break a foot when you're not home? It's very boring without you."

Jessie hugged her grandma, and plonked herself onto the nearest sofa. "How is everyone?" She loved getting news from here, as Juliet related things in interesting ways.

Parents were fine. Beverley, Jessie's older sister, who was dating Simon Wade—their father's attorney—was thinking weddings, Jeremy had just returned from visiting friends in Cape Town, and Lawrence had been on a tirade

5

towards the Barrymores again. About what, Juliet was not certain.

"Yes," Jessie's gaze dropped onto one of her shoes.

Lawrence had a distinct aversion towards all things Barrymore. But if anyone had reason to dislike them, it was Juliet and Taylor. Yet neither did, both preferring to ignore the rumours that reared their ugly heads with stubborn regularity, which, unsurprisingly, were often begun by Lawrence himself.

"How old is Simon, and are they in love?" Jessie veered the conversation away from the Barrymores, feeling guilty about keeping secrets.

"That you have to find out from your sister. How is interior design school?"

Jessie's eyes lit up as they roamed over the familiar surroundings; her gaze hugging the chinoisserie-influenced four-poster bed in soft sheens, the apricot canopy, pure beige wool carpet, and pale salmon brocade walls. "I'm sure Grandpa's love for beautiful things rubbed off on me. Are you disappointed I'm not studying business? That someone other than Lawrence should be interested in Stevens Textiles?"

"No, to each his own. Though, I feel Jeremy could show a little interest, instead, he drifts. But he's like grandpa, deep, complicated, and young, so we'll give him time. Beverley is a sweet child, and not interested either. Lawrence... Everyone must find themselves. Which brings me to a curious topic, your friend." Juliet changed her tone of voice. "Why have we not met this young man? Because every time I ask where you are it's John and Jessie this, they are going to that, here, there, everywhere together, but no sight of him."

Since that day a year ago, they had become inseparable, hence why she only came home for the monthly family dinners. Taylor was strict about that rule, no matter where anyone was, you let go of whatever was taking your time and came home to your family; to connect and give account. How did she tell them the friend she esteemed so highly was part of the enemy camp?

The astute blue eyes watched her granddaughter keenly. "It's obvious you care deeply for this young man and in the past, you brought people home for whom you cared less. Is there something wrong with him?"

"Nothing a renaming wouldn't cure." Jessie mumbled, then rising, she pretended to study the fine George III satinwood and marquetry demi-lune secretaire commode.

"What is he studying?"

"Textile production and printing."

"That's very nice, but what is wrong with him?" Juliet watched the drooping shoulders then patted the seat beside her. "Come, come tell me the truth about John."

Jessie sat down and admitted. "I have been hiding something and haven't brought him over because I fear the reactions, especially Lawrence's. You see, John's name is Barrymore."

"You mean…"

Jessie nodded. "Theodore's son,"

"But…"

"What happened, grandma? People talk but not always things that make sense, so all I know is that you almost married William Barrymore and our families cannot stand each other. I know it wasn't just the breaking of your engagement that caused this rift, but no one explains. John knows more than I do, but refuses to tell me. Says our friendship has nothing to do with the past. But that's not how everyone else sees it, is it?"

"Incredible, and this takes me back." Juliet's eyes shone brightly. "I knew Theodore's parents well. William was such a dashing man," she smiled then became serious again. "And Margaret was as beautiful as she was odd. I'm guessing the Barrymores don't know about you."

Jessie shook her head.

"Under the circumstances, is it wise to continue this friendship?" Juliet reached for the young hands. "How I would hate for them to break your heart."

"Neither of us set out to make this happen, it just did. And we have a rule, no gossip about the other's family."

"Then he took nothing after his grandmother, who had a vicious tongue…" Juliet stopped, as if realising she had broken a convention. "Of course, Barrymores is so much bigger than us. Which one is John?"

"Like me, the youngest. There is James, Mathew, Mark, and John. Why won't you tell me, grandma?"

"John is right. It's where it belongs, buried in the past."

"Funny, because Lawrence does a really good job of raking up the bones often enough."

Over dinner, Jessie studied her father. Every time she saw him, he appeared to have greyed a little more, no longer showing the blackness of hair both he and she had inherited from David, his father.

Taylor Stevens was fifty-seven and Jessie always felt immense pride when walking beside him. Not only was he a handsome man, but there was no one she knew who was as honest or kind.

She heard her eldest brother addressing her. "Sorry, Lawrence, what did you say?"

"I asked what you want to do for your twenty-first."

Lawrence had an avid appetite for things she often considered more suitable to Jeremy's age. Although, lately, he seemed to have lost some of his wild ways of former years. She still remembered her parents sitting up nights because of his comings and goings. She had been a little girl as there were ten years between them but she had known her brother was doing things that had their parents in nervous knots. He was a fine one to point fingers, which he constantly did at Jeremy, for whatever reason. Almost thirty-one, he was good-looking, taking after their mother, but rather conceitedly, he never let anyone forget how very *lucky* he was.

They enmeshed themselves in a discussion about birthday parties. Lawrence's opinion was that since she was a kid, she should enjoy a mad affair at NiteLite, one of the popular clubs in Johannesburg. Talk about a brother not knowing his sister. How was he not aware that she was no dancing queen, who would rather go sailing than to a disco.

Beverley was their grandmother's young version; blonde, kind, and brainy. But most, and that was particularly true of Lawrence, referred to her intelligence as *useless information*. It was far from the truth, Beverley had a deep love for the written word and Jessie always thought that she would have made an excellent teacher. But the six-years between them had placed them in different schools throughout their younger years, and prevented them from being closer.

That evening, Beverley suggested booking the date and inviting as many people as she could, but especially guys,

9

because, why didn't she have other male friends apart from John? And why hadn't they met him yet?

Jessie shrugged; even she was confused about the relationship at times.

Simon Wade. Just short of forty, he was handsome in an unobtrusive way, a mature charm she found pleasing and comforting, reminding her of his late father, whom she had always called Grandpa Milton, who had been David's attorney, so business stayed in the family as Simon became Taylor's.

Only three years apart, she and Jeremy had always been play mates, but in recent years he appeared to have become withdrawn and sad. She tried to get him to talk, not in a prying way, just so he knew she loved him and wanted him to be happy, because lately, that was the one thing he was not. Gazing at him, she knew that with his surfer-boy looks, he was the most beautiful of all Stevenses.

Returning from the dam, John gazed at the house's sprawling grey splendour, the imposing four-wing two-hundred-room mansion filling him with pride at what his family had accomplished. In today's modern world, it was overly pretentious, but he loved it nonetheless, even if sometimes feeling guilty that they had so much when so many had so little. Weaving his way through the precisely manicured gardens, he went to sit on the low wall outside the conservatory.

His eyes roamed over the sweeping lines and he knew Jessie would love closer scrutiny, no doubt going crazy over boss, finials, dentil trims, and pediments, not to mention the furniture. He smiled.

"And what is that wonderful smile for?"

"Hello, Aunt Monica. How was Paris?" He asked casually as she had just returned from a three-month trip, which she made at least twice a year to keep her apartment in the city aerated, as she put it.

"Fabulous and I miss it already. But the heavy snows were getting to me." She sat beside him. "What are you dreaming about?"

He laughed and pointed towards the house. "Just thinking about a friend and how she would love exploring this. She's doing interior design and knows every blessed architectural bit by name."

"Aunt Monica!"

She regarded the new arrival. "Hello, Mathew, you look good. How is Vanessa?"

"Hopefully, well."

"Hopefully," her brows went up on the well-made face. "Where is she?"

"Somewhere at the Skeleton Coast."

Her lips pursed disapprovingly. "Are you aware how very dangerous that desert is? Is she? People have been known to disappear, just like that," she made a hand gesture. "Without a trace. Why don't you demand she quit that silly TV job and marry her?"

"That's a rather chauvinistic point of view. But I would be satisfied with less travelling from her side, as I do enough myself."

John grinned. "I can vouch for that."

"Is she at least prepared to take time off for a wedding, and children? Don't furrow your brow, some women don't like them. And I do mean the children."

"I never asked but I'm sure Vanessa has no such hang-up. Now, can we stop discussing my private life? How is college, John?"

"Good."

"He was telling me about his girlfriend." Monica announced.

Mathew laughed and patted his brother's shoulder sympathetically. "Another love life; what's her name?"

"Huh…" he wondered what they would say if they knew, then decided not to test it, in no mood to explain the association. And the fact that Stevens Textiles was a regular topic of discussion and derision at the dinner table was not going to improve the odds in Jessie's favour, especially where Monica was concerned. She loved rumours and threats of scandals that could potentially obliterate them. He was not about to offer unnecessary ammunition.

"See? Dreaming again. An interior designer, and by the sounds of it, excellent. So, who is she?"

"Jessie Lewis."

"Then she would love this, there must be enough furniture to fill fifty houses." Mathew pointed towards the door. "Ask her over one weekend."

"And how do I convince her?" John recalled how petrified she looked the first time he suggested it.

"Tell her how much money we have and she will come running." Sarcasm laced Monica's words. "Other people's wealth gives some individuals whimsical ideas."

John burst into laughter, got to his feet, and went into the house.

He smiled as he looked down the dinner table and wondered what Jessie would make of his relatives; undoubtedly complain the moment she was expected to put on a dress and heels, as she was a jeans-and-running-shoes kind of girl.

"An odd bunch," Mathew said beside him and pointed left. "Though, I like those."

"Isn't it funny? Not a single Barrymore or Lennox among them, just mom's relatives." John pulled at his bow tie. "Is all this fancy dress really necessary?"

"I don't know about father, but Aunt Monica wouldn't have it any other way."

"Yeah, I know, she does relish in formal torture."

Mathew laughed. "Where did you learn that turn of phrase? But I admit, it's funny and better than that garbled mess Mark uses. God, what is it? It's not even any American accent I've ever heard."

"Ain't it?" John got to his feet. "I'm skipping the dance. Coming?"

A soft blue haze bathed the gardens where an array of trees cast picturesque shadows on walls, and a shrub nearby filled the air with a pungent fragrance.

Stopping next to the jasmine, John touched it lightly. "So sweet, it reminds me of Jessie."

"Which is more than I can say for that stench," Mathew waved an arm to dispel the smoke that drifted in the air. "What the hell is it?" Walking around the bush, he saw Mark leaning against the wall.

"Cigarette," Mark offered.

Mathew made a face. "Ugh."

"I'm glad you came outside to smoke it, mom will kill you if she picks this up on her drapes." John coughed. "What is it?"

13

"A special blend." Mark squashed the butt under his shoe.

"Have you finally decided what you'll do after graduating?" Mathew asked.

"Yeah," Mark said in the odd American drawl he had acquired during the four years he had been at NYU. "I started something part-time and make a fortune. Ever considered deliveries?"

"What kind?" Mathew queried.

"All sorts. People want things taken in a hundred different directions and there I am, offering top-notch service." Seeing his older brother's brows rise, he added quickly. "Don't worry, I'm not neglecting my studies."

"And Barrymores?"

"What am I supposed to do there? There's James, you, and next year, John as well. But I haven't ruled it out either."

"Father won't like it if you do."

"And I wonder about his wisdom of wanting four brothers working together." John commented.

"Know what I miss in America?" Mark said, "good Van jokes. Got any new ones?"

"Why does everyone think I have an aptitude for comedy? Even Jessie laughs at stuff I don't find funny."

"Ah, the famous girlfriend," James said as he joined them.

"Huh…" John was about to correct him then changed his mind. He had brought many an odd acquaintance through the front door during his high school years, and caused no ripples, but a Stevens friend was bound to cause a stir. He wanted to bring her here, so she could satisfy her curiosity, without any family member throwing whatever garbage in her face, which was particularly true of Aunt Monica, who would have no qualms doing so, along with having her removed. It was possible his father would do likewise but Grace would not care one way or the other, as she rarely partook in the scandalmongering that dominated dinners. "I see this turning into a grovelling exercise."

Mark placed a hand on his arm. "The trick to women is having them under control. Even James doesn't know how to go about it and that's why he can't keep a girlfriend. Women need fear and sex to stay in line. If you want this girl, put your foot down."

"Where, her neck?" Mathew asked sarcastically. "You do realise that weed you're smoking is turning your brain into porridge, right?"

"If that's how you treat the poor souls who cross your path, I feel sorry for them." John added.

Mark had a philosophy concerning relationships. Marriage was a business arrangement and passion entertainment. Women were not meant to work, more so if they were wives. His brothers stared at him as if he were a stranger and wondered where he had learnt such nonsense.

After furrowing his brow a few times, James turned to Mathew. "What's your opinion?"

Mathew looked blank. "Don't have one right now, this conversation dropped a level beneath me. Goodnight, guys."

"What do you think, little brother?" Mark asked.

"That you are hopeless and somewhat confused." John told him and he too left.

Mark glanced at James. "It seems the boys and the men have finally been separated."

"Admit it, Mark, you're just pulling our leg."

CHAPTER TWO

"Tell me again what I was on when I agreed to this?" Jessie asked as they neared the estate.

"Pizza. And, they think we'll soon be hitched."

"Nice," sarcasm laced the word. "I can't imagine who planted the seed and then fuelled the idea. Is it too late for me to wonder about insanity in your family?"

"There is the question of Grandma Margaret, who was known for bizarre behaviour, but that's another tale altogether. Just a hug here, a kiss there, one of those looks…"

"I'll give you a look all right. I'm not implying they're incapable of acceptance, but how did you explain my visit?"

"I told them your name is Lewis."

"What?" Horror spread on her face. "You got me here under false pretences! How am I going to avoid awkward questions now?"

"You worry too much."

"Hah!" She tried to calm the uneasiness that crept over her. "You know perfectly well people such as our parents always ask questions, lots of them. They want to know everything—including blood groups."

John roared with laughter.

"When the charade blows in our faces, and it will, I'll hold you personally responsible. Now, I also know I'm going to regret it dearly but for some reason I can't demand you take me back." She flashed her eyes angrily at him. "Let's see, James: twenty-eight, dark blond, brown eyes. Mathew: twenty-five, brown hair and eyes. Mark: twenty-three, dark blond, I don't recall the eyes. John, the maddest twenty-one-year-old I know."

He pointed to the tall iron gates in the distance.

"Oh, gosh, it's so much grander up close." She placed a hand on her chest. "I think I'm developing a heart condition."

"You'll be fine. You know, people have come, pretended to rearrange the furniture, didn't bother throwing anything out, and left it as crammed as ever. I wish mom would ask you to do something about it. But it's a waste of time, father won't let her. Or more correctly, Aunt Monica would have a conniption."

"And I'm hardly qualified to give advice on a house this size." It was old, grey, and magnificent, all four wings of it. The view instantly transporting her to an unforgettable summer she had spent in England with her family when she was fourteen. "When they ask, what shall I say my father does?"

"Make something up."

"And that's exactly when they'll ask questions I can't answer. Can't you see what we're doing?"

"Yes, having an adventure." Stopping the car, he turned to her. "Obviously, we can't tell them who you are because then they'd be suspicious of everything you did and I'd have to fight everyone, ruining a perfectly good weekend. To save ourselves unnecessary grief, we'll be slightly deceitful, and you get to tour the museum." He smiled encouragingly.

"It's just…"

The lies started at the front door when John introduced her to the butler, Mr Adams. She felt terrible, hoping she could be truthful, but imagining how her family might receive him one day, she bit her tongue and followed his example.

The interior was everything she imagined, and more, precious pieces on every surface and she felt almost dizzy as she tried to catalogue eras and centuries mentally.

She saw Grace Barrymore, the short blonde bob a perfect frame for the still beautiful face, who although looking younger, Jessie knew that like her own mother, was fifty-five. The curious and interested gaze regarded her firmly, making her feel shy. Not much flew past that powerful blue scrutiny.

"Mom, my best friend,"

"Hello, Jessie," Grace smiled warmly, extended a hand, and eyed the young woman with interest, liking the demure look of her. "Welcome to our home."

"So, this is she." Monica said from a wingback and an intense appraisal followed. The girl was casually dressed in a pair of jeans and silk blouse, and her expert eye told her those were designer labels. She also had a pair of Nine West shoes on, a matching belt, and a pretty decent handbag. None of the items were new, so she had not rushed off to buy them to impress. Good, she might have some means and taste.

Tea was served in the Louis XIV salon and Jessie struggled to keep her gaze on the two older women, simply wanting to look at and absorb everything. It was a gorgeous room; polychrome commodes, bureaux, gilded chairs, mirrors… No, she could barely focus on Grace Barrymore, who was enchanting, entertaining, and an absolute gem as a hostess and enjoying the company of another woman who was not Monica.

Now there was an extremely critical individual. If something wasn't to her liking, it was wrong, and this applied to every avenue, be it yard paving or the way one turned a collar. From the little Jessie had gleaned and John harped on, Monica sounded exactly like Margaret, who had been another strange character.

Naturally, it was Monica who asked what her father did. She was silent for a second and then told her that he was in plastics. Which was not a lie; Taylor had recently acquired Amalgamated Plastics in Durban.

Mark trudged in, draped himself over a velvet sofa, started on some interior decor conversation, and asked if she would be willing to do his penthouse in New York.

No one had to tell her interior design had not yet entered his mind; the blue eyes were hard to read and yet, it was all so easy to understand. Those designs were not what she wanted to inspire.

He beckoned to James, who appeared in the doorway, and told him to come have an audience.

She took a deep breath, trying to ignore the annoyance she felt.

James was quiet and polite, but after a few minutes, excused himself and disappeared.

"Mom, is tonight very formal?" John asked.

"It's such lovely weather that I asked for the summer dining-room. Something light will do, and the gentlemen don't have to wear ties."

The look of disapproval on Monica's face was instantaneous.

John saw it too. "Aunt Monica, if you're not careful, traditions and rituals will take you to the grave. But I appreciate the gesture, mom. Come, Jessie," he took her hand.

They walked through salons, chambres, salles, and corridors, stopping often to touch and study. Jessie wondered who, in prior generations, had been so taken with French décor, although, some rooms were the epitome of 40's and art deco. They reached a passage where 19th century animal paintings adorned the panelled walls and she was delighted to recognise the artist's name. When they reached the end, her hand ran over a wrought iron balustrade then stopping on the landing, her fingers slid up a marble column. "It's exquisite."

"Thought you'd like it, and I'll show you more after dinner and tomorrow morning." Pausing outside a beautifully polished door, he told her. "From today this is your room."

She made an incongruous sound. "Ah, the youthful dreamer. Please come in and show me what your mother meant by light."

"After I introduce you to Mathew,"

Their colouring was different, but Mathew was John's taller, mature, and more handsome version.

"Hello, Jessie." He neither smiled nor offered a hand.

She did likewise. "Mathew."

"When did you get here?" Mathew asked John.

"In time for tea."

Mathew's brows rose. "Are you ill?"

Jessie suppressed a giggle. It was common knowledge at college that he would rather die than touch the liquid.

John laughed. "I had to keep her company as Aunt Monica grilled and Mark gawked. You know how intimidating the Barrymores are."

"Absolute ogres," Mathew agreed then turned to her. "But don't let any of them frighten you. And I apologise, but I have to make a call." He smiled, raised a hand, and continued down the passage.

As soon as they entered the room, John threw himself onto the four-poster bed, and fixed his gaze on the sunburst roof. "I've always liked this room, and it suits you. What do you think?"

She glanced around the well-proportioned room, velvet sofas, delicate silk bedspread, Adam open armchairs, and exquisite ornaments. "Straight out of a fairy-tale."

He patted the place beside him and stretched out his arm in invitation.

As her head dropped on it, she queried. "What are we doing?"

"This," turning his head, he kissed her.

All the ingredients were present for a perfect romantic interlude; gorgeous setting, handsome boy, beautiful girl, and he did everything right, his mouth sweet and gentle. Jessie snapped an eye open and looked at him, he was as much in this as she was.

Over the past year, she had vacillated between wanting and not wanting at all, and at times imagined he might be in the same boat. Now, it felt forced, contrived, put on, and uncomfortable. Something was wrong between them but right now, she didn't care. In fact, a wave of relief flooded her and before he did anything else that was even more stupid than that kiss, she caressed his face, smiled, and sat up.

"I do love you but also knew it would be like this."

"Some things aren't meant to be, and lovers is not for us."

"You didn't feel anything either?" He asked between concern and relief.

"It was like kissing one of my brothers and we never have to do it again." Squeezing his arm reassuringly, she got off the bed, opened the small suitcase, unpacked the few items she had brought, and held up two dresses. "Which is it?"

John was good at putting outfits together, as he excelled in textile studies and pointed to what she should wear. Then after a few minutes, he announced. "I'm bushed, going to rest. You should do the same before dinner, which is at seven-thirty. Promptly."

This was not how she envisioned the weekend unfolding and she lay on the bed ruminating. The occasional fostering of romantic notions came and went, as he never showed actual interest in that avenue. So today, it wasn't just the surprise that he finally tried but that she had her concrete answer, numb disinterest. Turning a few times, she watched the lace curtains float gently in the afternoon breeze, a soft laziness enveloping her as her lids drooped slowly.

Being the only young woman at a dinner table had its advantages and she smiled with amusement as four bachelors vied for her attention, though, each had a different approach. James was careful with his compliments, seeming to take more pleasure in watching and listening. Mathew wasn't outrageous or extravagant. Mark had a way of giving double meanings to everything, which she found disturbing, and John was plain ridiculous.

After dinner, Mark annoyed her again when he asked if she could estimate a vase's worth. She had quickly realised there were pieces of dubious origins scattered among the treasures, a crazy practice from Margaret's days as lady of the house. It was as if he imagined she had come with a cash-register and put price tags on everything already. She was in no mood for his nonsense.

"Why does he do it?" She queried when John led her down a garden path.

"Because he thinks you're after my money. I may only be fourth in line but my inheritance is sizeable."

"Ah, of course," she made an odd gesture. "So is mine."

"But he doesn't know that. And who's ever heard of a rich Plastics Baron?" He teased. "It's usually Aunt Monica's job to scrutinise everyone with a magnifying glass, but he sure gives her a run for her money lately. I say it's grandma's fault; he was her favourite and she taught him weird stuff. But cheer up, he'll be gone on Monday so who cares what he thinks. How about a swim?"

She looked at the beautiful swimming pool area on the side of the house, white marble statues standing guard next to a fountain. "I have no wish to prance around half naked."

"Not here, we also have an indoor pool you haven't seen. And for your peace of mind, Mark is not into water sports anymore." Walking down the side of the house, he pushed open two wooden doors. "What do you think?"

"Not what I expected." She stared at the pool filling most of the room.

"It used to be a courtyard, but when grandma moved to the south wing after grandpa died, she requested all passages, doors, rooms, and windows be sealed off. We were all at school and in various swimming teams and mom hated watching us turn blue in winter, so father had it built, with only that door leading into the house." He pointed. "And just so you know, no one goes into the south wing, it's creepy there. Therefore, I won't be showing you that."

The freedom they felt in each other's presence turned them into children as they laughed and raced each other, and knowing they were making a racket, neither was surprised when Mathew peered in.

"Come join us." John beckoned.

"I don't want to intrude."

"Pfft. Besides, I haven't raced you in years." John grinned, which meant he had complete confidence in his own abilities.

Mathew drew closer and gave his brother a lopsided smile. "If I win, what's my reward?"

John scratched his head. "What do you want?"

"What did medieval heroes get?" Mathew asked curiously.

"I think they got a handkerchief. Or a kiss from the princess, or some such silliness."

Jessie blushed as two pairs of male eyes turned to her. She made a gesture, implying she didn't know anything.

"You'll be sorry." Mathew warned.

Sitting on the edge to watch, Jessie was engulfed in a blur. John wouldn't give up and kept losing, Mathew laughed and kept winning, and she reached a state of confused stupor. Not only her cheek and lips were smacked, but also a calf and thigh landed under his mouth.

"How am I doing?" John gasped.

She told him. "Not at all, shame on you."

"Is that so?" Reaching her, he pulled her into the water. "Let's see you do better."

She spluttered. "Wait until I get my hands on you. And it's unfair competition. Look at him, he's taller, stronger, broader, will be there long before me."

"Okay, two second head-start." Mathew conceded.

John laughed. "No way, she's trying to sucker you in. Ready…"

Mathew discovered how right his brother was, Jessie swam like a fish and was just as fast. "Now I know what you were doing," he wheezed. "You put me out of commission and then she finishes me off. Clever."

Jessie climbed out of the pool and wrapped herself in a towel. "Thanks for the workout, guys; I'm going to change."

"Thoughts?" John queried.

"Interesting," Mathew managed out of breath.

They spent the first half of next morning exploring one of the wings then went down to the dam with a picnic basket.

Jessie stared at the cute boat with the canvas sail and wondered if they were going to need a rescue. John waved her worries away, informing her that it could take four large adults. Regardless, she asked for a lifejacket, fearful of drowning in the overabundant mud. Now and then, their laughter travelled to the house.

From a balcony, Theodore looked towards the water. "This young Jessie," he said as Grace joined him. "What do you make of her?"

"I like her very much."

"She looks all right, but he's not the one I expected to bring someone home."

"Are you still on James' case? What does it matter if he's dating or not?"

"Gracie," he made a face, as if it was all self-explanatory.

"Oh yes, I forget. Barrymores chucked the title but still behave like aristocracy. Give the boy time to find someone to fall in love with."

"He'll be thirty soon, surely a woman has caught his eye by now. And the line must continue—"

"You are not doing this." She raised her voice slightly. "Don't impose expectations simply because of bloodlines. And Mathew is dating."

"I don't mind Vanessa. But did she have to be embroiled in the media? I am not a fan."

"I know what you're really complaining about."

"What's that?" He asked curiously.

"It's not the media, John's girl, James not dating, or marrying and having babies; you hate anything out of your control. Real life is not like that, Theo."

During lunch, Mark studied Jessie, as if she were an oddity. And to him, she was.

"Who's doing what tonight? I'm going to Shelley Barrell's get-together and everyone is welcome to tag along." James invited. "But I swear she is only interested in me because of Mathew."

"We're clubbing." John said quickly. He had registered Jessie's consternation at the mention of Shelley's name. Their grandmothers were friends and the last thing either needed was an unplanned reveal party.

"Mark?" James nudged him.

"Thanks, but I don't like your boring friends. I'm with John. You, Mathew?"

"I on the other hand, and due to my two left feet, will take a chance on James' boring friends." Mathew announced then turned to Jessie. "We have a basement brimming with objects I'd like to choose from for my place. Would you mind giving me a hand this afternoon? That is if John can be parted from you."

John made a face. "We are not attached at the hip. And although I was planning to show it to her sometime, it's not my favourite place, makes me claustrophobic. You can do the honours."

"Jessie?" Mathew pressed.

"I have heard so much about this fabulous dungeon, I would love to."

"I'll be outside your room at three; I expect you need rest after all that rowing."

For the second time, she couldn't fall asleep. Yesterday, John, today, Mathew… He fascinated her like none of the others and she wondered if it was because he looked like John.

As the doors opened, she thought the place looked like a lonely junkyard, a burial ground, where nothing was dead, and screaming to be let out. Pulling cloth after cloth, she uncovered treasure after treasure, her hands reaching out in recognition, as if they were old friends. "Oh, my goodness, some of these are worth more than an entire room upstairs, and I'm definitely underestimating."

"Some of this has never been upstairs. All Barrymores, but especially grandma, bought, collected, and dumped it in here."

"No wonder people and museums come here to borrow for exhibitions." She inspected a credenza and dresser in a corner with interest. "Wonderful Bressan."

27

"I'm puzzled," he watched her. "John has never told anyone who he is. Why you, or is it obvious?"

Familiarity surrounded him, and she put it down to him sharing his brother's looks. And just like John, he had intelligent eyes and a mouth that crinkled easily, displaying a carefree disposition. But while he was always well groomed, his hair appeared to be in perpetual disarray from his hands going through it so often.

"There is nothing obvious about us."

"How long have you known each other?"

"A year." She pulled a Chinese vase from a box. "This should be upstairs in place of that fake in the dining room. If I'm not mistaken it's from the K'ang Hsi period."

"Why haven't you come before?"

"Intense scrutiny is not my comfort zone."

"What made you change your mind now?"

"His pathetic begging, and the fact that I've been dying to see some of these pieces. But he basically blackmailed me."

He studied her for a silent moment. "Opinion,"

She told him seriously. "I shouldn't have come."

"We're not weird, are we?"

There was a lot to be said about that and she had heard enough to fill a couple of tomes. But like John, she had decided to let go. "I've only been here a day, so I don't know."

Mathew pointed to the vase in her hand and then to a table. "Put it aside."

She uncovered a painting and was sorry to see the masterpiece locked up, as mildew and rising damp were already taking their toll, and it would be an absolute nightmare to restore. The sofas and chairs weren't better off;

some of the fabrics had already faded beyond repair. An inspection of wooden legs followed and she made a face. They would have to burn a few because of termites.

James stuck his head in the door. "May I also get free décor advice?"

Jessie laughed. "Are you also looking for something special?"

"Which I would take where? I live here."

She nodded. "Of course."

James walked in and sat on one of the velvet sofas. "Carry on, I'll just listen."

It was near five o'clock when all three emerged. Patting their clothes, they made dust fly.

"Thank you, Jessie, that was informative." James told her and waved. "See you later."

"Wait," Mathew took her plait in his hands. "You're full of cobwebs."

Standing primly, she tried to ignore the intoxicating consciousness his proximity brought.

"Did anyone ever tell you that you have amazing hair?"

"I don't know about amazing but I am the only one who got it from my father. His is greying now so I stick out like a broken thumb amongst the blondes."

"I like it."

"Thanks." She took a step away. "I should go wash."

"Clubbing, huh?" He locked the door behind them. "An early night is what you need, you look beat."

"Can't, John wants dancing."

"Thanks for the afternoon, and I should pay you because you gave me excellent advice."

"Nah," she waved the idea away. "I'm just sorry for all the pieces going to waste."

"Mom has no problem ridding herself of clutter, but father won't let her touch anything."

When Monica saw them, she wanted to know what the verdict was because she liked her mother's stuff. Teasingly, Mathew told her that rats had made nests in half and fungi eaten the rest. Shock spread on Monica's face and Jessie realised Mathew had no patience for Barrymore junk, because although there was much to be appreciated, a lot of it was just that.

The evening did not begin smoothly. On their way down the stairway, Jessie almost rolled down the steps when lo and behold there stood Simon in the entrance hall.

"Oh my…" she exclaimed and grabbed her head. "What is he doing here?"

"Who is it?" John asked as he went down to help her.

"Simon. My sister's boyfriend."

"Why on earth would he be here?"

"Huh… I have no clue."

"Crap, he noticed me." John mumbled. "Okay, I'll go greet him and that should give you time to crawl out of here. Wait for me, we'll go down another way."

"Good evening, Mr Wade," Theodore greeted as he walked across then caught sight of John. "That's my youngest on the stairs, going somewhere no doubt."

And from bad it went straight to worse. Mark was hunting for clues in his bizarrely indirect way and she spent most of the time avoiding him. Couldn't they just ditch the weirdo? But inevitably, the dreaded moment he was obviously counting on arrived when she sat down to give her feet a rest. He began by complimenting her looks, telling her that she had a certain elegance that was rare in so many modern women.

She lifted a brow, wondering if he imagined her a fool.

"What is it you are really after?" He asked pointedly.

"Finally, or did you think I'd fall for flattery? I know you're wary of me, but since you've already decided it's money I'm after, I don't know why bother with this inquisition." She raised the juice glass to her lips.

Mark glanced at it and then her. "The puzzle is this; two personas are jumping at me and I'm confused. That's a problem because I'm never that where women are concerned. While I find you fascinating, I still want to know what you expect from my little brother."

"You seem to be an authority, why don't you enlighten me?"

"If I weren't leaving Monday I would soon know what your game is, because sometimes, I would swear there is an angelic innocence about you. Know what I find especially questionable? That you carry no identification."

Her eyes widened in shock. But as much as she was raging over his objectionable behaviour, she was also grateful for her last-minute decision, when she tossed her purse, along with her ID book, and driver's licence, into the bedside table drawer at College. "How dare you go through my personal belongings? I find it a repugnant violation, but clearly, I'm wasting my breath demanding an apology."

John joined them. "Getting to know each other?"

"Definitely," Mark said mockingly.

Jessie glared, hoping the disco ball above their table snapped from its chain.

"Don't you want to dance?" John continued, oblivious to the less than friendly looks.

"I'm tired." Jessie complained.

"Oh, I don't know, I think you're just getting started." Mark remarked in his cryptic talk.

He was now treading on dangerous ground. "I need to freshen up." Rising quickly, she disappeared towards the ladies' room.

"Why must there always be a bully?" She thought as she returned to the throng.

"Let's not disappoint John." Mark announced, pulled her onto the dance floor, and crushed her against his chest. "What's the matter, dear," he sneered. "Too close for comfort? And here I imagined you taking all the Barrymore boys on. Think I haven't been paying attention to your incessant flirting?"

She almost laughed, but once believed there was no one who could change a firmly held wrong notion. And where did he know her from, that he felt compelled to dictate? "You're hurting me."

"That's not all I want to do. But this is a warning, Jessie Lewis with the bewitching blue eyes," he looked straight into and through them. "Mess with my brother and you will be sorry." He leaned towards her.

Whether he meant to kiss her or not was not the issue. Her concern was over his assumption that he was free to do as he pleased, and why, because he was a man, her friend's brother, or a Barrymore? Swiftly lifting one knee, she landed a strategic kick to the groin, forcing him to let her go and double over. Unhurriedly, she went to join John.

"There you are, where's Mark?"

"Having the time of his life. May we go home now? He said not to wait."

This time, she did not like it one bit that she was having trouble with her thoughts. It was only fair a woman defended herself, because he had meant to hurt and humiliate her. Tomorrow was Sunday, was James about to do something that would keep her awake as well? No, he was quiet, respectful, and paid her just enough attention. How could four brothers be this different? Knowing sleep was impossible, she slipped into her shoes again and went in search of the kitchen.

The house was in almost complete silence but not darkness, appearing ghostly with all its riches in the soft lights of night, some waiting with outstretched arms. She got lost.

Peering out of a window, she noticed the lightning bolts a distance away. It would not be long before thunder clapped and rain inundated the estate. Trying to retrace her steps, she wandered through a hall and two salons before reaching one of the farthest rooms. She studied a German Meissen lidded vase; carefully turning it over, read AR, and returned it to its pedestal.

"Wondering if it's real?" Mark's voice pierced the silence, just ahead of the storm.

She jumped visibly. "What do you want?"

"No woman walks all over me."

"Then stop walking over them first."

He grabbed her wrists.

"I'm not impressed with your bullying." She tried to pull away but found herself in a vice. "You are giving me bruises."

"That's not all I want to give you." Pushing her against the wall, he held her prisoner with his body, bent his head, and his mouth slid towards her lips.

Jerking her head sideways, she tried to kick, but this time, he was expecting the offending knee. Instead, he hooked one leg around hers, knocking them both to the floor.

"I have no time for tarts and today you will know your place, on your back."

Her brain went into emergency mode. "Mark, be reasonable,"

"I thought this might be your style; tease and leave."

Suspicion turned to fear and that she knew usually put one at a disadvantage. She closed her eyes, hoping this was a nightmare, but his body's weight told her that no amount of dreaming would get her out of this predicament if she weren't smart enough. "I apologise," she began tentatively. Perhaps if she humbled herself and stroked his ego, she would divert his attention. "It was unkind of me. Let's start over,"

"The only thing I want to start is this." He placed his hands on her chest.

Whatever he did, she could not let him see she was terrified. "You're… good-looking, you hardly need force." A quick look around told her there was nothing nearby that she could use as a weapon.

"Some women know only one language, physical domination." As if this was the most natural situation in the world, he reached for the belt around her waist.

She tried to scratch and punch, her eyes burning wild and bright as she felt his hands slip along her body. "Stop!" Her voice rose sharply and she hoped someone, anyone, heard her.

"The thing about rain, it drowns out most sounds." He went on. "But be sure to tell John, and do call it rape. The police station is about three kilometres from here. Just turn left at the gates."

Her mind raced. *"Nothing is going to stop him!"* "I'm... John's girlfriend, and... pregnant."

He laughed. "Good try, but you forget, I've already been in your room and I know you're on the pill. So, which is it? Which brings me back to my original question, why don't you carry identification?"

As his hands went to the zip, she lifted her legs, and hit him full-force with both knees. Knocked off balance, he fell sideways, but she was no longer wasting time. Rolling onto her side, she catapulted to her feet, ran for the French windows, threw them open, and bolted into the drenched night.

Finding herself on the pier, she rushed towards the small boat that bobbed agitatedly under the pelting moonlit sky. Automatically, she grabbed the rope, climbed into the craft, and rowed to the centre of the dam, hoping as she did that he would not try swimming through the muck and mire. But perhaps a good drowning might be the best solution.

"Good morning," John greeted as he reached the breakfast table and glanced around. "Has anyone seen Jessie?"

"Master John," a servant said. "It seems Miss Jessie went sailing. One of the upstairs ladies says her bed was already made when they got to her room."

"Not another one." Monica remarked. "Young ladies are not supposed to run in the sun all day."

"That Miss Lewis is something else," Mark shook his head. "Who is having a grand time at our expense. Mark my words, she is going to turn this family upside down and inside out." He stood up, pointed to the ceiling then grimaced as he made a sudden movement.

"Too much dancing?" James queried.

"I should know better than to fool around with dangerous materials. I'm going out."

Walking outside, John turned a corner and saw Mathew. "What are you mumbling about?"

"You and Jessie used it last but I doubt you'd make such a mistake. The boat drifted. As you see, I'm not dressed for rescue missions."

"You didn't see Jessie?"

"Is she supposed to be in it?"

"I don't know." Reaching the pier quickly, John called out. Nothing stirred. "Do you suppose she hurt herself?" He asked.

"Now, one of us has to swim out there."

"Here," John placed his watch in Mathew's hand, took his shoes and socks off then pointed to a rock next to the weeping willow. "I'll go from the boulder, there isn't as much mud."

Jessie had cried for a long time, no longer from fear but anger and frustration. Why was he hell-bent on making her existence miserable? No one else in the family appeared that deranged, in fact, she liked everyone even if not knowing them. Theodore paid attention to things and Grace was just a mom. Monica, though meddlesome, she knew she could manage a decent conversation with. James was oddly quiet but in no way as intimidating as Lawrence, Mathew undoubtedly the heartbreaker of the family, and John, a kind and loving friend.

Mark was evil in his intent to do her harm and once she calmed down, she thought of indeed walking to the police station and having him arrested as he so tauntingly suggested.

Never had she seen the need to hide her identity, but now was glad John had suggested it, imagining Mark's wrath, and perhaps even the rest of the family's if they knew who she was. Would anyone believe her accusations? Police reports involved real names and when they heard hers, they would know she deceived them, assume she planned this all along, and presumably for monetary compensation. And exactly how did one tell a family such as this that one of their own was criminally bent? Oh, for the irony and shame of it all!

Slowly slipping into the bottom of the boat, she tried to close her eyes as rain soaked her through. There was no way she was returning to the house and risk running into him again. After lying curled for what felt like ages, she realised she had to start bailing the boat. Drowning because of an insane man was hardly the way to go.

John was calling her but it had to be a dream because she couldn't move or answer. She covered her face and slipped into a tighter cocoon but suddenly, he lifted himself into the boat.

The first thing he noticed were her dishevelled clothes. "Did you even go to bed?"

Managing to sit up, she held her knees against her chest. No one could make her tell this sweet gentle boy that his brother fell far below the line of decency.

"What's wrong?" Mathew asked as John threw him the rope.

"Have no idea, except that it looks like she spent the night out here."

"In the rain?" He noticed the sickly paleness. "Jessie, are you okay?"

She drew close to the comforting voice, and buried her face against his chest.

John hugged himself. "What were you thinking?"

"She's half frozen and so are you." Mathew told him. "You both need warm baths."

"I want to know what happened."

"So do I. But in the meantime, I hope neither of you catches pneumonia. Go, and I'll see to her." Mathew encouraged. As John started towards the house, he asked. "What possessed you? You know better than that."

"I…" Looking up, her eyes filled with tears. "I was scared."

"That's certainly true." He said. It was stamped all over her face.

"I need that bath." If only she could hide the shivers that ran through her body.

He saw them too and reached for her wrist.

She winced.

Pulling the sleeve up, he gasped. "Where did you get this?"

"Huh… I fell…"

He reached for the other hand. "These are finger marks. Who did this?"

She closed her eyes, trying to ignore his kindness. Was she supposed to tell him that his delinquent brother had left his prints all over her body? "I fell."

"No, something else happened, and since it was on this property, I want to know what. If you don't tell me, I'm going to question every servant until—"

"No!" Fear filled her eyes and voice. "It was my fault. I… wasn't tired, so I went for a stroll. I apologise for being stupid but I went outside the gates. A man walked by, thought I was a call-girl, and grabbed me. I fought him, ran, and climbed the gate. Afraid that he might follow me, I came to the dam."

The look on his face told her quite plainly he thought not much of what she had just said was true. "Then we'll call the police and I hope you can give them a good description."

"Please, no!" She knew lying caused trouble and here was the proof. "Nothing happened so I'd rather forget it. And I'd appreciate it if you didn't mention it either. I'm extremely embarrassed."

"This is an attempted rape!"

"And I don't want to discuss it anymore." Turning her back on him, she ran to the house.

"Did she say what happened?" John asked as both entered the bedroom simultaneously and she disappeared into the bathroom.

"Nothing that makes sense," Mathew said frustrated. "Go have your bath and I'll wait for her."

Jessie gaped at her body in horror. Dark marks covered arms, ribcage, and back. Tears welled in her eyes, not from weakness but outrage, her instincts telling her she should have him arrested and prosecuted, but the nightmare that that would unleash… Wiping the tears furiously, she climbed into the hot bath.

"Mathew," she said, surprised he was still there, and pulled the bathrobe tighter. "I'm okay."

He got up from the armchair. "I want to make sure."

She sat on the edge of the bed, feeling limp.

Sitting beside her, he took her hands and pushed the sleeves up. "Please talk to me."

Silence was not how one repaid kindness but what was the alternative? "I'm tired, I didn't sleep,"

"Jessie, this was a brutal attack! Whoever did this, belongs behind bars!"

Her sentiments exactly.

John walked in. "How are you?"

"Rotten." Catapulting to her feet, she threw her arms around his neck.

"Don't look at me." Mathew said as he got up. "She narrated some scrap of a scary story, which I don't like one bit. Some creep attacked her, look at her arms."

John did, and flinched in shock. "What's all this?"

Jessie's head dropped to her chest, a new wave of resentment filling her.

"Same information I got. How about breakfast?" Mathew queried.

John shook his head. "She couldn't possibly eat a mouthful right now."

"Have a good rest then." Mathew put a hand to her face, gave her a reassuring smile, and left the room.

John insisted, but she couldn't tell this thing to anyone, merely repeating the story she had chosen. It was true, the longer one told a lie, the more convincing it sounded. "Can we drop it now? I refuse to put either family through a circus."

Opening her eyes slowly, she saw Mathew sitting on the armchair again, his face resting on one hand, his eyes shut. But as if sensing someone was staring at him, he opened them and locked them with hers.

"I must get up," she said, and tumbled out of bed.

He sounded far away, as if talking inside a tunnel, and he held something cool to her forehead. "When last did you eat?"

"I never had dinner and—"

He finished. "No breakfast. You are light-headed. Don't make any sharp movements either or you'll give yourself a headache. I think you shouldn't go back to college tomorrow."

"We're going this afternoon." She did not want to spend another night near Mark.

"I know you're afraid but nothing will happen if you stay inside. Will it help if I promise to not leave your side?"

Except the danger was within. "Where is everyone?"

"There's only the three of us on the property, but don't worry, you're safe."

The mere fact that Mark was not in the vicinity made her exhale. But what if dissatisfied, he tried something later?

The afternoon was slow but pleasant, except for the times when she recalled the previous night, which was often, and her skin crawled with the realisation that things could be so much worse right now. Mathew allowed her to leave the room in exchange for having lunch on his balcony, which she enjoyed, as she watched the playful relationship between the two brothers. He was inquisitive about their relationship but never personal and when hearing they shared the same residence, he wondered if there wasn't complete chaos.

"You know how it is; there are always trouble-makers."

"That's certainly true, and I find it abhorrent that you found one right here. Jessie," a deep frown crossed his brow as he reached for her hand on the table. "Let's do the right thing and both John and I will stand by you no matter what, everyone will."

"Until you hear it's your brother." Shaking her head, she knew it was best she told no one about the assault or assailant. Tomorrow, Mark would be gone and no one else need feel upset. "I no longer wish to talk about it."

She felt better by the evening and although John and Mathew suggested she take her meal upstairs, she decided against it. Not with the intention of taunting Mark, but for him to understand that she would not cower before him.

Over dinner, he glanced her way a few times, and she couldn't describe the revulsion she felt at his apathy, as if this was common practice. If this were not John's family and Mathew had not been as kind, she would teach him a lesson he would not forget.

Halfway up the stairs, he appeared beside her. "Apparently, all good girls report criminal acts. This tells us quite clearly into which category you fall. Was this for the Lewis honour, Barrymore integrity, John's friendship, or did it just suit you to keep your mouth shut?"

She stopped and faced him. "No one who flits through life in such a careless manner and disregards what is right and proper can come to a good end. Now, stay away from me or I might still change my mind."

"You won't." He grinned. "You're also absolutely ravishing when angry and I have an erection the size of Manhattan."

Running up the rest of the stairs, she stormed into her room, banged the door shut, and leaned against it. But hearing him roar with laughter as he walked past, she opened it. 'By the way,' she began calmly. "At least you were right in one respect, my reason for being here. Except, it's not John's money I'm after, I don't deal in small change. I am going for the big time." She gave him a disdainful glance. "Next time you see me, I might just be Mrs James Barrymore." That should give him something to think about.

"You, manipulating, little… that's your game. Congratulations! You surpass my idea of a grasping wench. Pity though, we would make quite a team."

"Perhaps. But unfortunately, you are only third in line. Well, this is goodbye."

"And this is exactly the kind of deviousness I expected. I knew that sweet face and smile couldn't be genuine," he made a disdainful gesture. "But hell, you unnerve me because I'm so damn attracted to you. For crap's sake, I can't look at you without feeling horny. In the space of two days, I've become so infatuated that I've already lost control twice and the implications are beyond alarming. Just as well I'm leaving tomorrow, I would not be able to control myself a third time and cause an unredeemable scandal. Because, lady, I want you out of my head."

CHAPTER THREE

Switching lights on, Mathew glanced around the empty apartment, dropped his laptop on the nearest couch, and made his way to the kitchen. He peered into the empty fridge. This problem could only be attributed to Vanessa; she loved eating out, and he often found himself disposing of perfectly good ingredients because she found the task of preparing the odd meal or letting him cook one a chore.

Pouring himself a glass of wine, he went into the bedroom, thinking that an early night was exactly what he needed. He had barely removed his jacket when he heard the front door open.

"Hello, lover-boy,"

He returned to the lounge. "When did you get back?"

"Just arrived,"

To his surprise, she entered carrying a suitcase. "Finally ran away from the studio?"

Throwing her arms around his neck, Vanessa kissed him hungrily. "Hmm. Drove straight from the airport as I couldn't stay away another hour." Her fingers were already unbuttoning his shirt. "I've been in deserts too long. First it was the Namib, then the Kalahari, and you won't believe where I have to go the day after tomorrow." Kicking her shoes aside, she dropped the khaki pants on the spot then discarding the shirt in a rush, and stood in her underwear. "We went looking for one thing and uncovered another. It gives us little time together but I can't let it slip while the trail is still hot."

"And so are you." He grinned as she struggled with his belt. "How long this time?"

"If what we heard is true, it could be a while. We have to go all the way up to Zimbabwe."

"Why?"

Her voice dropped to a whisper. "Rhino poaching,"

"You have heard how dangerous those people are."

"Everything has its risks. How's your schedule?"

"As it happens, just returned from Thailand and am on my way to Japan."

"Good, it makes me feel less guilty." She ran her hands over his bare torso then with one quick movement the lace bra disappeared.

Turning in bed, his arm fell across her body. He hadn't dreamt it, she was here. Carefully, he got out of bed and went into the lounge.

"There you are," she said from the doorway a while later. "Rough day?"

"Mad week, the Union is threatening with a strike and I'm going over some things."

"Why do the peasants want to revolt?"

He regarded her for a second. "Sometimes I wonder how truly unbiased you are."

Dropping into the opposite couch, she stared at the papers spread across the coffee table. "Has the industry elected a spokesperson yet?"

"Simon Wade."

Her head cocked to the right. "There's an interesting development, Barrymores and Stevenses on the same team. Why him?"

"Because that is who the majority voted for. And besides knowing what's going on, he's also an excellent attorney, who made good practical suggestions when he was up at the house."

"What does your father say?"

"He's more concerned with a looming strike than Simon Wade or the Stevenses. Besides, he's not actually one of them."

"Still, where do you suppose his sympathies lie?"

"With the industry," he flicked a file as if it were contaminated.

"What's that?"

"The Union's ridiculous list of demands. We have always taken care of our people and don't feel threatened; nevertheless, father is nervous."

"You know how it is; gross exploitation went on somewhere so now everyone pays. There must be a great story in this."

"Don't you ever get tired of chasing headlines?"

"No," her green eyes glowed with excitement. "It's my adrenaline pump." Getting to her feet, she went to stand behind him, her hands running down his chest. "Come to bed."

"You have just returned from an exhausting trip and there is another ahead, go rest."

"And you are very stingy when it comes to love; do you actually feel anything during sex?"

He looked bewildered. "What kind of a question is that?"

"One that deserves your attention." She disappeared towards the bedroom then reappeared. "And another thing. Why haven't you ever slept with me?"

"What?"

"When I spend the night, you never do, always finding things to occupy your attention." She pointed to the papers. "Now and then, you stay a couple of hours, but then you're gone. And come to think of it, it's not just your bed."

Irritation was quickly rising. "I think the desert sands did something." One hand made a motion in the air.

"I dare you to come to bed and spend the entire night in it with me. You have never done. And now I'm curious; how many women have spent the night in this bed?"

"I don't know. Can we please drop this ridiculous conversation?"

"Is it? Sometimes I just don't know what goes on inside your head."

He was annoyed now. "You have priorities, so do I." Shuffling a bunch of papers, he grabbed a file.

"Call it whatever you like."

To calm himself, John chewed gum.

"Quite different when you're the one about to walk through the mincer, isn't it?" Jessie touched his chin, where stubble grew, something he was calling a disguise.

"Do you people ever talk about us?"

She shrugged. "No one is as preoccupied with the subject as much as Lawrence is, who gives it a frequent bash. But grandma and daddy drive him wild by refusing to quench his curiosity. According to him, the Barrymores are culpable of everything, from the weather to potholes. Here we are." She brought the car to a halt in front of the double-storey white edifice. "It's not as grand as yours, but it is home."

He gazed at the splendid pillars at the entrance, giant glazed windows, tiled red roof, and perfectly symmetrical banana and sago palms. "Perhaps I'll have a good time after all."

After introducing John to Samuel, she took him down the hall, along a passage, and entered the sunroom. "Hello, grandma." Helping Juliet up from the armchair, Jessie hugged her.

"Hello, darling. Oh, my goodness," Juliet gave the young man a cursory once-over. "If you hadn't told me, I would have known it anyway. You look just like your grandfather, except he wasn't as blond."

John smiled. "Both my brother Mathew and I have been told that, repeatedly, but he, more than me. How do you do, Mrs Stevens?"

"Please," Juliet said, her eyes twinkling. "I'm grandma. And, in another time, I would have been yours. But then, you and Jessie might have been related, or there wouldn't have been a Jessie at all. Did you know that I almost married your grandfather?"

"Conversations do their rounds at the dinner table, so I have heard some things. But I'm not much of a participant, it's annoying to constantly dig in dirt."

"Young and wise. And if you value this friendship, don't tell Lawrence who you are. It's unhealthy to dwell on mistakes made by others, but that's not how he sees it. Anyway, I for one am not angry and you are most welcome." Juliet's hands went out to him.

"Guess what, Grandma, I went to the Barrymore estate a few weeks ago."

"How did that go?" Juliet asked curiously.

"We didn't mention the Stevens name." John announced. "I don't know how they would have reacted but I didn't want to test it either and have them upset her."

Juliet made a sad gesture. "What did you think, you who love beautiful things?"

"Yes, priceless treasures in every room." Jessie said dismissively, her mind going down a dark tunnel. Heaven forbid anyone in her family ever dared make John feel that threatened.

"Serena, Beverley, come meet Jessie's friend." Juliet announced as she saw the family members in the doorway. "And there you are," she smiled at Jeremy.

Beverley grabbed John's hand. "I'm so thrilled to meet you! Talks about you incessantly, when she is around, and then doesn't have the decency to satisfy our curiosity."

Jeremy took an instant liking to John and as soon as Beverley began a discussion on gowns, cake toppings, and church services versus garden weddings, the two disappeared.

The foursome had fun at tennis and in the pool; guys against girls, as Lawrence, instead of being beside his father as he should be, told Taylor that he had important business to attend to, and vanished to parts unknown. Jessie wondered what could take precedence over the impending strike. But Lawrence's disinterest added to John's good luck. Without him, Taylor depended solely on Simon, so neither had yet run into them.

But Sunday lunch brought Taylor's interest to the fore. Jessie imagined him trying to place the familiar look, because, realistically, that so-called beard was no disguise.

As the meal ended, Samuel announced that Simon was in the study.

"Tell him to join us out here, I doubt it's top secret." Taylor told him.

John threw Jessie a furtive but anxious glance.

Because while Taylor had not yet made the association, she doubted Simon was so absent-minded as not to place him instantly, especially as he often met with Mathew. She jumped to her feet, grabbing Jeremy's hand, and then John's. "Just remembered something." All three disappeared around the corner.

"Unless he's stupid, which I doubt, he's going to unmask me." John stabbed a finger against his own chest.

"Huh… I'm thinking." Jessie said.

Jeremy stared from one to the other, recognising Jessie's *I'm in trouble* agitated state. "Suppose one of you starts explaining."

She told him breathlessly. "It's about who he is."

"Right now, I can't see anything worse than Simon or dad running into Union people."

"How about a Barrymore?" Jessie pointed at John.

Confusion registered on Jeremy's face. "Well… you sure know how to pick them. Okay, you get back there, and you," he turned to John. "Follow me to the garage and explain how this happened."

As it turned out, Simon saw John, shook his hand, and exchanged a few words, but wouldn't have recognised him even if he were the Prince of Wales for all the grease, oil, and dirt he had smeared on his face as they fiddled on Jeremy's Porsche.

"I don't know how you get me to agree to these things." Jessie grumbled as they dragged luggage and a box out of the car.

"You heard how many times he called, he likes me to look after his place."

Jessie glanced around the underground garage. "Looks pretty secure to me."

"It has nothing to do with that, I also leave food in the fridge, occasionally clean, and it feels lived in. Vanessa is not a homebody."

"I suppose." Jessie thought about the beautiful blonde woman she sometimes saw on TV. Ice was the word that came to mind. That woman was as tough as an iceberg and she could not picture her in an apron. As her grandmother often said, each to his own. Besides, she still had an assignment to get to and had barely come up with the concept. Getting an F would surely impress her father, whose only condition for letting her move into residence was, "no failing, any subject, ever," or her wings would be clipped. She loved and respected her father far too much to disappoint him that way.

For security reasons, the underground lift only went up to the foyer, where everyone then had to walk through and take the ones across the hall to go up to the apartments. As they exited carrying two overnight bags and a box, Mr Wilkins, the doorman, lent a hand and she marvelled how John sweet-talked the man into keeping mum about *the girlfriend.*

"You'll have plenty of time to work on that doll's house." John nodded towards the wooden box as they entered the apartment.

"It's not a house, just two adjacent rooms. Where's the bedroom?"

"Through there." He pointed.

Walking in, she saw the Chinese vase and two other pieces Mathew had chosen from the Barrymore basement. Staring at the king-sized bed, she opened a closet. "Whose room is this?"

John appeared in the doorway. "Mathew's."

"I can't stay here."

"First, he's absent, and second, the other room is mine."

"What if he doesn't like it?"

"The man who doesn't like you in his bed is a moron. Obviously, that excludes me, because we're friends."

"Honestly,"

A surprising routine developed from staying at Mathew's; Jeremy started joining them for the occasional lunch, then dinners, and outings. Jessie was pleased, they made the perfect trio. Perhaps Barrymores and Stevenses stood a chance at mending fences after all. Then slowly, she began seeing less of them. Which she was okay with, there was work to complete, and Jeremy looked happy.

Dialogue collapsed, the strike everyone had fought to keep at bay struck, and crazy mode went into gear. There were constant meetings and discussions, first to agree and then disagree over some minor point on the list, stubbornness and not common sense persisted.

"I need a rest." Mathew complained as he dropped onto the bed.

"Let's go somewhere." Vanessa's green eyes danced as she turned from the dressing-table clutching a handful of make-up brushes, mentioned a resort, and went into the bathroom.

He sniffed his pillow then took hers and did likewise. He dropped back onto his and half-buried his face in it. No doubt about it, there was a different scent, and he liked the giddy feeling it gave him.

"This strike," Vanessa asked when she returned. "How long do you suppose it will last?"

"It's all up to the Union, isn't it?"

"Did I tell you I'm doing a documentary on the Textile Industry?"

"No, you did not mention it."

"Two one-hour-long segments; one on the strikers, and the other on the hotshot bosses. Do you have clean house?"

"What kind of a question is that?"

"Don't get defensive, it's merely business."

"How could I think otherwise?" He detested how she made everything she did impersonal. Which was odd, as he believed people in certain careers had deep concerns for others. But not her, she relished ruffling feathers, something his father complained a lot about lately. Theodore loathed hype and distortions, which were plentiful, but especially when delivered by her. "Would you consider quitting TV?"

She regarded him. "Are you asking me to?"

"No, just curious."

"Good, because I plan to become a top-notch producer. And people are starting to notice. Not only that, I've been contributing articles to the papers as well."

That was news to him too. Then just for the hell of it, he decided to throw in a nugget. "It sounds incredibly busy, will children ever fit into your schedule?"

One shoulder went slightly up, and a vein twitched a little faster in her neck. He couldn't wait for the answer now.

"Definitely not… I'm way too busy to take time off to do nothing but wait hand and foot for small screaming humans. They are time-consuming, demanding, and once you have them your life is never the same."

"Which is as it should be. I'd love to have a few little Barrymores running around."

"And there is absolutely no guarantee that your kids will be anything like you."

"I'd never expect them to be replicas, whether in looks or personality, just a few characteristics here and there. What do you say?"

"About what?"

"Kids." He couldn't be certain, but it looked like the idea made her recoil.

"M… me?" She stuttered.

"Why not?"

"Your kids would be cute but I cannot sacrifice my career for nappies."

"Ever?"

"Well… I didn't… Not now." She composed herself.

"I didn't expect it to be straight away, but it is the natural course—"

She snapped. "This is so typical. I have barely begun to ascend the ladder of success and already there is a man trying to pull me down."

"That is not fair, and definitely not what I meant."

"Men say that as an excuse but secretly they do mean it." Whipping her head, she stormed out of the bedroom.

Jessie yawned as she pushed miniature furniture aside; she loved these peaceful weekends at Mathew's and it made her wish for the possibility of moving away from campus and sharing a flat with John, if they could find it. Then sense entered her head. Not a good idea, especially when both families discovered who the other tenant was. Rubbing her eyes, she got to her feet, stretched, and went to bed.

Turning, her hand touched a chest. 'Jeremy,' she mumbled sleepily.

A commotion followed, the light went on, and a male voice demanded. "Who the hell are you?"

"Mathew!"

"Jessie?" He stared at her incredulously. "What... I thought John was staying over, now I find you and—"

"Huh... John went out." She pulled the covers around her. "I thought you were away."

He reached for a shirt. "Vanessa got sick and we had to come back early. I dropped her off at her place as her cousin Rachel has just moved in with her and is an excellent nurse. I was exhausted."

This was a pretty mess. She got out of bed. "I'll take the sofa."

"No, stay. And who is Jeremy? Are you seeing someone else now?"

Before she answered, the front door opened. Running out, she walked straight at John and whispered. "Mathew is here. I thought he was Jeremy so now he's very confused."

"Mathew! We weren't expecting you."

"Clearly," Mathew eyed his brother oddly. "Who's Jeremy?"

John laughed. "Ah, Jess, been talking to the gnome in the doll's house again?"

"I'll take your room." Mathew eyed them disapprovingly then disappeared down the passage.

Jessie smacked John's head.

Mathew reappeared and threw a pair of pyjama pants at his brother. "Have you been fighting?" Then glanced at the discarded work on the living-room floor. "And am I assuming right that you left her alone the entire evening, or was it the entire day?"

"She'll live," John announced.

Without a word, she turned around, and went into the bedroom.

"Jessie,"

"What?" She answered furiously.

"Let me in."

"And if I say no?"

"I'll sleep on the couch and have a bad back for the rest of my life."

"Stop being melodramatic." She opened the door and pulled him in. "A fine muddle you got us into."

"I'm not the one who said Jeremy's name. Can we have this disagreement in the morning? I'm bushed."

"Don't cross the line." She told him as she climbed back into bed and pointed to the other side.

'Cross the line? you'd de-brain me with your doll's house."

Both burst out laughing.

As the morning glow tried to sneak into the room through the thick silk drapes, Jessie opened one eye and stared straight at John's face. He looked peaceful and handsome, but she was still mad. "John," she called softly, expecting him to be asleep.

"Hmmm…"

"Who's going to use the bathroom first?"

"Go drown in there for all I care."

Unceremoniously, she pulled the pillow from under his head and hit him with it.

He jumped up, grabbed the other one, and threw it at her.

Running out of its path, she bolted out of the bedroom, and straight into Mathew's chest. Cheeks flushed, her brain died, making it impossible to think or speak.

To her consternation, Mathew spent Sunday with them, not showing what she believed the required concern over Vanessa's state of health, although, he did go into his bedroom for about five minutes and she guessed he made a call. The poor woman might be contagious and he being wise by staying away. But she did find it unnerving that he watched her with much curiosity.

"Are you two alright?" He asked when John left the apartment to get ice cream from the corner shop, then elaborated. "I know you were fighting yesterday, problems?"

"What did John tell you?"

"Nothing."

"Join the club." She almost told him.

"Does this involve Jeremy?"

Why did things just get worse? She wasn't even going to try. "We don't really fight."

"That's good to hear. I have noticed how happy he looks lately."

"He does," she agreed reflectively. "But I doubt it's me."

"You know," a smile spread on his lips. "You're a little odd, but otherwise, nice."

Before she could ask what he meant, John joined them, and neither said a word again.

"I'm going to Portugal." Vanessa announced. "I'm doing a series on the Portuguese community and it makes sense I start with their motherland. How about coming with me? You're sort of off, and I hear it's amazing this time of year."

Mathew continued paging through the car magazine.

"Did you hear me?" She squeezed beside him on the sofa then pressed. "What do you say?"

"For your information, I have not been let off the hook because there's a strike on. In fact, I must sit at endless meetings trying to understand why people can't agree to something today when they will to next week. And is it on purpose or are you just lucky? Do they come to you or do you volunteer every time a new idea comes along? I travel enough as it is and am sick of it. Now I must be dragged to another corner of the world just because you happen to be there too? Can't you give this to someone else?"

"You work hard, it's fine. I do and it's not fine. Is it because I'm a woman? I love what I do and am damn good at it. I'm twenty-eight-years-old and this is the time to make a name for myself, now that the right people are taking notice."

"Notice? You bloomin' sit in their laps begging for it." He threw the magazine onto the coffee table.

"That's what you think I do?" Red suffused her neck and the green eyes flashed. "Why is it men think women need to grovel for everything they want?"

"Unfortunately, that is sometimes true, because men have not evolved enough. But that's not what I'm talking about. I mean you, personally, how you go about making your life insanely busy."

"Keeping score, are we?"

"No, but here are my observations. In a month, during which I was away twice, totalling seven days, I have barely seen you, and we only managed to meet once. Tonight, is the second time, and the month will be over in two days."

"I can't give up my life's dream. Want to accept it, fine; if not, let me know."

"What are you talking about? Every time I ask something work related, you have these... explosions."

There was no response, just a flurry of fabric and then she was back in the bedroom.

Staring at the carpet for a second, he got up and followed her. She was tossing most of her possessions into a small case, and he wondered why the desire to stop her was utterly absent, whether she meant to go for a day or forever. He crossed his arms and leaned against the wall.

Invisible daggers flew his way as she glanced at him. "I'm taking my property."

"Do whatever you want."

She acquired an antagonistic stance. "Why are you pressing me, wanting me to give up my job? But it's not just a job, it's my life; and sorry, I won't. You want me to be a sweet little wife, cooking dinner and vacuuming the lounge in a frilly apron; I refuse. Much less start producing little Barrymores in quick succession. I can't sit around doing nothing but having babies.' She pointed to her chest. 'I have never complained about your travelling and all the times you've been late or let me down because of work, but you find fault with everything I do. I realise I wasn't this busy before but that's because no one knew how talented I was. Now that they do, you want me to give it up. I will not."

"I merely suggested you not accept everything that is thrown at you. You are obsessed with making it big and slowly travelling further and for longer periods. How long will this trip be?"

"You think you're clever by using different words, but you are repeating the same thing men have been saying since the beginning of time, *you're a woman, you don't deserve an important job.*" She dressed in a rush. "I'm not ready to play house."

"I see," he retorted. "But you're the one twisting this, I was not suggesting marriage."

"Will you ever?"

She was good at spinning things and frustrated him no end. "Not the way this is going. And who would look after children with your schedule, a nanny? They need parents."

Fury filled her. "What the hell are we talking about children for if we're not even talking marriage? But my work is merely an excuse."

"For what?"

"If you loved me, none of this would be a problem."

He regarded her for a second. "I never said… and right now, I don't care."

"Precisely." And a minute later, she stormed in a whirl out the front door.

CHAPTER FOUR

Her twenty-first became a small affair. First, exams were stressful and she was in no mood for hordes of people plodding through the house. Then, Meghan couldn't make it; a grandparent passed away in Australia and she had to fly out with her parents. Third, her father got an early phone call; the Union asked for an emergency meeting and he, Lawrence, and Simon had not been seen since. She got the niggling feeling that her day was about to deteriorate.

And it did, when John announced matter-of-fact that he and Jeremy were going exploring Kwazulu-Natal during the holidays. She felt deeply hurt at being excluded; when had they decided, why didn't she know about it? When he asked if she minded, she lied. How could she say otherwise? Look at Jeremy's face, he was excited, laughing. She didn't know when but it had gone from a three-man club to two.

Now, she hoped the missing members managed to join her for dinner, to end the day on a better note. John would be gone by then, still avoiding Taylor's curiosity, Simon's keen eye, and Lawrence's suspicious nature but some things took time.

At four o'clock, seeing the three women paging through another pile of bridal magazines, she excused herself and went down to the stables.

"Hi Brutus," she greeted Beverley's horse and smiled when he didn't respond as he always did for his favourite person. Looking around the stalls, she noticed two others missing. Mounting Abram, she led him out and up the small hill.

Reaching the top, she gazed at the cluster of trees waving in the breeze at the bottom of the incline. There it was; the little house they had called headquarters. Now, it looked like a rickety shed, but it had been a centre of fun aeons ago. Lawrence, as the eldest, had always been their leader, but who, often told them to do silly things that got them all into trouble. Focusing her eyes, she saw the two horses grazing nearby.

Dismounting stealthily, she tied Abram to a hook on one of the trees and crept to the small abode, a mischievous grin on her face as she heard their muted voices. Swinging the door open, she yelled. "Surprise!"

Both looked up at her, indeed surprised, but not as much as she was, which quickly turned to shock as her brain absorbed the scene before her. Her eyes and mouth fell open, nothing having prepared her for this moment. Turning automatically, she ran out.

Jeremy was the first to recover. "Jessie, wait!" Calling after her, he scrambled to his feet. "Crap! Jessie!"

Without turning around, she cried. "Stay away from me."

"Jessie, please listen,"

Covering her ears, she screamed. "I don't want to see either of you, ever again. Don't wait to leave on Monday, go tomorrow, better yet, go today. How could you?" She sobbed.

"Jessie," Jeremy reached for her.

"Don't touch me."

"I'm sorry I've hurt you,"

She gave a hysterical laugh, rubbed her wet cheeks, grabbed the bridle, swung herself onto Abram's back, and left at a wild gallop.

"How?" Was all she thought as she reached the stables and dismounted, then, running into the house, the hall phone's shrill ring brought her to an abrupt halt. Mechanically, she picked it up. "Hello,"

"Hello, sweetheart. I apologise about today and I promise to make it up to you."

"It's okay, daddy." She sniffed.

"Are you all right?"

"Huh... I... received some bad news about a friend."

"On your birthday. And it seems we will be late again. We're getting somewhere and nowhere, if you can understand that. What kind of bad news?"

"A... huh... she's very sick."

"Sorry to hear it. Then I'll see you late. Happy birthday, baby."

"Thank you, daddy." Replacing the receiver, she ran upstairs, bumping into Beverley outside her room.

"What happened?" Beverley asked with concern.

"Daddy can't make it."

"Bummer. But cheer up, you can always have a midnight feast."

"Huh, no," Jessie wiped her wet cheeks. "Meghan is sick, I must go." Walking into the bedroom, she pulled a suitcase from the closet.

"What rotten luck; so, what are you doing?"

"I'm… going. Tell mom I'll be back tomorrow, or… ugh, I don't know."

"Would you like me to come with you?"

"No." Her eyes drowned in tears as she stuffed the case with clothes.

"Sure you're okay?" Beverley followed her from room to bathroom and back again.

"I'm not but no one can do anything about it."

It was the most miserable drive; incessant tears raced down her face, and she with no idea of direction. Parking in a side street, she let the unstoppable sobs continue. How could she be so stupid and not suspect? Now too she understood why nothing happened that time they kissed. That weekend at the Barrymores she knew, but as always, she had pushed it to the back of her mind and told herself she was being fanciful.

Staring blankly at passers-by, she speculated at either family's reaction at unearthing such news. It was too sickening to imagine and panic hit her with the realisation that she might have somehow caused this with her subterfuge. She gazed around, exactly where was she headed? In John, she had found all friend she wanted and neglected everyone else. *"I'm so stupid."*

"Jessie!" Mathew exclaimed as he saw her in the hallway.

Two giant pools looked back at him as she dropped the case on the floor. "Sorry, but I didn't know where to go. Just for tonight, huh… perhaps tomorrow."

He stared at her for a few seconds, then grabbed the case, and dropped it inside the apartment. Reaching out, he pulled her into his arms, and closed the door behind them.

"What am I going to do?"

"About what?" Concern creased his brow as he led her to the sofa. "Tell me."

She dried her eyes, only to have them fill again. Exactly what did she tell him? *"Oh, by the way, our brothers are sleeping together."* How would he handle that?

"Have you and John been fighting again? Is this about the holidays?"

"We are no more."

"I'm sorry." He commiserated.

"I should have realised a long time ago, but I'm such a fool, a stupid, blind fool."

"He loves you, he'll be back."

"Not to me, as I want nothing to do with him."

"What happened this time?"

She dropped her head against his shoulder. "If he calls, please don't tell him I'm here. I need to be alone, to think, to sort things out."

"Why don't you ever tell people what's going on? I can't help if you won't let me."

"Sometimes... I know I made a dreadful mistake." Yes, by getting involved with the Barrymores. Now, in the middle of complete bedlam, here she sat with another one. What trouble would he bring her? And would James be next?

They sat; she, crying, and he, holding her close.

"You look tired, which room would you prefer?"

"The couch is fine, couldn't bear to be close to his things right now."

Mathew merely watched her in silence, then getting to his feet, took her by the hand, and walked her into his bedroom. "Today, everything looks awful, but tomorrow will be better. Then, you'll make up and laugh about this rotten time."

"Except, there is nothing to laugh about." Two giant tears dropped from her lashes. "I don't know if I'll ever be able to tell you but I'm thankful you are letting me stay. But I shouldn't have come, Vanessa might not understand." She put a hand to her forehead. "I'm such a moron."

"Don't worry about her, we also sort of broke up, and she's in Portugal."

"Sorry about that."

"Don't be. We had been drifting, and evidently, I'm doing much better than you.' He touched her wet cheeks softly. 'Time is good. Goodnight."

Going to the bathroom, she took a long bath, crying continually as she recalled her birthday. How could a supposedly happy day start so badly and end exponentially worse? She and John would never be the same! She and Jeremy…

After getting into her nightclothes, she sat in bed staring at the phone. She had switched it off as soon as she saw both were trying to get hold of her.

Samuel answered. "Miss Beverley is out, is there a message?"

"Tell her that I'm fine and I'll call again tomorrow."

"Yes, Miss Jessie."

"Jessie?" Jeremy's voice travelled down the line. "Let me talk to her."

"Don't give him the phone." She commanded, but obviously, Jeremy had other ideas.

"Jessie, please listen to me. I'm deeply sorry because we never intended—"

"You stole my best friend," she accused through the sobs. 'You pretended we were a team, but it was just the two of you. I don't know what to do, except that I don't want to see either of you, because… you lied to me, both of you, and it hurts so much."

"Where are you?"

She disconnected.

It was horrible; an all-out war. Taylor and Theodore were strangling each other, James and Lawrence stood on a dusty road ready to draw their revolvers, and Mark laughed. Beverley paraded in wedding dresses, Monica handed out plastic Eiffel towers, and Juliet was dying of heatstroke. All she could do…

"Jessie, Jessie!" Sitting on the bed's edge, Mathew shook her. "What happened today that you are in such a state?"

"I can't…" she held her head. "Do you have sleeping pills?"

"No."

She dried her eyes and pointed to her chest. "When Vanessa left, did it hurt here?"

"Can't say it did."

"When it does, you tend to hate a lot too. I never did another person but tonight I'm so close I can't think." Shaking her head, she stared at her lap. "I don't want to hate anyone, least of all John or— I'm sorry."

"Why are you apologising to me?"

"Because he's your brother," she noticed he only had a pair of shorts on. "Go back to bed."

"I won't be able to sleep knowing you like this. I'll make some tea, it might calm you down."

Lying back in bed, she closed her eyes, but the images were too vivid to be erased. She knew some gays around campus but never given them much thought, but neither had she been oblivious to their challenges. A dreadful fear came over her. How was this going to turn out? Oh, she knew how. She and John were a fluke. In the land of real, neither family would accept the other, much less this new relationship, and if they were not strong enough, both would be crushed.

"Here," Mathew placed a steaming mug in her hand and sat on the bed holding another. "Do you always react this way?"

"Only when I can't do anything about it." She wiped the tears that lingered.

"He really knocked you out for a six and I'm going to demand an explanation."

"No!" Grabbing his arm, she almost spilled the mug's contents. "Say nothing as I don't want to hear from him for a very long time, if ever. And he's leaving so I don't want to delay him." Bitterness filled her voice.

"Talking usually helps."

"Not about this." And how she wished she could erase it from her mind, to be blissfully oblivious. But where to from here, and could they still be friends? In one fell swoop, she had lost the two most important people in her life, and that was the biggest heartache. Tears blinded her.

"You are not all right. Would it help if I stayed with you?"

She recalled his kindness at the estate months ago but couldn't answer.

Taking the mug from her hand, he put it down on the bedside table, threw the covers over, and climbed into his own bed. "Come here." He invited and stretched his arm out.

For close to ten minutes her body lay rigid against his, then, all fight gone from her, she exhaled deeply and closed her eyes.

She was uncertain of her whereabouts in the morning darkness then moving slowly on the pillow, felt an unpleasant drum in her head. Events returned to mind, her eyes filled with tears, and she dried them quickly. Why was she feeling sorry for them? They had hurt her. Getting out of bed, she went about getting ready for the day.

"Hello." Mathew turned in front of the stove. "How are you this morning?"

"I have a headache."

"Then eat and I'll give you something."

"Thank you." Sitting on a high stool, she watched him. "You can cook?" She asked more to make conversation than real curiosity.

"A few things so I won't go hungry, you?"

"A bit but I never have time to practice anymore, we're always too busy." That was when John was here, now he had found someone else to give his time to.

He realised where her thoughts had gone. "My cooking isn't that bad."

"No wonder some people commit suicide. It's the memories they want to wipe out." She pointed to her head.

"But it won't always be like that." He brought the food to the counter.

"I think I want to throw up."

"That's okay too." Sitting across from her, he helped himself to the scrambled eggs. "It'll take a while but you will smile again. My day is free, what would you like to do?"

'I can always sit here and have a headache." She rubbed her temple.

Opening a drawer, he took out a bottle, and placed a pill before her. "Finish your food first."

"I apologise for coming to disturb your plans, and please kick me out when—"

"I know right from wrong and it's right you stay. As it happens, father gave me off until next Monday as he imagines me heart-broken. Actually, he wants James to become more involved and sort of told me to get lost."

"Thank you, you're good to me."

A grin appeared. "I'm being totally selfish. I haven't done much since Vanessa left, so you came just in time."

After breakfast and painkiller, she found that sleeping was still a necessity to her shaken system. Sitting on the sofa, her head dropped sideways.

Seeing her, he walked over and carefully made her comfortable. "I'd really like to know what he did." The phone rang and picking it up quickly, he sat in the armchair.

"This is a surprise, you actually picked up. Don't you ever spend time at home?" Grace complained.

"Hello, mom."

"How's Vanessa?"

"I assume okay. We had a fall-out. Didn't father tell you?"

They spent some time discussing his distaste for Vanessa's way of life, the strike, and why John had not asked Jessie along. Grace said she suspected the two had split, because while John and friend were at the estate gathering hiking gear, she noticed he was upset. Mathew nodded, not much escaped her.

"Sorry," Jessie apologised as she opened her eyes. "I meant to go to the bedroom."

He told her about Grace's call and that he had enquired about John's forthcoming exploits.

She became frantic, wanting to know all sorts of things; did he say something, had they left, because she couldn't go home if they hadn't.

He watched the drowning eyes. "Then stay as long as you want." Rising from the armchair, he wondered if he should be pleased or troubled for not being truthful, since John and friend had already left. But an idea was forming, and he had to pursue it. "Okay, let's leave all of this alone and go do something. Anything specific you're interested in?"

"Please don't put yourself out because of me, do whatever you like."

He gave her an odd look. "I don't think so. Instead, we will do something we both enjoy, such as browsing through antique shops."

"There is a brimming basement at home."

"And where's the fun in that? I prefer to discover things on my own."

"What did you do before?"

"Vanessa dragged me around TV studios and film people. It's interesting for about fifteen minutes."

It was a poignantly satisfying day. There were moments when she smiled at something he said or showed her, then just as quickly, a reminder of John or Jeremy made her fight for composure. It was then he hugged her and said something so ridiculous that she had no choice but to laugh through her unhappiness. They returned home with no purchases, but she felt as if a considerable weight had been lifted from her heart.

"Mr Barrymore," Mr Wilkins, the doorman, called as they stepped into the foyer. "We are updating our records and would like a list of visitors allowed to go straight up, and those you wish to be warned about." He passed Mathew a register.

"All family members, and a few friends. I'll send the list down. And Jessie."

"Miss Manning?" Mr Wilkins asked curiously.

He seemed to debate the question, then said. "No, she won't be on the new list."

Walking a short distance, Jessie studied the frieze on a column.

A young man appeared from behind it, undoubtedly a security guard.

She smiled. "Hi."

"Hi." He greeted and walked over to front desk.

"Oh, Mr Barrymore, our newest assistant, Albert." Mr Wilkins announced.

That night, she cried softly, hoping Mathew didn't hear and that she wouldn't have nightmares again. How she hated having this secret, always imagining that someone could read her mind and see things she would also prefer not to know.

Mathew stared at the ceiling in his guestroom, his mind on a non-stop scheming bend.

He had been knocked breathless the first time he saw her, her enigmatic beauty convincing him there was perfection in the world, and when they found her by the dam and he held her in his arms for the briefest of moments, he had been tempted to never open them again. Then pushing his fantasy to the back of his mind—for what else could she be, he concentrated on work and Vanessa.

They had been dating for about a year and it was only fair he gave her a chance. But Vanessa had suddenly become hot property on the TV producers' lists and worked as if retirement loomed. After months of living past each other, he found himself disliking the situation greatly and as for her distinct lack of interest towards a normal family life, it only irritated him.

He realised Vanessa had an extremely busy schedule but that was because she made it so, and he would swear she purposely avoided what she perceived as a disagreeable development of events. When she went on about how he meant to end her starry life, he no longer cared if she went and never returned.

Fate had strange ways of dealing cards; he didn't need to go searching for her, she came knocking in deep distress, and the instant she stood outside his door, he knew he could never turn his back. She cried out for compassion and he found it oh so easy to give. He was also acutely aware that he was playing with fire by taking his brother's girlfriend into his house and heart, but right now, he couldn't help himself.

For a moment, he hated his brother. John caused this pain, forcing her arms to go so readily around someone else as she searched for the comfort denied, where it should have been promised.

Was it underhanded? Absolutely. But now was the only time he had and he was past caring. John was gone, she was vulnerable, her heart crying out for love, and he would give it to her in whatever form she needed. The possibility that the exercise might backfire loomed like a spectre but he was counting on it simply being too late.

It was a bright morning and tucked warmly in bed, Jessie fixed her gaze on the Chinese vase. But she didn't see it, her thoughts were on the man a few metres down the passage. And again, just like before, he was the comfort she sought.

Jumping out of bed, she called home and discovered that they had left. Shrugging, she decided to make the effort to not dwell on things she could not change.

"Today," Mathew said as they pulled away from the underground garage. "I'm taking you to Kensington. When father told me to take time off I thought I'd go nuts, now I see he was being insightful."

The day turned into an enjoyable undertaking. He was attentive and charming and often led her into conversations that made her forget all the upsetting things. They meandered through a dozen little antique shops, bought nothing, but returned home satisfied.

That evening, as she sat quietly, he asked. "What's wrong?"

"I'm merely hiding. I have to confront reality, and that is not here."

"You are not in my way and I like having you around. Besides, what is it you'll do if you go home? Think, and cry? You're on vacation, John is gone, so is Vanessa and neither of us has a schedule. Should father need me, he'll call." He sat beside her. "I know you're still shaken but I can already see improvement."

"Today was better." What did crying achieve anyway?

"Stay and I'll take you to some interesting places." He winked.

The phone's shrill barged into the moment.

He grabbed the phone, got to his feet, and took a few steps away, while never taking his eyes off her face.

Her face burnt, feeling as if he were touching her. She had always been drawn to John, yet, he never made her feel like this.

"So, what shall it be?"

"About what?" She asked confused, her cheeks still flushed.

He smiled. "About going or staying."

"I don't feel like going to face a cross-examination but—"

"It's settled then, you stay. Oh, that was James. He says we're eventually getting somewhere and the strike might be over soon. But don't let that stop you, you stay if you like, want, need, whichever. And on Friday, I'm planning a fantastic night out. All you have to know is to wear jeans."

Religiously, she called home daily and told tales of an illness that got better and worse in varying degrees, then asked herself. *"What is it I'm gaining from all these lies?"*

They discovered an easy friendship even if strained with pent-up emotions that were escalating at an alarming rate but both tried to hide, doing their best not to become too personal, giving the other space. She didn't know what he did when alone but she leaned against doors and walls a lot, closed her eyes as she recalled moments when their fingers touched, and hungered for him to kiss her with a sickening intensity. She was smitten, if not in love, and his gentlemanly restraint was driving her insane.

As predicted, the strike finally ended.

"But you don't have to go." He told her quickly. "Only thing is, you'll have to spend the days on your own. I really haven't given you time to think, so this is it."

She smiled, understanding full well he was begging her not to leave.

After a mindless weekend, she stayed Monday then thought it ridiculous to hang around any longer. He had been more than a friend and it was time she faced her own issues. On Tuesday, after saying goodbye in the morning, she packed her case, cooked him a meal, wrote a few notes, and went home.

Arriving to a darkened apartment, he knew instantly that she was no longer there. Sinking tiredly into the sofa, he saw the note.

"Mathew,

I apologise for not staying to say goodbye properly but I thought that if I did I might cry again and I don't want to do that anymore. You were a kind friend when I needed one and I'm grateful for your concern. I know I'll be all right now, thanks to you. Next time I visit, it will be without tears.

Jessie"

He read it three times, folded it, and slipped it into his breast pocket. What was he supposed to do in an empty apartment? Wearily, he dragged himself to the kitchen and discovered the meal she had left, her handwriting on the outside. *"Microwave 10 minutes."* Opening the fridge, he found a wine bottle with another label. *"Drink this one."* Smiling, he opened the cupboard for a glass and found a small cake. *"Sweet tooth, you'll enjoy this."* He roared with laughter; she was precious and he wanted her back.

After popping the dish into the microwave, he went to undress. Another note waited on his bed. *"Clean sheets. And I hope the pillow is dry."* Picking it up, her scent enfolded him. Lying on the bed, he hugged it to his chest. The phone rang. "Hello."

"Hello, Mathew."

Why hadn't Vanessa's voice ever done this to him? Oh, how he wanted her. "Didn't you like being here?"

"I did, but I can't take over your life." She told him shyly.

"Nonsense, what are you doing?"

"Nothing," she admitted.

"Then come back. We can even go up to the estate—"

"No, I couldn't."

"Okay, skip that thought. But the weekend is almost upon us and what am I supposed to do?"

She laughed. "What did you do before?"

"I was lonely." He announced seriously. "Please, Jessie."

"What do I tell my mother?"

"Do you still tell her everything?"

"Not specifics. But she worries if she doesn't know we are safe."

"You're a good daughter and I'm feeling guilty. Tell her you'll be visiting a friend and that you'll call every day."

"I'll think about it."

"Don't take long, I want to plan this weekend."

"Goodnight, Mathew." She told him softly.

"Bye, Jessie." He wondered what she would make of the fact that he couldn't stop thinking about her, that he knew for certain he was madly in love. The phone rang again. "Did you change your mind?"

"Yes. Hello, Matt."

Talk about a cold slap. "Vanessa… When did you get back?"

"This afternoon; how are you?"

"Well." He thought quickly, where had she gone? "How was Portugal?"

"Wonderful, I definitely want a holiday home in the Algarve."

"That good. How is the film?"

"Excellent." A pause followed. "Matt, I know you were upset when I left, so was I. The thing is, you took me by surprise. I don't know what came over me… and I want to apologise."

"I'll bet anything she's been at the studio the whole time." "Where are you?"

"At work."

Grabbing the pillow again, he inhaled deeply. "Yes, I think you should come over." Disconnecting, he called Mr Wilkins.

He put Jessie's notes away, took a shower, got dressed, and went to take his meal from the microwave. Savouring the last mouthful, he heard the key.

"Hello, Vanessa, you look good." He noticed the perfect tan.

Going closer, she offered her mouth.

He pecked the cheek.

Her eyes narrowed at the gesture then glanced around. "So, what's going on?"

"Cake?" He offered.

She pointed to her waist. "You know I don't eat sweets."

"Pity." Going into the kitchen, he reappeared with another piece.

"Why is it I get the feeling something is going on?" She fixed her eyes on the plate. "You baked?"

Looking at her, he hoped Jessie made up her mind quickly. But he would have to sit with the telephone directory and call every Lewis until he tracked her down. "Not me."

"No, you didn't." A peculiar nervousness filled her. "You are seeing someone else, and she did."

"Look," he put the plate down. "You were right. Your career is important; go pursue it. I do want a wife who can do mundane things, and not because I'm a chauvinistic pig but because that will make her normal. I want something different from what I grew up with and I am not embarrassed to admit it. I want children running around the place, climbing all over me, messing my shirt with their sticky fingers. I want to discuss dental appointments, how fast the kids are growing up, and where we should go for the holidays. But most of all, I want to be in love with my wife."

"Are you all right?"

"You see, Vanessa, what I want is called a life and that is not what we had. I am tired of fancy living but never living at all. Invisible hands do everything and you never know how. Why do you think I left home? I'm not saying we won't need help, because we will, but I want to try doing things myself, to repair the kettle and the toaster. I want my wife to tell me not to drop clothes on the floor because she must pick them up. Is that plain enough for you?"

"And what is the little woman's name to be, obviously not Vanessa." She eyed him uncomfortably.

"Well, she doesn't know yet."

"You're going to propose to a woman you just met?"

"I never said I just met her, I have known her for months."

"You cheated on me?" She looked like a fish out of water.

"Never, but our last conversation led me to believe that we were through. Or, at least, that you are unhappy about what I can offer."

"I'm sorry about that." She smiled tentatively. "I have thought long and hard and I admit, I overreacted. And we need to discuss all the things you want and I never considered—"

"I'm sorry too. Soon, you will find a man who understands you, your work, and you will be happy."

As she speculated over what had taken place in her absence and listened to endless virtues and talents, she also realised, she could not compete; Jessie was simply everything he dreamt about presently. "Staying home and having babies is not all women want to do nowadays."

"Neither does Jessie and I don't expect her to."

"I know I react far too quickly at times. I spoke harshly and I regret it, but somehow, I hoped… How did we get here, whatever this is?" She wasn't quite sure what else to say.

"You were absolutely right in one respect. If I loved you I wouldn't have seen everything as a problem, and would have found a way to make it work. I guess what I'm really saying, and apologising for is that I've been in love with Jessie for a while already, in fact, ever since I met her."

She bit her trembling bottom lip. "Well, you know where to find me, should you change your mind. A middle-class suburban life… I would never have expected it from a Barrymore."

"That's your problem, Vanessa. You assume the layer above yours is automatically better."

"I don't want to but I can imagine what went on while I was away."

"It's called love."

"Ah, yes, we never had that."

He stuck out one hand. "I'd appreciate it if you returned my key."

Fury appeared in the emerald eyes. Opening her bag, she took it out and dropped it on the table, refusing to touch him.

"One should not hang onto the past, however hard it feels." She stormed into his room and reappeared seconds later. "There was never much here anyway."

How true. "This was not the outcome I intended, and I mean it when I say I'm sorry."

"You're not sorry, you're in love."

He could tell she wanted to reach out, and pitied her, because this could have been avoided if she had been present in his life. Instead, she gave him the opportunity to open his heart. Then again, he might have been the absent one. But whoever was to blame, and perhaps neither was, this was the reality.

If only she could change his mind. But she knew him well, it was futile. "I'll survive, I'm very good at that, even more than you realise."

"Vanessa…"

Her hand went up. "Save it and don't tell me again how sorry you are. But one day, and yes, I hope soon, you will hurt as much as I do. And if I can help it, I'll do the hurting. Goodbye, Mathew." Turning around, she walked out of the apartment.

CHAPTER FIVE

Jessie soon discovered what monotony was. Not having John or Jeremy around to share in the activities all three enjoyed was a strain on her patience and she did not dare go near the stables or the little house, lest she recall and cry.

Beverley hired Mrs Pryce, a well-known wedding planner and Jessie wanted to laugh every time she saw the woman coming her way. On her first day at the house, she eyed Jessie curiously and asked, "who are you in the wedding party?"

"The maid of honour."

"What suggestions would you like to put forward?"

"None, it's her wedding." Jessie pointed to her sister.

"Huh-huh," Mrs Pryce said, scribbled in her book, and walked in the opposite direction.

"Didn't mom want to do it?" Jessie asked as Beverley stopped beside her.

"She politely declined and thanked me for saving her a mountain of headaches."

"You're not choosing weird dresses; I hate things that look like meringues."

"No, I'm going for simple lines. But at least on the day you get to wear one. What is it with you and the pants?"

"I can't go sailing or riding in frills."

"Fine. But you're also a woman, who should wear beautiful clothes. Romantic dinners are not the same in pants."

Jessie laughed. "What's the colour of this thing?"

"Blue. I'm lucky if I manage to get you into a dress at all so the least I can do is that you like it."

"Thanks, that's very accommodating."

Beverley surprised her then. "Please don't sit around waiting for them."

Jessie thought she was going to cry, didn't, and felt better for it. "You're right, nothing to stop me from doing what I want."

"Go somewhere; you look utterly bored."

Jessie phoned Mathew, to discover he was in bed with a cold. According to him, someone had fiddled with the thermostat at the factory and he was about to pay with his life for that someone's lack of judgement. She laughed and disconnected.

Entering the foyer, she greeted. "Hello, Mr Wilkins."

"Good evening, Miss Lewis."

She cringed every time someone called her that, "Mr Wilkins, please call me Jessie."

He smiled. "Yes, Miss Jessie,"

"Mr Barrymore told me he's ill. I brought medicine," she pointed to the large bag over her shoulder. "Is it possible I get into the apartment without disturbing him?"

Mr Wilkins nodded and pressed a button on the desk. "Albert, please bring key number three-twenty, let Miss Jessie into the apartment and then return it to the safe."

83

She felt uncomfortable riding the lift with Albert. He had an odd way of staring at her and she was convinced it was blatantly sexual. Shyly, she folded her arms across her chest, as he seemed particularly fascinated with that part of her anatomy, and when she stepped into the corridor and he purposely walked a step behind, it embarrassed her to know where his eyes were. To bring it up was probably further enticement so she chose to say nothing so he got no encouragement. Turning the key in the lock, he grinned knowingly, but what he thought he knew she had no idea.

Moving quietly across the lounge, she went into John's room to deposit the bag. She stood there a moment, feeling a slight pang of something then taking a deep breath, decided to be done with the past. Going to the kitchen, she moved about noiselessly as she prepared a tray.

She leaned against the wall, watching him as he slept. He looked peaceful, not as sick as he purported. Approaching the bed, she sat on the edge and gave him a gentle shake. "Mathew,"

Opening his eyes, an instant smile appeared on his face. "Did you only come because you thought I was dying?" He touched her hand on the bedspread.

"No, I came because I knew you're behaving like a small boy. Did you eat?"

Shaking his head, he sneezed.

"That's what I thought." Getting to her feet, she took the tray from the dressing table. "It's not much but you will feel better afterwards. Have you taken anything for this?"

"I don't get sick." He eyed the pills on the tray. "Did you come to kill me?"

"Why would I do that?"

"Revenge on all men. I never knew a cold could feel this awful."

"That's because you're doing too much and simply expect your body to cope."

"Now she lectures me."

She placed a hand on his forehead. "A little hot. Just eat everything." Turning, she picked the discarded tissues carelessly tossed around the bin and disposed of them in the bathroom.

A faint smile appeared on his lips.

"I see the threat of infection amuses you." Waiting for him to swallow the pills, she removed the tray. "Cover yourself and close your eyes."

"First she wakes me then she wants me to sleep."

In John's room, she touched everything with half a heart, feeling sad but no longer angry. Climbing into bed, the tears did come as the distinctive aftershave enveloped her, but strangely, it was no longer because she thought she had lost him, but for knowing that both were about to face uphill battles of gargantuan proportions.

"What the hell did you give me last night that you knocked me out cold?" He watched the beautiful Caribbean blue eyes turned up to him as she sat on the lounge floor looking through his CD collection.

She motioned for him to return to bed and disappeared into the kitchen. When she reappeared in the bedroom, she had a tray, and more pills.

"You don't want me to be conscious, do you?" Gazing at her, he wondered how such intense feelings had developed so quickly. But it had to be the fever because seeing her like this was driving him crazy; all he wanted to do was get her into bed. She smiled sweetly and he knew that she should leave. As if reading his mind, she turned around and walked out. No, it was not the normal fever's fault, but the one that rushed through his veins for her.

Lunch was an interesting affair and he had another taste of her stubbornness. He demanded to be let out of bed and she insisted he stay. She threatened to leave and he dropped back in defeat.

"I'll eat with you." She offered, went to get her own tray, and sat cross-legged on the other side of the bed.

He didn't say much, just watched her, studying her features, her movements, and adoring her smile. "Do I have to sleep again?"

"You may get dressed and walk around, just not out the front door."

"Is this how you treat all your patients?"

"You're my first. I'm the one who was on that side a couple of times. John is an excellent nurse." Her gaze dropped to the floor.

"What was wrong with you?"

Dismissing it, she left the room.

He felt an insane jealousy. John had a powerful hold on her heart, would she ever let it go?

"Mathew," she said Monday morning, as he was about to leave for work. "You're much better and it's silly of me to just sit around."

"What if I relapse?" He noticed she was already dressed and smiled a definite fake. "Pity you can't find something to do during the day, I like having you around."

"You're very kind but I must go, and I will call."

"I have a better idea. Give me your address and I'll come pick you up."

She felt light-headed. The family's reaction, not to mention his, would be something to contemplate. "Good evening, I'm Mr Barrymore. Is Miss Lewis ready?" "Who's Miss Lewis?" Samuel would ask. "The young lady who lives here." "You have the wrong address, sir. This is the Stevens estate." "What?" And Mathew would pass out right then. It was simply frightening to imagine. Grabbing paper, she scribbled something and gave it to him.

He glanced at it. "I've got this, it's your cell, which you don't know how to use." He accused. "I've seen how you receive calls. You either ignore it or switch it off."

They called each other back and forth over the next three days. Every time, she wanted to say so much more, to discuss things she couldn't begin to put into words, feeling a connection she had never imagined possible with anyone but John.

"How is your dancing?" Mathew asked Wednesday evening.

"What kind?"

He had booked at ELLA'S for Thursday night and wanted to know if she owned a dress, because he had yet to see her wear one.

Greeting her, Albert held the lift door open and rode in silence. When she took out the key Mathew had given her, she glanced at him furtively. He had the habit of grinning at random acts and she wondered if he was at it again. But no, he seemed to be behaving sensibly.

She stood in front of Mathew's mirror critically acknowledging her sister's impeccable taste in clothes. Beverley had chosen a white pleated blouson dress, daintily tied with a black ribbon at the waist, and she admitted that she did look different, somehow mature, and beautiful. She had wanted a long dress but Beverley insisted on a short one, saying her legs deserved airing. Jessie smiled as she recalled her sister waving hands and arms as if she were giving directions. Beverley had also tried her best at getting her into a hair salon, but she felt there were already enough changes for one day.

Hearing the front door open, she glanced at the time; twenty to four. Mathew was even earlier than he had promised. "I couldn't see properly in the other mirror—"

"Wonderful."

She turned, startled. "Albert! What…"

"I came to check that everything is in order, there was a prowler."

She exhaled and tried to hide her annoyance. "Thanks for the warning, but everything is fine."

He stared at her bare legs. "Very fine indeed and I'm glad I came in. Is Mr Big Spender taking the young lady out tonight?"

Displeasure appeared on her face. "You are not allowed in the apartments, unless there is an emergency."

"It is, this one." He held his crotch and took a step towards her.

Fear pressed her against the dressing table and blind hands opened a drawer, searching for something she might use as a weapon. There were a few books. She threw them all at him.

A flick-knife appeared in his hand and her eyes became riveted on the gleaming blade. If she made it across, she could lock herself in the bathroom until Mathew arrived.

Following her gaze, Albert leapt over the bed and with brute force pinned her against the wall, a heavy hand covering her mouth as she let out a scream.

Eerily, she recalled being in a similar situation months before; but as Mark had had no weapon, Albert flicked the sharp blade dangerously close to her face and neck. His mouth brushed her skin and her heart-rate vaulted.

With a quick movement, he knocked her off her feet, threw her onto the bed, and his full body weight pinned her down. She tried to kick but deplorably couldn't get the desired effect. Dropping his head, he kissed her brutally.

She thrashed and gasped. "Al—bert, this is a mistake. Please... leave now."

Ignoring all protestations, he stuck the blade into the fabric just above the belt. Her breath was knocked out as she imagined stab wounds across her abdomen. Instead, he slashed upwards, creating fabric slivers from waist to neck.

Her mind whirled frantically. *"Oh, God, he has done this before!"*

Clasping one arm behind her back, he stroked the throbbing vein in her neck with the blade. Then, with one movement, he tore the shredded bodice away. His eyes shone at the sight of her breasts in the white lace and one hand began running up and down in frantic caresses. "So, lovely,"

"Mathew... will be here soon."

He smirked. "Mr Barrymore is a very punctual man, home at six, Monday to Friday.'

Right there was her best weapon, but if she could grab the lamp...

As if guessing her thoughts, he reached out and knocked the lamp over, breaking it. Then resting the cold blade against her throat, his free hand started undoing his belt.

The front door opened, Albert stared at her, and everything moved into dreamlike state. Passing the blade to his left hand, he covered her mouth, and pulling the revolver from its holster, pointed it at the door.

Whether from shock or cold, she started trembling, and knowing there was no other way, she bit the hand covering her mouth. "Mathew!"

Albert dropped the knife, its sharp blade sliding past her shoulder, creating a bloody trail.

"Jessie?" Mathew called out.

"Don't come any closer, Mr Barrymore." Albert dragged Jessie from the bed and threw an arm across her ribcage. "Stand in the middle of the room."

Her lungs felt empty, but she doubted it was his grip. "P-lease, Mathew… Do as he says."

"I'm in the middle of the room." Mathew's countenance fell as he saw her in the doorway and took a step towards her.

"Huh, huh, huh." Albert shook his head and waved the revolver at him. "Against the wall,"

Her heart sat in her throat and it felt as if hours passed before they reached the door. There, Albert pushed her to the floor then fled down the hallway.

Mathew was beside her instantly, pressing a hand to her shoulder to stem the blood flow then led her to the bathroom. "Jessie," he called, but she wasn't listening. He threw a handful of cold water onto her face.

Opening her eyes in shock, she stared at him then tightened her grip around his neck.

"God, Jessie, I need to look at this. How—"

"The, he... had a... knife." She hiccupped, finding it difficult to breathe. "He... I tried but... he was too strong."

Carefully, he began wiping the blood from shoulder to waist with a damp towel. "I'm going to kill him. And then call the police."

"No!" She told him quickly. "Report him for breaking and entering if you wish, but I can't press charges."

"He must be punished."

She dropped her head dejectedly. "Please don't make me."

"It's not too serious. Obviously, the blade was razor-sharp." He said of the wound and searched for bandages and tape. 'Your lovely dress,' grabbing one of his shirts, he handed it to her. "I'm covering it but I think you need to wash, there's blood everywhere."

Looking down, she saw the shredded bodice and blood trailing down one leg.

He covered the cut. "Okay, you clean up, while I talk to Mr Wilkins."

"But you won't call the police."

"Jessie..."

She began to improvise. "Maybe he misunderstood. I was always friendly. He must have thought I was flirting..."

"Women flirt with me, I never attack them." He held onto a bloody strap. "This is serious."

"I know." How she wished to put the delinquent behind bars, but she couldn't be the one doing it. "I get myself into trouble without thinking. And I wouldn't be able to explain exactly why... what happened. I don't want to shame myself, my family, or yours. Please,"

"We'll talk after you clean up. Think about it carefully, reconsider."

She nodded and looked away, knowing she was not about to change her mind.

She felt better afterwards and wondered if she should go in search of him, but he was talking to someone in the lounge; doubtless, Mr Wilkins. Sighing, she sank onto the bed and cried softly. She was such a coward, blatantly giving a criminal an open road to continue perpetrating his disturbing ways.

Opening an eye, she realised four hours had passed since climbing into bed. Then seeing Mathew in the armchair, she raised herself against the pillow.

He went to sit on the bed's edge, pushed the shirt aside, and carefully lifted the bulky bandage. "Good, it stopped bleeding. Should we go to the hospital?"

She gazed at the cut. It had bled enough to suggest that it might warrant a stitch or two, but she couldn't bear to leave the apartment. If it bothered her in the morning, she would go to her doctor. "I think it will be fine."

Grabbing a can, he sprayed the red line then cut a gauze strip, and applied it to her shoulder. "You are very noble risking harm to warn me." He dried the tears that stuck to her lashes. "Are you hungry, do you need anything?"

Shaking her head, she threw her arms around his neck, holding tightly as she sobbed. "If he hurt you…" but she couldn't continue.

"And I'm so mad that he hurt you." Cupping her face, he kissed her, gently probing her intoxicating sweetness. "There is nothing I want more than to make love to you, but not like this, or under pressure. And John—"

"We are not the same."

"There will be no stopping me." He warned.

"I don't want you to, but there is one thing." She whispered.

"What is that?"

She wanted to tell him, but his touch made her feel a million things, turning her body into a mass of sensations, erasing all but the longing that grew within. She was a Stevens, he a Barrymore, how long could they last? Tonight, a day, a week, perhaps a month, a season was pushing it, but a year... She was already tempting fate.

No, there was no doubt, he was the one, and although hoping that she married first, she didn't see that happening with them. This was all they would have and she dare not walk away without knowing how they could be. "John and I didn't date, I've never really dated, except that one boy in high school, but I broke up with him the day he kissed me.' She was rambling. 'I've never slept with anyone either." Decided, that was the extent of her revelations.

"But you're on the pill." He reminded her.

"I have Dysmenorrhoea."

"Which is..."

"A fancy name for extremely painful periods,"

"Must we then wait for your wedding day?"

Surely, he was not proposing. As for waiting for her wedding... she would bet anything he would not be there. "Would you do that?"

"Yes, Jessie, whatever you wish. But then, dear God, tell me you'll marry me really quick."

One day, probably soon, she would cry, lament, and possibly regret her decision, but it would not be tonight. She shook her head. "Just love me."

"You have no idea." He whispered between buttons and kisses, his hands slipping into the black hair. Gentle but hungry hands began an exploration, probing exquisite places, discovering hidden treasures, delighting him as she awakened.

"Breathe," he reminded himself as he laid her down, his body becoming rigid with want. In featherlike gestures, he traced infinities down her stomach, pleasure filling him as her skin reacted to his touch, and he began a deeply erotic kiss, turning her into putty in his hands. Her skin heated, her breathing became erratic, and he thought he wouldn't be able to contain himself. Incredible, his little virgin was about to have her first orgasm. Moaning in ecstasy, he exploded and blended with her in a way he had never done with anyone else.

Never would he get enough of her, or this rapture he had craved but missed, and as minutes became hours during that first night of incredible discovery and mind-blowing fulfilment, he knew with every pore of his being that he would never, could never, love another woman as he did her.

Dawn arrived to find her blissfully asleep in his arms and looking at the tousled head, he recalled Vanessa's words. She had ranted about him not sleeping in this very bed an entire night with her. Here was the reason why, the only woman he wanted to wake up next to for the rest of his life.

Kissing a cheek, he carefully removed his arm from under her, got out of bed, reached for his phone, and went out of the room. "James. Are you okay alone?"

"I think I'll survive." James laughed. "How was your date?"

"Huh, well, I have a bit of a situation. The new security guard broke into my apartment." He gritted his teeth.

"You're kidding! Are you alright? Have you called the police?" Worry permeated James' voice.

"I'm fine; nothing was stolen so I'm not pressing charges."

"Why not, we can't encourage people like that."

"I know but I have reasons. Let's just say he won't be working in the security business any longer. Mr Wilkins filed a report and he's already suspended, and will be dismissed."

"But you're okay?" James insisted.

"Yes. Did you see the reports on your desk? I told you I wouldn't come in today."

"Are you going to the house then?"

"I would have liked to, but not this weekend. I have to take care of something." A smile appeared on his face as he peered into the bedroom.

"Should I come over? And why are you whispering?"

"Thanks, but I strongly decline your company. And I'm whispering because I don't want to awaken someone."

"Are you seeing Vanessa again?"

"No, we're over."

"May I ask why?"

"Because... we're just not right. Bye, James, see you Monday."

Going into the guest bathroom for his morning ritual, his mind drifted to his younger brother. Now, he really didn't get this fight. He understood quarrels between lovers but this puzzled him. They were close, best friends, who shared everything, so what could John have done to cause her such distress if they had never been intimate? He wondered if she would ever tell him, as she seemed adamant not to.

Returning to his bedroom, he watched her for a moment; here was something he had never known, a mystery. Snuggling down in bed again, he pulled her naked body into his arms.

She made a sound and opened her eyes slowly.

Pushing the glorious hair away from her face, he studied the beautiful Caribbean blue then began tracing her lips with the tip of his tongue.

She trembled, her mouth stretched into a smile then opened to let him in.

It was pure insanity, he couldn't get everything he wanted as fast as he wanted it. "Good morning. Did I tell you last night that I love you?"

"Did you mean it?"

"Every word, every letter…" He began dropping kisses on her face and neck then travelled to her breasts.

"A-aren't you going to work?"

"Not today." And he let the intense ecstasy that was to be with her fill him.

Closing her eyes, she felt his sometimes gentle and sometimes fierce probing, his mouth making the rest of her hungry for more. No, she had never imagined anything close to this rapture.

By Sunday, she felt as if she had been on a drug binge and was now a full-blown addict. She was crazy in love and there was no man on the planet, no matter what he did, who could turn her body, her mind, and her heart from Mathew.

"Bloody reporters,"

"What's wrong?" She queried as she entered the kitchen.

He dropped the newspaper in front of her and pointed to the front page.

It was a picture of Lawrence, Simon, and James with three Union men. "You're not glad the strike is over?" She pretended ignorance, knowing that wasn't what had upset him.

His finger dug into Lawrence's face and he began a tirade about the obnoxious lot; that if Lawrence was an indication to his siblings, then they were all terrible. David Stevens stole the machine patents he designed for Barrymores, and as if that was not bad enough, he then eloped with William's fiancée, Juliet Drew.

"My grandpa was no thief," she wanted to scream, hot tears pricking dangerously close, and her heart pounding in fear. Why didn't she know people believed such things? All she knew was that her grandmother had almost married William.

And then he said the one thing she had never wanted to hear. "I hate that lot."

Food untouched, she went to lock herself in the bathroom, turned the taps on, and wept. This was it; he loved Jessie Lewis, not Jessica Stevens, and the minute he heard... Why, because she had the misfortune of having a surname he despised? Then again, he was not doing anything she hadn't seen Lawrence do.

"Jessie," he called outside. "Are you okay?"

What could she tell him? She opened the door. "Huh, yes."

He pulled her into his arms, kissing her until she felt dizzy; making her forget what had made her cry, his hands soft and gentle, bringing more tears to her eyes.

"Tell me about your family." He urged later as he drew circles on her bare back. "I'd like to meet them."

"Yeah, right," now she knew something else too. Not only had the world of intimacy and love invaded their lives, but so had that of secrets and lies. It didn't take a genius to see which would eventually win. And in that moment, she learnt to take his mind away from all the things he should know but she refused to divulge, talking about everything bar who she was.

"John says you have a beautiful home." He said Sunday night as they lay in each other's arms.

She stayed quiet. Where was he going with this?

"Does it upset you to talk about him?"

"He has a place in my heart no one will ever be able to fill."

"And I'm jealous."

"There is always a little of us that belongs to someone else."

"Not me, and I want all of you."

"How can you be so certain? And basically, we've just met."

"Because the moment I saw you, I knew. It was then too that I knew Vanessa no longer mattered."

"And one day you will meet someone who will replace me."

"Impossible. You are a wonderful enigma and I adore unearthing all the little secrets. But why do you like keeping those?"

"I'm trying to understand what is happening to me. Don't want to start explaining to everyone else too."

"Take as long as you need, just don't ever stop loving me." He begged.

Her eyes became extremely bright. "But one day, you will."

"Never."

It was the first Friday after classes started and as promised, Mathew was waiting for her outside Residence.

Meghan did a double-take then pushed Jessie into a corner. "What the hell? Is that who you've been seeing, another Barrymore? Of course he is, he looks just like John."

"Please don't tell anyone. And I don't know how to tell him…"

"This is so much trouble, a hundred times worse than John."

"I know, but I can't."

Meghan took a deep breath. "Oh my, my my my… Never mind them, this is going to tear you apart. You are no liar, how are you going to hide, who you are, your family?"

Jessie's eyes filled with tears. "I don't know, all I know is that I love him."

Meghan nodded. "I can see. Okay, get your stuff, he's waiting. But you must do something, real soon."

"Jessie," Mathew began as they walked into the apartment. "Why don't you move in? I mean—"

"No! What would my parents say, yours? I wouldn't be able to concentrate."

"When you're ready." He dropped a kiss on her head. "What about getting married?"

"Are you crazy?" He would be when he discovered all the lies, and then kick her out. "We need time."

"Not me." He told her and walked into the dining room.

Was it possible everything was as simple as he made it out to be? The phone rang and she stared at it. "Mathew,"

"Answer it." He told her from behind the door.

"It might be your mother."

"For goodness sake," he appeared in the doorway, a large box in his hands, irritation showing. "Answer the damn thing and say whatever you want. That I let you stay, like before."

She lifted the receiver nervously. "Hello,"

"Jessie?" John greeted in surprise.

She stiffened, a silence falling between them.

"Are you still there? And why are you there?"

"Huh… Mathew said I could."

"Ah, I see, the next sitter."

She lowered her voice. "Where are you? Classes started already."

"I know, but Jessie, please let me start by begging your forgiveness. I'm sorry about what happened, how it happened… I didn't know how to broach the subject and I didn't want to ruin our friendship. But in the end, that's exactly what I did. And I apologise if I misled you, and at times I hoped, because you are an amazing person. Perhaps if you had ever been in love you would understand what I feel."

Her eyes shone unhappily; there was logic in what he said. "I'm trying to. Are you looking for Mathew?"

"I called your house, Samuel told me to try Beverley. I did but she didn't know where to find you, as your cell is always off. Then I tried Meghan, who talks funny. So I thought I'd let Mathew know. He can tell the family."

"Tell them?"

"Not about Jeremy. I'll do that in person when we return. It's just not going to be for a while."

She plopped onto the sofa, feeling faint. "What?"

"I've been doing too many other people's things, it's time I stop."

Her mouth dropped open in shock. "Where is he?"

"I realise that right now he's your favourite scapegoat but he had nothing to do with my decision."

"Have you both become idiots? Mere months from graduating and you decide it's all worth throwing away. And he has no excuse to encourage you, he has a degree, so he can do whatever he wants," her voice rose angrily. "Which isn't much anyway."

"Sorry, but neither you nor Jeremy can change my mind." He told her equally angry.

"Fine, do whatever you wish and see if I care." Her eyes brimmed with tears. "I hate both of you, and never want to see you again." She banged the phone down, and buried her face in her hands.

"Jessie?" Mathew called and dropped an arm on her shoulders. "Who was that?"

"John. He was going to tell you, but was glad to find me here." Bitterness laced her words.

"What did he do to you?"

"He's not coming back."

"Is he out of his mind? Why not?"

Wiping her eyes furiously, she told him. "He has been on a dangerous mission for a long time but I was too stupid to notice. What kind of moron am I? I never saw any of this happen. We will never get along again and I've lost my best friend."

CHAPTER SIX

Spring promised a blazing summer, and in three months, John had not come home or called again, neither had Jeremy. Many times, Jessie wondered what Taylor would say if he knew, because it was obvious he was becoming increasingly anxious about his younger son. Then, she wondered what the media would make of it. She and Mathew would keep the press running for months! John and Jeremy… it was just as well they were not around.

Love! Nothing could change the way she felt about Mathew. He, on the other hand, was worse, proposing every weekend, his countenance dropping when she gave one of the many excuses she had become so proficient at. Her stories for not spending weekends together ranged from slightly crazy to offbeat, and Beverley's wedding loomed like a fast-approaching tornado.

She hated newspapers. Every other week, there was something to upset Mathew about the Stevenses. He stared, snorted, and pointed with his judgemental finger. Most times, she was hurt and couldn't hide it. 'How can you be so horrible to people you know nothing about?'

"I know enough." He said sharply then was startled by her tears. "You are far too kind to strangers, who don't deserve it."

"I'm a nervous wreck," she thought as she drove home for family dinner. The wedding was a fortnight away and she was still trying to find an escape from the photographers, who would be present in packs; but could she break Beverley's heart simply because Mathew was about to discover her subterfuge?

As luck would have it and problems were not enough, he suggested going away during that specific weekend. She did the only thing she knew; smiled, said how sweet, and developed a massive headache.

To deal with the problem of recognition, she asked Beverley if she could also wear a veil. A short one, she explained, and pointed to her face.

Beverley looked at her as if she were high on something. "Huh, no, but a hat would look nice, maybe a Stephen Jones. And not black, it's not a funeral. Here," she gave her a sample of the dress' fabric.

Jessie liked the idea and bought a wide-brimmed one with lots of tulle, which she took to wearing in her college room so she knew how it moved and which were the best hiding angles.

"I'm so excited about next week." Mathew said Monday when he dropped her off at college.

"Huh… about that."

He stared at her, knowing one of her stories was about to make an appearance. "It took me a while to arrange with James."

"James is going?" Shock spread on her face.

"No, for me to be free on Friday. He has started seeing some woman who takes up all his time and is just never around. I almost went down on my knees."

"Sorry, but there is something that needs my immediate attention."

"Well, I can't stop you, can I? And I don't understand this hang-up. You never want to come home with me, but neither do you want me to go with you. So, Jessie, tell me what you do want." He stormed away.

Realising nothing would change her mind, he cancelled their reservations and decided to go to the estate, as he had not been there for some time. He wondered if she understood how hard her rebuffs were on him, because he never wanted to let go, his love for her so deep he would give her a piece of Venus, if she asked for it. And that was the crazy thing, she didn't, in fact, never asking for anything but his love; and no questions, because she didn't like those. It had taken John a year before he finally dragged her home, how long would it take him?

He entered the sunroom. "Hello, ladies."

"Good grief, where did you spring from?" Monica was the first to react.

Grace complained. "When last were you here?"

"I see father and James every day; don't they tell you how I am?"

Theodore glanced at his son. "No one can complain about the work but is out the door before anyone knows it, no longer wants to travel, and is always smiling. Something is going on in that apartment."

James nodded. "Must be a woman. I tried spying one afternoon, but disappointingly, he was alone. So, who is she?"

"Yes, darling, tell us about this new girl." Grace begged.

"And I thought I could hide it all." Smiling, Mathew sat beside his mother. "She is beautiful, smart, and very hardworking."

"How serious is this?" Monica queried with interest.

"I'm sure I've broken a few records when it comes to marriage proposals. Maybe I should go look at diamonds."

Theodore turned to James. "You're a fine one to talk, you too have been sneaking around."

James roared with laughter. "Okay, I admit, I am also seeing someone, who, as it happens, is a dedicated career woman."

"A woman's place is at home and that goes double for you." Monica announced. "Do you know what people will say if you marry a career woman? And professionals are hardly motherly types. Look around you," she leaned towards him, as if he wouldn't understand otherwise, and made a half-circle with one hand. "This is your son's inheritance. The one you don't even have yet. What is it she does anyway?"

"She's with a large corporation." James evaded and a frown appeared on his face. "Which is no one's business but mine."

"Every single time." Mathew noted. "But you know, Aunt Monica, it's not true women can't cope with motherhood and a career. Most do so extremely well. While men live only for work, women slot everything into their rightful positions. I'd say they are better managers."

"If this is what you're learning from the new girl, I don't like her already. What does her family do?"

"What happened to love?" Mathew countered.

"If she is from our circle, why not? If she isn't, then I already know what she's after."

"Money isn't all women are interested in either."

"You are so naïve it's almost sweet. Just be careful you haven't fallen for an upstart. There is nothing amusing about being taken for a ride and I know all about it from experience. I was married four times and three of those were disasters. I didn't know any better and ended up making my father pay those three good-for-nothings handsomely." Monica gave him a knowing look. "Mentioning money… the social wedding of the year is tomorrow; Taylor's eldest daughter is tying the knot."

"It must be such a joy to have a daughter as lovely as Beverley. Felicity Barrell says she is enchanting, witty, and smart." Grace said wistfully.

"Should be quite interesting," Monica continued. "I hear they are calling it a small and intimate affair. How small can it be with a hundred guests? Yet, I expected at least half the country to be there. Mrs Wade… I'm surprised she didn't aim higher."

"Most of our friends speak very highly of Simon. And from what Theo said, he sounds exceptionally intelligent and certainly proved his worth during the strike." Grace pointed out.

Theodore got to his feet. "Just a pity he became mixed up with that lot. Taylor inherited his father's business sense but Lawrence is quite reckless, with a penchant for danger, including high speeds. As for the other boy, I have no clue what he does."

Monica and James continued the conversation but Grace added nothing.

Noticing her silence, Mathew asked. "What do you think, mom?"

"It seems rather presumptuous that I should pass judgement on people I'm not acquainted with. For all we hear and say, they may be an admirable family, who barely give us a second thought. Why can't we leave them well alone? Gossip circulates and what we do know is that this hatred was somehow begun by your grandmother. She was cantankerous and sour about everything, so I have my doubts about her justification. But what I genuinely don't understand is why this generation persists in its pursuit. It all feels cheap and debasing."

"You sound like someone I know." Mathew mused as he thought about how upset Jessie became when he passed snide remarks. "Two good hearts. But I admit, they don't impress me much either."

"Hate is dangerous, no matter who it's directed at." Grace's hand went to his handsome face. "You are looking so happy and relaxed; I like you like this. And thinking of hearts, did Jessie manage all right with John's things? She offered to take them to you."

A smile crossed his lips. "That was ages ago."

"As I knew she would, which is why I forgot. Such a nice girl even if a little mysterious. I invited her over a couple of times this term. She's just extraordinarily shy and usually turns me down. Nonetheless, she managed to come once."

Mathew looked perplexed. "What? When?"

A smile appeared on Grace's face. "We had tea and chatted. She too has found someone, and for the few minutes she discussed him, it was as if sunshine emanated from her heart. Then just as quickly, the light went out, as if she were being tortured."

Mathew was bewildered. Why hadn't she told him that she had been here? The girl had more secrets than he cared for.

If possible, Beverley looked even more beautiful in their grandmother's old English lace dress and Jessie admitted, Mrs Pryce had done a splendid job. Everything in its perfect place, flowers looking as if they had been picked seconds before, and silk bows tied to flawless perfection. She had walked into the marquee and stared in amazement as the woman directed her people as if she were an army general deploying her troops.

She looked back at her sister. They had not seen each other too often in the last few months but they had talked a lot on the phone. Having lost Jeremy and John had brought them closer.

"One of these days, it will be you. What does Mathew say?" Beverley asked.

She had told her sister a few things but not all; she couldn't bring herself to. "Wanted to marry me yesterday, last week, last month…" Her eyes clouded over. "Is Simon right for you?"

"I wondered in the beginning then discovered how extraordinary he is. He's kind, sensible, and comforting, but more importantly, he loves me. Sometimes I thought I wanted wild ecstasy, but that is not always a guarantee to happiness."

"Yes, Simon will never break your heart. How I wish I was happy." Tears formed in Jessie's blue eyes and she batted her lashes furiously, trying to dry them away.

"I'm so disappointed Jeremy won't be here... Have you heard anything?"

"Not since John called to announce he was dropping out."

"Ah, yes,' Beverley said then took a moment to continue. "That birthday of yours sure disintegrated. I was right here." Both glanced out the window, just able to see the little house in the distance. "I saw you go in and come out. It didn't take a genius to figure out what happened. Besides, I saw them run after you, and I knew about Jeremy years ago. It was déjà vu for me, just a repetition of Alan Perry."

Jessie looked at her sister in shock. "Didn't he commit suicide?"

"And Jeremy blamed himself mercilessly ever since. I too stumbled on them, but they didn't see me and I never said a word. Later, I thought I had dreamt it."

"I was so angry and hurt. In one day, I lost both a brother and a best friend."

"I saw how freaked out you were, and that's why I kept my mouth. Now, it's different, the first anger is gone. And Jessie, it's not your fault. All I could see that day was self-recrimination. You thought; if I hadn't brought him here, this wouldn't be happening... Don't let it tear at your heart and you miss out on the love both have for you. Because right now, they feel worse than you do, and it might be the reason why they aren't here." Beverley glanced at a discarded card. "Why they only managed to send that."

As luck would have it, the papers printed a family portrait, but Jessie admitted with satisfaction that it certainly had paid off having worn the hat in advance; she had bent her head ever so slightly, thus, eliminating recognition. Nevertheless, she neared hysteria, waiting for Mathew to appear in their driveway.

CHAPTER SEVEN

Taylor Stevens studied the report. Months ago, he had become aware that money was disappearing from the business, and although paying attention to transactions, statements, cash, and credit flow, he was still none the wiser how it was being taken and by whom. Gazing at the private investigator and auditors' report, he couldn't find words to express his feelings. Honesty was important to him. That, had always been his motto in business dealings, which he had learnt from his father.

His face became grim. "This is correct?"

"There is no doubt. We couldn't believe it ourselves, but that is where most of the money went."

"Quite an impressive list. Let's see; Marula Sun, Wild Coast, Sun City, two Race Courses, Black Jack. Any gambling establishment he doesn't know?" Taylor glanced at the report again. "Five, seven, twelve, twenty-three, seventeen… and in the last year, progressively higher amounts." He pointed to the printout. "Thirty, fifteen, twenty-five, here's a good one, forty-two. Grand total,' skipping a few columns he passed a tired hand over his brow.

'One million three hundred and fifteen thousand Rand. Do you realise how much money this is?"

"It is considerable."

"Proof that it was taken is here. Now, for the culprit, there is no mistake?"

"None whatsoever, there is the envelope with the photographs." The man pointed.

"I wanted to know." Rising tiredly, Taylor shook the man's hand. "Thank you, Victor."

Entering the house that evening, Taylor found it almost deserted, except for Lawrence, who was in the study, and Samuel, who hovered in the background if no other servant was visible.

"Who would have believed it," he told his trusted employee. "Months ago, the house was filled with children. Where are they now?"

"It's the pattern of life, sir."

"I expected some changes, just not this many or drastic. I've lost all my children at once." Taylor glanced out the window. "It's going to rain, Samuel, you may retire."

"Sir?"

"I'll be all right, and so will Lawrence. Have a pleasant evening."

Samuel had been in the household too long not to know that Taylor's countenance asked for privacy. "Thank you, sir."

Lawrence looked up from the armchair in the study. "Hello, father, how was traffic?"

"The usual nightmare."

"You look tired. And worried."

"I received some shocking news." Pouring himself a drink, Taylor twirled the glass.

"What kind of news?"

"This." Taking the files out of his case, Taylor dropped them on the desk.

Lawrence paged through a printout uncomprehendingly. "What is it?"

"Perhaps the other envelope will explain." Taylor pointed.

Pouring the contents out, Lawrence stared then glanced at his father. "What's all this?"

"Since it's your handiwork, you tell me."

"It can't be right, a million three? I never took that much." Lawrence defended hotly.

"No, not at one go."

"What now, you want me to return it?"

"Can you?"

"I may have some, and there is my Trust—"

"Cut the crap, Lawrence. I know there is nothing left because I checked after I saw these. There is nothing, not a penny."

"I am a little old for lectures." Lawrence rose to leave.

"And I haven't even started." Taylor pushed him back into the seat with one finger. "Now, you are going to sit and listen, because if you had any sense you would not be in this mess. Has it even occurred to you that you have committed a crime? Embezzlement, fraud, and grand larceny." He threw a picture onto the desk. "But this is nothing." He pointed to the total on the printout. "You lost much more than this because your private accounts are depleted, the investments are gone, including the stocks I bought you. As for your Trust... how could you spend over five million rand in three years? On what, what did you buy, clothes, a car? You have been driving the same one for three years and I bought it." Taylor's anger rose. "We may have more than most but I'll be damned if any of my children waste it like this; on horses, card-games, and casinos.

"It seems I have two imbeciles for sons. One disappears to heaven-knows-where without ever setting foot in the family business, for reasons I can't conceive, and the other starts wiping me out because he's a compulsive gambler.

"And if I let you continue this way, we won't have to wait for the Barrymores as you keep telling me, you will annihilate us all on your own. I can't begin to express my disappointment in my sons, and it seems I can't do worse by leaving my daughters in charge because at least, both appear to have excellent judgement."

"Are you threatening me? Do you imagine that I will be frightened, fall to my knees, promise I'll never do it again, and be cured? It will never happen. Scream all you like, but who apart from me can run Stevens? Jeremy… Poor faggot, couldn't run a brothel if he tried."

Taylor looked at his first-born with distaste. "Typical, when cornered, threaten and insult someone else."

"It's no insult. What do you suppose he and friend are doing, working? Dream on, father. He doesn't want you to know, but I have for a long time. As for your daughters, think they're better? Just wait a while. Beverley, although damn sexy to look at is bloody insipid, an airhead, with what, an English degree? What does one do with that? And Jessie, those calm manners are not her. That little girl is a savage volcano and she will still cause you plenty grief."

"Listen to me you ungrateful pup! You have committed a crime and should be punished for it. As for my other children, keep your poison away from them. And furthermore, before you say another word, you are fired."

Lawrence burst into laughter then rising angrily, stood antagonistically before his father. "Want to have me arrested too? Go ahead. But you won't believe the commotion I'll cause in the media. I'll make enough money to pay all debt and open my own business." He snarled.

"Doing what, running a Bookie Company? You'll be bankrupt within weeks as you can't stay away from the shiny numbers."

"Go to hell, father! You caused this by keeping tight reigns on everything. Why couldn't you just let go? Control, control, that's all you want, until when, when I'm fifty? Then it's just too late. Well, have it all back!"

"Stevens Textiles was never yours that you should return it. Or did you think being born first automatically gave you privileges? You have to earn it, just as I did from my father."

"That's all very nice and dandy but I couldn't care less as I hate the damn thing; the machines, the fabrics, those endless floors, and all those people. Goodbye, father, and I hope your daughters have a whale of a time running it into the ground." Lawrence stormed out to the garden.

A few minutes later, he spun out the garage and down the driveway, almost crashing into the front gate before it opened.

Jessie was glad when Saturday evening arrived, feeling numb from so much spent energy, and was certain she had worn her fingerprints away. Mathew had dragged her to one of those out-of-the-way spots both liked and they had spent most of the day rock climbing.

"What are you looking for?" He asked as she rummaged through a cupboard in the kitchen.

"Have you seen a bag of plaster?"

"It's in the back, somewhere." He pointed. "What do you want it for?"

"I need to make a copy of a pressed ceiling border."

"Don't be long."

Finding the bag, she got to work then switched the radio on, in time to hear half of the news. "Top stories at this hour. It has been confirmed that the man killed last night during a car crash on the N1 was Lawrence Stevens, son of the textile giant, Taylor Stevens. A police spokesperson said Mr Stevens died instantly when he collided with the back of a stationary truck…"

Searching for her phone, she found it on the coffee table, where it had sat since yesterday, dialled the number through a cloud of paralysis, and listened to Simon tell her terrible things. Her eyes filled with unstoppable tears, she had to go, but what plausible explanation did she give Mathew? Wiping her eyes, she went into the bedroom and saw him fast asleep. She scribbled a quick note, kissed his brow, and walked out.

Reporters and photographers were camping outside the gate as she drove up. Thankfully, the security guards knew her car well and opened it before the flashbulbs exploded, but just in case, she had put on a beanie.

Her mother looked ill and didn't make sense, her father sat in a terrible silence and she knew she could never reach him there. Seeing their family doctor, she understood. And as the hours passed, she realised this was akin a Greek tragedy.

She had never been particularly close to Lawrence but he was her brother and he was gone. If she felt this wretched at his loss, how would she feel if it had been Jeremy, whom she loved dearly? Tears sprung to her eyes as she recalled the last time she spoke to him. She told him she hated him. Lie was all she did nowadays.

Within minutes, she learnt there had been a quarrel, and Lawrence, in a fury, spun out the driveway, down the road, and onto the highway at high speed. Five hundred metres later, he met death. Closing her eyes, tears ran down her face.

Would Jeremy consider joining Stevens Textiles? She couldn't imagine him wanting to. Although he had studied commercial law and business, he had made it clear that he refused to cross Lawrence's path. But Lawrence was simply an excuse; Jeremy had no interest in the family business. And where was he anyway? Beverley, with a BA in English could hardly be considered qualified, and she... the mere thought terrified her.

Monday, she called Mathew. He was upset. How could she just leave sometimes? Where did she go, what did she do? What could she tell him? All she wished to say was not possible.

"Typical," she thought as she gazed at the sky days later. Gloomy clouds everywhere and it hadn't stopped drizzling since early morning. She hated goodbyes, had ever since losing her beloved grandfather. Beverley and Simon sat silently and Juliet and Serena wept softly. Holding onto her father's arm, she squeezed it every so often, just so he knew she was still there, even if feeling that he saw no one.

She had always seen the church as a haven of peace, a refuge, never a place of sadness, because here, throughout her life, she had attended weddings, christenings, Christmas, and Easter services, always finding it a bright and happy place to visit, and had often entertained the idea of her own wedding. Now, even a remote hope of that was distant.

Glancing around from under her veiled hat, she wondered why some of these people had come. Probably imagined there was something to be gained from this misery.

Everyone wore black at the gravesite, looking like wet ravens. Taylor dropped his arms to his sides and Jessie quickly slipped a hand into his, pressing it a little, silently telling him that she loved him. He gazed down at her blankly, not aware of her presence.

She leaned her face against his arm and whispered. "We will survive, daddy."

Out of nowhere and through the dispersing crowd, they appeared. Dressed in black, they looked like brothers, and after exchanging a glance, walked towards her.

"I'm glad you made it in time." Jessie said, one hand caressing Jeremy's face as tears dropped, more out of thankfulness that he was there than the proceedings.

"And I apologise for not getting here sooner." Jeremy wiped his eyes. "What happened?"

"He had a fight with daddy and then took off at high speed."

She soon realised that although her father appeared to be thankful that Jeremy had returned, he also watched his younger son with an oddly curious expression. *"Must be wondering if he has what it takes,"* and conceded that as her grandmother had once suggested, she too had her doubts.

Seeing John leaning against a wall at home, she asked. "Are you going to stay?"

"That is the intention, which is going to be a challenge, my father barely speaks to me."

"He is very hurt. Will you go back to college?"

"What's the point, it's too late in the year. I just don't know what I should be doing."

"I suppose you know best." A silence befell them.

His hand went out to her. "Jessie, I despise myself for hurting you so deeply, but can't you at least try? Jeremy is hurting too and feels responsible for coming between us. Goodness, I miss you."

Gazing at him, she discovered that some pain did wane with time.

"There is responsibility in friendship, and although I have trampled all over ours I would appreciate the opportunity to mend it."

She dropped her voice. "And has it not yet occurred to you that you should not be here at all? If the photographers recognise you, it will be the Stevens-Barrymore war. Ready to pick sides?"

'You're right about that, but we still need to talk. For Jeremy's sake as much as our own, we cannot become estranged. In the meantime, I guess I should go home and try make right with father, but hell, I need your support. And shame, I have neglected mom… Will you come home with me, so we can talk away from all of this?"

"Do you believe it's possible to be the same again?"

"The only time things don't work is when people don't try."

"It's all strange and difficult, but we shouldn't say things we don't mean. And I too apologise for telling you that I hated you, I don't." Her eyes filled with tears. "But I don't know about going to the estate, I don't like misleading them" *"As if I'm squeaky clean. And Mathew will flip."*

"No pretences, we are exactly what we have always been, friends. Then can I count on you for the weekend?"

"You are the only person who within minutes, can have me in some insane tangle. Not that I haven't done enough of that lately."

Leaning forward, he embraced her. "Thank you, Jessie, and I'll call you during the week for arrangements."

She watched him walk up to Jeremy. Placing a hand on his arm, their eyes met in understanding, and then he was gone.

"John!" Mathew exclaimed in surprise and gave him a bear hug as he stood in the hallway. "Where the hell have you been? Come in. How are you?"

"Okay. The place looks great." John nodded approvingly.

"A bit of redecorating, sit." Mathew motioned to the sofa. "You're looking, er... rugged."

"It's all the sun."

"And the hair, and beard," Mathew eyed them curiously. "Been home already?"

"Father is so mad he'll probably tell me to get off the land. But I'll risk it over the weekend."

"You laugh... What happened in June?"

"Life. And you know what? I don't miss college, just Jessie."

Here came trouble. Was he supposed to tell him now or later? And when was later? They had been close, even if not intimate, but John was here and his return might be attributed to her.

As if following his train of thought, John announced. "I'm asking Jessie to go home with me. I love that girl and was a damn fool to hurt her."

"Definitely worse than I imagined. But now, I also want to know what she will do." "Yes, sure, give her a call."

"How's mom, who's to be married? Sorry I haven't really kept in touch."

"Mom misses you. As for marriage, women are more complicated than I thought."

"Is Vanessa giving you problems?"

"We broke up months ago, I'm seeing someone else." *"And I want you nowhere near her."* He felt like screaming. "Do ask Jessie along, mom seems to have taken a fancy to her."

"I intend to." Rising from the sofa, John took a quick look around. "Nice, it's looking like a home. I must go but I'll see you over the weekend. And then I hope to meet this new woman."

"Need a place to stay?"

"Don't worry and don't offer. From now on, I'm doing what suits me."

Mathew mulled over things after John left and liked none of the scenarios that spread before him. Why was Jessie so difficult, why did she drag on about telling their families, and when was she planning to become engaged? They had to have a serious conversation about the clandestine world she lived in.

But when she called, he moaned into the receiver. "I miss you."

"There is something I have to tell you, or you may already know, John is back."

"He came to see me." *"And said things I don't like."* "Are you on speaking terms again? Last time, you hated him." He pointed out.

"I know, but I can't stay mad forever. It's difficult to forget and accept many things but life is short and if we don't right the wrongs, one day will be too late."

"Why do they talk as if in riddles?" "What did he say?"

"He asked me to the estate."

"Did he come back for you?" He sat on the edge of the sofa.

There was a short silence. "We are drawn to each other but it's in a way few people understand. Neither he nor I ferment romantic notions towards the other and we will never be more than friends. Please don't be jealous, I love you."

"Good. What are you going to do?"

"It depends on you, and that is why I called. Do you want me to? If so, please don't tell them about us, as I haven't even told John. It would be too much and they would think I skip from one brother to the next."

Feeling at ease, he laughed aloud. "It sounds positively seedy. But say yes, the house is large, we can easily get lost."

"You have a dirty mind, Mathew Barrymore."

"You know me too well. When and where is he picking you up?" This should be an interesting answer.

"At college. I'm going back tomorrow morning, everyone is feeling better."

"Why, did you have an epidemic?" He wanted to ask. *"And when did they get back from wherever in Europe they were supposed to be?"*

Grace was so delighted to see John and hear he was staying that she forgot to be mad about his long absence. "Jessie, it's always such a pleasure to see you. And now that he is back,

122

I'm expecting to see you regularly as well. If he's busy, ask Mathew. That should give him a reason to visit his mother."

"Did I hear my name?" Mathew asked from the doorway.

"Hello, darling. I was telling Jessie that she must come more often."

"That would be nice." After kissing his mother, Mathew pecked Jessie's cheek, then sat beside her.

"Was Jeremy all this time with you?" Grace asked with interest.

John nodded. "We came back together. He's also at his family."

"Why does that name sound familiar?" Mathew queried and noticed the quick eye exchange, but neither volunteered an explanation.

At dinner, Jessie kept wondering what the Barrymores would say if they knew about Jeremy. Knowing about him was bad enough but when they heard who he was... Apart from that train of thought, she found it easier to converse, Mark's absence a welcome relief, and without Monica's eagle-eyed curiosity, it almost felt natural to be sitting there. And although James still studied her a little too intently, he also managed to not make her feel self-conscious.

"What is it?" Jessie asked with concern as John walked into her room later that night.

"I've been given an ultimatum. Either I return to college or... Father threatened to take everything away; credit cards, income, the lot."

"It would involve a lot of catching up, that's months' work."

"Newsflash, I'm tired of living my father's life. I want my way, good or bad."

"I understood you once, knew where we were both headed. Now, you have different priorities, and I'm afraid to say the wrong thing. But is the suggestion really so bad?"

"He's blackmailing me and I'm not going to let him. I refuse to end up like Lawrence, confined and frustrated," he said bitingly, then stopped. "Sorry."

"Perhaps he's concerned that something might happen if he can't keep an eye on you."

"That almost sounds nice, but no, he resents not being in control, dictating what he wants. But I'm past caring. Going to lead my own life and am not in the least grieved if he doesn't like it."

"I worry about you. How will you manage?"

"What, I'm useless? We came to stay so we discussed all scenarios already. We know perfectly well how families such as ours operate, so we also know your father is going to have a similar conversation with Jeremy, possibly discuss business. He has to decide what he wants to do; I am not influencing him in any way."

"Until a few months ago, you were stable, now, everything is upside down. Your father threatens to disown you and you don't even bat an eyelid."

"Lack of money has never frightened me. I hate this life."

"You are upset and don't really mean that, just think carefully—"

"What do you think I was doing all these months, merely having a good time?"

"I didn't mean it that way either."

Rising, he offered his hand. "I know, and out of everyone's opinion yours matters the most. How many times I wished I would fall in love with you, but as wonderful as you are, you can't change me." He smoothed the hair around her face. "But we have something many people never know, true friendship, and now even more than that, I feel as if you are my sister. We'll withstand love affairs, marriages, and whatever else may come. I'd say that is special. And now, I've upset you enough."

After he left her room, she realised how true his words were. They did have something no lover could break. Suddenly, she felt her spirits lift, to just as quickly have them drop. How she wished that neither family discovered this bizarre twist of fate.

Mathew appeared soon after and taking her in his arms, held her ferociously. "See what you do to me? I'm burning with jealousy. Don't you understand? You occupy everything in my life; my dreams, my thoughts, my nights, and my days."

"Oh, Mathew,"

"Jessie,' he said as they lay in bed. "I know you love me but there is this place you never let me into. Why is that? Are you embarrassed of who you are? Why is everything a mystery? It was exciting in the beginning but now I want to be here, always, without secrets. You know about me, but I know next to nothing about you. Why has John been to your house but not me? If you don't want them to know we are sleeping together, we won't. And we should have stopped a long time ago, by getting married. What's wrong with your family?"

"Nothing," she turned nervously.

"Then take me to meet them."

"I will." She said quickly, in no mood to be having this conversation.

"One more thing," he told her as he bent over the side of the bed and reached for his jeans. "Close your eyes."

Sometimes, she cursed her sixth sense and now was such a time. "Please,"

"Sshh," taking one of her hands, he slipped a ring onto her finger. "Go ahead."

Her eyes were already overflowing. 'It's beautiful.' She stared at the diamond.

"Like you, precious and rare." He kissed the tears away, holding her gaze lovingly. "Say yes, Jessie, because we are right. No, not right, perfect. We belong together."

"I love you." The knot in her chest barely let her get the words out.

Kissing her, his hands went into her hair, spreading it over the pillow. "Say you'll be my wife and we can tell them tomorrow."

"And your parents will think we are screwballs. I come as John's friend and leave as your fiancée? It's weird. Then they would want to meet my family. They can't, not yet, not while we're in mourning."

"Mourning?"

"No one can be so insensitive as to announce an engagement only days after a death in the family. Everyone is grief-stricken and now they're going to start celebrating?" Jumping out of bed, she threw her gown on.

"Who's dead this time?" He too jumped out and slipped into his jeans, facing her across the bed.

"I never told you anyone died before."

"But you have used every other excuse." His temper was disappearing fast.

"That's not true, ask John, he knows. Why do you think he came back?" If only she could swallow words.

"Here we go again. Don't you think it's all peculiar? What are you two hiding? What does my brother know that I don't, but should?"

"Not now, Mathew. I had an exhausting week. Give me time to think."

"More lies, because that's all you tell me. Let's see," he began counting off fingers. "A trip overseas, a sick grandmother, a death, and now I recall, a sister to be wed. Tell the truth now, is there a sister and a wedding?"

She merely nodded.

"When?"

She mumbled the date.

He stared incredulously. "But that's already past... Jessie," he raged. "I demand to know what's going on."

"You demand?" She shook with fear and fury all at once. "I told you I need time to work through stuff, but you are always pushing. I can't think this way, I need space."

"Have all the space you want." Bending down, he picked his shirt from the floor and threw it on. "But keep the ring, maybe it will help clear your head." Then he stormed out of the room.

That night wasn't particularly pleasant, but when morning came and she didn't feel better, it somehow became an insurmountable obstacle and she found that even putting her clothes on was difficult. Reaching the breakfast table, she hastily slipped the ring off her finger and into a pocket. "Good morning, sorry I'm late."

Mathew gazed at her, then at her hand, and she would swear he meant to do her an injury.

"Morning, Jessie." Grace greeted and motioned for the servants to come forward. "What would you like?"

"Only coffee, please,"

"Father made me a proposition." John announced.

All looked at him, and Jessie hoped he had reconsidered.

"And?" Grace encouraged with a smile.

"I politely declined. Actually, I wasn't so polite. In fact, this is farewell." John got up from his chair.

"Farewell?" Grace repeated the word as if not understanding it.

"Yes. I've packed my bags and am ready to go."

Theodore motioned for the servants to withdraw. When they were alone, he turned to his youngest son. "Our conversation was confidential."

"Of course it was. Why would you want them to know that among your many talents you have now graduated to blackmail, that you threatened to disown me?"

Jessie felt ill; whether from lack of food or the conversation, she wasn't certain.

But it was no longer a conversation, merely a pouring out of John's heart, and all he had bottled inside came tumbling forth. Resentment, denial, pretending... to be like everyone else, knowing he was not. What she could see was that no one else understood what he was rambling about. Wiping tears, she gazed at Mathew helplessly.

Getting to his feet, he reached for her. "This is a repetition of what you did months ago, isn't it? What did you do then, and what are you doing now?" He asked as the rest stared uncomprehendingly.

John fixed his eyes on Jessie. "I know we are not where we should be, but time will bring us together again. Strangely, being away from you also gave me purpose and courage. You see," he addressed everyone. "I'm no longer ashamed to admit that I am gay."

Theodore catapulted to his feet at the head of the table. "Get out! And don't come back."

"No!" Grace shook with sobs.

James put his arms around her. "Hell, little brother, just drop it like that."

"Heaven help us all!" Theodore thundered.

John's hand went to Jessie's hair. "Jeremy and I will be fine."

"And we have discussed this repulsive subject long enough." Theodore was barely able to control his outrage. Then he looked at Grace. The shock seemed to have flattened her as well as an earthquake might have done. "But for your sake, I'll allow him to come see you. Just warn me beforehand, I want him nowhere near me. My son, the... It's demeaning, humiliating, and disgraceful to our very name." And in a fury, he left the dining room.

John did likewise.

Jessie felt physically ill, swaying against Mathew.

"Heaven forbid the press got wind of it. They would tear us to shreds." James said.

"Why didn't you tell me?" Mathew asked as they drove away. She didn't answer, again making him feel locked out. It was as if she attracted enigmas. "You're right, the less we discuss it the better."

At the apartment, he stared at her as she sat on the sofa crying, unable to open her heart in ways she hadn't yet done, and clearly, could not. He wanted to reach out and hold her, but something lay between them. Until today, he had been annoyed many times, especially when he felt excluded, but now he was frightened. He watched nervously as she got up and disappeared into the bedroom.

When she came out, she had her case. "I have to go home, they need me."

But right now, he needed her, feeling afraid and broken by her refusal to share herself completely. He was sick of her silences, and her constant rejection of his intentions, but most of all, he wanted to tell her that he loved her until he could no more. "I'll take you." Hope was born again.

"I have to go to college to get my car."

And so, hope died a premature death. "Okay." He felt as if she had kicked him.

Neither said much as they drove away, each locked in their own scary world.

She arrived home to find Beverley and Simon still there, quiet pillars of support for Serena, who was the worst affected. Noticing Jeremy sitting on his own, she wanted to tell him about what had taken place at the Barrymores, to know if he was aware of what awaited him. His gaze lifted and fixed on hers, he already knew and was in no mood to discuss it with her.

Without a word, she went to her room and almost at once, Beverley appeared. They sat talking about Lawrence; how he had destroyed his life and fortune on the side while looking successful, how Taylor felt responsible, and Serena was shattered by her first-born's untimely departure.

Jessie recalled the breakfast scene at the Barrymores; no one could claim they fared better. "How is Jeremy?"

"Extremely quiet, I don't think he's going to stay."

"Not at home anyway. And he's certainly not going to try Stevens. He and John are headed for unspeakable heartache but neither seems to notice."

"How do you feel about it now?"

"I don't hate them and I expect we'll become reacquainted."

"Yes, you have a loving heart." Beverley smiled. "Amidst all this, I have some good news. I'm pregnant."

"That's wonderful," Jessie threw her arms around her sister and feeling the bulge in her pocket, pulled the ring out.

"Oh, my gosh, Mathew proposed! But why isn't this beautiful thing on your finger?"

Jessie stared at the diamond. "He gave it to me yesterday."

"You should be happy, you're anything but. You said yes, right?"

"I told him that I need to think."

"Are you crazy? I know you love him, and I'd say he loves you a whole lot too. What's the problem?"

"Hell is going to break loose when everyone finds out, but especially Mathew. I know I caused this, just don't ask me how. I've fallen in love with the wrong man. I mean, he's the right one, but... I love him beyond reason but when he discovers what I've done."

"Will you just tell me?"

"He thinks I'm Jessie Lewis. John's idea. I know I shouldn't have gone there in the first place but he was desperate and I—"

Beverley's hand went up. "Now starting from the beginning, explain what's been going on."

And Jessie did.

"Oh, God, this is a mess. And you must tell him, sooner rather than later."

"But that's my fear. Mathew will never accept me because they abhor us. You haven't heard how they talk, and

I particularly detest it when he does. Now he's demanding to meet my family. It's all so mixed-up and scary."

"Knowing about the bad blood between our families, would you still marry him?"

"I love him regardless, but they are different."

"If this stops him, then perhaps he's not worth it. Okay, I will understand if you tell me he went nuts about all the deceit. But if he loves you as much as he says he does, he will get over it. Now, I suggest you get a move on, unless you want to give him up without explanations. Jessie, you have to, before he finds out another way."

"Do you hate the Barrymores?"

"I don't know them so why would I? I know John, and he's nice, regardless of the intrigue. This is a predicament. Daddy gets upset when rumours do their rounds but I don't think he hates them either. Lawrence was a different story. Imagine if he had known…"

"Did you know grandma almost married William Barrymore, John's grandfather?"

"We all know this, just not the details. And it should have nothing to do with you."

"That's what we say, even John, but not them. I'm so scared."

After Simon and Beverley's departure, Jessie went downstairs, and stopped at the sight of suitcases in the entrance hall. She didn't have to rack her brain as to whose they were; the answer came down the stairs in jeans and a leather jacket. "So, you are leaving."

"You knew I would. I want a life and this is not it." Jeremy pointed somewhere.

"How can you break daddy's heart so callously? He has just lost his first-born and he needs you to give him a chance, Stevens, the family."

"It's because I care that I am leaving." He regarded her for a second. "You think you know a lot but you are young and I would say a little naïve. I refuse to be saddled with Lawrence's constraints. We might not have been alike in most things but he hated it and so would I. You also know what I am, how do you propose I explain it to my father? You don't want me to break his heart? Then let me go without making me feel worse than I already do. If I stayed, they would soon be pressing me to marry. How am I supposed to do that, and whose life do you suggest I ruin? There is only one person I want to be with and he is not female. I will not marry any woman for mere procreation. Being an uncle to yours and Beverley's children is enough for me."

"But they won't be Stevenses."

"A name isn't all that's important, Jessie. When you do get married, what will you do, refuse to give your children their father's name because you want Stevens to live forever?"

"If you gave it a chance, I'd say, he tried. But you won't even attempt."

"One day, you will understand. And it saddens me to hurt everyone, but it's little compared to the misery I would cause by staying. How long do you suppose it's going to be before our pictures become front-page news? I don't want to be home when that happens."

CHAPTER EIGHT

"Hello," James greeted as he walked into the chic apartment.

Turning on the sofa surprised, Vanessa's shoulder-length blonde hair bounced about her face as she smiled. "Hello. Why back so soon? And lunch?"

"We never got that far. John is back and it's a complete disaster."

"Oh, gee," her mouth twisted a little. "What happened?"

Bending over, he kissed her mouth long and hard, instantly feeling aroused. "Mmm. I'll tell you after I do this." Falling over the back of the sofa, he landed with his head on her lap, his hands reached out, and unbuttoned her blouse.

"I have to be at the studio in an hour."

Ignoring her protestations, he continued undressing her. Then tearing off his clothes, he pulled her onto his lap.

"Honestly, must we do it on every piece of furniture?" She complained but her mouth quirked upwards as she did her blouse's buttons again. "So, tell me."

"John's return was the expected calamity. I knew nothing good would come from his dropping out but even I couldn't imagine what was going on. He arrived yesterday with that pretty girl of his and everything was calm. Father calls him into his office and about an hour later, he emerges highly ruffled and makes a bee-line for her room. We assumed they were dating but it turns out there is nothing going on. Mathew was also there, which is surprising as he hasn't been home in a while. What is stranger, is that I got the distinct impression his visit had nothing to do with John's return. Then this morning, over breakfast, John drops his bombshell. Mother was in shock, Jessie cried, Mathew, I don't know, not to mention that father kicked him out."

"Wait… What? Why?" Her green eyes were round with shock.

"He's gay."

"Holy crap,"

"Apparently, Jessie discovered this bit of info around June and went to cry on Mathew's shoulder."

"Ah, Jessie!" Vanessa eyed him oddly. "Mathew's intended."

He lifted his brows. "Are you sure?"

"Oh yes, told me all about her. Some college kid, twenty-one, and pretty smart." Vanessa told him bitingly.

"That's her all right. Well, well, what do we have here?"

"In my business, secrecy equals trouble. What's this kid's surname?"

"Lewis."

"Then what happened with John?" She queried eagerly.

"He went on for a bit, while none of us followed, except Jessie, hence why she looked absolutely gutted, and then father told him to get out. He did, on his way to someone called Jeremy. Who, as it happens, is the same guy he went on holiday with, and whose Porsche he was driving today. I was curious where he had got it and asked. It must be another college kid, because it came across as if Jessie might also know him."

Vanessa looked pensive.

James continued. "Personally, I don't care about his choices, and well... whatever. But it's all very bad news. Which is why, you are not to breathe a word of this to anyone."

"Heavens no," she agreed. "But as soon as I have an hour or two to spare, I'm going to pay college a visit. You never know what turns up."

He wondered if she felt compelled to go after Jessie because Mathew had tossed her aside. But as if guessing what he was thinking, she turned around and kissed him.

"Mark!" Grace got to her feet. "Why didn't you let us know you were arriving today?"

He embraced and kissed her. "How is everyone?"

"Not well." She told him sadly.

He pulled her to the sofa. "Why have you been crying?"

She wiped a slow tear. "John. Your father hoped he would return to college and so did I, but it was a lost cause. Made up his mind and just walked out. We never knew, had no idea, and poor Jessie was devastated."

"She has been around?" Curiosity filled his voice.

"A few times, but that day, she came with John and left with Mathew, in tears, and all over breakfast."

"What happened?"

"John is gay."

A hand flew to his forehead. "You're kidding... of course you're not."

"Your father is in a fury and has cut him off. But for my sake, he's allowed to visit when Theo is not here. Imagine, now my son has to make appointments to see me."

"What about Jessie, they looked okay together."

"John's insinuations, she merely played along."

He held her hands in his. "Does anyone else know about this?"

"It's possible Mathew and James told their girlfriends."

"How is Vanessa? And good god, she's in cahoots with half the press."

"Mathew broke up with her months ago and we haven't seen her since. There is a new girl and he's constantly talking about marriage."

"He was always a homely type, and James?"

"In the months they have been dating, neither has yet brought his girlfriend home. Mathew says his is funny, and James' is some career woman who never has time."

"I think it's good I'm back, I might have to help my brothers get some perspective back into their lives. When did this happen?"

"A week ago."

Turning the corner, Jessie wondered if she should go home. Last weekend had been spent listening to Beverley repeatedly telling her that she had better enlighten Mathew, soon. She went as far as calling him, wondering if telling him over the phone was easier. All she had been able to mouth was to ask how he was doing. Then, in a mental blank, she pushed the lying monster aside yet again.

She crashed into someone. Apologising profusely, she gazed at her victim. "Mark!"

"Hello, Jessie." He steadied her.

"Wh-what are you doing here?"

"I did graduate months ago, I just stayed in the States looking for new business opportunities. I'm planning to export our fabrics."

She nodded. If he stayed on neutral ground, she might manage a conversation. But that still didn't explain what he was doing here.

"How are you, really?"

"Fine," she held the books tightly against her chest.

His eyes fell on her left hand. "Engaged! When did this happen? Mother never mentioned."

Thankfulness filled her for having been a little vain that morning. "Yes, it's recent. I'm very busy and there's a meeting," she pointed to a door.

"Who's the lucky guy? Obviously not John. And what the heck, Jessie, why did you pretend you were dating?"

"Our business. Goodbye, Mark," she turned to walk away.

His hand stopped her. "And here I believed you were after James. Though, this guy must be loaded too." He stroked the ring.

"Think whatever you wish." Flicking the long black hair over her shoulder, she ran down the steps.

"Can we start over?" He asked beside her.

She stopped abruptly. "As what, I don't trust you."

"Look, I came to apologise. I go crazy when people push my buttons and that day you did a very good job. I knew you were up to something; it just never occurred to me to consider an innocent prank. Forgiven?"

What was it with all the Barrymore men? Looking at him, she could tell he was sincere. But be that so, he still made her nervous, because if he had lost control once, he might again. And no matter the brushstroke used, this was an already messy canvas, and no amount of whitewashing would repair it. "I'll give you the benefit of the doubt, but now, I really need to go."

He gave her one of those charming Barrymore smiles. "Thank you, that is all I wanted."

She wondered if he was satisfied with her answer, as he kept agendas and wrote notes to himself. Her life was twisted enough as it was, ever since meeting the Barrymores. Leaning her head against her car, she hoped he was as genuine as he purported, because if there was a person who could freak her out...

"Jessie."

"Ma- Mathew!" And right there one of those unwanted complications had reared its head. Tremors ran through her.

"How are you?" He watched her eagerly.

She nodded, trying to calm herself. "You?"

"Couldn't you call to ask how I'm doing?"

"I've been studying for exams. And I did, but you don't believe me anymore." She accused.

"What do you expect from me? You are always doing things that don't make sense. I want to marry you, yet I scarcely know enough." He saw the ring. "Have you told them?"

"Only my sister,"

"Okay, we wait a while, but you are wearing it." Taking a step closer, he took her face in his hands and kissed her.

She was unable to fight, she didn't want to. Dropping the books to the ground, she threw her arms around him.

"How I love you. Get what you need, let's go home."

"Does it have to be this weekend?" She asked as they lay in bed later.

"I told them that I proposed, you accepted, and if they have anything to say, to keep it to themselves. And no," he added as he saw her wide eyes. "I didn't tell them it's you."

"I'm so scared I feel sick."

"You do look pale." Smoothing the raven tresses, he dropped a kiss on her nose.

"They will be shocked and ask why we didn't care to mention it."

"It was hardly the right time."

"You know Mark is suspicious of me, James watches me funny. But I'll bet if something isn't to your Aunt's liking she will be the worst one of all."

"Well, you sure have them down to a T. But please don't worry, I promise it will be all right. And you know mother loves you." He smiled.

"Actually, I feel as if I'm about to step into a grinder." Her hands went up to his face. "Just promise me one thing."

"Anything,"

Her eyes became bright as she told him softly. "When you do stop loving me, try not to hate me too much."

"Why do you say such things?"

"Because we don't know tomorrow. Look how many people start off with good intentions, meaning well, deeply in love; see where they end, ripping each other apart."

"We'll never be like that, you're just talking crazy. You wouldn't perhaps want to avoid all this suffering and elope?"

Looking up from her book, Grace stared at them in surprise. "Oh, I'm so glad you brought Jessie along." Rising, she kissed the young face then turned to her son. "And where is the mystery lady?"

Suddenly, Mathew became a little boy. Huh—"

Grace cut him short. "Don't tell me you broke up again. I thought you said you love this girl so much."

"I do love this girl." He gazed sheepishly at his mother and then adoringly at Jessie, his arm encircling her waist possessively. "Mom, close your mouth."

"Jessie?" Opening her arms, Grace embraced her with pleasure. "Then why keep it secret?" She turned to Mathew. "Oh, honey," she said emotionally. "What a celebration, you have made me extremely happy."

This was only happening because she was Jessie Lewis. The moment she became Jessica Stevens would Grace's reaction still be the same? Guilt gnawed at her. Again, she had used poor judgement by coming here under false pretences. Fear gripped her, he had to know. And if he must be mad, or even break it off, so be it. "Mathew…"

Grace placed herself between them and steered them to the stairway. "Listen, you two, go get ready for dinner. This surprise I cannot miss."

"Pity we don't have time," he murmured against her face as soon as they were in her room. "I'm addicted to you."

She placed a hand against his chest. "I need to tell you something."

He glanced furtively at his watch. "Does it have to be now? I'm waiting for an important call."

"This is also important."

Regret filled him as he leaned against the wall. "I'm listening."

Turning her back on him, she took a deep breath, her hands twisting nervously. "It's about who I am."

"I know who you are."

She swivelled around. "You do?"

"You are the love of my life," he took a step towards her.

She raised her hand. "Please don't touch me while I'm trying to say this. And that is not what I meant. It's about where I come from."

"I don't care if you come from a long line of street sweepers."

"If only." "I know I've done a terrible thing by letting it get out of hand, something I regret deeply. But it just happened and it seemed right. As you say sometimes, perfect."

"What are we talking about?"

"Things you have to know."

"For goodness sake then, get to the point."

"When John first suggested it, it seemed so simple, but that's because neither of us expected it to turn out this way. I should have said something months ago but I was afraid, still am, and it's not fair to either of us."

Someone knocked loudly. "Mr Barrymore, an urgent call from Thailand."

"Thanks, I'll be right there." He turned to her. "Jessie, I can see you are troubled, so I do want to hear what this is about. But now I must take this call and then we need to be downstairs. Please get ready and we will discuss it later." He dropped a gentle kiss on her lips. "I'll see you in ten minutes."

Standing in the middle of the room, she wondered why she had rambled on. Must enjoy punishment because she sure had dragged out her own suffering. This was categorically not the time but at least he had agreed to talk afterwards. And if he could not accept her for being a

Stevens, could she simply go her way and never cross his path again? The prospect made her feel quite ill.

"Are you dressed?" Mathew asked outside.

"In a minute," scrambling to her feet, she rushed into the dress.

Theodore helped himself to a drink and turned to Grace. "What does this girl look like? And why were proper introductions not made before today?"

Grace chuckled. "All I'm saying is that you will be surprised."

Monica glanced around curiously. "I hope he chose someone worthy of the Barrymore name."

Grace turned to Theodore so she didn't blurt out what she thought. "Where is James, it's as if he has moved out as well."

"I won't be surprised if he also announces something before long." Theodore pursed his lips. "I don't understand why everyone does such unorthodox things nowadays."

"This younger generation, no consideration whatsoever," Monica went to the drinks. "Mark, seen any of your old friends?"

"I don't have many here. All I'm interested in right now is to find my niche. You may have heard that I'm moonlighting in father's office."

"How did you become interested in exports?" Monica continued.

"It's a logical avenue for excellent products. Besides, it's not a new idea for us, it's just that we're going over the ocean now."

Theodore watched his son proudly. "What an addition to Barrymores."

"Any nice girls in America?" Monica queried.

"I suppose, but I'm particularly taken with one right here; met her last time I was home."

"Care to elaborate?" Monica pressed.

An odd expression passed over Mark's semblance. "Not really."

"What is with you boys? always hiding women."

"It's called privacy. We are adults and entitled to our own lives, or are we not?"

"Of course." Grace's thoughts flew to John.

"As long as it's within the boundaries of decency." Theodore announced.

"Mathew, darling, there you are!" Grace called and the other three turned to the door expectantly. "Is she hiding again?"

"A blushing bride, how awful. Give me a fighter any day." Mark commented and pouring himself a drink, took a swig.

Theodore stared, then blurted. "I'll be—"

"Good heavens, when did this happen?" Monica prided herself in knowing everything. "Incredible."

"Jessie!" Mark choked on his drink.

Smiling mischievously, Grace extended her hand. "I said you'd be surprised."

"That's hardly the word. Anyway, congratulations," Monica kissed the air around the young face.

"Likewise," Theodore hugged Jessie and looked at Mathew. "Why the secrecy?"

"I wanted to, but she drives me nuts. Mark, no congratulations?"

"Huh, well, yes, of course." Mark shook his brother's hand and then turned to Jessie.

The finger of fear ran through her, had he meant what he said days ago? She decided to take him at his word.

He leaned in to kiss her cheek and whispered. "I'm astonished, only second best?"

Monica looked at her watch. "This is ridiculous, where is James?"

"Let's give them a few minutes more." Grace suggested.

But ten minutes later he hadn't arrived yet.

"I can't pretend to drink the entire evening." Monica said displeased.

Grace shook her head. "Okay, they are probably stuck in traffic."

Jessie felt as if her nerves had moved to the outside. But it was no longer anxiety but an actual sick feeling in the floor of her stomach. Lifting her eyes, she noticed Mark studying her. She took a deep breath, feeling like throwing up.

"Are you okay?" He asked, something resembling genuine concern on his face.

She didn't know if this was better. "I think so."

"Here," he poured water into her glass. "Drink some, you look pale."

"Thank you."

James entered the room. "Sorry we are late, traffic was crazy. Remain sitting, we all know each other."

Everyone gaped.

"I don't think I can ever be this shocked again," Monica complained.

"Why didn't you tell us?" Grace asked stupefied.

"Hello, Vanessa." Mathew shook her hand.

Vanessa dazzled as she smiled; the white silk dress moulding her perfect lines like a second skin. "So, this is Jessie." Her gaze rushed over the younger woman, as if she had just been fork-lifted off a mud puddle.

Glancing at the beautiful but cold creature, Jessie knew instantly that neither would ever like the other and given the opportunity, Vanessa would crush her.

Looking away, she caught Mark's gaze again. She had made a mistake when indulging her bruised confidence in men, but he had frightened and hurt her and she had not known how else to strike back. Now, however sincere he was, she was so very confused about his good intentions.

Mark turned to Vanessa. "You and James, weird, go figure."

She, in turn, gave Jessie a cold glance.

Mark noticed and decided to say what was on his mind. "It's hardly the same."

Naturally, Vanessa could not follow his line of reasoning.

Jessie fixed her gaze on the intricate silver napkin ring and wondered why he had made a distinction because it did look like the same thing.

Grace intervened. "I can't get over this. We thought we were meeting two strangers but both turn out to be family friends already."

"That remains to be seen." James said.

"What are you talking about, old man?" Mark asked curiously.

Jessie glanced at Mathew, who was in silent mode, and she knew why. He was delving into the upstairs conversation.

"Did you hear, Mr Barrymore," Vanessa turned to Theodore as the entrées were served. "Lawrence Stevens gambled all his money away, so there is suspicion that he might have committed suicide."

Jessie watched her. What could this woman know of Lawrence's life? But wasn't it to be expected of people who were in the limelight? And with Vanessa part of the media, she would doubtless hear more bizarre accounts of what was speculated.

Vanessa continued. "Taylor has quite a task ahead of him, no heirs."

Theodore regarded her. "He does have another son. Obviously green, but with training, he should learn something."

"He wants no part of Stevens. And the reports on his life are far from glowing."

Jessie's hand rolled into a fist, who had this woman been talking to?

Grace frowned, this was a happy occasion, no one needed an initiator in their midst. "We shouldn't be talking about sad families but discussing gayer things."

Theodore gave her such a cold look that she bit her lip.

"What else do they say?" Monica joined the instigation.

"Taylor is selling huge chunks of his holdings, including the plastic plant in Durban."

"Jessie's father is also in plastics." Mathew remarked.

"Really," Vanessa arched a brow.

Jessie looked up and saw Mark watching her again. He smiled.

"This is a farce." James announced.

Vanessa placed a hand on his arm to calm him down. "Let me take care of it." She turned to Mathew. "What do you think of your future in-laws?"

"Haven't met them yet; they are in mourning." Mathew told her.

"How sad, Jessie." Grace sympathised. "Who died?"

Vanessa opened her mouth, but Mark intervened. "Stop it. Can't you see she's not well?"

Jessie stared at the elaborate setting, a dreadful premonition filling her. And just as if a thunderbolt had struck and a cloud of doom gathered above her head, she knew they knew. Why the cat-and-mouse conversation. Resting her clammy hands limply on the table, she asked. "What do you want from me?"

"We could start with the truth," James invited.

Mathew stared at his brother. "What are you implying?"

"Ask your fiancée why you haven't met her family."

"They were away."

"Is that how she kept you in the dark? But, kudus, she did not lie about the death." Vanessa declared. ·

Mathew turned to Jessie. "What are they talking about?"

Like a pack of hyenas, they were onto her, and likewise, would not let go. Looking at James, she knew why he was doing it. He was in love and would do anything Vanessa wished, including hurting his brother. She felt sorry for him, because right now, he was blinded by the blonde green-eyed charms, while Vanessa still had her eye, and heart, if she had one, elsewhere, and this was the punishment she had chosen to dish out.

Mark told Vanessa bluntly. "We are not interested in your theories."

That only upset her more. "How interesting; John, Mathew, and now you."

"I'm warning you, shut up." Mark commanded.

James hit his right hand on the table, startling all. "I may not be head of this household yet but I will not tolerate this masquerade. Come on Jessie, or don't you have the guts?"

"Say nothing." Mark told Jessie then turned to Vanessa. "You are a vicious bitch."

Vanessa gasped, Grace and Monica stared incredulously.

Mathew shook his head, as if he were trying to clear it of hallucinogens. "Everyone, sit down. Jessie, explain."

Vanessa produced a photograph, making sure Jessie saw who was in it then placed it before Monica. "Please do and tell us who that is."

She gazed at the two happy faces. How had Vanessa found that snapshot? Where had she been? And was this how people behaved at the dinner table? She had never seen it at home, even when Lawrence was at his worst, as her parents usually put a stop to his malicious tongue. She had thought James was odd, but never seen him as mean. With Vanessa's goading, he might become dangerous.

"We are waiting." Theodore encouraged, as he stared at the photograph Monica passed him. He pushed it across to Grace with one finger.

"John, Jeremy!" Grace recognised.

"I'm sorry," Jessie began as she rose to her feet and fixed her gaze on Mathew, "but this is what I was trying to tell you. There is no excuse for lying and I should have been forthright a long time ago, if not that first weekend when John brought me here, but I was afraid. I'm not sure why he did it, but in a moment of pure lunacy, he gave me an assumed name, which was supposed to last only that weekend. I know I cannot possibly apologise enough but I never intended harm."

"The fact remains that you are here." James accused.

"And congratulations," Vanessa added venomously as she pointed at the photograph disdainfully. "You and your brother have set a wonderful path of destruction over this family."

"Your brother?" Grace stuttered in shock.

Jessie's eyes filled with tears. "And you think I wanted this to happen?"

"Is this the same boy John left college for?" Theodore asked, momentarily unable to think of anything else.

"And there are no words to express my distress. This is not—"

"Come off it, Miss Stevens." Vanessa said theatrically and a gasp arose around the table. "What exactly did you expect when the Barrymores uncovered your secrets?"

"Is this true?" Theodore demanded.

"I was afraid of being found out but I'm not ashamed of who I am."

"You… lied," Mathew began in a strangled voice.

Jessie's eyes filled with tears as she saw the hurt in his.

"When… when where you planning to tell me? At the altar?"

She felt as if she were being suffocated. "I'm sorry."

"Sorry can't change anything, can it?"

She dropped her head sadly, how right he was.

Monica glared at Grace. "And you thought they were not dangerous. My mother was so right, you are filth, worse than, and now your brother…" Unable to hide her disgust, she rose from the table and pointed to the door. "Go on, run along and tell mommy and daddy that their vile scheme was only half-successful."

Theodore spoke again. "Miss Stevens, I would appreciate it if you left at once."

Nothing she said or did could change the hurt she had brought this family, or prove the remorse she felt for having done so. She picked the photo from the table then turned to Grace and said simply. "I am sorry, Mrs Barrymore."

"So am I, honey, so am I." Grace answered sadly.

"Are you going to do nothing?" Mark asked Mathew.

"Mark, it's your turn to shut up." James told him.

"And none of you know what you're doing."

Mathew got up.

"Don't." Monica begged as she placed a hand on his shoulder. "I would hate to lose a second nephew to another Stevens. Heavens above, unhappy with self-destruction, they are trying to drag us along, just as they did in the past!"

Getting to her feet, Vanessa ran to Mathew. "Sorry you found out this way, but it was my duty—"

"You're a hazard, and I'll be damned if I want anything to do with you. Stay away from me, as far away as possible. And from now on, when you visit this house, let me know, so I may go elsewhere, preferably, another hemisphere." Mathew told her furiously then strode purposely away.

Incensed, Vanessa bit her lip.

Mathew ran upstairs and stopped in the doorway. "Why?"

"Lie or fall in love?" Jessie asked as she quickly packed her case.

"I chose to love you, now, I choose to stop. But did you me, or were you simply looking forward to what my name could do for you?" He asked savagely.

"And I need it to change what about me? But if that's what you believe then you don't know me."

"Did I ever? And when were you going to tell me?"

"I don't know. What I do know is that you think I've done you a terrible injustice because I'm a Stevens. Well, I'm sorry, but I can't change who I am. I knew this day was coming, knew it the first time you said you loved me, also knowing it would end this way. So, as you look at me now, what has changed except a word on a piece of paper?" She almost laughed. "Jeremy was so right, a name isn't everything, but where you're concerned, it's the only thing.

"You think Vanessa did this out of the goodness of her heart? She wants you back and this is her way because she knows James is her pawn. He's so in love he'll do absolutely anything to get her, including hurting you, but evidently, neither of you can see it because a threatening Stevens is in the house. But I'm wasting my breath. Goodbye, Mathew." Walking past him, she stopped on the landing.

Mark was leaning against the wall, listening. "Do you need me to drive you home?"

"I would appreciate it if you called a taxi."

"I'll ask Adams to take you." Mark told her as he watched Mathew walk to his bedroom and slam the door shut.

Jessie jumped visibly; the sound of the end. "Why are you being kind? I realise now that you must have known too but it's not even important how you found out."

"That's college for you, kids talk and I won't lie and say I wasn't stunned or didn't feel upset when I first heard. It's true I don't like what your name represents, but these things can be fixed. Unlike them, I've had time to think about it logically, therefore, my question is this, will you marry me?"

"W-what?" She asked stupefied.

"You heard right. I asked if you'd marry me."

"Why, live where, and parade in front of them as they insult me? Were you not paying attention downstairs? You'd be thrown out of this house faster than John was. And to tell the truth, I don't care to see another Barrymore for a very long time, if ever again."

"They are in the throes of shock and emotion, it tends to blind people. Besides, I'm like John in this; I don't care what my father thinks."

This was proof that all Barrymores were insane. "No, Mark, I will not marry you."

"One thing I know," his voice softened. "You have far too much of this damned love emotion and I'm willing to bet that you would soon learn to love me."

"I love Mathew, but I'm no longer good enough for him; I accept that. And it was naïve of me to believe that he would somehow see past everything." She started walking away.

He walked beside her. "Please reconsider. I know where you live now, so I'll keep calling until you agree."

She stopped. "If that's a threat, I'm no longer scared. James is doing it for Vanessa, and Mathew... He's hurt, confused, and not ready to deal with any of this. Your motives I'm not certain about, as you always have hidden agendas and I plainly refuse to be part of them." Then she turned and ran all the way down the stairs.

"Miss Jessie," Adams waited with the car door open.

"Thank you, Mr Adams, but if you don't want to..." she gulped.

"It was a rather silly prank." He closed the door and climbed behind the wheel. "But I am sad to say that the place won't be the same without you, or Master John. Where to, Miss Jessie?"

"To... Mathew's apartment." And this was how it ended. It was her fault she hurt this much but what could she do now but bear it? Like the romantic fool she was, she believed love conquered all.

At the apartment, she removed every vestige of her presence and left the ring and key on the dressing table.

Adams merely watched in silence as she packed her possessions into a box and after loading it into the car, drove her to college. "Are you certain you'll be all right, Miss Jessie?" He asked concerned.

"I'm not, but neither of us can do anything about it." It was then that the unstoppable tears began.

"Goodbye, Miss Jessie."

The flood was such that she never saw the extended hand. Then she ran out of the building and up the hill. The wind picked up, the trees swayed, and out of nowhere, raindrops started falling. She stayed right there as it grew into a downpour. And as thunder and lightning pierced the sky, it felt as if they went right through her, mirroring the very state of her soul. As if tempting the bolts, she sobbed, and screamed one word repeatedly. "Mathew."

It was there Meghan found her, drenched to the bone, almost delirious, slumped against the tree. After making her take a hot shower, Meghan climbed into bed with her, to hold her close so she would stop shivering.

"I'm sorry it turned out this way." Meghan said sadly in the morning.

Jessie leaned over the side of the bed, grabbed her discarded wet jacket, dug in the pocket, and held the picture in her hand. "Vanessa Manning had this. Did you talk to her?"

Meghan stared at the empty spot on the noticeboard. "The TV star? No. But I heard she came around a while back. I had classes so I never saw her. Someone must have shown her around, and of course she snooped. Which means, she was onto you."

Jessie wiped her overflowing eyes. "My life is over."

"Come, let me take you home." Meghan offered.

The minute she walked in the door, Jessie ran to her room and locked herself in.

Meghan refused to divulge any information, pretending ignorance, instead mentioning a terrible cold Jessie might have picked up, then asked Samuel to drive her back to college.

"So, that's what Mathew and company thought." Beverley hugged her.

Jessie nodded sadly, her eyes brimming. "Why are you here so early in the morning?"

"Because you are not all right and Meghan called me."

Jessie broke down and cried for a long time, trying to explain the immense hurt. "It was that awful Vanessa. She's playing James like a violin and the fool can't even see it, neither can Mathew." She wailed. "I know I took too long to tell him but I had finally decided. I didn't stand a chance."

"I'm so sorry."

"That's what I said and Mathew told me it doesn't change anything. And she had this." Jessie flicked the photograph onto the bed.

"That's mine." Beverley grabbed it.

"No, it's the one I had."

"The snake is a thief as well? She came to see me a few days ago, with flowers for Lawrence. Please, as if I believed her. We attended the same school; different years, we do not know each other. She discussed pointless stuff then asked to see my wedding album, where that picture's twin happens to be. I added it because they weren't there. I couldn't guess any of this or know she was mixed up with James... In other words, she was double-checking. I could punch her."

"Not as hard as I'd like to, but I won't cheapen myself and use the same tactics. Now that I'm gone, she's going to be the kind shoulder... James is going to hurt as much as I do and I'm not going to feel any pity." She sniffed. "I know there is no excuse for not being truthful, but I never hated anyone, and I never intended to do what they said."

"He might come to his senses."

"Before we went to the house, he told me he didn't care what they thought. It's not true, he does, all he lives for. I'm just never going to see him again and I think I don't care." But she did, and hurt so much she thought her heart would explode.

Within two weeks, she asked her father to let her go to Europe. He offered to help, realising something was going on with his youngest child. But she wasn't going to repeat any of her pain to anyone else.

"How can you just go? What about Christmas, New Year?" Beverley asked later.

"You think it's easy for me? This is my life, everything I know, but I have to let it go." Jessie's eyes burnt. "I know they worry, but I can't tell them, and neither can you, not after Lawrence and Jeremy. The Barrymores losing their minds is more than enough."

"You should give Mathew time to think, to make a decision—"

"I'm making it for him."

"You love each other. Go work it out, scream, throw things around if you must, but please don't leave it like this."

"The only Barrymore on my side is John and what can he do? What have I done, to me, Mathew, both our families?"

CHAPTER NINE

Walking east on Kotze Street, John entered Best's Employment Agency.

"Just in time," the receptionist waved an envelope. "Mr Best left this before he went out of town."

Taking the envelope from her, he tore it open and glanced over the page. "This is great; I'll go see them now. Thanks, Cathy."

Jeremy had suggested they wait for the new year to find jobs but why snub potential opportunities? Moreover, Taylor might decide to cut Jeremy off too and then where would they be?

The mere image of Jeremy brought a smile to his lips, which was instantly replaced by a frown. Lately, he had started worrying about Jeremy's health, noticing the continuous paleness, weight loss, colds and flu that hit one after another, making him swing between thankfulness and concern as the endless ailments came and went.

They had travelled great distances in Natal and not everyone reacted favourably to exhaustive schedules, as Jeremy proved when he collapsed with bronchitis and was admitted to a local clinic, hence, they had missed Beverley's wedding. Both had been upset about the incredibly inconvenient timing, but the doctor had been quite plain, ignore a hospital stay and continue at your own peril. Passing the pharmacy two blocks away, he bought vitamins. That should boost Jeremy's system.

A deep silence greeted him as he entered the flat and dropping the bag on the kitchen table, he went into the bedroom. Jeremy slept peacefully. Passing a hand over the forehead, he felt no temperature. He might be getting better after all. Leaving the room silently, he closed the door and walked back to the kitchen.

Later, Jeremy found him stretched out on the sofa. "Something smells good. Why didn't you wake me?"

Throwing the magazine aside, John sat up. "You looked like you were enjoying the rest. And no more junk food. How can you eat all that grease and stay this thin?"

"I don't eat that much."

"Lately, no." John agreed. "And from now on, you are having nothing that doesn't come straight from the ground and onto your plate. Some good news, I found a job. It's at a printer's shop, and only three blocks from here." He passed him the envelope. "Do you suppose Jessie will speak to me if I call?"

"If she doesn't bash the receiver in your ear in the first two seconds, she'll talk."

"Very comforting. How are you really?" John asked as they went into the kitchen.

"Okay, just this permanent lethargy makes me feel sick." Picking one of the vitamin bottles, Jeremy sat at the table.

"I want you to take all of that. I should call my mother… but first, Jessie."

Samuel informed them that if they needed information they should call Beverley, which they did straight away, and she invited them for lunch; there were things she needed to discuss with them, because she had no idea what to do.

"Mathew and Jessie!" John exclaimed when she told them. "Wow, I can actually see it."

"Then you probably picture that disastrous evening better than me too."

"Alone amongst the wolves, and Mathew did nothing?"

"What can I say, I don't know him. What I do know is that she loves him. But that witch knew exactly what to do and it must have sounded like Jessie cavorted with the devil. I understand that he felt betrayed, because she deceived him for a long time, but the reasons are obvious."

"Do your parents know?" John queried.

Beverley shook her head. "And I suggest we leave it at that."

"She told me we would live to regret the day…" John announced sadly. "I guess this is it."

"The damage is done, and I'd say near impossible to repair."

"I don't understand Mathew's behaviour, unless of course, he too was poisoned by grandma's venom. That woman couldn't endear herself to anyone, except Mark. I think it's time I go make a house-call."

"That might not be advisable, he must be raging mad by now." Beverley reached for Jeremy's hand. "Amid the pandemonium, some good news, you are going to be an uncle."

"What do you want?" Mathew asked between irritation and anger.

Pushing past him, John stared around the lounge; empty cans on every surface. "Interesting look."

"Don't get smart. And I blame you for the nightmare I'm living. You knew who she was, so what the hell were you thinking when you took her home?" Mathew raged as he pushed the dishevelled hair out of his face.

"What the hell do you mean?" John retorted sarcastically. "She is my best friend."

"Out of the hundreds, nay, thousands at college you choose a Stevens… great choice." Mathew threw at him.

"Because she's Jessie." A gentle smile appeared on his lips. "They are not what people say they are, and everybody deserves an equal chance, unless proven to be creeps, which, they are not. And I didn't tell either of you to fall in love."

"I did, hook, line, and sinker, I don't know about her."

"Did she tell you she loved you?" John made space on the sofa and sat down.

"So she swore."

"Jessie is no liar."

Mathew regarded his brother as if he were an idiot. "This is your professional opinion. She ripped my heart out, tore my life apart, I wanted to marry her."

"Why don't you?"

"Are you on drugs? Me, marry a Stevens! But how did you know I was talking about her? Has she been begging for intercession? I refuse to capitulate."

"That was some investigative work and I would be very weary of Vanessa from now on."

"She lied to me, for months on end. Why didn't she tell me, why didn't you?"

"Because I didn't know, and I couldn't care less what her name is. Now, as far as I'm concerned, the problem is easy to solve. Trivialities shouldn't matter between people who love each other."

"You speak from experience."

"If that's your best shot at Jeremy, you fail dismally."

"That's another thing… he had to be a Stevens too?"

"These are good people and if you're implying Jessie set us up, you are dead wrong. I started the relationship with her, which I did out of curiosity anyway. Grandma painted this dark picture, and I cannot grasp it. And what difference does a name make?"

"That's just dandy but I can't go from this to that." Mathew snapped his fingers.

"Interesting, I thought you just admitted that you fell in love. How did you go from this to that?" John snapped his fingers.

Mathew glared at him. "Don't get cocky, this is different, our sworn enemies."

John glanced around the room, shook his head, and got to his feet. "Doesn't this situation deserve some time, effort, even some calls?"

"Why should I? Why doesn't she? To apologise, to explain why she did it."

"Do whatever you want; I just came to see how you're doing." John walked towards the door.

"And of course, Miss Calm is doing exceptionally."

"I'd say worse than you."

"She brought it on herself." Mathew spat angrily.

"Of course, she did. The fact that she regularly heard you cutting into her family had nothing to do with her trying to delay the inevitable. And I don't know what she said, as I

161

knew nothing about this until two days ago. What I do know is that she is devastated, which is why she's gone, just up and left the country."

Mathew felt strangely empty. He had counted on a confrontation, wanting to scream at her for a long time, to accuse her of all her wrongdoings. Then she would cry, and he would feel better knowing she also hurt. Instead, she had left him alone with his anger, with no one to vent it on except John. If she had been serious about this relationship, she would have stayed and faced his wrath, whatever the consequences. But this was her way, to hide or run.

"Know what surprised me the most about this?"

"I'm not even going to ask."

"Too bad, because you're going to hear it. It seems you too inherited a most unhealthy Barrymore, or rather, Lennox trait. I know grandma imprinted us all with the hatred that consumes hot and deep but if you never trust me about anything else, trust me on this, it is unfounded. So, if you ever come to your senses, give me a call." John waved and walked out the door.

All at once, Mathew heard her. *"When you stop loving me, try not to hate me too much." "I can never hate you,"* he told her.

"Damn you," he slammed his fist against the wall. "I have broken a promise." How he hated her for turning his life into torment. Since she left, he had not yet been to work, Christmas would be spent alone, and New Year…

How peculiar that Mark had read her so well, even knowing that she was hiding something, when all he had seen was the woman of his dreams. Then she had come out of them and into his life, and he had known happiness beyond comparison. Now, what was it he had?

Why did she wait for Vanessa to do what she should have done? Then, no one would have been any the wiser, and neither been subjected to the humiliation both had suffered. Staring around the lounge, he realised it mirrored his life perfectly; a total shamble.

Christmas came and went, ditto New Year, and he refused to spend either with the family, asking to be left alone.

When he returned to work, it was as a means of salvation. Labouring harder and longer than he had ever done, he grasped travelling as a vessel of escape, finding excuses why he should be the one sent away. Suddenly, he did more than a group of men, never seemed to rest, arrived at work long before anyone, and left after everyone else.

"Mathew," Theodore entered the constantly busy office. "Your mother wants you home this weekend."

"Why?"

"It's your birthday. Call and discuss it with her. By the way, how is the new printing programme coming along?"

"Very efficient, scary too. Where Mark found that contraption, only he knows."

"I'm certainly impressed."

"He sure does a lot of that lately. Nevertheless, I still believe that monster is dangerous."

"Are you serious?"

"Pay heed, father, or you will be sorry. I swear it's out for blood."

Theodore laughed. "You make it sound as if it has a mind of its own. Anyway, call your mother."

Grace was upset and told him so. He tried to dodge and used work as an excuse. Sick of pretences she told him to get himself home because she wanted to talk to him. Unless he wanted her to go to Barrymores and have words in his office in front of friend or stranger.

The concerned look on her face told tales, especially as he had lost weight, but there was nothing he could do about it. When he walked down the passages, he swore he heard Jessie's laughter coming from the indoor pool, then heard her describing something. It was pure torture because he wanted her out of his head.

"Theo tells me you have it in for one of Mark's machines." Grace said, trying to divert his attention, because if there was anyone who understood how he felt, it was her.

Mathew gave a short laugh. "He must have ordered it from outer space, because it is sci-fi efficient. As for his helpers… an extremely competent pair."

She reached for his hand. "Have you heard from John?"

"He came to see me before Christmas and then sent a gift. Something I have no idea as to its purpose. Jessie would probably know…" his voice trailed off.

"Mathew, you can't pretend nothing happened. It's unhealthy and I worry about you. Call her."

"I'm fine, mom. And can't you see I no longer care? Besides, John told me she was out of the country. It seems they have made peace again."

"Such is love. Why don't you give it a chance?"

"With a Stevens?" Rising, he left the room.

He had done about ten laps in the indoor pool when he realised someone was watching him.

"Reliving happy memories?" Mark asked sardonically.

"Don't you start."

"You tell everyone not to mention her, but here you are, where you had so much fun."

"How do you always know so much about everything?"

"I make it my business to know. Did it ever occur to you that you made a huge mistake letting her go?" Leaning against the bench, Mark lit a cigarette. "You all became too emotional and never looked at the situation from a business perspective."

Mathew waded out. "Is that what you saw, business? I can't wait to hear what kind."

"Feudal lords did it, kings, countries. In America, mafia bosses still do it."

Mathew reached for the towel. "What are you talking about?"

"Mergers, consolidation, coalitions, a union."

"What?"

"For your information, they were not the only ones who knew who she was. I too had found out and was still trying to figure out what to do with the information. Of course, I had no idea she was your fiancée, but it hit me during drinks. When they arrived and began that inquest, it all became so clear. No jokes, you should have married her. Imagine Stevens Textiles incorporated into Barrymores. It's where it belongs anyway."

Mathew was gaping. "This is what you thought about as the vultures ripped and then nailed down the coffin? Who are you and what have you done with my brother?"

"There are times when emotions should not be let loose, and that day was definitely one of them. And more is the pity where you are concerned because you are quite the business mind, better than anyone I know, and that includes father. Take it at face value, it's a compliment. Barrymores is massive, but with Stevens Textiles, it would become colossal."

Mathew went to stand within centimetres of him. "You only see dollar signs everywhere you look, don't you? Even while you defended her, it was all you were thinking?"

"Among other things. She is also bloody good to look at and that never hurts when it comes to the bedroom. But what am I saying? You know that better than me."

Mathew grabbed him by the collar. "You make me sick." Then turning, he walked away.

"I didn't tell you the best part."

"Keep it to yourself." Mathew threw over his shoulder.

Later, as he sat in the upstairs study, he saw Vanessa's feet appear at the door. Ignoring her, he concentrated on the papers before him.

"I know you are upset, but you don't have to be rude."

"Whatever you are looking for, it's not here."

"It may surprise you, but all I want is in this room."

Looking up, he stared at her. "How interesting, I thought it was James, along with money and prestige, of course."

"Why are you like this, because I saved you from a miserable relationship?"

"What do you want from me, a medal for public service? Go harass someone else."

She entered the study. "Do you know what will happen if I marry James?" Her green eyes flashed.

"Yes, you'll be out of my life forever. What a relief." Leaning back, he locked his hands behind his neck, a disdainful look on his face.

"I hate you, Mathew Barrymore." She spat.

"The feeling is mutual."

"I'll make your life hell when I marry James."

"Knock yourself out, and good luck."

Whipping the blonde hair, she stormed out of the study.

The patterned muslin floated softly as the breeze blew in through the open window and sitting on the rocking chair, Beverley put a hand out and felt the fabric, one of the latest beauties out of Stevens Textiles. A quick glance around the room told her that everything was in its perfect place. Simon had not been certain about the yellow walls but eventually relented and let her follow Jessie's advice that a child's room should be a place of fun, of bold colours, and interesting patterns. Although he wouldn't admit it openly, she knew that he liked it very much.

Reaching into the polished oak cot, she pulled out a fluffy toy, an adorable grey walrus with felt teeth; a gift from Jessie. Beverley had stared at the postmark for a long time and wondered what she was doing in Oslo. There had also been a small note, but it barely said how she was. Holding the toy tightly against her chest, she started rocking herself. A phone rang in the distance and hearing footsteps coming up the stairs, she stopped.

"Madam, your sister," The cleaning lady announced.

Beverley took the receiver from her. "Thank you, Bettina. Hello?" She greeted eagerly.

"Hi, Beverley, how are you?"

"Huge," Beverley laughed. "I can't wait to get this over with."

"How much longer?"

"The doctor says a few weeks, at the most three. I suppose you won't be back."

"No."

"Jessie, if you keep running it will haunt you forever. Please come resolve this."

"There is nothing to resolve." A short silence elapsed. "I played with fire and got burnt; now I live with the scars."

"He loves you."

"He loved Jessie Lewis; she doesn't exist."

"Will you stop rationalising and do something? It's impossible to hide all that damage."

"I have other things to think about and I make sure I'm always busy."

"That's during the day. What about when you're alone? It's been months, please come home."

"It's complicated to explain, and I no longer want to."

Beverley thought she heard a sob and her heart went out to her sister. How easy could it be so far away from home and hurting as much as she knew Jessie did? 'I see John and Jeremy every few weeks,' she began tentatively. For all she knew, Jessie didn't want to talk about them either.

"I miss them so much. How are they?"

"Okay, I guess."

"You guess? I thought you said you see them."

"It's Jeremy. He's lost a lot of weight, and sometimes I think he's ill. He's been going around with colds and flu for ages and nothing seems to make him better."

"I'm sorry to hear it. Is daddy still upset with me?"

"Just missing you, everyone does."

"And I miss you. But I have to do this." Jessie's voice shook. "I have to go now but I will call next week."

"Give me your number, it will be easier for Simon or mom to let you know."

"It would be tempting to give it away and I don't want anyone to know where I am. I need to be in control of something right now."

What was the use in pressing her? "Then don't forget to call."

"I won't. And tell Jeremy… tell him that I know now what he meant when he left and I'm not mad anymore, at either of them. Sometimes we must do things no one understands."

"What's wrong with you?"

"It must be something I ate." Jeremy complained as he returned to the bedroom and lying on the bed, closed his eyes. "I feel like death warmed over."

"This week it's something you ate, last it was the heat, the previous the cold, not to mention you never do anything. I no longer believe you are rundown. I've been pumping you with vitamins for months and still no change. You are always tired, no longer go out, and all you do is sleep. Something else is wrong, make a doctor's appointment."

Reaching across the bed, Jeremy touched John's hand. "I can't explain what's happening, I just feel awful all the time."

John squeezed the hand. "It's probably some bug you picked up in Natal and your system can't flush out."

"Maybe. Have you called Beverley lately?"

John smiled. "What's with you and this baby?"

"Do you think I'd make a good father?"

"You would and who knows, you might still get married." John told him a little sadly, but Jeremy's gaze told him more than words ever could. "I know some guys who do it just for the kids and then—"

"Selfish bastards. I told Jessie and now I'll tell you; I can't do that to anyone. I love you and that's the way it is. Do you wish to be married?" Jeremy asked curiously.

"Same set of rules applies here. The only girl who ever came close to tempting me was Jessie, but nothing worked as I imagined. I'm afraid you are stuck with me."

"Honey, don't move so much." Serena said for the umpteenth time as they sat in the sunroom having afternoon tea.

"Why is this baby being difficult?" Rising, Beverley stared over the garden. "And I can't imagine going through four pregnancies.'

'One forgets." Gazing at her daughter, Serena smiled. "You have dropped, your time must be close."

"Mine is, what about the baby's? Grandma, what was it like to have babies in your day?"

"Painful and nightmare-ish. We didn't have fancy machines to tell us that everything was going right. You went in with your eyes closed, so to speak."

"Is that why you only had daddy?"

Juliet was still for a few seconds, then looking at her granddaughter, said. "Taylor wasn't an only child; I had another son and daughter."

"What?" Beverley asked in shock.

"Yes, Andrew and Beverley. That's where you got your name."

"Why is this the first time I hear about these people?"

"Because they are dead. Andrew died a cot death, or so they said. But he was in hospital, so your guess is as good as mine. He was my first-born and your father never knew him.

Beverley came after Taylor. She was three when she died and was the apple of my father's eye. He succumbed to a heart-attack on the same day."

Walking the short distance, Beverley hugged Juliet. "That is so sad, grandma. Why didn't you ever tell us about them?"

"Because it took forever to get over the loss and then… it was just too painful."

Serena nodded softly, understanding well what Juliet meant.

"Mom," Beverley made a helpless gesture and looked at her feet. "My water just broke."

Cool calm Simon became frantic agitated Simon and Beverley eyed him suspiciously, wondering if he could drive them safely to the clinic. But before the day was over, Simon and Beverley Wade were the proud parents of a baby girl.

"She looks like Jessie." Serena exclaimed.

"She does." Taylor agreed and grinned. It was the first time in months.

Juliet peered at the small bundle in Beverley's arms. "What a little beauty. So, what are we to call her?"

Beverley smiled. "We had already decided that if she was a girl we would call her Juliet. I hope the two of you get along."

"Thank you, sweetheart." Juliet kissed her granddaughter's cheek. Then bending over, she brushed her nose across her great-granddaughter's forehead for the first time.

"What's the verdict?" Jeremy asked casually as he sat across the wide mahogany desk.

Dr Langley gazed at the beautiful young man. "Do you have medical aid, and how are you financially?"

"That can only mean it's serious." Jeremy smiled ruefully. "Medical aid, yes. As for finances, I guess I'm okay. How much do you think I'll need?"

"It's hard to say, and I wish you had come sooner."

"Before we go any further, give me a name I understand."

"Wouldn't you prefer to have someone with you? And how I wish I never had to tell anyone… You're young, with such prospects."

Jeremy stared straight ahead, then rising, went to gaze out the window, his hand resting on the curtains. The trees were bare and the grass not been green for some time, a few birds flew by, and he watched as they fought over a crust of bread as soon as they landed on the windowsill. "Did you know my father made this fabric?" He asked softly. "You see, I read the pamphlets you gave me. Of course, they couldn't verify anything, but I made the effort to read what I could find and kept coming up with only one candidate. Yet, I still hoped you would call it something else." He turned towards the doctor. "How long do you reckon I have?"

"It's hard to guess and that's what I would be doing whatever I said. But nothing is clear-cut and that is especially true when we deal with the human spirit. And you must fight, every moment is precious."

Minutes later, Jeremy walked out and down the street, his gaze riveted on the grey pavement blocks. Then glancing at the sky, he noticed it too was grey. The colour he would be seeing a lot of from now on, no doubt. Idly, he walked home, deep in thought, in a world of sudden fear.

Entering the flat, he glanced around its neatness. Unable to formulate logical thoughts, he sat at the kitchen table for close to fifteen minutes, then leaning back with the chair, he pulled out a large envelope from a drawer.

When done writing, he took his wallet and emptied it. A few credit cards, driver's licence, a couple of notes, and a sealed envelope. He flicked the old thing in his hand. Years ago, when he was still a schoolboy, he had loved someone with a sickening intensity. Alan Perry was beautiful, smart, funny, and Jeremy worshipped him. Then one day, for no reason he could fathom, Alan took his own life, and this was all he left behind.

Jeremy refused to open it, hating Alan passionately for being a coward. Why was death the best way out? Was he the reason Alan couldn't bear to stay alive? Why couldn't Alan have trusted him enough? No matter what, he would either have been there, or left him alone if those were his wishes. He twirled the enveloped again then grabbing a knife, he slit it open, took out the thin parchment, and read it through…

"There you are." John greeted as he entered the bedroom. "What did the doctor say? The sooner we know the better."

"I have a surprise for you." Getting off the bed, Jeremy handed him the thick envelope.

"What is it?" Tearing the edge open, a bunch of keys appeared in John's hand.

"I went down to the Traffic Department and transferred the Porsche to your name."

"Why?"

"Because you drive it more than I do. And here," Jeremy grabbed something from the table. "This is yours too. Must just sign and take it back to the bank."

John stared at the papers, credit cards, keys, car registration form, and lastly at Jeremy. "What's going on?"

"When last did I visit the bank? Okay, this afternoon, but now I never have to set foot in it again." Jeremy disappeared into the kitchen.

John followed. "What did you hear at the doctor that you found it necessary to do all this?" Placing both hands on Jeremy's shoulders, he felt an unusual trembling.

Taking one of John's hands, Jeremy drew it across his chest. "I'll be all right."

"I'm asking one last time and then I'm calling the doctor."

"Are all Barrymores this stubborn?"

"I'm serious, Jeremy."

Jeremy swivelled around, his eyes filled with tears. Nothing could prevent them from falling now. "I could have a couple of years, but I'll probably never make it." He rested his hands on the kitchen counter.

"Have you been for a second opinion?" John tried to hide the fear that suddenly crept over him, the fear that told him to reach out and never let go.

"I don't have to, I know he's right."

John enfolded Jeremy in his arms. "So, what's the name of this disease we are to dread?"

"AIDS," Jeremy sobbed against the loving shoulder. "And I may have infected you."

When he read Alan's note, he felt as if a black-hole swallowed him up. Alan had been diagnosed with HIV-Aids and the knowledge that he might have infected Jeremy, whom he loved, pushed him over the edge of sanity. Alan refused to suffer for years because the disease was already affecting his brain, and equally, refused to watch Jeremy give up his life to be saddled with his care. Now, here he sat, in the same predicament with John, simply because he had been the coward six years previously.

Weeks of gruelling tests followed, as they visited doctor after doctor, but only the faces changed. They climbed out of a pit merely to fall into a deeper one as the reports piled up. The diagnosis stayed unchanged, and as for the prognosis… they could only attempt to stretch time.

Mathew stared at his brother in surprise. "Come in. Where have you been?"

"Working," John glanced around, everything was back in its place. "How's things?"

"Busy. I've just come back from a trip to Japan and have to return in about two weeks."

John sank into a sofa tiredly. "How's mom?"

"She misses you."

"I've also been running around lately, but it can't be helped."

Mathew saw an expression he could only describe as sad. "Is everything alright?"

"I'm okay but Jeremy is going through a rough time."

Mathew pursed his lips. "Jessie's brother, the supposed gnome."

John smiled at the memory. "We laughed like crazy at the mix-up and you should have seen her face when you told me to go to your room; threatened to saw the bed in half. I wonder how she's really doing."

"You don't know?"

"Even Beverley doesn't know if she's telling the truth when she says she's fine."

"Why would she lie? Forget it, wrong question."

"You really have it in for her, don't you? But whatever your feelings, I worry about her. It can't be easy to be so far away, and alone."

"Where is she?"

"I told you, overseas."

"I assumed she had gone for a short spell, that she was back somewhere."

"You don't know Jessie; she suffers in silence.' He mused. 'Now for what brought me here. Is my Golf still at home? I need it as I'm selling the Porsche."

"Are you two in trouble?"

"The car is. We stay in Hillbrow and driving one of those is not advisable.'

'You have a point there. How much?'

'Seven hundred thousand and we already have a buyer. We could get more if we waited a while longer because it's in excellent condition, but I want it out of the way."

"Sure you're not in some kind of trouble?"

"Will you stop? I simply wish to sell a ridiculously expensive car and would like to know if it's possible I get mine back, if not, we'll buy something cheap."

"Why didn't you just go home to get it?"

"You forget, I'm no longer worthy of the Barrymore name."

"Don't you miss your life? This is your home, your family."

"Money, luxury, and comfort, that's all we really are. None of it matters, Jeremy does. Now more than ever."

"What's different now?"

"I doubt you'd be interested. Can I call you in a few days?"

"Don't worry, I'll get the Golf myself. How did you get here?"

"The Porsche, it flies like the wind."

"And you know what flying did to Lawrence."

"Why, Mathew, I thought you didn't care."

"Whatever you do, you are still my brother."

"Just a pity you can't find it in your heart to forgive Jessie."

"She's different."

"And according to some, a bad seed," John shook his head. "When will you let go of the chains that bind you? You are a slave to your name. But who knows, you may still find the courage to follow your heart and become happy, because that's exactly what you're not."

"Just what I needed, a sermon from my baby brother."

"What bothers me is that you are pretending she was never part of your life. Jessie is the most loving person I know and I'm deeply disappointed she's not part of our esteemed family. Her love radiates to all around her and I'd say that's what the Barrymores need. Except for mom, I don't think one ounce of goodness flows in this family."

CHAPTER TEN

"This is not happening," John thought as he watched Jeremy's face barely visible beneath the bandages. Then dropping his head on the bed, he asked with difficulty. "Will he be all right?"

"I don't expect so, son. He's badly broken up." Dr Langley told him.

"How, why?"

"The paramedics say bystanders told them he jumped. You know how bad full-blown AIDS is."

"And I refuse to believe it. We have money, he was well enough… He was no longer contemplating suicide."

"But he had?"

"When he first heard, he considered taking an overdose of pills, a painless end." John turned angrily. "But then he read an old friend's letter and swore he wouldn't do the same to me… And why would he jump, chance survival, all this suffering, risk infecting others. No, not Jeremy. We decided extra time was important." The unstoppable tears fell again.

Dr Langley's kind hand rested on the young shoulder. "Is there someone you would like to contact?"

"No more time?" His chest hurt. "His family doesn't even know about the AIDS."

"And he's not going to die from it."

John grabbed the phone and waited a few seconds. "Beverley, please come…"

"Huh…" Jeremy moaned weakly.

Taking the bandaged hand where only fingertips were visible, John touched the partially covered face softly. "Sshh, don't talk."

"I… don't… have time…" Jeremy said very slowly. "Have to go. Please, doctor… my last request…"

Nodding, Dr Langley left the room and closed the door.

Forty minutes later, Beverley swept in like a ghost. Face drained of colour and eyes red, she made a beeline for her brother, touching him gently. "Oh, my darling…" she cried.

"Tell dad…" Jeremy rasped.

Beverley no longer tried to hide the heartache that made her feel as if she were standing on the edge of an abyss. Not only because Jeremy was gone but because this truly was the end of the road for their father. Who, instead of coming to bury his son, decided to hold his life choices against him in death and refused to see him to his final resting-place beside Lawrence, especially after hearing about John's identity.

Serena and Juliet stood like automatons and she could no longer see past the blank stares etched on their faces. Simon had wanted to stay away, obviously for Taylor's sake, but for hers put his feelings aside and accompanied her in her time of need. And she was upset; the most important person was not present, and Taylor refused to wait for her to either call or turn-up.

John stood a little aside, as if uncertain that he should be there at all, or wondering why anybody else was, and Beverley noticed that he no longer shed tears. Doubtless, he had done enough of that four days ago after Jeremy died in his arms, as she stood holding both their hands, with a hurt so deep she thought she would never be able to feel anything normal again.

As proceeding ended, she could tell he was filled with way too much anger and grief, because he too had begged to postpone the funeral, wanting Jessie to attend, but no one listened. And who knew where she was and how long it would take to find her? She showed him the Christmas cards that came from Oslo. He merely stared, mumbling that he couldn't understand Jessie's business there. She watched him as the casket disappeared. Never had she felt so much pain emanating from another human being.

He turned to leave and was startled by Mathew. So was she. This certainly was a surprise. Why was he here?

Striding purposefully, John stopped in front of him, his chest tight with emotion. "Came to gloat?"

Mathew watched the pallid face with concern. "Are you, all right?"

"Should I be? And what is it you're doing here?"

"I read about it in the papers, but you never called and I didn't know if you needed someone. You never talk to me anymore, and I worry."

"You used to have a heart, then decided to lock it away when discovering Jessie wasn't up to your standards, and because of you, she's absent. So please, spare me the sympathies. I'm almost ashamed to call you brother." John turned to walk away.

"Jessie and I have nothing to do with this. And I am sorry that you are hurting."

"That's just swell, but now I have places to go."

"John, please, wait." Beverley called behind them and both turned to look at her. "Oh, honey," reaching out, she took his hand, the tears rolling down her face.

Mathew inclined his head. "My deepest sympathy, Mrs Wade."

She gave him a quick glance. "Thank you," then turned back to John and enfolded him in her arms. "Please come home with me, you need company."

"You don't care that I am a Barrymore?"

"How can you say that?" She chided.

"If it had been me, no Barrymore would have consoled Jeremy." John's gaze stopped on Mathew accusingly. "But I do have to go say goodbye to my mom."

"Yes, do that, bring whatever you need, and I'll drive you to the airport—"

"You're leaving?" Mathew asked in consternation. "Where are you going?"

Deep concern furrowed Beverley's countenance. "And perhaps it's too soon."

"I have to, but I will see you tonight." John walked away.

"Today, he hurts far too much to notice the loving gesture, but one day, he will thank you." Beverley said.

"Why isn't Jessie here?"

"I don't have her number." She glanced at the handsome face. "Why do you hate us so much? I'm sorry, that's your business. Goodbye, Mathew." She turned as she heard Juliet and Serena approaching.

"Good heavens, William Barrymore!" Juliet exclaimed.

"No, ma'am, Mathew, and my condolences on your loss."
He extended a hand.

Juliet shook it lightly. "Thank you, son, but does your father know you are this side of town?"

The jibe affected him oddly. Was that what people thought, that he was devoid of individuality and only did his father's bidding? "I wish I was meeting you under different circumstances." He shook Serena's hand and then Simon's. "Where is Mr Stevens?"

"He refused to come." Beverley told him, her eyes brimming with tears.

"John!" Grace rose from the sofa in surprise, her heart going out to him. He looked pale and gaunt. "I'm so sorry."

"Disgusting," Monica cut icily.

"What do you know?"

"I know it's immoral."

"Know what is immoral? The poison you spread about people who deserve better, the hatred that controls your life, and the wicked jealousy you inherited from your mother. You hated her, yet, you're the same. What is it you covet the most about the Stevenses?"

"They have nothing I want."

"Then let me enlighten you. They have what you only dream of, warmth, kindness, and love. No wonder you couldn't stay married, you are as cold as this marble floor." He pointed to it with the tip of his shoe.

"John! I understand grief, but that is no excuse for rudeness. Apologise to your aunt."

"As soon as she apologises to Jessie. But I just came to get a few things, I'm leaving the country."

"What… why?"

"I need to get away." He disappeared out the door.

"We have known nothing but misery since meeting that awful girl."

"Monica, why don't you take a trip somewhere? Paris should be lovely this time of year." Grace told her and leaving the room, rushed upstairs.

"Don't look so worried, mom, I'll be fine." John told her as she entered his room.

"Where are you going?"

"I'll know when I get there."

"Are you okay?" Mathew asked from the doorway.

"Not yet, but you didn't have to follow me."

"That is not how it looked earlier."

"Who knows," John threw him a glance. "You might actually be redeemable."

"Hey, bro," Mark said as he peered into the room. "I won't be a hypocrite; this could very well turn into a blessing in disguise. Maybe father will let you come back home now."

Before anyone could stop him, John punched Mark.

"Calm down." Mathew pulled John away.

"Ah, the prodigal son returns, or is he leaving again?" James pointed to the suitcase.

"Spare me your thoughts. As for that creepy woman you date, I suggest you wise up. But you won't." Grabbing the suitcase, John walked down the passage.

"What is he doing in my house?" Theodore asked as he appeared on the landing, then turned to Mathew. "Please be so kind as to remove him from my presence."

Mathew's gaze never wavered as he declared. "You don't want him here, do whatever you wish. I will not throw my brother out."

"It will be my pleasure.' Mark said as he rubbed his chin.

"Don't be an ass, and learn from your brother," Theodore told him angrily. "Family always comes first. He may no longer meet with my approval, but he is still your blood." He pointed to John. "Get." Then noticing Grace's stricken look, he felt immense pity for her. "But for your mother's sake I will tell you this; the day you marry a woman is the day you will be allowed back."

Congratulations streamed in from every corner and Grace wondered why people they were barely acquainted with were interested in an event that neither improved nor damaged their circumstances. Within the family circle, everyone seemed pleased, with perhaps the exception of Mathew. But it wasn't that he was displeased, his mind was elsewhere, and Grace had a good idea where.

She recalled that other short-lived engagement. *"A year ago."* She had been so pleased then, yet, how sadly it had all ended. Life turned and twisted in different directions, and often for the worst.

When she saw the date, she thought James and Vanessa extremely insensitive. But she had already realised that Vanessa was not interested in anything that was not self-serving and being the centre of attention was doing nothing to diminish her narcissism.

The merry-making went on for hours and as Grace thought she should spend a few minutes in quiet reverie to the approaching changes, she became alarmed to see

Vanessa watching Mathew with an interest that should not exist. He in contrast, seemed oblivious to the attention.

Later, as she walked through the gardens to alleviate a pounding headache, she found him sitting on a bench.

"There you are," she sat beside him and took his hand. "Once, yours was small and fit in mine, now it's the other way around." A gentle smile spread on her lips. "What are you doing out here?"

"Why does it still hurt?"

"Separations always do."

"It's a year ago, and I still feel the same."

"Were you at least polite at the funeral?"

"She wasn't there and as I understood it, she didn't know Jeremy had died. I thought she only hid from me, but it seems she does from her family as well." He fell silent.

"Does this engagement bother you?"

"Not in the least."

"Please remember that she is to be your brother's wife and I don't want to see you at loggerheads. Your grandmother started enough feuds."

"No, I'll let her do all the screaming, and eventually she's bound to make a fool of herself." Rising, he pulled her up with him. "I'll leave as soon as they are done with the toasts." He pointed to the house, where, except for the south wing, every other light appeared to be on. "Has John contacted you yet?"

"Not a word, spoken or written. He left so full of anger, I haven't stopped worrying."

"And most of it directed at this family."

'Sometimes, I think I didn't do enough for you boys."

"No, mom, you did much more than I saw many others do. And if any of us turns out bad, it will never be your fault."

"I loved spending time with all of you. Not that it was easy, I had to fight your grandmother every step of the way. She was a firm believer in armies of nannies and rules that could fill an encyclopaedia. I hated it as I could never do a thing unsupervised. After she died, I had the time but no longer any of you. I came from a home where doing things for ourselves was encouraged but she often banned me from attempting anything remotely mundane. She even frowned at me making the occasional cup of tea.

"Once, she caught me making my own bed and it felt as if I was about to be ex-communicated. That's why today I have an aversion for interfering in anyone's life, most of all my children's. I remember well what it felt like being reprimanded every time I did something she didn't approve of. On the other hand, Grandpa William was a sweet soul, who purposely went against her, so I could have my little victories. I still believe he died willingly just so he could escape her."

"Now, you are the lady of the house and unlike grandma, fair. Vanessa is too much of a hothead to rule anything."

"Don't let your brother hear that. He is deeply in love and she can do no wrong."

"I'll stay out of their way." Slowly, they walked back into the house.

"I was about to go look for you. We would like to make our toasts." James announced and placed crystal flutes in their hands.

"May you have all the happiness you deserve," Theodore told them proudly.

"Since I'm the best-man, I'll make one too." Mark added. "May the next Barrymore generation be better than this one.

Let's face it, brother," his voice dropped so only the immediate family heard him. "We are a bunch of bastards."

"What awful things come out of your mouth at such inappropriate times."

"Maybe, Aunt Monica, but true."

"My turn," James began. "To my beautiful wife-to-be, may we have all our dreams fulfilled."

"I'll drink to that." Vanessa agreed.

Walking over the gravel, Mathew became aware of a shadow near the bushes. Stopping next to his car, he asked. "What do you want, Vanessa?"

"How did you know it was me?"

"Your perfume. What is it this time?"

"You can't ignore me forever. For goodness sake, we have slept together."

"In bad taste if I reminded James, don't you think?"

"Don't you even care a little anymore? We used to have fun, laugh…"

"That is hardly love."

"Ah, love! How could I forget Jessica Stevens? Don't tell me you're still pining for the little liar."

He grabbed her arm. "She may have lied but she was no… Stay out of my way, married to James or not."

"And you should be careful how you speak to me; I'll be the new mistress."

Digging his fingers into the flesh, he told her. "Not yet, you're not. This is my mother's home, and don't you try usurping her position. You even blink the wrong way and I'll be all over you."

"Like this?" She asked huskily and pressed her lips against his.

He pushed her away in disgust. "You are explosive, and I wonder if James has any idea what he's getting himself into. Goodbye, Vanessa, and have a nice life." Getting into the car, he drove away without a backward glance.

"Miss Manning," Mark greeted. "How very interesting, you have just become engaged to one brother and are having a rendezvous with the ex?" He laughed and leaned against a column.

She turned quickly, hoping the semi-darkness didn't show her face. "It's not what you think."

"I didn't think anything, I just got here."

A sigh of relief escaped her. "So, what do you want?"

CHAPTER ELEVEN

For some peculiar climatic phenomenon, March began as an extremely wet affair, raining daily, contributing nothing to make the wedding preparations any easier. Grace imagined going mad in the next few weeks as Vanessa dropped off little lists, somehow imagining her a fairy godmother who could wave a wand and meet every silly detail on those ridiculous rolls. And when she thought she had come up with the basics, Vanessa's mother and aunt appeared with a schedule to rival a royal household.

The guest-list now approached four hundred names and Grace prayed the day came and went quickly. Then, just as she believed they had a decent programme together, Mr Manning appeared. He walked up and down stairways, peered into rooms with a grin of satisfaction, and almost broke two priceless vases with his clumsy ways.

"Spare no expense," he said as he walked from room to room. "I'm paying."

As she watched him telling the servants to remove an 18th century Kurdistan Persian carpet because he didn't like it, Grace understood the urge to pull out one's own hair, and people who said they wanted to scream at something.

"It clashes with my baby's colour scheme." He boomed.

Nearby, a phone rang. She went to picked it up. "Grace Barrymore."

"Hello, Mrs Barrymore."

"Jessie?" Grace stopped in surprise. "I'm so glad you're calling. How have you been?"

"Okay. I saw the wedding announcement and wanted to congratulate you."

"Thank you, but I'm not the one getting married, and I'm barely surviving." Grace laughed. "Why haven't you called before?"

"It took me a long time to pick up the courage."

"I know. How are you really?"

"Sometimes better than others but I'm okay now. I have a wonderful job and it keeps me busy."

"Where are you?"

"Suffice to say, I'm freezing. There is nothing like South African weather."

"True. Though, it has rained a lot lately and it's driving Vanessa nuts."

"Regardless, she will make a beautiful bride. Mrs Barrymore, I never had a chance to apologize properly. I'm so sorry for what happened, the lies I told."

"Honey, stop, it's all in the past and I never hated you or your family."

Jessie sniffed. "You can't imagine how good it is to hear someone other than John say that. Have you seen him lately? It's been a while since I called, and they must think I've enlisted. I miss him, Jeremy too. But I'll call them soon."

"Good heavens, she still doesn't know!"

"I realise it came across as if I plotted and fixed things, but I never did. My only interest was for John to meet my family because he is my best friend. And I dreamt about seeing your house…"

"Jessie, I know that despite accusations and insinuations you are not to blame for how things stand. But remember, family is so important."

"And I haven't been a very good member of mine. I must still congratulate my sister; you wouldn't know what she had."

"But…" *"Where on earth has this child been?"* "That was months ago. She had a girl and if I'm not mistaken her name is Juliet."

"Grandma's name," Jessie blew her nose. "Sorry, I have a cold."

That was no cold, she was crying, and Grace's heart went out to her. "When are you coming back?"

"Not any time soon."

"Then promise you will call home, they must be terribly worried."

"I sent Christmas cards. But I apologise that I couldn't bring myself to send you one. Mrs Barrymore, do you think me forward for calling? After everything Jeremy and I have done."

"Don't be silly, and I wish you had long before today."

"Huh… how… is… no, I should go now."

"Mathew is fine. Works far too hard and is always going somewhere."

"Well then, I will let you get back to the wedding preparations, and congratulations again."

"Thank you, and promise you will call again, because it's not the same without you." *"And I wish it was your wedding."* Placing the phone on the desk, Grace sat there a few minutes, knowing how much pain Jessie would soon be feeling, as soon as she heard of Jeremy's death and John's departure. Heaven alone knew where he was and she too worried constantly.

Beverley watched Juliet move around the living room, grabbing, and pulling things as she went. "But you are a handful. Turn out like your aunt too, always climbing something." Smiling, she picked up the little girl and handed her to the babysitter. "Thank you." A nearby phone rang. "It's all right, I'll get it." Leaving the room, she grabbed the phone in the passage. "Wade residence,"

"Hello, Mrs Wade. How is life treating you?"

"Jessie! Where have you been? Good grief, do you know how anxious we were?"

"Okay, I'm sorry, and I'll try calling regularly." Jessie laughed a little nervously. "How is Juliet?"

"How do you know her name?"

"I called Mrs Barrymore an hour ago and she told me. Then she started on the importance of family. All I wanted to do was congratulate her. So, how's everyone, and is Jeremy better?"

Once Jessie knew, no one would be able to get anything else out of her. Beverley opted for a detour. "Any plans to come home?"

"As I told Mrs Barrymore, not in the near future."

"Still that bad. I said it before, why can't the two of you sit down and have a screaming match? You might still not speak to each other afterwards but at least feel better."

"I no longer have expectations regarding the situation."

"Maybe you should." Beverley thought back to Jeremy's funeral. Then again, he hadn't been there to see Jessie but because he cared enough about his brother. "What about a short holiday? It might be what Mathew needs. If it doesn't work then, I'll never mention it again."

"I want to get over this, not relive it. And I certainly don't want to explain, least of all to him."

"Where are you?"

There was a silence.

"London."

"What happened to Oslo? That's what the postmark on the Christmas cards said."

"I was there for a while, visiting a friend. Then I sent her the cards to post."

"You are so paranoid. Don't you have a cell number?"

"I do, but…"

"If it makes you feel better, I'll memorise it. What are you doing in London?"

"What else do I know? I joined a small up-and-coming Interior Design company. So, who does Juliet resemble?"

"You." They spent a few minutes chatting then when Jessie asked about John and Jeremy again, Beverley finally announced. "I'm afraid I kept the bad news for last. We were anxious to contact you but had no idea where to start."

"Grandma?"

"She's fine. It's Jeremy, and I don't know… Huh, he died."

"Stop fooling around, Beverley."

"I wish I was."

"But… what… he was fine the last time I called."

"That was months ago, last year, and I told you he was sick. But he didn't die from any illness."

"What happened?" Jessie cried uncontrollably.

"He fell from their balcony. The police say it was either an accident or a suicide, but John and I refuse to believe the latter explanation. Then, some guy swore he saw a man with him on the balcony just seconds before he fell. The police say he has a record of lying so we shouldn't take a drunkard seriously. But murder... it makes even less sense."

"Where was John?"

"At work. I knew the press would make something of it, so I told daddy about John. No amount of begging helped, he simply refused to see his son buried."

"How... is John?"

"I don't know; he flew to Australia and said something about fulfilling a promise. He was devastated, angry, and hurting far too much to go off on his own but no one could stop him."

Sighing tiredly, Grace got up early, her thoughts squarely on the previous day. The wedding had been the planned success, even if she often imagined that the Mannings' very presence was enough to ensure a cataclysm. It couldn't be denied, Vanessa had made a dazzling bride in her masses of silk and chiffon skirts, and the boned bodice embroidered in pearls and rhinestones was nothing short of breathtaking and Mr and Mrs Manning nodded their undeniable pride as everyone oohd and aahd.

Grace sighed again. It was time to attend to the dozens of guests staying at the estate and she noticed with amusement that most were somehow related to Vanessa. There were rooms to change, pillows to fluff, and broken pieces of something or other to pick up after someone no doubt.

Walking down the passage, she recalled having studied Mathew's date, Carol Cummings. Curiously, she liked the young woman's sense of mischief. With sparkling brown eyes, Carol possessed the most interesting spiky hair, smiled easily, and her infectious laughter rubbed off on all around her, especially Mathew. Cheerfulness was exactly what he needed after so much gloom. However, today, Grace couldn't help but feel they were mismatched, and she wondered how long Carol would stick around. The last four hadn't lasted longer than a month each.

Walking past one of the salons that were never used, she saw the open door. Going to close it, she heard voices inside.

"You can't possibly be serious, Rachel." A male voice said.

"Rachel," Grace did a few mental calculations. *"Oh, Vanessa's cousin, the lovely nurse."*

"You think because she married James it's over? Not likely." Rachel said. "Young Jessie got to her and she despises her with a passion, more than any Barrymore ever could. Vanessa was as mad as hell and being on the conceited side, could not believe Mathew replaced her. Of course, at the time, she had no idea who this girl was and went into a deep depression, feeling all miserable as she tried to work herself to the bone. Then one day, what did she do? Dissatisfied with her little life, she tore my engagement to shreds."

"Surely she feels something for James."

"Mostly, status, because who do you suppose initiated the relationship? And when he helped fill in the gaps a couple of months later and she went digging at college, she went berserk. She's like a bloodhound and once she was on that girl's scent there was no stopping her. This marriage is a farce but not where James is concerned. Tragically, he does love her, and I can't help but pity him. She is trying to spite Mathew because she swore revenge, and she meant it."

"If anyone heard you, they'd say it's sour grapes."

"Of her? please," Rachel continued. "I don't care how rich or poor she was, is, or will be, what I am concerned about is what she does to people, because she obliterates anyone who crosses her path. And didn't you see this morning's headlines? Quite a feat making the front-page two ways. From now on, she is on the warpath towards all things Stevens. But she does look radiant in white, don't you think?"

Grace decided she had heard enough but as she walked downstairs, although sounding outrageous, those words had a nasty ring of truth to them. Vanessa had taken immense pleasure in delivering the blows that drove Jessie away, and she had that bad habit of staring at Mathew. Time would tell, and she hoped that none of it was true.

Going a little faster, she saw Theodore in the blue salon. "Theo, you won't believe—"

"I already know." Throwing the newspaper down, he left the room in an unmatched fury.

Appropriating herself of the discarded paper, she turned to the front page. As Rachel said, there were two main items, a huge photo of James and Vanessa, and the main article written by Vanessa Manning. "STEVENS AIDS SUICIDE."

"Oh, dear lord," Grace placed a hand on her chest and sat down to read it. Five minutes later, she couldn't control her racing heart and the indescribable fear that was suddenly suffocating. "John…"

The trip had been long and dreary, and he felt that seeing another train in the next hundred years was too soon. He hurt everywhere and couldn't wait to just have quiet days for a while. But that had to wait; there was something he must do first.

He was leaning against the street-lamp when she appeared around the corner, her arms full of giant rolls, cushions in plastic bags, and a case swinging at her side. As he watched her struggle with the lock, he noticed the long hair had been replaced by a shorter style and that she no longer looked like a girl. His heart leapt.

Running across the street, he offered. "May I be of assistance?"

There were rolls and bags all over the pavement as she stood staring at him in shock. "John!" Then throwing her arms around his neck, she burst into tears.

"Hello, Jessie," he hugged her tightly to him, hardly giving her space to breathe, his own eyes filling with tears. "I have missed you so much."

"I… I can't believe you're standing here. How did you find me?"

"I recalled how you dreamt of coming to Howard Bracken's School of Interior Design. So, after wandering around Oslo for a week and thinking why the heck you went there, I figured this was your destination. Only, when I got there, no one wanted to tell me if you were still a student or if you had left. I almost had to bribe one of the girls who remembered you to tell me where you had gone." He pushed her a little away.

"You were always a smart Alec. I was there, but only six months. It was crazy hard." She wiped her overflowing eyes. "I eventually called home and Beverley told me. I can't even begin to express how I feel." Embracing him again, she swallowed the sobs.

"How do you think I feel? And I'll never believe he committed suicide."

"Then it must have been an accident."

"How, he never left the room."

"Well, the third option is the most implausible because who would want to hurt him?"

"If I knew that, I'd be sitting in jail."

"Come," she opened the door. "It's Sunday, how did you know I'd be here?"

He picked the things from the pavement. "I didn't. What's that girl's name? Kate. She gave me the address, so I thought I'd come have a look, but here you are."

"I have something to sort out. Dump that stuff." She switched a few lights on and went to stand in front of him. "I can't believe you're here. Called home lately?"

"Not since I left."

"I eventually picked up the courage and called your mother, just before James' wedding."

"That's certainly no surprise. And good luck to him, he's going to need it.' He gazed at her warmly. 'Why didn't you tell me about Mathew?'

"I made such a mess."

"Exactly the kind of situation Vanessa thrives on. That woman is spooky."

"You've lost weight. Don't tell me you travelled through the Australian Outback on foot."

"Was there a while then went exploring a bunch of islands. I eventually went to India and travelled to Turkey by train. Then took a boat to Greece, and finally flew to Oslo. I swear I brought all the Indian dust with me." He glanced outside. "It's a nice area."

"I was fortunate to get this job so quickly."

He watched her with interest. "Your mouth smiles but not your eyes. I know what happy looks like and this is not it."

"We grow and change all the time."

"Aren't we tragic? It was the saddest time of my life, but I wouldn't trade it for anything, you?"

"Knowing Mathew? Never."

"The hair suits you like that." His hand went out to touch it. "A real woman."

Smiling, she sat at a desk, opened one of the rolls, and taking ruler and pencil started drawing. "How long are you staying?"

"Didn't I mention? I'm not returning without you. I found a nice hotel and tomorrow I'll start looking for work. I haven't seen a cent from my father since the day I left home but I inherited from Jeremy before he died. There are things even your family knows nothing about, the reason why we sold his car. We needed the money to begin some expensive treatments."

"So, he was sick. What was wrong with him?" She fixed her gaze on his face.

"AIDS."

The ruler and pencil dropped. "That's not possible."

"We also wished, hoped, and prayed, but it was. Jeremy finally discovered why Alan committed suicide and it was awful watching him amidst all that regret. And remember Beverley's wedding? That was the first time it got out of control and he had to be admitted to hospital, with bronchitis. We just didn't know why it got so bad."

"And you?"

"I'm okay."

Jessie wiped the tears that had gathered, and rising, put her arms around him. "Then how sure are you that he didn't kill himself? I've heard how bad it can get."

"And he would have done it right, left a note for no one to touch him, and jumped from the tenth floor. That's how tall our building was." He regarded her intently. "Are you dating, in a relationship, or engaged?"

"As if there is time. Besides, I still hurt too much."

"That's what I thought. So here goes. Will you marry me?"

"What? Why?" She asked blankly.

"Because that was Jeremy's last request, that I find and marry you. He wanted us to be together again."

"Which we can do anyway. You can't go around promising impossibilities to dying people, even if it was to my brother. He was probably delirious, not quite there anymore. Many people take marriage as a temporary state, I don't. I want to do it once, and with the right man."

"And if you believed there was hope you wouldn't be thousands of miles away."

"Are you out of your mind? I can't decide like that at a moment's notice. You appear unexpectedly, after being heaven knows where, I've barely had time to ask about your health, and you're proposing?" She eyed him. "Are you sure you're not in love with me and feeling embarrassed concocted this tale?"

Taking her by the arms, he kissed her. A moment later, he let her go. "How was that?"

"Awful. Will you get a grip on yourself?" She told him angrily. "Apart from the fact that it sounds bizarre, that I don't want to marry you, and that you have lost your senses, this is the most preposterous— People don't go around doing things like this!"

"I suppose I can't expect you to agree today. Look, I've had a long time to think about things." He moved a few papers. "Jeremy said you would need protecting from fortune hunters the minute he was dead."

"Stop," she placed a hand on his forehead. "No temperature and you don't appear mad. Then again, this is probably how it manifests." She threw her hands up. "I'm going home as I can't possibly work now. Want to tag along?" Snapping elastic bands on the rolls, she stared at him. 'You do realise you sound demented.'

She asked about the trip, where he had been, what he had seen. She found it interesting, but he couldn't say that he did in the retelling. Because just recalling the reason to visit a specific place filled him with painful memories.

He stared at the small house, the neat garden, and the medium-height wall. He would have guessed her living in a high-rise. "You're not married…"

She laughed. "Don't be crazy." Opening the door, she called. "Elaine, I'm back."

"No doubt about it, something's going on. Who's Elaine?"

"My housekeeper. Hello," she called again.

A woman appeared. "Miss Jessie, I thought you said two o'clock."

"I did, but he dropped in and I couldn't work after that. Elaine, my friend John,"

"How do you do," Elaine responded, stared at him for a second, then led them to the kitchen. "If you had called I would have started lunch."

"We're fine and will do something ourselves. Thank you for coming out today, you may go enjoy the rest of the day."

"Thank you, Miss Jessie."

"Hello." Jessie greeted again and turned to the corner, her voice soft and warm. "John, meet my sons."

He turned pale in shock. There were two of them and identical.

"This is Jeremy," picking the nearest little boy out of the playpen, she kissed his face. "And John," putting her hand out to the other one, his chubby little fingers took it, and after kissing him, she turned to John. "What do you think?"

"I… can't." He told her with difficulty.

"Jeremy, John, meet your Uncle John."

"U-uncle?" He stuttered. "How?"

"I could draw a picture, but I'll pass." Unceremoniously, she placed them in his arms. "I'll make us coffee so long."

"You named them after us." He noticed with emotion. "Mathew's twins! How do you tell them apart? How old are they?" He couldn't stop staring at them. "If only Mathew knew—"

She swung around. "Mathew must not know. This is why I left, not just because of him. And he's not going to know about them until I'm ready. I refuse to have anything to do with him if all he cares about is two little boys he has never seen."

"Your mom, mine… What beautiful replicas."

She smiled sadly. "How can I forget? I see him every day."

John dropped his tone of voice. "How did you register them?"

"They are Stevens."

"Now, we really need to go back. Whatever my feelings about my father, these babies deserve their rightful name. And if Mathew won't give it to them, then let me."

"Here we go with crazy talk again. But you know, I was tempted to register them as yours. So, the only way they will be known as Barrymores is if he marries me, out of his own free will."

"Which will never happen if you don't go home." He pointed out. "Mathew loves you more than he cares to admit so you have to be near him, your family, mine. Whatever the past, it has been changed, erased forever. We are one now." He held the little boys tightly to his chest. "They are adorable."

"I still don't understand why I should marry you."

A frown appeared on his face. "I'm beginning to think that Jeremy's request says more than his words did. I know it sounds nuts, and I told him as much, but he begged that I do this one thing."

"You are not doing this to me." She took one of the babies. "You just came to mix me up and I hate you."

"No, you don't." He leaned against the kitchen counter, the baby in his arms exploring every inch of his face.

"Only you can have me in this state within minutes of showing up."

She slept fitfully, unable to stop thinking about his reason for having travelled immense distances. For countless months, she lived a lonely existence, gone through the inevitable sleepless nights, unstoppable tears, and suicidal inclinations. And most mornings, she awoke with pangs of fear as she imagined what Mathew would do if he discovered her pregnancy, but never did she feel the apprehension John had brought today, which didn't even make sense.

Everything was hard, especially emotionally, and when Beverley complained of morning sickness, heartburn, swollen feet, and a dozen other little things, she knew exactly how it was but been unable to share.

She wished Mathew changed his mind. That he came for her, told her he made a mistake, that she meant more to him than any name, that everything would be all right, but most importantly, that he loved her.

Over breakfast, John asked. "How on earth did they happen?"

"I forgot to take my pills when Lawrence died." She gazed at the small brown heads. "Knowing that I was responsible for another life kept me sane. Then, they were born, and I no longer had time to feel sorry for myself. It felt as if a crater swallowed me whole but now with Elaine's help everything runs smoothly."

"You have never been selfish, but this... They are supposed to be making bonds, and you are depriving them of theirs, especially with their father."

"Don't start."

"I just hope you come to your senses."

Within days, she suggested he move in with them, and suddenly, they were back in their college days, again the best friends who could share everything. How had she survived?

Having children in his proximity brought out the comic in him and he often had Elaine in fits of laughter. She had taken an instant liking to him but sometimes, she watched him curiously, seeing a remarkable resemblance between him and the little boys she adored. Realising her confusion, Jessie gave her an edited version of the past.

Knowing that her services were much desired, Jessie managed to wrangle a job out of her boss for John, who, although not a decorator, was the best colour co-ordinator and fabric designer they had come across and who had a knack for pleasing some of their most difficult clients.

John brought comfort and security, and at his insistence, Jessie saw her way clear to start dating.

"You'd swear I have a disease." She told him one evening as another man left and both knew he wouldn't return

"Well, this little test-run confirms my suspicions; it's not so much that they are weird, it's that you give no one a chance. I've been watching you, every guy has a defect."

"Why do you do this?" She closed her eyes for a second, as if sweeping a few thoughts away. "I called Beverley this afternoon and she told me they know about Jeremy's AIDS. It was in the papers a while back and of course, they denied it. Then she went through the boxes you left in her house and found the medical reports and medication. She half-suspected it but daddy didn't take it well at all."

"Perhaps I should have told them, but it seemed irrelevant. And how did the papers find out? Only Dr Langley knew our real names."

"I don't know if he had anything to do with it, but Vanessa wrote the article."

"Why am I not surprised?"

"And I think it's time you called your mother, she must have been anxious ever since. Probably thinks it's the reason for your departure."

"I'll call tomorrow, any messages for Mathew?"

She pointed the wooden spoon at him. "Don't get smart."

He took her free hand. "As I see it, you are never going to fall in love again. There is something wrong with every man and I know what it is, he's not Mathew. So, either marry me or let's go home."

"Not yet. I can't face him and say nothing. I'm angry, very angry. I know I'm the one who walked away, but I had to. He on the other hand never made a single attempt at finding me."

"He has no idea where you are."

"I don't care, he could ask." She stormed out.

CHAPTER TWELVE

Watching Vanessa and Monica on the patio, Grace's brows went up. Why was it those two got along so well? Perhaps because both were also difficult to understand. "Good afternoon." She said and sat opposite them.

"Where were you?" Monica asked half-interested.

"At lunch with Mathew and Carol. Wonderful person, don't you think?"

"If you like that sort, it won't last." Vanessa dismissed.

"Interesting you say that," Grace remarked. "They got engaged."

Vanessa's face turned white. A sudden brightness marring the disdainful gaze she had had but a few seconds ago.

"Just like that?" Monica asked.

"Theo and I were there, Carol's parents were there, and that's it."

"When... I mean," Vanessa struggled to formulate words. "W-when's the wedding?"

"They haven't set a date. Carol is extremely busy and not the kind of woman to be rushed into anything. Mathew..." it was best she left things unsaid.

"At least there's one thing to be thankful for, she is no Stevens." Monica declared.

"No, she is not."

"And I find it disturbing that you liked that girl so much. But what is to be expected of someone who isn't a Barrymore by birth?" Monica patted Vanessa's hand warmly. "Child, you have more potential than you realise."

Monica would take Vanessa's guile as a good trait.

Grace on the other hand, was becoming concerned at her responses regarding Mathew. Rachel had been onto something. Did she warn her son? But which one and what did she tell him? She got to her feet again. Better go do something constructive. "It will be nice to have another young woman around." She smiled. These two must never think they intimidated her.

As she passed the study, the phone rang. She went in and answered. "Grace Barrymore."

"Hello, mom, how are you?"

"John? Dear God, finally! Where have you been? I've thought about you almost every moment of every day."

"I'm fine, mom."

"Are you really? People have been saying things and I don't quite know how to tell you because I have no idea if you know about it."

"If you mean about Jeremy's AIDS, I do. And let me set your mind at peace; I'm fine."

"I'm so grateful to hear it." She said with tears in her eyes. "But where are you, what are you doing?"

Instead of answering, he asked. "Mom, do you, like everyone else, hate Jessie?"

She took a moment to respond. "At first, I thought I would, then, a strange thing happened, I knew Vanessa hoped I did. I know what kind of a family we are so although not condoning her subterfuge, I understand it. Why do you ask?"

"I like to make sure I know you as well as I say I do. How is everyone?"

"Your father is always busy, Monica is about to go somewhere, and Vanessa is constantly on TV. James works harder than I've ever seen, Mark runs between the US and here as if he holds shares in some airline, and Mathew is probably close to becoming fluent in Japanese. Oh, and he's just become engaged."

"What about Jessie?"

"Never mentions her. She's gone and he either doesn't want or doesn't know what to do about it. He has no idea where she is anyway, apart from the fact that she's somewhere in Europe. He's lonely and Carol is great fun."

"But does he love her?"

"I don't know. Where are you?"

"England. Mom, I'm very busy and I have to go, but I promise I'll call again."

"Do you want to be there? I miss you."

"And I miss you." Disconnecting, he glanced over the large work-area, seeing Jessie pouring over some blueprints. He dreaded telling her about Mathew's engagement now, because it would break her heart. She lived in hope, dreaming that he would come, but how she planned for him to find her, only she knew. Sometimes, he felt like doing something, but what? She would not take kindly to him meddling.

"I know you called home, so?"

He was startled; he didn't see her walk across. "Everyone is fine." Getting up, he pretended to busy himself in a discussion with another co-worker.

Barely entering the kitchen that evening, she cornered him. "Okay, you have avoided me long enough. Out with the bit you don't want to tell me. Did something happen to Mathew?" Worry poured out.

"Nothing like that, he… huh… got engaged." Seeing the blue eyes fill with tears, he reached out and hugged her. "I'm sorry."

But clearly, she felt emotional, because she started sobbing. Immediately, loud wailing arose from the playpen.

"Look what you've done now." Gently pushing her away, he went to the children, both stretching their arms towards him. "There, there," he said soothingly as they dropped their heads on his shoulders. "Mommy is a little sad, but she will be fine. It's all right, I'll take care of them tonight."

Wrapping her arms around them, she asked sadly. "I'll never have a real family, will I?"

"I am here, and you know what I keep telling you."

"What did I expect?" She asked herself. *"That he would leave everything, ignore who I am, who he is, and come chasing after me?"* She was naïve and her head full of romantic nonsense if she convinced herself of the like. Mathew was not John, who was trustworthy, dependable, and didn't give two hoots about anyone's name. She tossed, turned, and eventually arose in the morning with dark rings under her eyes.

John watched her keenly but said nothing, merely going about feeding the boys in silence.

"One of these days they'll start calling you daddy." She remarked.

"And what's wrong with that, unless you don't want to encourage it. Jessie, let me be their father if they can't have Mathew. You need help and I want to give it."

James watched Vanessa from the bed as she busied herself with her morning ritual. There was such a sensual look to her that he often thought she would have made the perfect pagan priestess. He loved walking into a crowded room with her on his arm, especially when she wore one of those indecent creations of hers. At once, he saw lasciviousness in men and envy in women. Men lusted after her, few controlled themselves, and some even dared to suggest indulgent liaisons. As most women hid such titbits from their husbands, she delighted in telling him about her rebuffs, making certain he was aware how many persisted.

Now, his mind was not on strangers but themselves. Six months had passed since their wedding and he was beginning to see impatience in his father; Theodore wanted grandchildren.

He had made it his duty to pay attention to her cycle, making sure they made love at the right times, and knowing she used no contraceptives should make it a straightforward process, right? No, nothing had happened thus far.

As promised, she had toned down her schedule, but it was still much busier than he liked, because she had a knack for cramming things into tiny spots of time. If there were children to be raised, she had to be home, as that was one custom from his grandmother he refused to bring into his family.

"Vanessa," he called, as she passed the bottom of the bed in her silk teddy, and patted the sheet in invitation.

"I have a meeting."

"You will be sorry if you miss this."

"What are you up to?" She watched his face. "Okay, five minutes." She climbed in. "Whaa…"

"Oh, found it already?" He moaned.

Greedy hands pulled the gold choker from under her body and dangled it in front of her eyes. "Thank you for the lovely gift, it's gorgeous, but I have to go." She put it on.

He loved how the gold caressed her bronzed skin. "We have to start thinking about children."

"We'll see."

But as December approached, there was nothing to see. Perhaps not intentionally, but his urgency annoyed her. He couldn't figure her out, becoming unapproachable, and as for making love… Undercurrents flew, the relationship strained, and the tension was something all developed a healthy respect for, standing well clear of their mounting spats.

Watching them at the Christmas table, Grace trusted they wouldn't start one of their now frequent rows, which never made sense because she had no idea what they were so uptight about. Fortunately, Carol was also present and had a certain flair for bringing relief to strained situations with her sparkling personality. Nevertheless, Grace wished her good luck trying to calm a savage Vanessa. The latter, had taken to staring at the other woman in open dislike and Grace hoped she didn't transfer her exasperation from James to Carol.

"Madam, telephone," a servant announced beside her nervously.

"Cut off whoever is on the other side." Theodore's displeasure was as plain as day.

Grace watched the man's face. That suggestion was something he did not want to do. "Who is it?" She queried.

The man glanced at Theodore. "Master John, madam."

"Wonderful, I'll take it here."

Theodore opened his mouth but saw his sons studying him with curious interest, their gaze almost daring him to take this one pleasure from Grace on a day she believed family was all important. "Okay, let him speak to his mother." He waved in irritation.

As soon as Grace took the instrument, she put the speakerphone on. 'John, darling,' she greeted with pleasure. "Merry Christmas."

"And to you and everyone at home."

"Likewise," Mathew answered. "How are you? We haven't seen you for so long it's as if you moved to another planet."

"Hi, Mathew, congratulations on your engagement. And to you, James, on your marriage,"

"Thanks."

"When are you coming back?" Grace daren't say home as Theodore watched.

"I wanted to months ago, but I have a problem."

"Do you need money?" Mathew queried.

"No, I have a great job and make more than I can spend."

"Then?" Mark threw in.

"My wife is excruciatingly difficult. God, she drives me insane."

There was a stunned silence.

"Well, I'll be," Monica said stupefied.

"Congratulations," Grace smiled a little disconcerted. "So, what's the problem, doesn't she like South Africa?"

"Very much, she just doesn't want to go there."

"I don't understand."

"Neither do I, but I'll do anything for her, including freezing to death."

"I'm glad he has finally come to his senses. What was that before?" Monica mumbled.

"I heard that, Aunt Monica. And it seems you always have a lot to say, but being Christmas, I won't tell you what I think."

"Where is your wife?"

'Right here, and about to commit murder. Mine, from the looks of it. She didn't know I was calling you so she's running around in a nervous haze."

"Put the girl on, we are just normal people."

"That's not what she says."

"Wow, a girl with sense," Mark noted.

"What's her name, honey?"

John made a strange sound. "Huh… Are you all right?" He asked someone in the background.

"How could you? I'm totally unprepared." A female voice said.

"Who is she?"

"Jessie. That's why I came here anyway, to find and marry her. It took forever, but here we are."

Either intentionally or otherwise, all eyes were on Mathew, no one knowing what to say.

"You are dead, John Barrymore."

"Stop planning my demise and watch what your sons are doing. How do they get things out of drawers? They are going to kill each other. Give me that."

"Ta." A baby voice answered.

"Yes, ta. You are such naughty little boys."

"W-what, what's going on?" Grace found her voice again.

"Your grandsons, mom, forever pulling things out of drawers. There are two of them, twins, and a handful."

"You have twins and didn't tell us?"

"Considering how relations stand between our families, Jessie said no one would be interested. I tend to agree."

"I understand about the others," Grace looked at everyone around the table. "But me?"

"Mom, you know how difficult she is. Come say hello."

"I will call your mother another day, leave me out of this conversation." Jessie told him angrily.

"See how it is? I'm lucky she actually said yes. But I maintain it was the wine." John laughed. "Anyway, merry Christmas, everyone, and a very happy New Year."

"Goodbye, honey, and congratulations." She heard the click on the other side. "Well, will there be anything to beat this wonderful surprise?"

An eerie silence filled the table. James glared at Vanessa, Mark scowled, and Carol watched Mathew with undisguised interest.

"That girl was determined to get a Barrymore, eventually did, and now has already produced two more. Quite a feat if you ask me. So, what are you waiting for, Vanessa? By rights, you should have had the first Barrymore babies." Monica told her.

"You know what is sick?" Vanessa asked heatedly. "It's that all four fell under her spell and in differing degrees seem to be in love with her. Even you, James," she accused. "The way you go on how it's such a shame she is a Stevens because she's so damn beautiful. I hope she has picked up twenty kilos and looks gross."

"Vanessa," Theodore addressed her. "All we expect of you is a Barrymore heir. If she already has two, it shouldn't be too difficult for you. Only," he turned to Grace. "Why did he marry her? And why did he go through that repulsive period, causing pandemonium in this family, probably hers too, live with her brother, and then go back to her? From being queer to being married to a Stevens, I don't know which I find more troubling."

"But you will keep your promise, won't you?"

"What promise?" Theodore asked blankly.

"The one you made when he left. That he would be welcomed back when he married."

"I said that?"

"You did." Mark concurred flatly. "Do you keep it?"

"Heaven help me and the things I say without thinking. But you know how I feel—"

"I have often kept my mouth even when I didn't like what was said, but today you are all going to hear my thoughts on the subject." Grace announced. "Personally, I don't care what the surname is because Jessie is a lovely girl and it is utterly unfair we judge her because of it. So, she married your youngest son; what do you want now, when they already have children? He will never listen to you and do you know why? Because he's as stubborn as you are. You were the same, never doing what was expected.

"We are married today because your mother told you she didn't like me and although I know you loved me, you also felt obliged to spite her. Otherwise, you would have been hitched to that silly Rebecca Simms and been ditched the same way she did her last five husbands. Let the boy be, he's settled down and sounds the happiest I've ever heard."

"How they must have laughed behind our backs, telling their friends what a great catch she made."

"Knowing Jessie, they know as much as we did this morning." Grace covered Theodore's hand with hers. "Give the girl a chance, all she wants is happiness, and if she found it with your son, so be it. And remember," she gave him a beguiling smile. "We have two grandsons, two innocents who shouldn't pay for past misdeeds. Let them grow up without guilt for being whatever they are."

"I still don't like it."

"And I can't do anything about that. I'm merely asking for the same courtesy we have accorded Vanessa and Carol."

Later, Grace found Mathew on the terrace, staring over the garden. "Where is Carol?"

"Swimming."

"Oh, Mathew, please don't pretend. Why didn't you marry her?"

"Not after what she did."

"And what did she do, told a few lies, concealed her name, or was it the fact that your brother was gay? One hates an act not the person and Jessie is difficult to hate. You should have done what he did, gone after her. Now, let go of the past, especially the one that doesn't concern you. This constant digging back is destroying you. And stop making decisions to please this family, because it is you who must live with them. Can't you feel your heart rebelling against your head?"

"You never said much before, why now?"

"Because I am sick and tired of this thing."

"Do you like Carol?"

"I do, she's interesting and entertaining."

"Vanessa?"

"Tiresome and nasty, but if I dig deep enough I may find some good."

"But Jessie, you always liked her."

"Simply because she is who she is. I've heard many stories about the Stevenses, flattering and otherwise. Know what I think? Not worth repeating or remembering because Jessie disproves every single one. The bad are based on gossip and the good don't measure up."

In the space of three months, Stevens Textiles underwent a revolution, a nasty and unexpected one. More was the disbelief because as a company, it had always been well-respected, and as career advancements went it was well sought-after. Taylor had learnt good principles, fairness, equality, and promotion from his father, and to that he had held since his seventeenth birthday, the day he was allowed to walk into the factory as a member of Stevens Textiles' workforce; where he began as an apprentice to one of the printer mechanics.

Over time, things changed, modernised, and he was proud that equal opportunities allowed quite a few women to build good lives before it was fashionable to do so. So now, he did not understand the recent upheaval.

Four accidents had taken place in the last ninety days, and as he looked back, he noticed that they had become progressively worse. The first man got himself stuck in a machine, was almost pressed into pulp, and came out looking like a plumb, bruised from head to foot. Another lost a thumb to a falling metal plate. A third received severe burns to his arms when a burner went haywire, and the fourth lost a leg when he was squashed against a wall by a rogue computer arm.

But the surprise to beat all others came when one of the warehouse's security guards called him in the middle of the night. Nemesis, a retired police dog, was going crazy over something. It could only be bad because Nemesis was not moved by anything.

Forty minutes later, Taylor stood alongside Peter, the security guard. 'What are we looking at?' He asked as he peered into the box that was supposed to have fabric cleaners but was filled with small tinfoil packets.

"Drugs, sir. Nemesis wouldn't have made such a fuss if they weren't."

Taylor stared at him flabbergasted then phoned Simon and told him to call whomever he had to in the police force to come investigate and cart the garbage away.

The boxes had come off the Durban Harbour, from Nigeria. Taylor could not understand why, as Stevens Textiles had no dealings with the West African Country. Major Patterson, the man in charge of Narcotics, seemed sceptical about a mix-up and Taylor liked none of the scenarios he saw running through the Major's head.

As if all of that wasn't enough to give him insomnia, resignations began landing on his desk. What did he have insurance and security for? His employees were spooked, people coming close to losing their lives, and drugs were becoming the second commodity on the premises. Exasperated over things he could not explain, he went to see Major Patterson.

Realising the man was sincere, the Major decided to tell him a few things as well.

Rumours from narcotic investigators had begun filtering through and all agreed that although unable to prove it, Stevens Textiles appeared to be involved. Two weeks back, a group of teenagers had been arrested in possession of cocaine and fingers were slowly pointing that way, which was all a mystery, as the same investigators couldn't find a shred of evidence to support the accusations. And the accidents, he continued, might also be connected to the drugs because drug-lords did not take kindly to people messing with their merchandise.

Taylor cringed at the idea of being mistaken for a pusher. 'I know you have no reason to trust or believe me, but why would I do this? I am as concerned as you are about where this rubbish is coming from and the harm it wreaks in our community. And if anyone in my employ is responsible, I want him behind bars. No matter who that person is.'

Major Patterson grinned. 'I was beginning to think I had to bust you because although we know something is going on, we don't know who is involved. You mentioned people resigning, what positions are available?'

"One designer, two executives, a couple technicians, a printer, a few labourers, a cook," Taylor passed a hand over his eyes. "And the list is growing."

Major Patterson tapped his chin. "I'll send someone undercover. I like this young man and promised to bring him back from Natal at the first opportunity. He seems the perfect candidate because not only is he an unknown face around here but he's also an excellent narcotics detective, who happens to have a bit of a graphic design background. Naturally, you can't expect him to be as good as the professionals working for you, but as a cover, it's adequate."

Few things escaped Bruce Murray's intelligent brown eyes. He was tall, athletic, and had a way of studying people with immense concentration, as if trying to guess the reason behind their decisions, or ulterior motives.

As cover, one position was as good as another so Taylor let him go to work in the printing department. Unashamedly encouraging hard work, long hours, and taking an open personal interest, he also realised that as the Major alluded, Bruce had genuine designing talent.

"What have you learnt so far?" Taylor asked one evening as both looked out of his office window and over the factory roof.

"A couple people are on illegal substances and someone here is dealing. It's still too early for anyone to trust me so no one talks. As for the accidents, haven't seen anything suspicious yet. Then again, I don't sleep here. But more than likely it's one of your executives."

"Why do you say that?"

"Because of your security system. Everyone uses their cards coming in and going out." Bruce held his own up. "Every name and number is registered twice, including times. The printouts are open to scrutiny and not one person was here after hours before those accidents. The executives on the other hand, punch a code to override using their cards and it seems they all share the same one. How can I tell who left at six and who left ten minutes later?"

"But I have known all these people for years. Except for three men I recruited after my son's death. Phillip Fourie, Alan Ming, and Harry Stander."

Bruce checked in the book he always carried with him. "This is exactly my point. These people come and go as they please and I have seen them around at all hours. The thing is, their offices are all up here, while I'm mostly down there. I need to spend a few nights around here." He followed Taylor to the desk and sat opposite him. "I need to ask a lot of questions without anyone becoming suspicious."

"All I see is the corner they are forcing me into. Lawrence wasn't exceptional, but he lent a hand. Now, I have almost everything back on my desk and it's hard to keep up." Taylor announced tiredly.

"Lawrence was supposed to take over, right?"

"That was the intention."

"Let's tell everyone I am your heir; a distant nephew, cousin, anything. That way, you give me free reign to come and go. I must learn fast and work even harder, especially overtime." Bruce said pointedly. "Introduce me to your executives; let them know that I will be their next boss. It will annoy them, perhaps even make someone nervous and precipitate the clues we are looking for."

"I like none of this." Taylor shook his head then pointed to a few designs. "Why did you quit?"

"I wanted adventure and joined the force."

Bruce told Taylor to suspect all, and not to be blindsided by friendship, because sometimes those turned out to be the worst. He was introduced as a distant relative and the assumption that he would be regarded suspiciously was proven correct.

No one was pleased with the turn of events, especially those who imagined Taylor beaten and hoped he sold the family business for lack of heirs. But the young man strove to please and endear himself to anyone who gave him five minutes, and although some were reluctant to befriend him openly, most accepted the status quo.

To further make the role believable, Bruce was also introduced to the family, where a friendship soon developed between him and Simon. Then one Sunday, as they sat having family lunch, Taylor caught Bruce watching Beverley with a fascination that seemed a little dangerous.

"Are you in love with my daughter?" Taylor asked without preamble Monday morning.

Bruce became flustered. "I, that is… I'm sorry, Mr Stevens, I didn't mean any disrespect. And I'd never… My personal feelings will not detract me from my duties."

Taylor nodded. "I know, and I didn't mean to embarrass you, but things are what they are. Pity you are so taken with this police business, you are a good hand to have around."

"Thank you, Mr Stevens." Bruce said as he left the office.

"Yes, sir," he thought as he walked away. Lately, his life was a muddle because even he forgot that this was not a real job, and he had been a policeman more years than months here. But worse, so much worse, Beverley… Every time he was in her presence strange things happened. Her long blonde mane made him want to reach out and touch it and her beautiful blue eyes mesmerised him in ways no others had done before. Being in love was as painful as it was pleasant.

An amazing kaleidoscope of colour appeared as Bruce entered the gargantuan storeroom, shelves from floor to ceiling. He never knew there were so many hues of blue, shades of brown, and intensities of red.

"Do you smell something?" He asked as he glanced at a printout in his hand.

223

"It always smells here." One woman told him. "It's all the chemicals. No smoking, see?" She pointed to the sign on the wall. "I'll get you a mask from the closet outside."

"Thank you," he glanced at her nametag. "Lorinda, but I'll go. I need the air."

Finding the closet locked, he gave it one smart kick, in case the door was stuck; then looking up, saw the notice on the wall "PLEASE GET KEY FROM OFFICE". Walking across the fifteen metres, he greeted the woman behind the counter. "Hello, Estelle, may I please have the key to the gas masks?"

She laughed, reached for a key on a giant board, pulled a file over, and told him to sign.

"GAS!"

Most of the city heard the explosion.

Bruce was flung across the room and against a wall by the intense force, cutting his brow open and dislocating a shoulder instantaneously. He felt the warm blood pour down the side of his face and the excruciating pain in his shoulder, but he also knew that he was the nearest help those women had. "Estelle," he staggered to his feet in bewildered shock. Running past the scorched door, he saw her in a heap, killed by flying glass. Leaning against the wall, he wiped his eye then raced towards the raging fire. Before getting close enough, he knew that no one had survived.

Sirens went off, workers evacuated, and dark noxious clouds rose from the building. Looking up, he saw the sky. He was still struggling one-handed with the extinguisher when fire-fighters appeared beside him.

"Come along." One man put an arm around his shoulders.

He winced and pointed to where flames devoured everything.

"No one could survive that. We'll take care of it now." The man let go of him as a paramedic appeared. "Check his arm, it might be broken."

"Good heavens," Taylor said in shock when he saw him. "You were in there? You're bleeding, your arm…"

"It's dislocated." Bruce swayed against the ambulance.

"Sit down, son. Let them take a look."

"Mr Stevens, was there supposed to be any gas?"

"In a room full of chemicals?" Taylor stopped. "They mean to ruin me, don't they?"

Wearily and in a lot of pain, Bruce lay back on a stretcher. "It's sabotage, arson, intent to do bodily harm, malicious damage to property, and murder. These are serious players in a game with no rules, so whoever left that gas knew exactly what would happen when someone flicked a switch. What a mess, and as usual, innocents died."

"Did you hear about what happened at Stevens?" Mark asked as he joined the family for dinner.

"So did the whole of Johannesburg. It's been bad luck all the way this year." James said. "The death toll was four, and twelve injured. The smoke was so thick it reached downtown. Even the heir apparent was hurt."

Theodore nodded. "I heard something at the club. It seems Stevens found himself a distant relative. Must be from his wife's side because he has no one out there. The boy apparently knows nothing about textiles but is an adequate designer and quite willing to learn."

Mark turned to Vanessa. "You were there, how was it?"

"Apocalyptic. Tried to ask a few questions but Taylor was completely focused on his heir's well-being, and the loss of lives. I guess that's commendable. Got pictures of him but he was so sooted and bandaged that I couldn't see much."

"Do we have to discuss this?" Grace cut them off. "We should be feeling sorry for the family not gloat over a disaster that could have happened to anyone." She turned to Mathew. "Where is Carol?"

"At a symposium in Cape Town."

"And when is this wedding taking place?" Vanessa asked with interest.

"Give us time."

"You seem to have a lot of that."

Irritation filled him. "Butt out, I'm not your assignment. Excuse me."

"What's his problem?" Vanessa queried.

"The same one he has every time we discuss the Stevenses." Mark informed her. "It's called Jessie."

"Then he should just get over it. She is his sister-in-law for crying out loud." Vanessa's voice rose sharply.

Mathew bobbed gently in the water when he heard someone push the door open and then wade in. Turning, he saw Vanessa. "I'm not in the mood."

"I just want to talk."

"I don't like what you say."

"I have noticed. So, what am I doing wrong?" She moved closer.

"You seem to forget that you are married to my brother. And don't play dumb, because that's something you're not. You are always asking, where was I, why am I late, where am I going? Who are you, my wife?"

"I should be." Her hand went to his face. "Why did I only find out afterwards how much I really care? Damn it, Matt, I love you."

"Which I can't help. Besides, you made your choice."

"No, I made a mistake, and you didn't give me another chance." She kissed him.

Astonishment kept him immobile, then, he pushed her away. "Are you mad?"

"Yes," her eyes filled with tears. "When he touches me, I close my eyes and pretend it's you. I just never imagined that it would get this bad."

"If you're not on something you should be because this is no talk for a married woman to be having with her brother-in-law."

"I'm going insane, all he wants is babies." She made a helpless gesture. "Why didn't I know what a good thing I had?"

He looked her straight in the eye and took two steps away. "This is absurd."

"I know you never loved me, because it's always going to be Jessie. She came along and messed with your mind. But tell me now, Matt. Do you care for Carol as you cared for me, or as you did for Jessie? The answer will indicate your marriage's success."

"Carol is not you. She is kind, sweet, and warm-hearted. We understand each other."

"Have it your way, but if you are not careful, you will end up as frustrated as I am. And then perhaps you'll come knocking on my door. I just hope I will have the strength to turn you away as you're doing me now, so you'll hurt as much as I do."

"If you hate it that much why don't you get out? I assure you, James may not think so, but he will survive."

"You don't understand," she shook her head. "Then I'd never see you. I need that desperately, even if I can't have you."

"Get a grip, Vanessa, and perhaps you should try having a baby. You might be very happy once you do and forget all about me. But you don't really love me; you are just peeved things didn't go your way." Turning, he walked away.

"You are intelligent, Mathew, and yet, about things that really matter you know nothing."

CHAPTER THIRTEEN

James watched Vanessa as she slid off the bed after stretching like a cat. Once, he enjoyed and teased her feline moves but now it was just another morning, another wave of wasted ideas, and another unpleasant day. The situation was getting out of hand, but what exactly was he supposed to do, to first, get her to cooperate, and second, to appease his father? It wasn't as if he were trying to coerce her but there was no teamwork taking place, not even a discussion, because she simply turned livid the moment he opened his mouth. Oh well, here it went. "Is there a date I can pencil in?"

Vanessa flicked her hair with an angry gesture. "I'm sick and tired of this nonsense. The time is right, the temperature is up, this month, the next. Just let me be."

"I don't want to let you be, I want a child. I need sons to carry my name into the future."

"What about what I want?" She hit her chest. "You think I'm an incubator, my sole purpose in life that of producing miniature Barrymores. And if you wanted kids so badly perhaps you should have married that Stevens brat." She told him sarcastically.

"Perhaps I should have as it seems she does normal things without complaining. One would swear I'm asking for some preposterous thing."

"Babies take a lot from a person. They are demanding, irritating... what would happen to my career?"

He sat in the wingback chair. "Don't act coy, you know it's like this in families such as ours. I said you could do whatever you wanted, and that still applies. I'm not antiquated and I don't much care what anyone says on that subject. But now, give me my heir and don't profess ignorance. I'm telling you, I want a child, and soon."

"Or what," She shouted across the room.

"I don't know. We have been married how long and what has happened? Nothing. It's just not possible, unless you can't have any. Go see a doctor, go find out what's wrong with you."

She gasped. "You can't be serious! And how do you know it's me?"

"I assure you, nothing is wrong with me, or any Barrymore, even my gay brother has already produced offspring."

"Don't be an idiot, that has nothing to do with it and you know it. You want me to go to the doctor, I will, as soon as I see your results." She slammed the bathroom door shut.

She ran upstairs, undressed quickly, and climbed under the shower. Then wrapping herself in a bath sheet, she lay on the bed, unable to stop the thoughts that had taken over. What exactly could she do about it now? A slow tear slid down the side of her face.

Someone was touching her, his hands running up her naked body, kissing her but never quite becoming passionate, always holding something back, just like…

"Hmmm, Mathew," she murmured and put her hands up to his face.

The flick of a switch bathed the room in light.

James towered above her. "Mathew?"

She got to her feet and pulled the towel tightly around her. "Sorry, a slip of the tongue."

"That is no slip; a wife knows when her husband is making love to her." His eyes narrowed. "Have you been sleeping with my brother?"

"You were kissing me differently."

"And your mind flies to him?" He asked incredulous as he jumped to his feet.

She shrugged. "It felt like him."

"Tell me the truth now, how long, just how bloody long has this been going on?"

"It hasn't!" She denied indignantly. "If you don't believe it, that's your problem."

"And now I realise I have more than anticipated." He pulled a paper from his pocket. "When I asked you to go to the doctor, I had already been. There is nothing wrong with me and I can father a dozen children should I wish. Or did you think I was afraid? But your results should be interesting, I know you received them today."

Shock spread on her face.

"But it's not my children you want, is it? So, if it's Mathew's you're waiting for and there's still nothing, then we're back to the original problem, you." He pointed accusingly. "Damn you, woman, what the hell have you been up to?" Grabbing her by one arm, he shook her.

"Stop behaving like a spoilt brat," she demanded.

"A brat, huh?" Pushing her aside, he stormed to the tallboy. "I'm going to kill him."

Vanessa gulped as the shining black object appeared in his hand. "James, put the gun down, you could hurt someone."

"And you, two-timing… should be the first. Instead, I'll make you suffer to see him dead."

"You're wrong, we have never. Not since we broke up."

Pointing the gun at her, he saw the fear in her eyes. "What did the doctor say?"

"You have no right to spy on me." She threw back.

"Apparently, but I merely called the station to take you out to lunch and your PA checked the diary to see where you had gone. When she told me you went to the doctor, and then home, I thought I'd better rush… And for what? Just to discover you've been cheating."

"Why won't you believe me?"

"Because I know you've been lying since the beginning." He said tiredly and sank into the chair. "Never loved me, yet, I hoped a baby would change things. I was so pleased when you called me that first time… But just a ruse, right? You wanted him back. Tell me one thing, are you pregnant, and if so, by whom?" Then rising quickly, he turned to leave the room.

She bit her bottom lip nervously. "I can't have children."

The words arrested him in mid step. "Huh… Why?"

"It's about what I did years ago."

He waved the gun around in irritation. "Stop the rigmarole, tell me."

"I had tubal ligation done."

"What?"

"Sterilisation,"

He stared at her as if he had never seen her before. "I know what it means, It's just… You have known all along that you can't conceive and chose to hide it from me? You let me hope and dream in vain, while knowing how important this is?"

"I couldn't tell you, you don't know what happened."

"I don't care what happened, why wasn't I told? And naturally, it's irreversible."

She nodded, her eyes filling with tears. "I didn't know I would need children to save my marriage."

"Damn you woman, how could you? How old were you? And why the hell would a young woman do such a thing? Was it because you hate them? You are cold, Vanessa, cold and brutal!"

"I started out life wanting the same things all women do. Get married, have babies, a nice job… but then, it all went wrong. One night as I walked home, I was raped, gang raped!" The tears blinded her. "I never reported it because I knew them. They were supposed to be my friends, my neighbours. If they had threatened to kill me, I wouldn't have cared, but they threatened to hurt my parents and I knew they meant it. How I prayed I would die, but I didn't." She wiped her eyes with a shaking hand. "Then just as I thought I was getting better, I discovered I was pregnant.

"Whose was it? And was I to have this child and be constantly reminded of the brutal attack that was its creation?" She covered her face for a second. "I got rid of it, my shame, and of what could make me have more. Never again would I suffer the same pain. Know what, James? Three years later, it happened again. But that time it was only one creep and I was not scared, so I nailed him like the bastard he was, and thankfully, there was no fear of babies, because I couldn't have any. It was then that I congratulated myself for my good sense." She stared at the floor for a moment. "Then I moved here and met Mathew.

"Everything went well until he started talking children. I freaked and ran, not realising I loved him. When I returned, I tried to patch things up, but Jessie was in the way and had two things I didn't, his love and the ability to have babies. I became sad, depressed, and bitter." She made a gesture. "And messed with Rachel's fiancée. But he was a loser anyway, so it was better she found out then. I didn't know what to do. Then one day, I saw you in town and the idea just hit me." She made a face. "I needed you because under what pretext could I come back here? There was Mark… but no. I hoped that if she went he would return to me, but he didn't, he loved her, still does, just won't admit it. He didn't marry her because she's a Stevens, but he loves her and hates me for what I did. And as much as I love him, I hate him too."

"Half your friends are in the movie business, whose script did you swipe? Give me a sad story and I filled with pity forget everything? I forget nothing; in fact, I'm having trouble believing anything that's been spewed from your mouth. So now, I want to hear him say that he has not touched you. I need him to validate part of your story, because the other half, I suppose he knows nothing about?"

She shook her head. "You are the first person I told."

"What an honour." He told her sarcastically.

"James, let's start over, with no lies, no secrets—"

"And you had the gall to point fingers at Jessie, to use me like a puppet."

"I didn't have to do much, you all hate the Stevenses enough, I just had to point out she was one. Of course, even I couldn't have foreseen the relationship between John and Jeremy. That was the bonus."

He shook his head and placed a hand over his brow. "I can see clearly now too. Had he married her none of this would be happening because your hope would have died. You would have gone your merry way and I wouldn't be in this mess.' Then stuffing the black object in his belt, he opened the door and ran down the stairs.

Driving at breakneck speed, James arrived at an almost deserted factory. *"Should have flushed the phones down the toilet,"* he thought then asked two technicians working on a printer. "Have you seen my brother?"

"Which one?"

"Not Mark."

Funny way to ask for someone. "No sir. Is there a message?"

"I'll deliver it myself." He ground out through clenched teeth then walking up and down some aisles, he sat down in a corner. Wasn't this a dandy situation. But he had known all along nothing was right, just ignored the gnawing. The question was, could he believe her? Hearing the slow drone of Mark's monster, he went to peer at it, a slow whoosh rising from its gargantuan stomach.

"James, get away from there." Mathew said from the top of the stairs.

James waved a hand in front of the gaping hole.

Mathew ran down. "Stop that, the damn thing is dangerous."

"What's it going to do, eat me? But you don't really need me out of the way. Did you at least give me a second thought?"

"What?"

"Why is it everyone reacts this way when confronted?"

"James, I have no idea what you're saying."

"Didn't my wife already fill you in?"

"They said something upstairs and my cell rang but I haven't had time to call back. What does she want anyway?"

"Who gave you the right to sleep with my wife?"

Shock appeared on Mathew's face.

"Should consider a career in acting,"

"Vanessa and me… you are insane to even consider it."

"Are you saying you didn't?"

"I most certainly am." Mathew made a wild gesture. "And where the hell did you get this idea?"

"Vanessa. Did you know she's still in love with you?" James queried tiredly.

"I don't know what this is about, but I swear nothing happened between us. I don't want to start trouble but if she suggested—"

"No, she denied it most vehemently."

"Then why?"

"Today, she called me Mathew when I was making love to her."

"I swear, James, I didn't go near her. We hardly speak."

"Oh, the things she told me… My marriage is basically screwed."

"I'm sorry but I don't know what else to say."

"Quite the manipulator, you know. Inveigled her way into my life to get near you, then used us all to get rid of the threat, Jessie. Made me so angry that I even brought a gun." James pulled it from his belt.

"For goodness sake, put it away."

"It's not loaded." Stuffing it back in his belt, James leaned against the machine. "What does a man do about a wife like mine?"

"I don't know. James, move."

A formidable suction followed an incredible gush and Mathew watched his brother almost disappear into the machine, feet first. He heard James scream, he screamed, and instinctively grabbed his arms, trying to drag him out, because if he let go, he would surely die. 'Help,' he needed to throw the switch, but the contraption was too powerful and he too far from the panel. "HELP!"

"Let me go…"

"I can't, I won't. HELP!"

"Hey," one of the technicians asked at the other end. "What's going on?"

"Come, quickly." Mathew shouted.

The man ran across the floor and stood transfixed by the scene for a second then hit the large blue button. Everything moved in slow motion, the engine taking an eternity to come to a standstill.

"Get an ambulance and ask whoever is around to come take this thing apart, now!" Mathew ordered as he saw his brother's ashen face. "James, can you hear me?"

The technicians quickly set about opening the machine, unscrewing, and lifting panels.

"Look at me." Mathew begged as he noticed blood reaching his shoes.

James' pain-filled eyes couldn't get a fix on his brother. "Are you… in love… with Vanessa?"

"No."

"If I die, will you marry her?"

"I will not, and you won't die. But please don't talk."

"I can't feel my legs," James' voice drifted.

"Hush now," Mathew passed a hand over the matted hair. "I hear the ambulance. Just try to stay awake." But he knew James couldn't.

"It's a nightmare," Mathew thought as he paced the hospital lounge. Everyone disappeared towards the theatre and no one deemed it important to inform him of whatever progress.

Grace was the first to reach him. 'Mathew!' She said anxiously. 'We drove as fast as we could. Where is he?'

"In there," he pointed then asked darkly. "Where's Vanessa?"

"She drove herself, what happened?"

"That damn machine I warned everyone about." He glared at his father. "Didn't I tell you it was dangerous? You won't believe how quickly it happened, his legs, blood everywhere..." Seeing Grace's face, he stopped, then turning, noticed Vanessa. "Why are you late?"

"I... I..."

Grabbing her arm, he took her a distance away. "I don't know what the hell happened tonight, but I hold you responsible. As soon as he comes to, you are going to straighten this nonsense, is that understood?"

"I didn't... I mean..."

"Shut up and listen. How could you say we are having some kind of affair?" His eyes darkened ominously.

"I didn't, it was a slip of the tongue."

"I don't much care for your explanations. To even imply— are you out of your mind? And don't make yourself comfortable because if he dies I'll kick you out myself, do you understand? I told you more than once to stay away but it seems you didn't take my warnings seriously. I suggest you do."

"But Mathew," her eyes filled with tears. "It was a horrible mistake."

"He came to the factory with a gun. Thankfully, the damn thing wasn't loaded. What if he were so out of control that he wouldn't listen to reason? And I'd also be here, in the morgue. Is your thirst for retaliation such that you want me dead? How can you look at yourself and know the trouble you've caused?"

"I tried to warn you—"

"Which wasn't necessary, as this should not be happening. In future, keep your thoughts to yourself and me out of them. And don't go anywhere because you are going to stay by his side like the devoted wife you are, night and day."

"That's not fair." She told him angrily.

"You are either quitting or asking for leave, understand?"

She opened her mouth, but words wouldn't come.

Letting go of her, he went to sit beside his mother then after what seemed like an eternity, he saw the doctor. He jumped to his feet. "How is he?"

"You did a brave thing, son. If you hadn't been there," the doctor made a gesture. "Well, it's an absolute miracle he wasn't killed outright. But the gun also helped save his life."

"What gun?" Grace asked in shock.

"The one he carried in his belt." The doctor continued. "It became entangled in the pinions and prevented serious damage to his abdomen."

Vanessa broke into sobs and took refuge in Grace's arms.

"If the torso had gone through those rollers, we wouldn't have been able to do much. For now, we have saved both legs and feet but there is considerable damage. His spine was also twisted so we have to wait and see." The doctor stopped a moment. "I wish I could say everything will be fine but there are no guarantees. He is critical."

"Mr Stevens, did you see today's papers?" Bruce asked as he walked around the office with his bug detector, then switched it off when all read clear.

Taylor pointed to the chair. "What do you make of it? Think our boys started at Barrymores as well? Our woes could involve the entire industry. We had a strike a few years back and who knows, someone might be vindicating himself?"

"Anything is possible, but it says most people thought the machine was dangerous."

"Then it must be an accident." Getting to his feet, Taylor closed the office door. "I see you have been spending a lot of time around the offices, any suspects?"

"A few people are hooked on something or other. I found traces of cocaine and heroin in the men's rooms and took the liberty of sending a package to Major Patterson for tests." Bruce pulled a paper from his pocket. "Received the results today; almost pure, and according to this, Colombian, but with African traces. It's being mixed in Nigeria, which explains those first boxes. Now we need to find out how it gets here and how Stevens is involved."

"Stevens is not involved."

"Someone is making sure it looks that way. Think about it, it's the perfect cover as well as means of transportation." Bruce pointed to the map on the wall behind the desk.

Taylor glanced at it, coloured strings following the intricate web-like pattern of roads. "I see what you mean."

"There is a connection between here and dealers around Johannesburg, just don't ask me to explain it. I'm running out of patience, but no one is dying to confide in his future boss. In fact, some of those executives have become pretty nervous."

"Shouldn't you arrest the people on drugs?"

"I'd blow my cover. Besides, I'm trying to get some myself. Then I'll be part of the inner group."

"Please be careful, I would hate for anything to happen to you again." Taylor smiled and glanced at the portfolio Bruce always brought into the office. "Certain you don't want to leave the police force?"

"Don't talk like that, Mr Stevens. I'm confused enough as it is."

"Police work has to be some of the most dangerous."

"No more than this factory. I keep wondering what's next." Bruce told him and left the office.

Glancing out the window casually, Taylor saw the workers he had hired to rebuild the storeroom and extension putting their tools away. Ever since that first accident nothing had gone right. He was more than tired of it all. His phone rang. "Simon," he greeted surprised. "I thought you had already left."

"Had to cancel, Juliet has tonsillitis. I received the insurance papers, should I bring them over?"

"Yes, please, I need a lift home too. The garage came to get my car, as I can't stand that rattling in the dashboard. I could have asked Bruce, but he has to go see..." Taylor stopped, realising he couldn't mention Major Patterson. Bruce said the office was clean but he felt better taking the extra precaution. Replacing the receiver, he busied himself with a heap of files.

A distant rumble startled him. Concerned, he hoped the predicted weekend downpours held off, as the extension floor was still wet, and the roof only halfway across. Getting to his feet, he went to look at the sky and noticed a man on the roof. Probably one of the workers who had forgotten something.

"What the..." Turning, he grabbed his jacket, left the office, and went in search of the fire escape ladder. It took him a few minutes to reach the top, and then he stood flabbergasted for a few more. He walked over to the man and raised his voice above the drill's din. "What the hell are you doing? And who are you? You're not one of the workers."

The man turned around.

"Harry? What on earth!"

"I saw you leave."

"The garage came to get the car... Why am I explaining myself to you? What everyone does here is my business.' Staring in shock, Taylor realised the wrought damage. "Does this explain everything that has been happening for months?"

"Sorry, no time to chat," Harry pointed. "Jump."

"Why would I do that?"

"Jump, be pushed, or shot, your choice."

"You are mad. How could you do this? People died."

"So? People die every day, from this or that, it doesn't make much difference."

"I can't wait for the authorities to get hold of you, and watch you squirm when justice is dealt."

Without warning, Harry landed a hard fist on Taylor's jaw, making him falter, as he tried to keep his balance. Harry hit him again, forcing him to his knees, then, kicked him in the stomach and back. Falling flat on his face, Taylor was unable to move for a few seconds. It was all the time Harry needed to push him over the side.

Taylor screamed as he hit the iron beam, breaking the right femur, and dislocating the right shoulder instantly. Trying to grab onto something as he dropped fast, thoughts flashed through his mind, *"is this how Jeremy died? Did Lawrence feel pain?"* His body hit the still soft and wet floor, pain shooting through every muscle and bone, every inch of flesh.

Not certain if he had been out seconds, minutes or hours, Taylor opened an eye with difficulty and felt the odd paralysis that constricts any type of movement. Where was Bruce? With superhuman force, he started dragging himself towards the phone, had to warn Simon.

Harry grabbed the phone out of Taylor's hand, pushed him face down onto the wet cement, and with extreme care aimed at the back of his head…

Stopping the car in the open parking, Simon glanced at the sky. "I hope it doesn't rain just yet."

Beverley also looked up. "It looks okay here."

They were supposed to have gone to a friend's game farm for the weekend, but Juliet's tonsils had thought otherwise and made the child develop a high fever. But as sick as she was, she wanted to see her grannies. When Simon mentioned he needed to drop insurance papers at the factory, Beverley was keen to see the place again.

A man's scream startled them both.

"What on earth?" Simon tried to pinpoint its origin.

Beverley pointed to the factory. "It came from there."

Bruce closed another door. He was sick of going through people's drawers and finding nothing, copying hundreds of telephone numbers, calling them, and discovering they belonged to mom, grandma, or uncle. Scanning the grey clouds, he noticed two men on the roof. "What is he doing up there?" He mumbled as he recognised Taylor then froze in horror. The man he couldn't identify hit Taylor. Not once but twice, kicked him, and then pushed him over. Reaching for the gun he carried strapped to his calf, Bruce ran to the lifts.

Racing through the yard, he stormed into the factory. "Beverley! Simon!" He exclaimed, taken aback by their presence.

Harry swivelled around as he heard voices and fired once, hitting the target full force. Simon's blood spread over his chest and splattered Beverley's pink dress. He staggered, pushing his wife against the metal column, where she hit her head and fell. Harry aimed again, and two shots went off simultaneously. Bruce dropped to his knees with a hand on his shoulder, the red soaking his shirt as if it were a bubbling brook.

"Beverley," Bruce called.

"Hmmm..."

"Thank God you're safe." He sucked in a painful breath and noticed Taylor's twitching hand. "Help your father, he's alive… and call… Major Patterson… Sorry, I'm going to… pass out."

Beverley arrived at the hospital in deep shock, unable to recall how she dialled the number her father mumbled before he too became unconscious. Then she sat cradling Simon's dead body against hers, hoping that if she closed her eyes the horror would be obliterated. Instinctively, she reached out to Bruce's heart, feeling the life that still beat there, her eyes glued to Harry's contorted face in death. Security guards and emergency personnel rushed towards her, but she couldn't let go.

It was then she burst into the sobs that didn't stop until Major Patterson entered the factory with what she would always recall as a small army. Then he ordered a doctor to inject her with something that had her travelling in a world of detached suspension in seconds. In one night, she had lost a husband, didn't know if her father would survive, and her friend was in surgery having a bullet removed from a fractured shoulder. She looked up blankly as a man stopped in front of her.

"Beverley?"

"Mathew," she recognised tiredly. "Huh…" her voice trembled, and her eyes filled with tears. "Simon is dead."

Visibly shocked, he took her hand in his. "I'm so sorry to hear it, how?"

"Shot, daddy is in theatre… so is Bruce."

"Why?" He asked disconcerted.

She couldn't answer; instead, she let the sobs tumble forth.

Gently, he put his arms around her, pressing her body against his in comfort. "Is your mother here?"

Shaking her head, she cried. "Why are all these things happening? Why was that man so hell-bent on destroying daddy? I know it's a bad dream. Only, I can't wake up."

Pulling her to a sofa, he sat her down. "I keep saying I'm sorry, but it doesn't quite express what I feel."

Her gaze fixed on his. "No, you are glad someone is taking fiendish delight in our extermination."

"That is not true."

She continued as if talking to herself. "If daddy dies, Bruce is all man we will have left. Is that what you want, to see us wiped out? Well, you're getting your wish."

He realised she was becoming hysterical. "You are grief-stricken therefore I'll forget you ever said it. And I don't hate you like that. We too are amid a tragedy; surely, I can't blame you for it. Have you contacted Jessie? I was going to call you because we don't have John's number either."

She gazed at her shaking hands. "I can't remember..." She broke into tears again.

Seeing Juliet and Serena enter the lounge, Mathew very gently walked Beverley over to them. "I know my condolences may not mean much but I offer them with all sincerity. Please look after her, she is not well."

"Jessie," the receptionist called as she entered the shop. "Message," she waved a paper.

"Who?" Jessie queried, but probably Mrs Maya, who couldn't quite make up her mind over the bedroom furnishings.

"Your mother. She also asked for John, but he's not in."

"Mom?" Only Beverley knew this number. "When?"

"About two hours ago. Do you need the number?"

"No," sitting at her desk, she grabbed the phone, feeling odd tremors of fear run down her spine. Then she dialled and waited a few seconds. "Hi mom, what's going on?"

"Sweetheart, is it possible you come home right away? There has been a terrible accident, daddy, Simon, and Bruce. Poor Beverley is so full of tranquillisers she no longer knows what's going on."

"What happened to Simon, mommy?" She felt like a frightened little girl.

"He's dead. Do you suppose you could make it before the funeral? Daddy and Bruce are still in intensive care and we don't know what to do with your sister. Juliet doesn't understand, and it's just as well. Huh," there was a short pause. "There is also very bad news for your husband. James too was involved in a serious accident at Barrymores and they fear for his life. Even if he lives, he might never walk again. Beverley mumbled about Mathew wanting to contact John and I had quite a task getting this number from her."

Jessie felt physically ill. "But… what is going on back there? How can all these things be happening?"

"I don't know. Will you come?"

"Yes," Jessie wiped her eyes as the tears welled.

There was no way she could work after that, but she did manage to call the airline and book their seats. Then she went home and cried until John arrived, her cases already half-packed. And through her tears, she eventually explained the little she knew.

CHAPTER FOURTEEN

"Feels longer than four years," Jessie thought as they disembarked from the plane.

To their horror, the airport's arrivals hall crawled with reporters, all expecting comments on the tragic occasion… neither said a word. Both dressed in black from head to foot, John held her hand, as each carried one of their sons. It was the photograph that greeted every Sunday breakfast table.

"Like peas in a pod." Grace said misty eyed.

Theodore glared at the picture and the rest wondered what was going through his mind. Vanessa took one look at it and excused herself.

Mark stared and said cryptically. "What a fool."

Mathew spent a second on it, his face betraying nothing.

Before breakfast ended, John stood in the doorway. "Good morning, father. Am I welcome, or should I just turn around and leave before we get into an argument?"

Theodore looked at Grace. "You will have to excuse me, I have things to take care of."

"At least he didn't kick me right out." Smiling, John embraced Grace warmly and then his brothers.

"How I've missed you.' Grace appropriated herself of one hand. "And why did it take a calamity to bring you back? Where are the boys? I so want to meet them."

"They were exhausted, and after what's going on over at that house… it's a disaster area."

"And we are very sorry for them." Grace announced.

"Yes, and I wish I could say welcome back under different circumstances."

John's brows knitted in surprise. "Thank you, Mathew."

"I know we didn't part on good terms and I apologise for being a jerk." Mark told him then asked curiously. "Here to stay?"

"I'd like to, but I don't know about Jessie. How's James?"

"Not well, drifts in and out of consciousness."

"Certain it wasn't sabotage like over at Stevens? Beverley is shattered. She watched her husband die. Fortunately, Bruce was there to prevent any further calamities."

Grace nodded. "I can well imagine. I'll take you to see James after breakfast but remember, he's heavily sedated and doesn't recognise anyone. Now," Grace brightened up. "Please tell me about my grandsons."

He told them how much fun the little boys were, except when they were screaming their heads off. That he had photos, which he passed around. Grace was enthralled and then stopped on Jessie's portrait.

Following her gaze, John grabbed a slice of toast and said. "Yes, a real lady now."

"Very nice," Mark agreed, flicked through them then passed the wallet to Mathew.

John watched him with fake disinterest, seeing the muscle twitch beneath the handsome jaw. But he also knew what it meant. He was as mad as the day she left.

"Please come to dinner after the funeral." Grace begged. "Your father needs cheering up and perhaps the children will do that."

Jessie estimated that half of Johannesburg's law fraternity was at Simon's funeral, everyone shocked, and Beverley still in limbo. Curiously, she watched how Bruce held onto her sister protectively, with Juliet in his arm. Love permeated everything he did but Beverley wasn't even aware of where she stood.

After everyone left, she and John stood at Jeremy's and Lawrence's graves and it was then that the tears came. How long ago it all seemed and yet it was just yesterday. Her thoughts turned to her father; she was beyond grateful that he was still alive and not being judgmental over her choices. John placed an arm around her shoulders, as if sensing that she needed reassurances. She gazed at him thankfully, this friend who had already done so much more than was required.

To Jessie's surprise, Bruce was in the hospital room when she entered. Taylor had asked to see her, and she wondered what he needed to discuss with her. Had she had an inkling, she might have packed her bags and run.

"Hi Bruce," she gave him a charming smile. She liked him, but she especially appreciated the way he cared about Beverley and Juliet. She turned to her father enquiringly. "I thought you wanted to see me."

"I do. But since I'm about to discuss some difficult things, and make even harder requests, it's only fair you know the truth."

She became alarmed as he explained that he was about to give part of Stevens Textiles away. Maybe it wasn't a giving away per se, but it sure felt like it to her. Because how could he simply hand his executives a 5% share each under a new management system he was working on with the attorneys? That effectively placed 40% of Stevens Textiles in strangers' hands. What about the other 60%? For now, it was all still in his name, but if something should happen to him again, it was to be divided between the four remaining family members.

What about Bruce? The truth came out, her hands sweated, and two hours later, she felt dazed and frightened. Then she realised what else he was doing. If he had told her none of that, she would have said no, but letting her *in* on the secret, effectively wiped out her own will. It was highly irregular and unfair, because he was blackmailing her with his own mortality. She wanted to scream no, but grateful that he lived, she would not dare.

She went home, wrote her resignation, and sent it to London. John would have no problem doing likewise because how long had he been trying to get them here? All she had ever wanted was to be an interior designer, find a good man, get married, have a few children, and be happy.

Strapping the boys in the back seat, Jessie placed a hand on her chest to calm her thumping heart, then, wiping clammy hands on the jeans, she wondered if Mathew would be present. The mere thought did strange things to her, turning her on like a volcano. The very idea of being in a house where he often was, and where they had made love, was making her volatile. One minute she wanted to hide and the next she became viciously angry. What would she say? was there something to say?

"We'll probably hate each other on sight." She said when John asked how she felt as they stopped a distance away from the front door.

"Sure, he's mad, so are you, now resolve this thing. And please relax, or you will explode." He told her as he let the children out. "Boys, if you break anything in this house, I will take your toys away."

Both stared at him, then glancing at each other laughed.

"Now, let's do this thing right. Boys," John reprimanded.

"Why is the road full of stones?"

"It's the driveway, stop kicking them around."

Jessie wished she could swallow an anvil to put stop to the peculiar feeling in her stomach. The mere atmosphere made her feel faint.

"Jessie!" Grace called from the doorway and embraced her. "We should not wait for things like this to return us to our family, and I am so glad that you are part of mine now."

"Thank you. Huh, your grandsons."

Grace fell to her knees, her eyes full of tears. "My darling babies."

"Jeremy and John," Jessie pointed above their heads. "I wanted to dress them differently, but this was apparently the wrong day for it."

Grace was enthralled with her little boys.

"Who's around?" John asked, wanting Jessie to calm down.

"I arranged so no one would be here until later. Monica is away for the weekend, the men are still at work, and Vanessa is over at the hospital. Come inside, darlings," Grace invited. "It's so good to see you again, Jessie."

"Boys, what did I tell you earlier?" John asked as he saw their small hands already reaching for a vase.

"They are so beautiful, Jessie. Yet not one little bit of you in them."

"This is all misleading," John told her. "They only resemble Barrymores, their character is thoroughly Stevens, which is the best combination that could ever be."

"Come sit with grandma." Grace patted the seat on either side of her.

After an hour, Jessie felt as if she had never been away, finding the familiarity she had always enjoyed in Grace's presence. Then, she became aware of someone in the doorway. Looking up, she saw Mark.

"Wow, the next Barrymore generation." He offered his hand. 'Welcome back. I have to admit; the place has not been the same without you."

Before she could answer, Theodore appeared. Embarrassment filled her, even feeling that he might owe her an apology. He nodded at her dismissively and she refused to feel anything, telling herself she was not doing this for her benefit but her sons'. Then he sat down and watched quietly, leaving all the talking to Grace.

The boys became fascinated with the silent man. Slowly, they leaned against the sofa, then sitting on the floor, they touched his shoes and pants, and finally his socks were inspected.

In contrast, they almost ignored Mark, who tried to start conversations. "What are they doing?" He queried.

"Making sure he's sturdy." John informed with a laugh. "They do it to things they like. Though, they usually break them."

"What's your name?" A small voice asked.

"Theodore, but grandpa to you."

"I'm Jewemy, he's John. Mommy says," his brother giggled and both nudged closer. "I love Elaine,"

"Who is she?"

"Elaine cooks. I don't like bwussel spouts… John hates cawlky flowers. Mommy says," Jeremy pointed a small finger and tried to imitate Jessie. "Eat them or there is no Channel."

"Channel?"

"I like swimming. Mommy says we're champions."

"Good, I like champions." Theodore told them. "Would you like to see our swimming pools? We have two."

The boys grinned, and both put two small fingers up. "Two."

"One inside." Rising from the sofa, he offered his hands. "I'll see you all later."

"And there you have it," Mark remarked. "He wanted James' but these will do nicely."

"Honestly, must you always talk this way?" Grace chided.

"It's the truth. But why do they always say, mommy says?"

"Every time John tells them something, he says that, as if I'm some book of rules."

As they walked up the stairs minutes later, all the feelings she had suppressed were back. But above the turmoil, was fear. Nothing had changed and to protect her sons she would have to lie again. She realised she was supposed to be John's wife now, but it was a silly sham of a marriage and she was beginning to think that she owed the Barrymores nothing. This was as bad an idea as when she first came here.

As if aware of her inner fight, John took her hand.

"I shouldn't be here." She whispered.

Stopping, he told her. "Someone must end this insane Barrymore thing and I guess I've been elected. They will learn to accept all things Stevens and realise you are the best thing that will ever happen to them. Don't worry so much, everything will be all right."

"That's what you said last time and look what happened then. You and the boys must come, not me."

"For goodness sake, relax."

She had lived this scene a long time ago and felt exposed.

Mathew walked up the stairs and stopped, seemingly debating what approach to take. He hugged his brother then turned to her. "Jessie," he nodded.

She responded likewise. "Mathew,"

"Congratulations on your marriage, and sons."

Her throat was bone dry. "Thanks."

"Where are they?"

"Last we saw of them they were headed for the pools with father." John told him.

Mathew's brows lifted slightly. "Go down and meet Carol."

"Going to freshen up first," John smiled, took Jessie's hand in his, and squeezed it.

What had she expected? A celibate man who had buried his head in the sand because she left? *"Grow up, this is life."* She told herself. Still, she hurt more than even she could put into words.

As they mingled during drinks, Jessie watched Carol with a certain amount of interest. Surprisingly, she couldn't bring herself to dislike the attractive woman with the cute shorn brown hair and bouncy personality. Then, she tried to guess what each was thinking. Theodore, I don't want her here. Mathew, I wish she wasn't here. Carol, why is she here. Mark, best not to delve. As for absent Monica... I will not be in the same house with this parvenu. Oh yes, she was quite the mind reader. Thankfully, Grace led most conversations as everyone else had too much going on and couldn't think of normal things to discuss.

"Mommy, Mommy," the boys stormed in and ran to her. "We saw ducks." John told her breathlessly.

"And a boat," Jeremy added.

"How exciting," she draped her arms around their shoulders as they clung to her.

"Here they are." Mathew bent towards them. "Hello, young men."

Two little faces turned up to look at him.

Her heart skipped a beat. What if she said, *"Mathew, your sons,"*

"You look like daddy."

"Yes, I do, and you are?" Mathew offered his hand.

"John."

"Very pleased to meet you, John." Mathew stroked the brown hair then turned to Jeremy. "Hello, Jeremy. I'm your Uncle Mathew."

She felt limp, then, every other emotion rushed in and pulled her apart. Almost unable to battle the knot in her throat, she told the boys. "Let's go wash," and turned her gaze to John.

Until this moment, he had not known how utterly she loved his brother. He tickled Jeremy then took her hand. Reaching the stairway, he watched both boys run up the stairs. "I'm sorry." He told her softly.

Her eyes drowned. "Look at what he's lost. Why can't we just fall in love and be done with it?"

"It's a nice dream."

Dinner passed reasonably well. She took part in conversations, smiled, and even gurgled a few times over something Carol said, but as hard as she tried, she could not look Mathew in the eye, fear telling her he would guess at the secrets she kept. She had done it before; he would expect it again.

After dinner, she and John took a stroll through the grounds then stopped on the small pier.

"Take me around." She asked and took her shoes off.

Reaching the centre of the dam, John leaned back lazily. "You have to talk. Neither of you will heal if you don't."

"As if he wants to talk to me. He's only doing it in public to be polite, I can tell he's dying to rip me up."

"Precisely, and which should have been done years ago. You felt abandoned and he betrayed. If I had known, I would never let you leave."

She snorted, disbelieving. "Imagine if I had told him I was pregnant. He adores children and would have accused me of entrapment. All I wanted was for him to love me, not be under obligation. Now, as far as I'm concerned, he has no rights. Let him marry Carol and have his own, these are mine."

"I know we agreed to always tell the truth, but they are little and one day they will say something strange. What will happen then? And you heard John this evening, he recognised Mathew from the photographs. Obviously, everyone thought he meant me, and it's lucky we do look alike."

"They are my children." She stood up in the boat. "Where was he when I needed him? Didn't even endeavour to discover where I was; simply closed the door on me as if I was yesterday's garbage. I needed him desperately and I hate myself for the way I still feel but I am not letting him break my heart again. But most importantly, he is not going to mess with my sons' heads and tell them Stevenses are second-class citizens. I will not have my children poisoned with ridiculous grudges and malicious resentment and if I ever hear any Barrymore… that's the last they see of them."

"It's no longer sixty years ago and no one is going to try change things to what they were before, except perhaps Aunt Monica. But she isn't here and who cares what she thinks? Look at father, if he still hated you, or me, we wouldn't be here."

"I'm supposed to fall down on my knees and say thanks? I know what he's doing, tolerating us for your mother's sake. And perhaps James' accident made him evaluate some things, just as my father did. Life is brief, and all your father wants is to have you back. Don't imagine he's doing me any favours." She dove into the water.

"You're crazy." He shouted and rowed towards the shore. "What's your problem?" He asked as she reached him dripping wet. "Do you feel better now?"

"No, just wet, cold, and miserable,"

"Here." Removing his jacket, he placed it around her shoulders.

Beverley sat primly in her father's hospital room, wondering what he was about to propose. Jessie had been bamboozled into starting at Stevens in January, so his summons had her more than concerned. If he asked anything as outrageous as that from her, could she say no?

His hand went to her pale face. "How are you?"

"Better. But when I think and realise that it could still be so much worse…" her voice trembled.

"Thankfully, I'll be home soon. How is Bruce coping at Stevens?"

"He doesn't discuss it with me but he's busy. He does however have time for Juliet, and I'm glad because she doesn't really understand."

"Bruce is a good man. Now, you must stop feeling guilty and give him a chance."

She stared at him uncomprehendingly.

Taylor took her hand. "There is no shame in love, and I can tell you have deep feelings for him."

"Daddy, are you okay? I have barely buried my husband and it sounds like you're encouraging me into another man's arms."

He watched her for a second. "The timing is yours to pick but I know you love Bruce in a way you never did Simon and it's good, because it's the way it's meant to be. But you are riddled with guilt. I'm just sorry I didn't have the patience to wait."

Beverley gave up trying to decipher Taylor's ramblings. None of this made sense, it was bizarre, and it must be the medication's effect.

She left soon afterwards; feeling a little hurt but mostly confused. All this time she believed that she and Simon had happened naturally, instead, he, the old goat, had played cupid and got the ball rolling. Why? Because he somehow got into his head that she was too sheltered and unable to find a man on her own... Gawd, for the gall of some parents and their pre-set buttons. And although denying any future intrusions, she was already seeing his fingers in affairs that did not concern him.

Stepping outside the hospital, she smiled, the first time since Simon's death. At least he had done one thing; he had set her heart free.

Bruce glanced out the window and saw John and Jessie walk past. They sat at the end of the garden on a bench and he watched them for a few minutes. He liked both and although thinking that they made an attractive couple, he often thought that something was amiss. He returned his attention to the papers on the desk.

He couldn't understand it. Harry Stander's flat had been meticulously searched for clues, dusted from top to bottom for prints, and still they had nothing; except for a few grams of heroin and cocaine. Men who had worked in narcotics for years shook their heads helplessly. How could a novice have acquired almost pure shipments, where, or have planned the attacks at Stevens Textiles without making a mistake or being suspected? There had to be a connection somewhere, but he could not see it.

Despairingly, he gazed outside again. Having Jessie around was doing the family good, but especially Beverley. In the last few days, he had seen her smile and once even heard her laugh.

"Very busy?"

"Beverley, come in." With practised movements, he shuffled all papers together and threw them into the briefcase. "I was staring out the window."

She peered outside and sat on the chesterfield. "I see."

"Are you sure those two married for love?"

She was intrigued, queried further, and he went into a discussion of the two. How it didn't look like a marriage, but more like a brother-sister relationship.

Perhaps their friendship had transferred into their marriage, she suggested then asked with a smile. "Do you like to spy on people?"

"I've done more stake-outs than I care to mention." He almost told her. "Watch them, you'll see. But you haven't exactly had time to think of ordinary things. You do know that Simon's death was not your fault."

"I didn't understand when John blamed himself for Jeremy's death, I do now." And she proceeded to give him a family history lesson.

"As I said, people don't change that drastically. But, it's their business." He held her gaze for a moment. "Would you like to go for a walk?"

"I have a better idea, let's go riding."

"I see those horses get so excited when you go near them, especially Brutus."

'And I'm sorry I haven't paid him much attention lately. I was planning to have him moved to a stable near home but after Major Patterson came to see me the other day, I decided to sell the house and move back here again. It's not safe for Juliet."

Bruce sighed inwardly. He had begged the Major to make her see that all was not well. That she might be in danger living alone. Who was to know who Harry worked for and what else they might try? Because there was no way Harry had concocted it all on his own or without instigation. "I'm glad you're doing your best to move on."

"It's just difficult."

He glanced around. "Where is the saddle?"

"We don't need one." She had already opened the gate.

"Well then, let's see if I can still do this." He adjusted the bridle and with one agile movement was on the horse's back.

"Very good, where did you learn to ride?"

"I grew up on a farm," which was true, but he had also done it a thousand times in the Natal midlands while working on the trafficking squad. Seeing her arms raised to him, he swung her up behind him.

She pointed to their left. "To my favourite spot."

They rode in silence, the pounding of the hooves restricting conversation.

"I see," he said as he slowed to a trot and glanced at the thick bushes and trees.

"My hiding place. Lawrence used to tease me about silly things; braces on my teeth, funny looking legs, limp hair, and a million other things." Sliding down the horse's side, she disappeared through the greenery.

Following her blindly, he found himself inside an almost perfect circle reminiscent of a maze. "Nice."

Collapsing on the grass, she invited him to do the same.

Falling backwards, he closed his eyes in pleasure, and asked. "Am I mistaken if I guess that you napped here?"

She made a happy sound. "Fortunately, Samuel knew where to find me." Rolling onto her stomach, she gazed down at him. "Is it all right if I kiss you?"

He snapped his eyes open.

"I never thanked you properly for saving my life. I meant to, but I was in shock and then I just forgot. Thank you." Bending her head, she kissed his cheek then very slowly pressed her lips against his. "But that is what I really want to do."

He sat up, surprised.

She followed suit and dropped her gaze. "I apologise, I'm being forward."

"Beverley, look at me." When she did, he thought his heart might burst as he saw the expression in her eyes.

"I have wanted to do that for such a long time, even before Simon died. Does that make me a bad person?"

"Just human."

"Jessie!" James exclaimed, shocked that she was standing in his room.

"Hello, James. How are you?" She stopped beside the bed, holding her handbag tightly to calm her nerves, and wondering why she had come. Then she glanced at the contraptions surrounding him, it looked agonizing. "I'm very sorry about this. Are you in a lot of pain?"

"I no longer cry." He took a shallow breath.

"Can I do something?" Unexpectedly, her eyes filled with tears.

Seeing them, his hand went out to touch hers. "I see you will have enough for the both of us. But before you say anything, I need to tell you something. But lord, I don't know how."

"I know why you did it and it no longer matters."

"You don't understand, I have nightmares, and I wondered how I was going to ask you to come see me."

She smiled now. "Well, here I am. Apology accepted, and let's leave it all well alone."

His breath and sigh were deep enough to fill a set of healthy lungs. "How did you know I wished you would come see me?" He asked curiously.

Feeling more at ease, she pulled the chair and sat down. "I decided to go on a hunch. Guilt is a terrible thing, so you need to stop thinking about the accident as punishment. Stress does not help with recovery."

"You're a good person, and it seems everyone misjudged you."

She shrugged. "Maybe just a little."

"That day when Vanessa came from college and told me who you were… I went nuts. As you know, grandma saw to it that we learnt to hate the Stevenses well. I was suspicious of her intentions for about a minute, but I certainly did not expect a blatant set-up, even though I knew she was not in love with me."

Jessie covered his hand with hers. "Don't say anymore. Now, we carry on. But surely, she has changed, she seems so devoted."

CHAPTER FIFTEEN

From the terrace, Jessie watched the three walking away from the dam. Every Saturday, she handed her sons over to Theodore and within minutes, the three disappeared until after lunch, when they returned for the boys' nap.

She felt better now that she had started visiting James, because oddly, he was the one who gave her strength to return here every weekend, to accept that she was starting at Stevens Textiles in the new year, and to manage a semblance of normal in Mathew's presence.

Pulling a chair under the umbrella, she sat down, leaned back, and closed her eyes, Theodore's reaction at seeing her arrive alone instantly coming to mind. Whether with disapproval or commendation she was not certain, all she knew was that he looked stunned.

John had freely given his time in the first weeks, then, without ceremony, announced that she must carry on whatever routine she saw fit. He had also begun frequenting his old hangouts and reacquainted himself with old friends; that information she was in no rush to part with.

Monica had of her own accord left for Martinique, as the latest arrangement seemed to upset her sensibilities. She still had to see Jessie or the boys but had no intention to do so any time soon.

A smell she recognised and disliked reached her. Opening her eyes, she watched Mark.

"Hi." He greeted.

"Why are you here?"

"Is that why you chose Saturdays to visit, because I'm usually not around?" He pulled a chair and sat down.

"It's the only time your father has."

"Christmas is in a few weeks, have you decided where you will spend it?"

"Haven't discussed it yet but we'll compromise."

"How was Christmas in England?"

"Cold and wet."

"New York has beautiful white ones, though, quite terrible at times. How's your father?"

She studied him, expecting him to be mocking. "Much better, he's coming home this weekend."

"A pleasant thought, your eyes glow when you're happy." He squashed the cigarette under one shoe. "Would you come with me next time I go to New York?"

"What?"

"Damn it, Jessie! I regret the mistake I made before, but you know how I feel and if you wanted to marry a Barrymore that desperately why didn't you pick me; I asked, remember? You think John has changed because he fathered a couple of children? By the way, where is he?"

She jumped to her feet.

He followed suit. "Get real, Jessie, you are a passionate woman, he's queer; how does he satisfy you?"

He never saw the hand that struck him across the face. Turning around, she took a step away but grabbing an arm, he pinned her against the wall.

His hand went up the side of her neck and face. "I'm curious now, which of the two do you prefer? Then again, neither has a backbone. So, don't you think it's time you gave me a chance too?" His lips brushed hers.

With a violent movement, she turned her head sideways. "Leave me alone."

"Or you'll do what? As I recall, last time you did nothing."

Pushing him bodily, she put some distance between them. "This is not years ago when I stood to lose because I was frightened of exposure. And apart from that, I didn't want to break your mother's heart. But if you are deluded that you intimidate me, then I suggest you sober up. Now, get out of my way." Cheeks flushed and eyes burning, she shoved past him. Good behaviour had never been his forte, but for the family's sake as well as peace, she had hoped. *What do I do, tell John? But who would want to believe such a thing?"*

"I have noticed that you seem fearless, but I think you're just an act." He called after her.

"Get lost." She threw back at him, ran into the house, and bumped into Mr Adams.

"Miss Jessie,"

Seeing his face, she knew he had overheard. "Please, Mr Adams, not a word."

He inclined his head politely. "As you wish."

Turning away, she carried on down the passage, down the stairway, and straight into Mathew.

"Hello." He steadied her. "Where are you off to in such a rush?"

"None of your business." Blue eyes flashing, she yanked her arm away and continued her run out the house.

Brows lifting, Mathew stared after her, then turning, strode up to his room. Opening the balcony doors, he waited. There she went. "Hey, Jessie," he heard Mark call from the terrace. She didn't turn around, instead, she made a wild gesture and carried on her way towards the dam. He frowned as he heard Mark's laughter. What was that about?

"There you are," Grace said with pleasure as Jessie entered the blue sitting room later that morning. "Been out to the dam again?"

"I need sun." Sitting down wearily, she became aware of Mathew.

"You look tired," Grace noticed. "Do you rest?"

"Not always. I need to tell you something. Daddy asked me to stay to join the business." Whatever reaction she imagined, didn't transpire. "I dislike it intensely, but I'm too much of a coward to refuse."

"What does John say?" Grace invited.

"He's pleased we're staying as he had been on my case for a long time."

"I meant about Stevens."

"Says I must do whatever I want, but this is not exactly it."

"What about Bruce?"

"He might not stay much longer, Stevens is not his cup of tea." That was about as much as she could say anyway, except if she started on all the scary things. She shivered unconsciously. "Daddy needs someone… I wish I could say no, but I can't."

"It's only logical that if one has no sons then one must depend on daughters. Has John mentioned what he will do?"

"He may be considering Barrymores."

Mathew spoke for the first time. "A bit of split loyalties, wouldn't you say?"

"Why, we don't have to discuss work. Whatever each does is none of the other's business."

"You think it's that simple?' Mathew continued.

"I'm simplifying it. Excuse me." Rising to her feet, she disappeared out the door.

Grace regarded Mathew. "What do you make of that?"

But before he voiced his opinion, Theodore appeared in the doorway, the boys trailing behind.

"Hello," Theodore greeted and glanced at his watch. "We had a fantastic morning."

"Oh, darlings, don't even try sitting anywhere." Grace said, horrified at their clothes. "What did you do? And that means you too, Theo."

"We started a garden down by the cottage." Theodore provided.

"You want to see?" Jeremy asked eagerly as he turned to Mathew.

"Yes. What did you plant?" Mathew asked.

"Cawots and beans."

"And flowers," John added.

"Who's going to eat those?"

Both giggled. "Mommy likes flowers."

"I didn't know she eats them." Mathew teased.

"She makes them pretty." Jeremy placed his grubby hands around Mathew's neck.

"Sweethearts, don't touch anything." Grace begged.

"Leave them." Mathew helped both to his knees. "And who is going to look after this garden?"

"Grandpa. Rain makes them grow."

"I'll go change so long." Theodore announced. "Now, you two, promise you will eat all your vegetables, take a good nap, and then I have another surprise. But I'm going to ask mommy to stay tonight for that."

"Yepee." They shouted and threw their arms around Mathew's neck.

"What is so exciting?" Jessie queried as she re-entered the room, the picture they made going straight to her heart.

"Jessie," Theodore eyed her eagerly. "Would you consider staying until tomorrow? There is something I'd like to show them, but we need dark for that, unless of course, you have prior family commitments."

The irony of the situation hit her then. Once, he kicked her out, now, he almost begged her to stay. True, it was only for one night, but soon he wouldn't be able to part with them. She wondered how wise it was. But seeing them sitting on their father's knees, she knew she couldn't decline. "We have to leave before lunch, I promised my father we'd be there when he gets home."

"Absolutely," Theodore grinned with pleasure.

"Come on you two, let's go clean up." Jessie put her hands out.

"I want Uncle Mathew to wash me."

"He has other things to do."

"I don't, and it will be my pleasure. See you later, mom."

"Yes, honey." Grace told him quietly as she watched them go.

Bathing the boys was an amusing experience for Mathew and he soon discovered that it was a job not to be done in ordinary clothes. With a wet shirt stuck to his torso, he turned to Jessie. "You haven't a drop on you, what am I doing wrong?"

"They know who they can take advantage of."

"Is that so?" He glanced at them, both waiting to be wrapped in bath sheets.

After drying and dressing them, they sat them down at the small table where lunch awaited.

Jessie asked. "Would you mind helping Jeremy, they are sleepy after such a busy morning."

He did in silence.

"Now, to bed." She picked John into her arms.

"Story, mommy," he begged as his head rested on her shoulder.

"But you are so tired."

"Please." Jeremy implored as Mathew dropped him on the bed.

"Thank you, Mathew."

"Shout if you need an extra hand." Leaving the room, he leaned against the wall outside.

"So," Jessie asked. "What story today?"

"Daddy," they said in unison.

'But I've told it to you so many times. Did I tell you that I used to sail a lot back then?"

"Does daddy love us, mommy?"

"Yes, my baby, he loves you very much."

"And you, mommy?"

"Do you want to hear this thing or interrogate me?"

Mathew walked away.

"Where's John?" Grace queried as they sat down to lunch.

Jessie shrugged. "Said something about a surprise."

"And where is Carol?" Mark asked.

"Visiting her parents," Mathew turned to Theodore. "What's your surprise?"

"Remember my father's train-set?"

"I thought half the pieces no longer worked." Mark noted.

"Had someone come have a look and a few modifications were made."

Mark turned to Jessie. "This you have to see. It's a beautiful miniature town with rivers, roads, and parks, even lights in the windows and street-lamps, and when you turn the lights off," he pointed to the ceiling. "There are stars and a moon."

"It sounds lovely." Jessie said, wondering how it was possible to change one's character so fast. Just hours previously, she had absolutely detested him. She looked at Theodore. "But they are a little clumsy and I would hate for them to damage it."

"I'll be there, it's my toy." Theodore grinned.

Grace laughed. "That's what he wanted, playing partners."

Jessie noticed Mark's gaze again. Why did he make her feel as if she wore nothing, again bringing that aversion she always felt in his presence? Of all brothers, he was the oddest and she was past trying to figure him out.

"Vanessa took an apartment close to the clinic," Grace informed her.

"Riding in and out more than twice a day must be exhausting. I just can't believe she quit her job."

"Which she should have done when they married," Theodore said disapprovingly.

"What's important is that she has dedicated herself selflessly." Grace noted. "A few months ago, they couldn't stop bickering and it was all rather tiresome."

"Most people have redeeming qualities." Jessie smiled in general then her gaze stopped on Mark. "And there are those who don't possess one good bone in their bodies. I'm sad this happened to James, and to hear that he may never have children is simply heart-breaking." Would she have been better off without her sons? The mere thought of not knowing the little boys who gave her so much joy made her eyes fill with tears. Years ago, she had been angry with James, but now... No one around this table knew it but they were becoming fast friends and she felt his loss deeply.

Looking at her, Theodore did something no one expected; he patted her hand. "I know people do things we find hard to forgive, but I'm glad to see you are not harbouring hard feelings towards James. I didn't want you here before either, but now it seems foolish, considering circumstances."

"He's not really apologising or telling me I'm welcome, he's merely doing it for them." "My father asked me to start at Stevens in the new year. Will I still be welcome then?"

Theodore was visibly surprised. "What about that Murray fellow?"

"As you know, there are no guarantees in life. So, my question remains."

Theodore took a moment to answer. "There is no secret our families never got along but things have become somewhat different. Personally, I think you have no idea what you have agreed to. Certain your father didn't hurt his head?" He saw her face. "I don't mean that as an insult, it's just a strange decision for a businessman, and a good one at that, to make. Years ago, I wouldn't have cared one way or the other, but today, your success is part of my grandsons' future, so I must wish you well."

Grace felt like crying; why didn't he do this years ago? But Monica's absence had contributed to his tempering of heart, not to mention the pain he felt when imagining James at death's door. Turning to him, she smiled accord.

Mark's mind went down a different tunnel. He didn't know how but he had known that whoever married her would eventually end up controlling Stevens Textiles. He had said as much to Mathew years before. He wanted to laugh if he didn't feel like crying when he pictured John in the role.

Mathew saw the situation differently, but before he could dwell on the subject further and formulate an actual opinion, a horrible racket came up the driveway and stopped meters away from the dining room windows.

"What on earth?" Theodore got to his feet.

"It's some kind of motor-cycle," Mark informed them.

"John!" Mathew exclaimed.

"What?" Jessie strode outside.

John sat astride a ferocious looking thing. "Isn't it fantastic?" He accelerated a few times then switched the engine off. "Imagine the fun the boys will have."

Jessie stared at him open-mouthed. "This is a death-trap and I will not have my sons killed because you have no sense."

"Just a few rides up and down."

"Read my lips, NO, end of discussion. You know how I feel about bikes, and this one appears particularly dangerous.' She wrinkled her nose at the ugly skeleton. "You take them anywhere on this thing and you will wish you were dead."

"I can even have a sidecar put in." He pointed.

"Put anything you like but stay away from the boys. I asked you to buy a car; instead, you bring this monstrosity. How are we supposed to go anywhere when it rains?"

"Bikes are fun."

"Then have it on your own."

"It's an investment, a classic, and only twenty thousand."

"You want it, keep it, but I forbid you to take the children on it. You have an accident, you stand a chance, they don't." She stormed back into the house.

"Honey, you will listen to Jessie and not take the boys on it, please?" Grace asked.

"She worries too much. Sees them with a little temperature and rushes to the doctor."

"It's only right, they are little." Grace scolded.

"Why is she still here? I went home, and they told me she's staying until tomorrow."

"I'm showing them the train set tonight." Theodore announced.

"They'll love that. Are they asleep?"

Mark eyed the bike a little closer. "If you didn't wake them already."

"Let me go then. Tell her I'll be at the usual place should she need me, and I'll see you tomorrow at the hospital."

"You're leaving?" Mathew stared at his youngest brother.

John started the machine, lifted his arm, and rode down the driveway.

"That guy becomes stranger with the passing of years. I'm going out." Mark announced and walked towards the garages.

"Do you suppose they are having trouble?" Theodore queried.

"Jessie never mentioned, and why would she." Grace put her arm through his. "Show me the garden you started with the children."

"Shouldn't we be discussing…" he saw her face. "I guess not."

Mathew gazed after them then walked into the house. Faint laughter and screaming reached him as he walked down the passage. It came from the indoor pool and he realised, Jessie made most of the noise. Since being back, she had smiled, even chuckled, but never laughed like that. Pushing the door open, he saw all three in the water, two little boys making a big splash around her. He stood there a moment. She loved those boys with all her heart; it was obvious in everything she did.

John noticed him. "Uncle Mathew, come swim."

"Has John left?" she asked.

He stopped at the edge. "Said he'd be at the usual place."

Jeremy got out of the pool and took his hand. "Come play."

Mathew grinned. "Okay, give me five minutes."

Jessie told Jeremy to get a ball then averting looking at Mathew's bare chest until he was in the water, asked. "What shall we play?"

"Anything,"

"Two teams, John and I, you and Jeremy."

"What's this game called?"

"Throw-ball, catch-ball, whatever, we'll make it up as we go."

"What does the winning team get?" Mathew asked curiously.

She took a moment to answer. "On Monday, ice cream from Heavenly Ice."

"Okay, Monday six o'clock you're buying. Where is it?"

"Rosebank, don't you know your own town?"

"Not all the sweet shops and ice cream parlours."

"And what makes you think I'll be paying? Focus, I'm starting."

She cheated outrageously and never batted an eyelid when caught.

He shook his head with a bemused look. "I hope you're not taking these practices into Stevens Textiles."

"What practices?"

"Cheating. What is that?" He asked as she passed the ball to John.

"The rule says."

"No more rules."

"Sore loser," she made a face.

"You are not setting a good example."

"And they know we're playing. But I think we must stop, they're tired."

"Yes, let them sit this one out, only you and me." He helped Jeremy to the edge.

She helped John. "Don't cry foul afterwards."

"Stop talking and hit me with your best shot."

And she did. Having powerful arms, the ball hit him on the side of the head, right on the ear, making him dizzy for a couple of seconds.

"I win." She yelled behind him.

Turning, he wondered how she got there so fast, then, another picture entered his mind. He recalled racing John, and that kissing her had been the prize. Dropping his gaze, he saw the hairline scar Albert's blade had left on her shoulder, a testament of her love for him. His stomach turned, and he was glad water covered him. "Fine, a bet is a bet."

"And don't you forget it because we will be waiting. Come boys, time to get dressed."

Mark was nowhere to be seen at dinner and she thought all the better, enjoying her meal without having to be conscious of his presence. She was sick to the core of his advances and hated the idea of having to tell Grace that she had a lunatic for a son.

Mathew found her sitting in darkness on the terrace. "Aren't the lights working?"

"I prefer it this way."

"Why so quiet?" He sat down.

"Thinking,"

"You do have a lot to consider." He looked in her direction. "I meant to ask, what's going on between you and Mark? I've noticed the two of you can barely have a conversation without ruffling the other's feathers."

"And I told you that it's none of your business."

"Just like it wasn't before?" A silence followed. "Why, Jessie?"

"Why what, lie, pretend, conceal? And which lie did you like least, the one about my name? That one hurt deeply, didn't it? What can I say, I'm just heartless." She announced sarcastically. "I accept responsibility for all of the above and whatever other evils you imagine I committed."

"Before, I wanted you to admit that you were wrong. Now, I just need an explanation."

"Why?"

"I need peace."

"Of course, you do, because heaven forbid that you should have to explain yourself."

"I'm not the one who lied."

"No, you simply changed your mind when my name became something you loathe."

"I was stunned, in shock. Why didn't you explain before it got out of hand, before Vanessa?"

Jessie made a small sound. "She knew what she was doing, planned her revenge and executed it perfectly. It's the kind of person she is, vindictive. As for the embarrassment you endured, and perhaps still do with my presence; I can't ignore what I did but I somehow imagined that you would have a little compassion. But none of this is important anymore, is it?"

"Why didn't you write, call, anything?"

"You don't know me, but I know you, and I knew you had no intention to mend whatever we were. Had I said anything else it would have made everything worse and today we would be fighting like cats and dogs. Separation was inevitable, so I did the only logical thing. What do you want from me now? I'm still who I was, or am I somehow more acceptable because your brother gave me his name? Is that why you speak to me? It's just ink on paper, nothing has changed." She rose. "Goodnight, Mathew."

"Wait," He stood in front of her. "What do you mean nothing had changed?" *"Hell, do I really want to know?"*

"I'm in no mood for this."

"Yes, just like you weren't then. You knew you couldn't hide forever, yet, you never made the attempt."

"All this is beyond repair and in the past. I lied to you, of that you don't have to remind me. I know you resent me for deceiving you; it's no more than I do myself, for I've obviously caused you great distress. So please, don't feel obliged to go against your nature because your pity is the last

279

thing I'm trying to persuade. If you're merely doing it for civility's sake, then let me put your mind at rest, I do not need your banter. Now, let me make something else also clear, I'm here for my sons' sake, not mine, and certainly not for yours."

She left Sunday without seeing him or Mark again and was glad then wondered if she should ask John to drive them around, but she already knew the answer.

"What are you doing here?" Theodore asked surprised.

John leaned against the door nonchalantly. "Looking for a job."

Theodore studied him, and John could tell he was not going to like what was going to be said next.

"After blowing twenty thousand on that worthless piece of junk, I'm not surprised you need employment."

John took a deep breath, trying not to lose his temper.

"Your wife is starting at Stevens." Theodore pointed out.

"I could have a job there too, but I'd prefer it here."

"Then it's yours."

"I have to mention though, I may be going back to the UK for a while. We left everything as is."

"Take however long," Theodore regarded his youngest. "Would you consider living at home?"

Oh yes, the old man was hooked. "I'd rather not even suggest it. Is Mathew still in the same office?"

"Look in James' as well, he shuttles between the two."

Walking further down the passage, he heard Mathew's voice. "Knock, knock."

"What brings you around?"

"Came to ask father for a job."

"What about Jessie?"

John knew what he meant but pretended not to. "She and the boys were on their way to some ice cream place."

That brought their wager to mind, and that he was supposed to be there to pay for it. "Where are you on your way to?"

"To see some friends, have a few beers, and go home whenever. Mr Stevens is finally back but not ready to socialise, so there is only Bruce, who, for some reason, has moved into the house as well. Nice guy but only has eyes for Beverley. If love were a disease, we'd already be dead."

"But, she's just lost her husband."

"And it was hardly romance central, no offence to Simon. Bruce has her head spinning."

"Everyone deserves to be happy."

"They do. So, when are you going to make yourself happy? You're like a stray puppy in need of a good home. Why don't you lighten up and pursue your heart's desire?"

"Philosophical too, what next?"

"Next, I'm going to race my bike. Jessie is a bit of a nut, needs to lighten up too."

Leaning his forehead on the glass, Mathew tried to peer inside. Unable to see much, he walked in, glanced around, and saw them sitting in a corner. She said something and both boys looked up. They were ecstatic to see him and he automatically placed a hand on their hair.

Jessie told him they had been shopping; neither had enough clothes and she thought it important to keep the promise—whether he turned up or not, and John was busy with an estate agent looking over some places, as they planned to have their own house.

It occurred to him then that his brother wasn't being completely honest, but to whom he was lying and why was still to be decided.

"Ice cream," Jeremy begged.

"Just now," Mathew beckoned to a waiter, pointed to something on the menu, and asked for four.

"What did you order?" Jessie asked curiously.

"It's a surprise."

"I can imagine, something totally decadent."

"You know me too well." He smiled. "So, how is Grandpa Stevens?"

"He can't walk, and we sit on his wheel-chair."

"Well then, you'll be completely familiarised by the time Uncle James gets home. Have you been to see him?"

Both shook their heads.

"Would you like to?"

They nodded eagerly.

"Good. If mommy doesn't mind, we'll go after we leave here." He turned to her. "Where are you spending Christmas?"

"At home, and New Year with you, I mean… Pity James won't be home either."

"Yes, I'm afraid he's going to be in traction for a while."

"It's heart-wrenching and it must be extremely difficult on Vanessa."

"Days ago, you told me how horrible she was, today, you feel sorry for her. I don't understand." He commented.

"When did you try?"

He opened his mouth to respond but saw the waiter. "This is what I ordered? Is it too much?" Glancing at the boys, he saw their eyes bulge in delight. "Thank you. Wow, there must be half a kilo here, so let's eat as much as possible. And Jessie, don't tell me I'm ruining their health, I'm feeling guilty as it is."

Suddenly, she had no desire to be there but somewhere dark, where she could cry. She was playing dirty tricks, and what was it she was doing this time, revenge? How, by making him fall in love with his sons and then snatch them away? This was a dangerous game and there would be no victors.

Mathew glanced at her untouched bowl, she loved ice cream. "Are you okay?"

"If it's all the same to you, I'll go home now." Getting to her feet, she kissed both boys, and grabbed the shopping bags. "See you later, sweethearts. And please be good to Uncle James."

A breeze blew her hair about, but she didn't notice, Mathew called out but she didn't hear. Quietly, she started walking down the street where a taxi had stopped. Reaching the vehicle, she asked the driver if he would take her home.

Mathew was aware that something had changed, recognising that look; the one he had seen before, the one that cried out to him, and he ignored. As he watched her eyes lose their life, he knew she wouldn't ask for help, and as before, simply walk away.

His chest became tight at the realisation that he did want to help this time, all three of them. Taking a few steps towards her, he stopped, turned around, and glanced at the boys. They too knew something was happening and looked at him for reassurance. Deliberately, he offered his hands, knowing as he did that he was making a silent promise. Feeling small hands in his, he tightened the grip, and watched her get into the taxi and drive away. All at once, he understood her plight. She was lost and so was her heart; all place she had in there belonged to these little boys.

Getting out of the taxi, Jessie stopped, baffled, she had no money. An oddly familiar sound came up the driveway. Turning around, a car stopped within centimetres of her.

"Jessie," Mathew called.

She took a step towards the door and a welcome void enveloped her.

"…are you all right?" Beverley called.

Carefully, Jessie opened her eyes and saw her sister on the edge of the bed. "What happened?"

"You fainted. Are you ill, or how about pregnant?"

For a second, Jessie forgot that she was a married woman, and gave her sister a look that said, how would that be possible? Then she gathered her senses together. "I was fine and then felt awful, what does that mean?"

"Not sure. Mom has already called the doctor and he'll come past on his way home. By the way, Mathew is outside."

"Why?"

"You forgot your handbag at some place and he was returning it when you passed out."

"Tell him I'm fine and he can go."

"Wow, word for word. He also threatened to wait until you see him."

"I'll send him away myself." Standing up, Jessie swayed against the bed. "What is wrong with me?"

"That's what we all want to know. Stay still, I'll let him in."

"Don't you understand English?"

Beverley ignored her and walked to the door. "Mathew."

"I won't be long." He closed the door behind him. "Are you feeling better?"

"No, but it's probably not serious. I'm just very tired and feel dizzy when I stand up."

"Then don't until the doctor gets here. Apart from that, what else is wrong?"

"Nothing. It was kind of you to return my bag, but you don't have to be here longer than is absolutely necessary."

He opened his mouth, closed it, and pulled a chair close to the bed. "Why did you run out? You frightened the boys."

"What do you care? I don't feel well and that's all. The doctor will come, give me something, and I'll be fine again."

"I'd like to help if I can, or should I say if you'll let me? As you said the other night, we don't have the best basis for a friendship, but we can try. Are you and John all right?"

"Why shouldn't we be?"

"Because it's as if you're leading two different lives. Is that why you are so sad? Your marriage is in trouble and he's not really making an effort, is he?"

She realised what he implied. But she wanted none of his good intentions because his proximity only complicated things. "It's kind of you to offer but I can manage. And you shouldn't waste time meant for Carol on me."

He rose to his feet. "Is it still all right I take the boys, or would you prefer I didn't? It's also a little late."

"Today, tomorrow, you may take them wherever and whenever you want."

"That's very considerate, thank you. But John should be here, do you have a number?"

"He's looking over some property and will be back when done. Goodbye, Mathew."

"Please call if you need anything, the boys…"

285

"At least the Barrymores will never hate them. Imagine if he knew they are his. He would take them away for fear that I couldn't look after them."

The doctor came and told her to get herself to his consulting rooms the next day, so he could draw blood; but from a basic test, it seemed she was anaemic. The results confirmed it.

When leaving London, neither had imagined they wouldn't return, although, John had hoped. Now, having gotten his wish, she noticed how quickly he volunteered to return to take care of their unfinished business.

"But you won't be here for Christmas," she complained.

"Or New Year, but one of us has to do it." The sacrifice felt minimal.

"Your mother invited me and the boys to go spend time with her."

John smiled. "Let me guess, for the time when the men go on safari?"

"Yes. Have you been?"

"Every year as far back as I can remember, when I was around. We pack the day after Christmas and stay in the bush until New Year's Eve. Father hunted once, had us all in tears, so never did again. Now, it's just a sightseeing and unplugging from the world kind of trip."

"Sounds nice. But shame, neither you nor James will be there this year."

"Yep, things are a-changing."

"Jessie!" Grace kissed her warmly. "I'm so happy you agreed to come. Did John get away all right?"

Jessie nodded and ruffled Jeremy's hair. "All went well."

"Sebastian," Grace addressed one of the younger servants. "You are okay with solely looking after the boys and keeping them amused?"

Sebastian grinned. "Yes ma'am, I have already planned our adventures."

"Yepee," the boys danced, as they liked Sebastian very much.

"Well, then," Grace smiled, "we seem to have a success."

The week was halfway through when Jessie, sitting in the conservatory, opened her eyes, and looked straight at Vanessa. For a moment, neither knew what to say.

Jessie greeted her politely and then steered the conversation towards James' health. It was possible she knew more than Vanessa did because James discussed intimate details with her as their friendship was now well-cemented and he valued her opinion, but for conversation's sake, she asked general questions.

The other woman seemed surprised that they were staying at the estate and managed to get a jibe in about Grace having a soft spot for her. Then, done with chit-chat, she asked if John had gone with the men on safari, and not waiting for the answer, disappeared again.

Realising Vanessa was spending a few hours around the house, Grace asked her to join them for lunch.

"That wasn't too bad." Grace said later when she walked into the indoor pool and sat on the bench. "I'm glad you chose to let sleeping dogs lie, as this one is particularly vicious."

Jessie knew that was a warning, not only not to start trouble but also for her own comfort. "I won't lie and say I've forgotten, but if she wants a confrontation, she will have to start it. All she's getting from me is hello and goodbye."

When the men arrived on old year's afternoon, the boys ran across the yard, and threw themselves at them with delight.

"How long have they been here?" Theodore queried as he kissed Grace.

"Since you left. Jessie needed rest, John is gone, and I wanted company."

"I wondered why you didn't complain about being left on your own this year. Actually," Theodore winked and hugged her. "I thought you had a young man stashed somewhere."

"Two of them. We had a most enjoyable time and learnt a lot about each other. Vanessa came around…" Grace smiled. "No blows. They were very polite, we had lunch, and then she left."

"Good." Theodore tickled John. "And what did you do all this time without grandpa?"

"We played with Sebastian. He made me a boat."

"Did you sail it?"

John's eyes dropped sadly. "It's in the middle of the dam. Mommy said she'll get it later."

"I'll get it now." Mark offered and received a wide grin as reward.

Walking around the side of the house, Mark made his way to the water. To his chagrin, Jessie was on the pier, the small boat in her hand.

"I was coming to get that."

"Thank you, but it wasn't far. How was the getaway?" She asked politely even if disinterestedly.

"Nice. I thought a lot about you."

"Don't start."

"Why are you always so surprised that I have feelings for you?"

"Because you have a twisted mind and I don't appreciate it."

"I could change, as many people apparently do. John obviously did, and what about my father? Once, he didn't want you here, now, it's all he thinks about. You are very smart and couldn't have found a better weapon to become acceptable to the Barrymores. Just remember, should you and John ever part company, dear father-in-law might just turn against you again. And remember, he's a very powerful man."

"If you're trying to frighten me it's not working." She rolled one hand into a fist. "And say rubbish to me again and I'll break your nose."

She was dreading the compulsory exchange of pleasantries that went with the turn of year and thought it a great pity that Grace couldn't hold one of her parties. But with John out of the country and James in hospital, she wouldn't. *"It's always easy to get lost in a crowd."*

She eyed Mark with distaste. He was rude, crude, conceited, and as she often thought, she couldn't reconcile the fact that he was related to his brothers.

As luck would have it, he was the closest one at the stroke of midnight. She offered her hand, which was shaken, and as she thought it was over, he pulled her into a bear hug and smacked her cheek. Trying not to make a face, she turned quickly to her sons.

"Pity your daddy couldn't be here." Mathew said beside them and all three stared at him. "Happy New Year," he shook her hand and ruffled the boys' hair.

Blankly, she gazed at Carol. How could such an impersonal touch do this to her? It was as if he poked her with a hot rod in her very soul.

CHAPTER SIXTEEN

Gazing at the glass tower—as she called the executive block—Jessie wondered what everyone made of her father's idea. Primarily, she imagined, more than feathers would be ruffled. Just months previously, Taylor introduced Bruce as heir apparent, and now, he dropped her on them like a bomb. For those who were frenetically trying to get deals together, she imagined her presence was both unwelcome and unacceptable, for they had stuck out their necks in pacts with institutions not necessarily above board, and if failing, not only their careers but also their very lives could be in jeopardy.

Taylor wanted her to start in the factory, as he had done at seventeen. Why? Doubtless to find out what she was made of. He was in for a rude awakening. True, it wasn't as if she were asked to sit in his chair, lead board meetings or make deals, but everyone knew what it meant.

To appease her misgivings, she had daily lunches with Bruce, who was still around but police business was incrementally taking priority and he did not have time for a frightened and intimidated woman. She noticed the looks of suspicion and knowing grins. Everyone knew she wouldn't last.

Months ago, she was in England, leading a perfectly normal life, doing what she loved. Then, all hell broke loose, forcing her back, and here she was about to start something she had neither the training nor the inclination for. Did parents know what they did at times?

As if her very greenness was not enough, Bruce announced within weeks that he was leaving. Some leads had come to fruition concerning the drug trail and he was tasked in their pursuit. He hadn't yet told Beverley he was undercover, and Jessie became nervous for his part because she knew only too well what revelations could unleash.

She also became anxious over her father's safety, when he eventually returned—and she hoped it was soon. Bruce quickly pointed out that he and Major Patterson had already solved the problem, and not only for Taylor's sake but her own, or did she forget that she too was on her way to the top? Two of the security guards were under-cover policemen, replacing those who had accepted bribes from Harry Stander.

To alleviate January's slowness, she learnt workers' names, what each did, and discovered that most enjoyed working there. It was interesting seeing what she had learnt at college applied in real processes, machines, and chemicals, and that helped pass time, but evenings were utter loneliness.

There were the boys, Beverley, the rest of the family, and James... yet, she found it exceedingly difficult to share anything pertaining to John, or Mathew, and both were constantly on her mind. Her father was encouraging and pleased with any progress, however small, but slowly, a chasm was opening in her heart.

Twice, she saw Mathew as she faithfully visited the estate, and twice John called her, merely saying everything was going well and gave no specific details. She wondered what Theodore made of his absence.

"Another empty night," she thought after putting the boys to bed. How long could a person be lonely before snapping? Someone knocked and walked in. "John!" Her arms flew around his neck as she kissed his face a dozen times. "Why were you away so long? Come tell me everything."

One of her old clients was having issues with all sorts of mix-ups and the woman was threatening to sue the company if someone didn't fix it. Hardly the thing that would look good on anyone's resume. Now, she had to go to London.

Eagerly, she grabbed the chance to escape for a while. Taylor might be back at the office now, but that didn't improve her dislike of the situation. And while she prepared to leave, John announced that he had found them a home. A good turn of events, because most people did not understand their family workings.

"It's the first time I'm leaving them." She realised.

"They will be fine; play with Juliet during the day and I'll pick them up after work. And I promise I won't forget Saturdays. You are just a born worrier, when did I ever let you down?"

But a few days later at the airport, the boys looked scared and so did she. What if something happened? They started to cry, and she wanted to stay. John pushed her away with determination, keeping the boys close. When they started sobbing, he bent down, picked both into his arms, and walked away.

Friday mid-morning, he walked down the passage and leaned into Mathew's office. "Can I ask a favour?"

"Sure."

"What are you doing this weekend?"

"Just a bit of work,"

"Where's Carol?"

"On an all-girls weekend, whatever that means."

"Are you going up to the house?"

"Maybe, why?"

"I forgot about a friend I need to see and told Jessie that I would take the boys."

"I don't mind picking them up and dropping them off."

John shook his head. "No, my friend is out of town, so I'm asking you to baby-sit the whole weekend."

"And Jessie?" Mathew asked.

John shrugged. "I promise, they are no trouble at all."

Mathew noticed that they were easy to please but imagining them starting waterworks as John was ready to leave within five minutes, he offered ice cream.

Watching them, he noted that they ate like Jessie, and sometimes when they smiled, the same dimple he had loved so much appeared on their faces. Shaking himself mentally, he took the empty bowls away. "Go brush your teeth."

After their bath, they watched in silence as he opened their suitcase.

"How long does he expect you to stay?" Mathew asked. "Whose pyjamas are these?"

"Mine." John jumped onto the bed.

"Right, the two of you sleep here and I'll take the other room." He saw their faces drop. "What's wrong now?"

"I don't like big bed." Jeremy complained.

"Story,' John tugged at his sleeve.

"Give me a minute." He disappeared into the bathroom and reappeared in a pair of shorts. "What?" He asked as they giggled. "You've never seen your father in underwear? So, what type of stories do you like?"

"Where's mommy?"

"In England. You know, where you were born. Don't worry; you have daddy, grandma, grandpa. Don't you like playing with your cousin, what's her name?"

"Juliet. Sometimes she cries."

"And I'll bet you have something to do with it. Remember, gentlemen always make ladies happy."

"Where's Auntie Carol?"

"Away, but I think you change the subject on purpose." Mathew sat on the bed's edge. "How about a Jonathan story?"

"Who's Jonathan?"

"A little boy who lives on a farm."

"Does he have an elephant?"

"And when last did you see an elephant on a farm?"

"On TV."

"Forget I asked. But that's a jungle not a farm. Jonathan—"

"Not there, like mommy." Jeremy pointed to the space between himself and his brother.

"Like mommy." Mathew crawled between them and both snuggled close to him. "Jonathan has a little dog named Boone," he began and went on for a few minutes, then glancing down saw both were fast asleep. Smiling, he bent his head and kissed first the one's brow and then the other.

Strange, it was the first time he kissed a Stevens voluntarily, and stranger, they didn't look dangerous or like thieves.

Grace stared at them in surprise. "Where's John?"

"Busy. And we're staying until tomorrow."

Grace passed a hand over Jeremy's hair. "These are life's blessings."

"My boys," Theodore called from the door. "Where's John?"

"I brought them. Now go play, father."

Theodore beamed, took hold of the boys' hands, and all three walked away.

"What troubles you?" Grace queried. It was curious; she had always seemed closest to John, but ever since Jessie left their lives, Mathew was the one she had drawn closer to.

"I'm thinking that I should get married and have a few of my own."

"All this time," she gazed at him tenderly. "Your life is in confusion and you don't know what to do, do you? Slow down, honey. Please don't rush."

Sunday afternoon arrived with no sign of John. Mathew frowned heavily as he walked around the apartment, hoping his brother was merely late. However, at seven, John called to announce that he was stuck in some small-town Mathew had never heard of.

Carol appeared a little later. "Did you miss me?" She asked at the door.

"I didn't have time." Standing aside, he let her in.

She saw the duo playing on the carpet in a corner and followed Mathew to the sofa.

He sat down, grabbed a toy car, looked it over a few times, yanked a wheel out, and started searching for a new one in a box.

"I was wondering," she began. "How about setting the date? We don't need a fancy wedding, just family and friends."

"We can't right now, I asked James to be my best man."

"He could use a wheel-chair for a few hours."

"And you know as well as I do that he's in unbearable pain."

"Why don't you ask John? You're much closer to him."

"I won't ask John because I asked James. I can't break his heart now, as standing at my wedding is the goal he's trying to achieve."

"Yours, maybe, what about ours? Are you really committed to this relationship?"

"Of course, I am." Taking her hand up to his mouth, he kissed it. "But with James' absence I'm also inundated and have barely had time to breathe. I apologise, you probably think I don't even give you a second thought."

"Do you?"

"All the time," turning to her, he straightened a few wisps of spiky brown hair, but then he was looking at a pair of blue eyes.

The phone rang an annoying long drone and taking a few steps with the aid of his cane, Taylor answered, "Stevens."

"Mr Stevens, I have some information I think you might be interested in." No introduction, straight into business.

Out of habit, Taylor turned the answering machine on. "What kind of information?"

"I know this will interest you. Is it possible we meet? Do you know where Benny's Bistro is?"

"I'm not sure."

"You take the off-ramp to…" the stranger explained. "Could you come right away?"

"Wouldn't it be best if you came to see me at the office?"

"I'd never make it that far, and it took me a while to shake off my tail."

"What are you talking about?"

The voice dropped to a murmur. "All I can say is Harry, and unexplained events. I'm taking a huge risk, come see me, alone."

"How will I know you?"

"You don't, I know you. You want this, come get it, but if I see any cops in the area, I'll think you called them and split."

"How do I know this isn't a trap?"

"Why would I invite you to a public place? I'm waiting until ten, if you don't show up, I'll never call again and burn this lot."

Taylor glanced at his watch and disconnected.

"Where are you going?" Serena asked as she saw him adjusting his collar.

"To visit an old friend I haven't seen in ages. Where is Bruce?"

"Want to take him along?"

"No, this is a friendly get-together." He dropped a light kiss on her face.

Walking up the stairs, Bruce was angry. The security guards at the gate had called him four times in the last hour. The first, he heard how Taylor told them he didn't need backup because he was going to visit a friend. Second, they were on Taylor's tail. Third, Taylor had made them. And fourth, he had given them the slip.

He noticed a blue haze on the wall and looking out the window, saw the police-car stop outside the door. They couldn't be from his department, so what were they looking for? He ran downstairs again.

Samuel had already answered the door and stood in the hallway with two officers.

"Thank you, Samuel, but I'll take care of this. May I help you?"

"I'm Detective Nkosi and this is Detective Roets. We need to see Mrs Stevens."

"Everybody has retired, may I help?"

"It's a delicate matter and we need to see Mrs Stevens." Roets emphasised as he took a quick look around. "It's about Mr Stevens."

"What about him?"

"Can you describe Mr Stevens' car?" Nkosi asked.

"Black BMW, grey leather seats, registration… what's happened to it?"

"Nothing, but unless someone else was using the car and Mr Stevens' ID, he's dead."

All colour drained from Bruce's face. "What?"

"I'm sorry, sir. Are you a relative?"

"No. Yes. I mean… how?"

"He's been shot." Nkosi said. "There was another man with him in the car, killed the same way. Do you know where Mr Stevens went and why?"

"No." Bruce put both hands to his head. "He's still convalescing from a fall."

"We are aware of the incident. Is it possible we speak with Mrs Stevens?"

"Damn." Bruce smashed a fist against a table. "Are you absolutely certain?"

"Sir, we don't know Mr Stevens personally, but we have seen enough photographs to positively identify the face."

"Where did this happen?"

"Outside Benny's Bistro parking lot, do you have any idea why he went there?"

"No. You said there was another man… do you know who he is?"

"We haven't yet identified him."

"Where are the bodies?"

As morning arrived, he felt like crying. Then he called John, he needed Juliet out of the house. It was a pit of misery, three distraught women, servants in endless tears, and he at a loss.

"What about Jessie?" John asked.

"I haven't had time, and it's better you do it."

John agreed, but he wished to anything on the planet he didn't have to.

"This is absolutely going to kill her." Was all Mathew managed to say when he heard.

John sat in Mathew's apartment, feeling as if he were being dragged through a nightmare, staring unseeingly, three children playing at his feet. He had chosen the apartment because two reporters had seen fit to camp outside their townhouse, and a media circus was not what he intended to put the children through.

Surprise had filled Mathew when he saw Juliet. Following his gaze, John apologised and said he hoped it was okay.

Mathew shrugged and stared at the cute little girl who looked so much like her absent aunt. "Have you called Jessie, or is she due back?"

"I did but she wasn't at work, or the hotel. Front desk said she mentioned going to see someone; so probably Elaine. She'll call back eventually."

The phone rang, and Mathew grabbed it. "Hello,"

"I just heard." Carol said. "What in heaven's name? It's utterly unbelievable."

"Yes. Listen, we're expecting a call from London."

"Jessie?"

"John left this number as he'll be staying a few days."

"Don't they have cell phones?"

"They do, but with this back and forth… Jessie is not very good with those."

"Then I won't be seeing you over this weekend either."

"Probably not. He's alone with three kids, so I'll stick around."

"Three?"

"Jessie's niece is also here."

"I see. Okay then, until whenever."

He dropped his tone. "Do you have a problem with this?"

"Of course not, say the name Jessie and you're running."

"What's that supposed to mean?"

"Exactly what I said."

"This is not a good time."

"And don't I know it."

"What's the matter with you?"

"Nothing." She banged the receiver down in his ear.

He stared at the instrument then went to sit with John again. "Do you always understand Jessie?"

"No, she's this mystery."

"Doesn't that bother you?"

"It's kind of fun to be surprised, though, Jessie really springs them on you. And tragedies hit her hard."

"Then she'd better bounce back real fast because father was already predicting Stevens' demise. I can't help but agree that neither she nor Bruce is equipped for such a task."

"And I'm sure neither will actually run the place, which makes this so much sadder. Those executives wanted to be in control, they might be getting their wish. I wonder if any of them is responsible?"

"You can't be serious. These battles are done in boardrooms, with lawyers and bankers, not with guns."

"I've heard of worse. And what was Stander all about?" John's cell phone rang, he answered. "Hello."

"Hi," she greeted. "What's going on that I got a mountain of messages?"

"Where were you?"

"I went to see Elaine. She has a new job but doesn't look happy. So I asked if she would prefer going to South Africa and continue working for us." She laughed. "She almost flew through the roof."

He watched Mathew and the children disappear into the kitchen. "Jessie, huh… I have bad news about your father."

"He's worse?"

"No," he paused. "He died last night." Her voice broke and heart-wrenching sobs reached him. How he wished he could be there to hold her.

All Mathew saw in the situation was that it was a catastrophe, which was strange as he had never thought too well of them, but this inexplicable event touched a chord. They were somehow tragically doomed, and he felt fearful as he imagined more dreadful happenings. Something he never imagined feeling where any Stevens was concerned.

"Then it's three to the estate this time." He said matter-of-fact.

John gave him a peculiar look and raised his brows as he glanced at Juliet.

He got what John was thinking, but looking at the little girl, he couldn't get it right to hate or dislike her in any way.

"There is hope for you yet." John announced. "Years ago, you wouldn't have taken the boys in, much less Juliet."

"They are my nephews, I couldn't do that to you."

"You kicked Jessie out."

"She left."

"You gave her no choice."

"What's wrong with you? This is your wife we are discussing." Mathew said irritated.

"And before that, she was to be yours."

"I realise we find ourselves in a peculiar situation, but she married you and I..." Mathew scratched his head. "If you had included her as you should have done, instead of going all over the country, she wouldn't have come to me. My point is, I didn't know who she was, you did, and obviously, it didn't matter. If you imagine it was easy sitting at that table and hearing things I never envisaged, think again. Today, I accept that she didn't do it on purpose but at the time, it sure as hell felt like it. And this is not a conversation we should be having with each other."

"Why not? I love you both and I want you to find a way to get along."

"Most men would dread having their wife's former fiancé within a hundred meters of them."

"I'm not most men and you are not anybody. But tell me honestly, do you still hate her?"

Mathew considered the question. "Hate is a strong word, and I don't dislike her either. It's just that everything is different."

"Come on guys," John called.

"Now now, daddy John." A voice reached them.

"Why do they call you that?"

"I'm daddy, and I'm John. They put the two together and there it is."

"Come to think of it, you're a weird family in general."

Grace was the first to be surprised when Mathew entered the house.

"John wanted them to have a respite from what's happening over there. Miss Juliet Wade." He introduced as she held tightly onto his hand.

"The boys are Barrymores but this beauty is a Stevens." Grace's hand went to the little girl's chin.

Shyly, Juliet hid behind Mathew.

"And you have a way with children." She smiled then became serious. "How is Jessie, or haven't you heard?"

"She's arriving this afternoon and John will take her straight home."

"Poor family, hitting one misfortune after another. It's almost as if someone is systematically eliminating them."

Mathew glanced down at the children. "Should we be discussing this?"

"I apologise." Grace turned to the boys. "Grandpa will be really surprised, he didn't think you would come today."

Mark walked by then stopped dead in his tracks. "Whoa, Jessie's niece?" He stared straight at Juliet and didn't wait for a reply. "Your desire to atone is going a tad far."

"What is wrong with you?" Grace frowned.

"The way he and John carry on we'll soon have the entire clan coming to tea. Then we'll say how sorry we are we didn't like them before, but everything is okay now, they can visit whenever they wish." He announced sarcastically.

"In case you haven't noticed, your nephews are half Stevens."

"And I don't mind anymore. Though, why couldn't she have been a McCormick, a Vermeulen or a Markowitz? No, she had to be Stevens."

"And what's wrong with that?" Grace went on. "Neither she nor these children did a blessed thing to one of you. And if this perverse grudge had not been in full swing years ago, she would be married to Mathew today. Why does anyone wonder why she suppressed the truth? This was the reason, the fear of facing this contempt all of you possess. Now, you listen to me, Mark Barrymore," she warned. "You ever pass snide remarks about anyone named Stevens again and you'll answer to me.

"Don't you dare say another word because Jessie has more capacity for love and forgiveness than you could hope for and I've had it with this bizarre feud. Any of you want to hate them, do so in private. I will no longer listen, but especially not at the dinner table how any Stevens did what to the Barrymores. You don't agree, tell me, so I may start taking my meals elsewhere.

"Whether you like it or not we are united, and I will no longer sit apathetically by as you criticise any member of that family, alive or dead, is that understood? Now go do whatever you were on your way to do and leave these children alone." She turned to the boys and pointed to where Theodore stood. "Go on my darlings, grandpa is waiting."

Then she turned to Juliet. "Would you like to stay inside with me?"

The little girl merely tightened her grip on Mathew's hand.

"Should she change her mind, you know where to find me." Grace left.

"I no longer mind about Jessie and the boys, but the others… I refuse to share anything with them." Mark glared at Juliet. "And don't be fooled by father's apparent acceptance of things. If she crosses him, and she will, it will be a very hot day in hell indeed. When that happens, on whose side will you be?"

Jessie didn't agree with most things Theodore said, but on this day, she did. He had suggested that her father had no idea what he was doing when he asked her to start at Stevens; the will proved it. Taylor had taken a detour into insanity and completely lost his mind.

"There has to be another," she kept saying, but the attorneys assured her otherwise. "How am I supposed to run a business this size?"

"Everyone in that building knows what to do, they'll help you." One of the attorneys suggested.

But she knew better. At the reading, she had already seen more resentment than willingness to lift a finger, all astounded that Taylor had done such a thing. How was it possible that a kid, who barely knew how to operate the lift to the executive office, was to run a company like Stevens Textiles?

"Hello," John poked his head into the room. "Are you okay?"

"Those people in that glass tower are not welcoming me with open arms. You heard them; all shocked senseless. God, why did he change everything again? And what power do I really have with 15%? They are going to do everything possible to influence mom, grandma, or Beverley every time. Just like sharks, waiting to devour any little fish unfortunate enough to cross their path. Oh John," she threw her arms around him. "I'm so scared."

"Your father sure surprised a lot of people. I imagined Bruce in training… he's not even mentioned. But at least there is a way out."

"All ammunition they need to undermine my authority is to simply shoot me down. And of course, daddy knew I'm going to fail, which is why he added that funny one-year clause. How am I supposed to even last that long?"

"Stick to existing business. You might not grow, but at least you'll be safe."

"Daddy should have left you in charge; you seem to know all about it."

"It's the Barrymore trait; we all have good business sense, although, James is a bit on the I don't care side."

"And after a year, they are going to bring their statements and figures, point their autocratic fingers at me, and kick me out."

"You are just frightening yourself, and all before you've even begun. You are usually good at what you do."

"All I ever wanted was to lead a normal life, now… I have no idea what's happening to it."

He rubbed her shoulders. "How is the investigation going?"

"No one knows a thing. All they have is an unidentified body and a few packets of heroin and cocaine. What was he doing with a man who had drugs?"

Very slowly, life began to follow a pattern. Jessie didn't always enjoy being right and on this occasion loathed it tenfold. Somehow, the higher echelons soon had everyone believing that she was there to make life miserable, and those Friday meetings were enough to phase anyone with less determination than she had right now. At times, she locked herself in the bathroom to control the helplessness she felt as she watched what went on around her. Not one friend or kind hand stretched out to her. People she had once believed her father's friends now regarded her with apprehension.

For moral support, she asked all family members, including Bruce, to join her at those awful meetings. Juliet's advanced age meant her ideas were outdated. Serena had never given counsel. Beverley put on a brave face, sat demurely, and pretended she understood what they discussed. Bruce did but could no longer help, as Major Patterson refused him participation due to his involvement with Beverley. The last thing they needed was for Narcotics to be accused of personal gains through corruption.

Bruce's perceptive nature also told him that something untoward had just begun and he couldn't help but wonder where Taylor's head had been when he thrust Jessie into the lion's den. Then again, Taylor had no idea he was not going to be around to train Jessie.

Since her return from England, John had been ferrying the boys around. She gleaned from them that he barely spent ten minutes at the estate himself, Mark was in the US, and

Mathew spent a lot of time with them. He made them laugh, taught them things, rowed, swam, and plain gave them a good time. She loved her father, it was only right they did the same; all gathered memories to be filed under fun with my dad. But some form of selfishness prevented her from opening her mouth and giving him the privileges he deserved.

As she drove to the estate for the first time again, it felt as if she were about to embark on yet another unknown voyage.

"Darling," Grace extended her arms and embraced her warmly. "How are you?"

"Better."

Grace hugged the boys. "Sweethearts, grandpa is outside. I'm glad this tragedy hasn't influenced them negatively, but Mathew helped a lot. He always makes their visits so interesting nowadays."

"Huh, yes, I must thank him."

"You look exhausted. Go sleep for as long as you need and stay the night. I'll have Adams bring your meals." Grace studied her daughter-in-law. "What is it John does all this time on his own?"

"He's working on new designs."

"Jessie, know this. I will never take anyone's side, be they related to me or not, if they are wrong."

"I know." Jessie hugged her.

Walking up the stairs slowly, she studied the tip of her shoes. Then, he stood there, as if waiting.

"Jessie,"

"Hello, Mathew,"

"I'm sorry, but I feel as if anything and everything I say is not enough."

"Do you mean that?" Her eyes filled with tears.

"I do."

"Thank you, and I appreciate your kindness towards the children." She told him softly and walked away.

CHAPTER SEVENTEEN

"What is it?" James asked inquisitively as John deposited a beautifully wrapped box on his lap. Just the mere fact that he was in the entrance hall at home already made him feel better.

"It's from Jessie, there's a card."

James pulled the ribbon and open the lid, revealing a folded cashmere blanket. Taking it out with care, he placed it on his lap, and patted it. "Perfect," he read the card, and didn't even try to hide the tear that ran down his face. "Where is she?" He asked emotionally.

John squeezed his shoulders. "Busy. But I'm glad you discovered what she's all about."

"Tell her I love it. She's a good girl."

Vanessa whispered beside Monica. "God, she's not even here and still they discuss her. I hate it, hate her."

"Sickening." Monica agreed.

"What are you two mumbling?" Mark asked.

"An awful episode I had in Martinique." Monica dismissed then turned to James. "I am so glad you are home and hope you will be back on your feet soon." Bending, she kissed his brow. "Barrymores needs you."

"I doubt it and Mathew isn't doing too badly alone." He said without malice. "But thanks for being here, Aunt Monica, it was not required."

"It's right I am. Besides, I still have to meet my great-nephews." Her mouth twisted slightly.

A sad expression appeared on James' face. "Yes, if one can't have sons then one must treasure nephews."

"Oh, darling," Grace embraced him lovingly. "Don't talk that way. We must always hope."

"James, old man," Mark added. "Doctors aren't always right, and I'd say it's far too early for anyone to give you a final prognosis. But you're also correct; those kids are cute and fun to have around."

"Egad." Monica moaned. "From the sound of it, it's probably better I move to France."

"That would be best." Mark told her seriously.

Vanessa positioned herself behind James. "What can I do for you?"

Putting a hand back, James slid hers off the wheelchair handle. "Nothing, your duty has been done. From now on, the nurse will see to all my needs. Go do whatever you wish; including returning to work as you have been so desperate to do."

Vanessa looked uncomfortable as she threw Mathew a furtive glance. That snippet was the part she had meant to keep secret for a while longer, especially if he was going to be on her case about duties and all the nonsense he adhered to. What no one was aware of was that James had chosen to shut her out, excluding her from everything he considered important.

Everyone stared when Monica appeared in the finery she was accustomed to for dinner.

"Was there a blaze while I was away, and all your clothes were destroyed?" She queried.

"But I told you we no longer have such formal dinners."

"One should be constant, Grace. Ah, Carol is here. I heard you were away."

"Just a few days in Rome."

"I was there over Christmas. Wish Johannesburg was as gay," Monica announced then continued. "Didn't John stay for dinner?"

No one answered.

"I suppose I should stop making such references seeing he's a father now. What did they say about Taylor's death? It's the one thing I miss while away, a South African newspaper."

Everyone looked from her to Grace.

Monica's perfectly made brows arched upwards. "What?"

"You are excused since you did not know, but the Stevenses are no longer discussed as if they were the scum of the earth, particularly not at the dinner table."

"Who made this rule?"

"I did." Grace looked her straight in the eye. "No one has a problem with it."

"You mean we are not allowed to say anything about the people who robbed us blind?"

"That's right, and I would say they hardly took bread from our mouths." Grace glanced around the room meaningfully. "There are a million topics to discuss; the Stevenses are no longer an option."

"Well, she certainly tenderised you. What about the rest of you? Carol?"

"She doesn't bother me."

"She should, she almost married Mathew. Then again, even Vanessa."

James glared at her and Vanessa shifted in her seat uncomfortably.

"Can we drop all this nonsense and have a good evening?" Theodore requested.

"I can't get over the fact that you always hit the nail on the head." Monica told Mark.

"Good heavens! What are you wearing?" Monica asked aghast.

Theodore stopped whistling and jumped the last two steps. "My play clothes."

"Okay," Monica sank into the corner armchair as if defeated "I think you should explain a few more things before I leave."

"Grandma!" Two little boys threw themselves against her.

"You're nice and early today. Hello, darling."

"Sorry I wasn't here for James' homecoming. How was it?" Jessie asked.

"Quiet. Boys, this is Grand-Aunt Monica." Grace pointed to the armchair. "Jeremy and John," the boys giggled. "Sorry, John and Jeremy."

"Hello," two sweet voices greeted.

Having had no idea what the boys looked like, Monica stared. "Talk about genes."

"Aren't they beautiful?" Grace smiled her pride. "Go play, grandpa is waiting."

Jessie stopped and glanced at Grace, as if for moral support. "Mrs Cooper, how was Martinique?" What else was she supposed to say?

"Fine. I heard about your father's passing, a pity really."

"If you mean it sincerely then I apologise for doubting you and thank you." Jessie turned to Grace. "Has John got here yet?"

"Haven't seen him." Grace watched the pale face. "I think you should go give Theodore a hand. And do me a favour, give these to Mark, I just saw him walk past." She placed a bundle of fabrics in Jessie's hand.

As soon as Jessie was out of the room, Monica commented. "One of these days she will be calling you mom and Theo dad and I can't believe he fell for this gooey stuff. She has the Barrymores exactly where she wants them, under her spell. Did you know that in the Middle Ages they believed women with black hair and blue eyes, or was it green, were witches? How long have I been gone and look at what's going on?"

"Jessie, a witch? Don't be absurd. If you can't see she's a sweet child, then you are blind. But this might also explain your mother's behaviour, she had those exact same looks too, didn't she?" Grace made sure Monica understood.

"Mark."

"This is a surprise."

"Hardly, I'm here almost every Saturday."

"I meant you addressing me first. Did I tell you how sorry I am about your father?"

"Everyone does. I'm just not sure if they mean it."

"I don't know about the others, but I am sincere. How are you coping at Stevens?"

"Not as well as I'd like." Gazing at him, she realised who she was speaking to. Hardly the person she wanted to have conversations of any magnitude with. "Your mother sent these."

"Not exactly confidant material, am I?"

"Sometimes I don't know what to tell you."

"Grandma solved the problem by reciting rhymes."

"Really?"

"Ask John. Anyway, thanks for these, and I'll see you later."

She stared after him then heard Monica's laughter. That she felt vulnerable was no doubt due to Monica's humiliation, her behaviour hurting deeply, but more because Mathew had not come to her rescue. He sat there as if mummified, and now she knew that he had been traumatised. Tears stung her eyes at lost opportunities. Once, she had believed that they could beat it all. She was wrong. Racing up the stairs, she went towards her room.

"Jessie."

She turned quickly and watched James push himself in the wheelchair. "Hello, welcome home. How are you?" Bending, she hugged him.

"Much better now that I'm home. Thanks for the blanket," he patted it on his lap. "It was thoughtful of you. And thanks for the lovely note, I appreciate your inspiring words."

"It's nothing. I was going to the bedroom, but I think I should rather go outside." She glanced down the stairs. "Want to go somewhere?"

"I wouldn't want to bother you."

"No bother and I need to get fresh air. So, where do you want to go?"

"The dam, haven't seen it in months."

Turning, she pushed him towards the lift that had recently been installed for his benefit.

Finding him a good spot under the willow, she sat on the large boulder nearby.

He smiled. "This is so crazy."

She grinned and pointed to the house. "Do the others know we've been dating?"

His laughter broke over the water. "If Vanessa hears you she'll think it's true." Then he became serious.

Seeing his semblance, she told him quickly. "Please don't tell me again how you deserve this."

"I can't help but despise myself for causing you so much unhappiness. I need to tell you something today, the reason why I went to the factory." He was silent for a second. "I wanted to kill Mathew."

One hand flew to her mouth. "What? Why?"

"Because I thought he was sleeping with Vanessa."

"No!"

"He didn't, but not from lack of enthusiasm on her part."

"I'm sorry, and I wish I could say I don't believe she would try. Why don't you take her somewhere?"

"All this has been a strain on her, and I admit, she pretended pretty hard she cares. Now we're back, I'm useless to her, a cripple, so who do you think she wants? She's sneaky, persuasive."

"Trust her a little, offer her a second chance."

"No, we're done. And speaking of chances, where's yours?"

"There is John."

"Substitutions are never good enough. I know, I'm one. It's true he and Mathew look alike but it's not the same, is it?"

"We move on, and so must you then. You didn't break your back and that's good. I know you're doing physiotherapy, so you might recover sooner than you think. How's the swimming?"

"Used to love it, now bordering on detesting it."

She smiled. "You know what they say; no pain, no gain, and you have so much to reach for. Ask Vanessa to participate."

He shook his head. "Didn't you know? She's already planning her big career comeback. How is it going at Stevens?"

"The same nightmare I mentioned before. Everyone is suspicious and refuses to accept me into the club."

"Give them time."

"You don't know these people." She sighed. "How I wish daddy hadn't done it. I'm like a blind man in a crystal shop. Imagine what I'll do in a year."

"Did you take the manuals as I suggested? You already have an idea how the factory works, so now, go through the financial statements for the last two years and memorise them if necessary. If you know that, it's an advantage they don't expect. Do you understand what they talk about?"

"Not completely."

"Then start reading. It will be hard but better than if you know nothing. It's tough running any business but ten times worse if you feel illiterate. And this one has departments, people in charge of all sorts of things, they come and go, run around, and do things ad infinitum. Try to focus and understand, even if it's only one thing at a time."

Mathew regarded the scratch on the car door, then hearing small feet running on the gravel, he looked up.

Jeremy was chasing John, both making a racket. John tripped, fell, and dropping his head on his knees started crying. "Mommy,"

Jeremy stopped beside him. "Sorry."

Getting to his feet, Mathew walked towards them. "What happened?" He asked kindly as he noticed John's scratched knees.

"He chased me and I fell."

"And I'm sure he didn't do it on purpose. Come along, we'll go put some plasters on this."

"Me too." Jeremy held up a finger.

"Yes, let's go cover all the wounds." Mathew picked John into his arms, while Jeremy chattered beside him all the way up the stairs, and into the bathroom.

"How is that?" He asked as he cleaned and patched the small knees.

"Better." John announced happily.

"Let's wash the hands and face too. How do you get so dirty?"

"It comes naturally."

Mathew laughed. "Where did you hear that?"

"Mommy,"

"She's right. But it's also fun. Do you like coming here?"

Jeremy nodded. "Mommy can't play."

"Why not?" Mathew queried as he sat Jeremy next to the basin and busied himself washing the small hands.

"She reads books. And she cries."

"I think it's because she's very sad for grandpa." Mathew suggested.

"Like Uncle Jeremy and Uncle Simon."

"And Uncle Lawrence." Added John.

"That's right. Have you seen their photographs?"

"Yes."

"Good. One day I'll also show you grandpa William, and of course the Mercers."

"What's that?"

"Not what, who. They are grandma Grace's family."

"Are they dead?"

"Some of them. Okay, all done." He put them both down. "Come again when you have more accidents."

"Thank you, Uncle Mathew."

He grinned as they ran out the room.

"There you are," Carol said as the boys whizzed past her. 'I should have known."

"Needed something?"

"You promised to take me riding."

His hand flew to his temple.

"I know you forgot. Forty minutes and still no sign of you, I come looking and there you are, with her kids."

"What's wrong with them?"

"Nothing, except that they are hers and you are always around them."

"They needed a little mending."

"Then let her or someone else do it." She told him sharply.

"Are you jealous of her, or is it them?"

"Both and I no longer care if you know it."

"Then how about having one of our own?"

"Are you serious?"

"Why not?"

"I'll tell you why not. If we had kids, they wouldn't be like those two. Those are hers and John's. Yours and mine would be different, so stop dreaming."

"I have noticed for weeks that something is going on, only I have no idea what. Would it be too much to ask as to why you've been fermenting?"

"And then you'll hate me. Not that I blame you."

"What are you going on about?" He closed the door behind her.

"I have been trying to fall pregnant for the past six months."

"What?"

She gave a nervous laugh. "Now, I can stop imagining and trying."

"You're pregnant?"

"Perhaps then you would marry me, but I no longer want to fool myself. It's never going to happen, and it's all her fault. If she hadn't come, we might have stood a chance but with her here, you can't."

"She's my sister-in-law—"

"Isn't it all so interesting. Two of your former girlfriends married to two of your brothers. I should also go cry on Mark's shoulder and marry him. That way I too could join this curious group of women you Barrymore men are slowly collecting. We could be called Mathew's leftovers."

"All explanation I find for this ridiculous conversation is that you lost your mind. You tried to fall pregnant without my knowledge?"

"As if you were paying attention. And admit it, somewhere along the line you wished it would happen. I see the wistful looks, which is why we will never work. So, here's my deal, I'm infertile, barren, whatever you want to call it." She leaned against the door tiredly.

"How do you know?"

"I went for tests. Saw three doctors and all told me the same thing. If there's one thing Barrymores treasure above money and power it's children, but I can't produce the required quota. My fallopian tubes are shot to hell."

"Carol,"

"Don't say anything, it's only right I tell you now. And here's your ring." She deposited it in his hand. "I know where this relationship is going, nowhere. I'm sorry I deceived you, but I wanted to save this so-called engagement. Now I see what an impossible task I set myself. There was nothing to save because nothing ever existed. You have gone through the motions, but you were never in anything. Deny it all you like but you are a one-woman man, and she's not me.

"Your heart belongs to the mother of those little boys, who you wish were yours. I know because I never had it, and because I see it in your eyes every time you look at them and at her. That is why you adore them, because they are hers, not because they are your nephews. But now you do have a dilemma, as there is your brother to consider. Even if the gay rumours persist, and I've heard enough about that from all sorts of people, she is still a Stevens. Once, her name was enough to stop you, but now... What will stop you now?" She swung the door open and walked out.

He stood staring after her as she walked into her room. It crossed his mind to call her back, to go after her, to tell her that it didn't matter about the babies she had been trying to have for him. About to step outside his door, he saw Jessie at the end of the passage, two small figures appearing behind her.

"Mommy, look," John showed her the plasters.

"What happened?" She went down on her knees.

"I fell. It was very sore."

She kissed his face lovingly. "Poor baby. Good plaster work, who did it?"

"Uncle Mathew."

"Did you say thank you?"

"Yes."

"Me too, mommy." Jeremy showed her his finger.

Smiling, she kissed the fingertip. "Better?"

Both nodded and threw their arms around her.

James appeared around the corner. "Hey," he greeted with pleasure then feigned horror at seeing the boys. "Been at the wars again? I hear grandma calling, go see what she wants. And don't run in the house, you'll fall."

"Okay." They shouted and raced down the stairs.

James smiled. "I love those kids. Considering putting them up for sale?"

She made a tinkling sound. "You don't have enough."

He took her hand. "How's work?"

"Somewhat better since I followed your advice. But it's such minuscule difference I've barely noticed. Oh, and two resignations."

"You'll survive it." He looked around. "How about a walk? I need to discuss something."

"Sure. Warm enough?"

"Stop mothering me. That way." He pointed to the lift.

She ruffled his hair then straightened it again. "Yes, sir."

Mathew closed his mouth after the door and like a thunderbolt, Carol's words hit him; creating a jealous rush so intense, his heart began beating a wild tune. And indeed, this was a much larger predicament, because not only was she still a Stevens, but worse, a Barrymore as well. Aware of what he had lost, missed, and would never have again, he placed a trembling hand on his chest.

Bruce had some information. Martin Williams, the man who died with Taylor was a small-time dealer, who on occasion worked for Harry Stander. Once Narcotics got into his PC, there was enough evidence to establish that much. A kilogram of cocaine and a few packets of heroin also linked him, and the smart Alecs worked for a big shot named Peter Moss, whom Narcotics had had their eyes on for a while.

Unfortunately, Moss got himself killed by Murder and Robbery during a recent shootout. As Bruce explained, these people dealt in all sorts of things and one department didn't necessarily know what another was doing. Moss didn't only traffic in drugs but also in stolen goods, hence his eventual run-in with Murder and Robbery, and demise.

The hard work now was proving that Peter Moss had been involved in Taylor's death. Narcotics were sieving through his place and Bruce had seen a few suspicious entries on his computer. There were references to Harry and Martin and two initials that appeared a few times, ST. They could stand for anything but under the circumstances, chances were good that it was for Stevens Textiles. What they couldn't figure out was; if he was using Stevens for distribution, what was the motive for the killings? Was it blackmail, extortion, or something else altogether? And who had they been blackmailing, as Bruce would swear in any court of law that Taylor had never met the man.

Jessie asked. "If you can prove that Peter Moss was involved, and he's dead, will all this craziness end?"

"Yes and no," Bruce said. All danger to Stevens Textiles seemed to have ended but Narcotics had to continue following the drug trail, because the death of one drug-lord only meant career advancement for another. Shipments were still getting into South Africa, they just didn't know how. To follow the shambles to its successful conclusion, Bruce had to go.

Jessie shrugged, what was she supposed to say? She had already accepted that nothing would ever be easy again.

Beverley's second wedding was the opposite of the first; yet, Jessie saw now what had not been present before, an affinity between two people who truly belonged together.

When returning from their honeymoon, it seemed as if they had been together forever, as they connected and understood each other in ways Jessie had only seen in her grandparents.

Discreetly, they moved into a new house and Bruce returned to his original undercover work. Then, Beverley went about setting up a study and Jessie thought that apart from the file room at Stevens, she had never seen so much paper in one place.

"What on earth is all this for?" She asked curiously.

"I'm going to write."

"Never heard of computers?"

Beverley gave her an odd smile. "I need to take a lot of notes, do research, visit places, interview a bunch of people."

"I wondered when all that scribbling was going to catch up with you. Anything specific?"

"I'm going to uncover the story that needs telling."

"And what would that be?"

"The Barrymore-Stevens saga."

"What?" Jessie said in shock. "That's all we need, to lose everything else to the Barrymores… when they sue us for defamation. What possessed you?"

"All I want to do is set the record straight."

"You're crazy! You can't!"

"Says who? I'm sick and tired of unintelligible gossip and I refuse to have my daughter grow up in the shadow of something that happened decades ago, which is a mystery, but everyone whispers about anyway. There are already two from both sides, more might follow, is it fair on them? No ancient feud should keep our children from walking anywhere with pride. You, more than anyone, should appreciate what I'm trying to do."

"Will the Barrymores? They don't take kindly to criticism."

"Then I'll be extra careful and double-check every bit of information. No one is ever going to call a Stevens a thief or a liar again."

Looking at her sister, Jessie saw a determination that hadn't been there before. Who knew, perhaps the fruits of her labour would pay off.

"Jessie," Serena greeted as she reached the top of the stairs. "I was going to call but I'm glad I found you here. I've been thinking, why don't you and John move back to the house? There is so much space now that Beverley has moved here, and you are always rushing about; it would save a lot of trips with the boys, unless you want to take them to a nursery school. But I'd suggest getting them a private tutor first. Please discuss it with John."

"Thanks, mom, I will." She liked the idea, but John was another story altogether.

To her surprise, he agreed, under the condition that they did not sell the townhouse. Without opposition, she gave him the keys, somehow knowing that he was complying for reasons of his own.

CHAPTER EIGHTEEN

It was hard to see deeds people who had been at this game forever were committing behind her back, and instinct told her that it was a scheme to dispose of her. Although suspicions abounded, she had no proof. She knew it wasn't all of them but how did she differentiate between disdain and tolerance?

For hours on end, she thought, imagined, studied, and paged through files, manuals, statements, and memos. And at the end of each day, she stared at the mountains accumulated without success. If it hadn't been for James, she wouldn't even have been aware that something was wrong.

Like every Saturday, she sent the boys in search of their grandfather, then running up the stairs, she knocked on the door.

"You!" Vanessa hissed.

"Hello to you too." Jessie smiled. "Is James in?"

"Shameful hussy, have you absolutely no remorse?"

"Excuse me?"

"He's crippled, damn you. All I have."

"What—"

"You are determined to destroy everything, aren't you?" Vanessa screamed. "I hate you, how I hate you."

Grace stopped in her tracks as she came down the passage and Mathew opened the study door to see why the woman was in hysterics.

"Will you calm down and tell me what I'm supposed to have done?"

Vanessa snorted. "You poisoned my husband against me."

"And how did I do that?"

"Nothing has been the same since you've become friends. Talks about you nonstop and refuses to try. Damn you, Stevens, you made every man in this family fall in love with you. Aunt Monica is so right; you are a witch, weaving magic over every Barrymore male."

Concerned, Jessie took a step towards her.

Vanessa put her hands up. "Don't come any closer, lest you contaminate me. I gave up everything and now, I'm stagnating. I have nothing; no career to speak of, and soon, no husband." She accused. "And stop this miss pretence act, because you are a liar. But I caught you out. James regrets the past, not me." She turned to Mathew. "We were good together, weren't we? but then..." she swung on Jessie again. "The witch came along and all of you fell under her spell. It's aberrant because you never liked Carol or me this much." The green eyes flashed in Grace's direction.

"Vanessa,' Grace tried to intervene.

'Only, sweet Stevens here couldn't hold onto John tight enough and he chose her brother," Vanessa laughed merrily. "So, she ran to Mathew, and his bed, turning his head in such a way I could barely recognise him. How was she, better than me? And after your gay brother..."

"Don't talk about things you know nothing about."

"Hell, Mathew, men are fools."

"You have no right to speak about Jessie this way."

"I can say whatever I like, I'm part of this family." Vanessa looked around. 'By the way, where is your queer husband? Absent again? I wonder why. And there comes the other one." She pointed to Mark. "The one who lusts after her like a wild beast in heat,"

"W-what?" Mark asked perplexed.

"Don't feign ignorance, you're just like the others."

"What's going on?" James queried as he appeared from the lift.

"Don't deny it, I saw the divorce papers." Vanessa yelled. "You want her."

Surprise spread on his face. "Good God, Vanessa, how does your mind work?"

"You're always talking, whispering, laughing... you're in love with her."

"And you are mad. I do want a divorce, but not because of her, because of you. I am deeply embarrassed to admit that my love for you made me blind once, but no more. You are cunning, conniving, and cruel, and I will not let you destroy anyone else. We were mean and calculating and I no longer want to be your peon, because that is what you do with your murmurs."

"Murmurs, what murmurs? It's what I see. You're ruining me, stripping me of everything I am, and I hate you. I've had enough of all of you. Barrymores indeed, bunch of nutjobs."

"Well, what are you waiting for? pack your bags and go. Go prey on someone else, not on Jessie, my brother, and definitely not on my nephews. Don't think I haven't seen how you constantly entice them into dangerous situations; down the banister, into the dam... What the hell, trying to get rid of them?"

"You saw wrong." Vanessa defended hotly.

"That's not all I saw but we'll leave it there. Thankfully, both have more sense than you give them credit."

"All your heads have been turned."

James put a hand up. "Enough."

"What I've had enough of is this sick family." Before anyone could stop her, Vanessa pushed the wheelchair down the passage, where it overturned and fell down the stairs.

There were wheels, blankets, James, and Mark racing after him.

"I'm okay." James said and getting to his feet with Mark's help, took two steps and leaned against the wall.

"This is your doing." Vanessa ran towards Jessie.

"Don't you dare." Mathew warned as he pulled Jessie into his arms.

Vanessa turned to James. "You can't walk, you're a cripple."

"Sorry to disappoint, dear, but I have been able to do so for a while already. Which is how I discovered what you were up to."

Turning on her heels furiously, Vanessa went back into the bedroom and slammed the door shut.

"Oh, James," Grace cried as she embraced him.

Disentangling herself from Mathew's grip, Jessie disappeared down the stairs.

"See what happens in life?" Grace said. "Things are not always what they seem. Was Jessie's crime so serious that she had to be ostracised?" Then she followed Mark, who was helping James back into the wheelchair.

Mathew grabbed Jessie's discarded bag, walked to her room, and tossed it onto the table. He stared at the bed and closed his eyes. Her hair spilled over the pillows, her eyes burned, and he could feel her touch on his skin. How she had loved him then. Why couldn't he forget? Turning, he saw some of the boys' toys. John had everything in the world.

"There you are. Are you okay?" James asked as he reached the boulder near the willow.

"I'll recover." Jessie told him. "But what are you doing out here? You should get an electric chair—for Vanessa. But I meant an electric wheelchair."

"I've ordered one. Sorry I frightened you," he glanced at her fondly. "I meant to have it out with her privately but when she started on the past, it hit me what a ruckus she likes to create."

"And I find it hard to believe that anyone would purposely endanger children's lives." Giant tears filled her eyes.

"I apologise for that because it might have been my fault. As things stand my chances of fathering children are practically nil, so unless Mathew and Mark produce their own sons, the boys will become my heirs. She was secretly gloating because now I can't point fingers. But I can because I should have had them before the accident. That would have made it more bearable. She robbed me." He announced bitterly and gazed over the water. "But this is where we find ourselves. So, I've decided to follow your advice and go away for a while. Naturally, she thought I meant to take her but when I told her I had no intention of doing so, she went ballistic."

"Surely you're not going alone…"

"Oh, no, not alone. As everyone discovered today, I can already stand for minutes at a time, so I no longer need a burly nurse to carry me around. Miss Vidal is a wonderful companion, with immense patience, and a treasure-trove of amazing tales. A well-travelled young woman too. Did you know that she's half-French?"

"With a name like Antoinette Vidal, what else could she be? Where will you go?"

"As if there is a shortage of places, it's just that you are far too busy to even think of them. I've decided on a cruise."

"Won't you pine for Barrymores?"

"The one good thing about this accident is that sense was knocked into me. I'm not a leader, Mathew is."

Jessie nodded as her thoughts wandered. Yes, Mathew, her sons' father, the man she adored with all her heart, and who once loved her. Now, he had other things on his mind, and by the sound of it, a whole lot more was coming.

"Where does your mind go?"

She made a dismissive gesture. "I'll miss you."

"Years ago, had anyone said that we would be close friends, I'd have said they were off their rockers. What is it with love, why does it make people do such crazy things?"

"You don't have to tell me."

"The one thing I do regret is that I won't be able to help you, because you can't struggle like this. Please promise that you will hire someone."

"I'll see." She glanced away. "Thank you for looking out for my sons."

"It was my duty. Oh, for goodness sake, kiss me and be done with it."

Bending over him, she kissed his cheek.

All I Ever Wanted   Jessie   Athina Paris

Deliberately, he took her chin and almost pressed his lips against hers. "Vanessa was right on one count, you do have strange powers over the Barrymore men." He watched the blue eyes intently, looking for things that might exist. He smiled, having his answer. As much as he liked her, she was not the one. "May I keep in contact with you while I'm away?"

"I would be hurt if you didn't."

James looked up. "Hi, Mark, coming out for fresh air?"

"Rather cold out here." Mark noticed. "Actually, father is looking for you." Then turning around, he walked back.

Reaching the front of the house, James commented. "Interesting, Mathew is up a tree."

Jessie glanced at the red kite floating in the wind.

"More than ever, I see what chaos I created. John doesn't even pretend to act like a married man, is never here, and when we ask as to his whereabouts you hardly know the answer. What kind of marriage is that?"

"One that suits us fine." She said, staring into the distance.

The following week, Antoinette Vidal moved into the room next to James', so she could familiarise herself with his more personal habits, relieving the male nurse who had handled all those needs during the night.

Jessie noticed with pleasure that she never took nonsense or an excuse, and yet there was gentleness in everything she did. Then, she also knew something no one else did, and went around the house smiling smugly to herself.

And through it all, both Mathew and Mark watched her with fascination. Both wondering why she still managed to look happy. Only sometimes, when she thought no one noticed, sadness filled her eyes.

Now she was positive someone was up to something. But what was it they were doing, who was doing it, and how did she unearth her suspicions? A knock at the door disturbed her thoughts. In exasperation, she threw the file into the corner. "Come in."

"Mrs Barrymore," the attractive secretary stood awkwardly inside the office and closed the door. "Huh, I don't know, what I mean is—"

"Don't feel embarrassed, Miss Fischer, when do you want to leave?"

"Oh, no, that's not why I'm here," Miss Fischer said quickly. "But as I said, I don't quite know how to tell you..."

"They say honesty is the best policy, I have found it to be devastating."

"Mrs Barrymore, I worked for your father close to seven years and my loyalty to him and this company is absolute. I believe everyone deserves a chance, but that is not what you're getting. I don't want to resign like some of the others, those who have nothing further to gain by staying, because it seems it has come to that. I know this doesn't mean much, as I rank nowhere in importance, but I am here to tell you that you have total support from me.

"I see you struggle every day, wondering who is doing what and why. I sense it too, and it's disgraceful. I know about the offer they made your father, but he hoped Jeremy would change his mind. I saw how upset they were when he refused point-blank to sell, and later, their smugness when he had no choice but to delegate responsibilities as he simply could not cope, and then actually dividing 40% among them, giving them more power than they deserve. Now, it seems it has all gone to their heads.

"You were thrown into a hornet's nest and being young, they think they have a good case for outsmarting you. You need help, Mrs Barrymore, good help, and I am sorry to say that you won't find it within these walls. My knowledge is limited but I do know most of our customers. It's a pity I don't know more because they need to be taught a hard lesson."

"Thank you, Miss Fischer. You have no idea how long I have waited for someone, anyone, to say those words, but as you see, this is what we've come to, me against them."

"It's mutiny."

"Very well put and my feelings exactly. Unfortunately, they are right, I'm simply ignorant."

"I know some consultants, should we try a few until you find the right one?"

"Not yet. First, I am going to figure out what this is." Bending over, Jessie picked the file from the floor. "Do you know someone named Clive Richmond?"

"Yes, but he doesn't work here anymore, he emigrated to Canada just last month."

And then she knew how they planned to destroy her. Clive Richmond had taken a million Rand of her father's hard-earned money and abandoned the sinking ship. She had read and memorised manuals, but never considered taking a closer look at the contracts that landed on her desk. Stupidly, she had put her signature to papers she should not have touched.

Miss Fischer told her it wasn't creative doctoring but a blatant crime; but much good it did them knowing it, he was gone, and she was never seeing that cash again.

She called Beverley to hear if Bruce was available because she needed a professional's advice, wanting to know how to go about pressing charges. He was out of the country, embroiled in undercover work again. It was a fact, troubles multiplied.

"Is James around?"

"No, honey, Miss Vidal took him out." Grace announced then added. "I'm so pleased you told him to hire her."

"I had a small influence."

Grace smiled. "Hardly, he takes everything you say very seriously."

"He shouldn't, or I'll make an awful blunder, just as I'm doing with the rest of my life. I have so many problems I no longer know what to do about any. Where did they go?"

"She asked what he wanted to do before leaving for Durban on Monday and he told her he wanted to visit old friends. With Vanessa gone, he has become a new person."

"I'm glad. Is it my imagination or is the house extremely quiet?"

"Theo and the boys are at the Newtons, they've just had a new foal. Mark is in Cape Town and only due back in a couple of days. I'm also on my way to the Newtons, but Mathew is here. Do you mind being left alone?"

"It suits me fine, I have work to do. Enjoy the foal." Waving, she ran up the stairs.

She had known there was a rough road ahead, what she could not handle was that to prove herself, repeatedly, she would have to fight criminals among the men who had once called themselves her father's friends. Grabbing the briefcase, she left the room, walked down the passage, and lifted her hand. She stopped. "What am I doing?"

The door opened. "Jessie!" Mathew said surprised.

For a second she was transported to the past. Only this time, she was before him without tears. Who was she kidding, with their track record, she would be shedding those pretty soon. "If you don't want to I'll understand, but please help, I desperately need a professional's advice."

"Huh, come in," he closed the door behind them. "What is this about?"

She opened the briefcase, took out a few files, and stuffed them in his hands. "This."

"I can't see these, it's unethical." He told her in shock.

"Damn ethics. You know me, I'm no business person. Given the chance I may be, but that is not today. So far, I've lost Stevens over a million rand; know why? I have no idea what I'm doing." She announced. "And they are doing it on purpose. They want me out and this is the devised scheme. How much must I lose before they are satisfied? Five, ten, or how about total bankruptcy?"

He eyed her quizzically. "Even you couldn't lose that kind of money."

"No?" She pulled a thick file from his hand. "This deal; there are no suppliers, the factory closed seven months ago, only I didn't know it. This one; I was sold junk we don't use, for the highest price they could get. And this one; the same smart Alec skipped the country. I understand the wording, because it all sounds right, but I have no idea who these people are, where the places are on the planet, or even if they exist. Which is why, Mr Clive Richmond had no problem singing praises to some Indonesian silk producer—that never was—and then hopped on a plane to Canada.

"Do you see what's happening?" She sat on the sofa tiredly. "Mathew, you know this, probably even deal with the same people." She pointed to a few files. "I need to know if those are swindles, if I'm being taken in again, for how much, and by whom. I may have no right to do so, but I am begging, please help me. Once, the Barrymores wanted us ruined, and perhaps still do, but this is so much worse; my own people are doing it."

"Do you know how much trouble—"

"I don't care. They are not going to make a fool out of me, even if I am one. And now I dread to think what else I signed that's going to blow up in my face."

His eyes fixed on the blue ones that stared suppliantly at him. "How can I know if anything is amiss unless I have inside information? It could take weeks."

"Would you, please?" She pulled some disks from the briefcase.

"God… they are going to throw us both in jail." A faint smile crossed his lips as he sat beside her. "Have you given this idea any thought at all?"

"I have no one else. John wants none of Stevens, Bruce is out of the country. And I can't ask your father or Mark, they'll think I've gone bananas, and it's possible I have, or at least on my way. If I go to lawyers, all they can tell me is that everything sounds legal. I know that! I'll even pay you."

"Then they'll really lock us up." He stood a moment then sat down again. "Okay, I will have a look at these, phone around, and give you my honest opinion. After that, it's up to you." The fact was that he couldn't say no because over the last few months, she had crept back into his heart, and although knowing that he could not touch, he still wanted to be close. As unorthodox as this insane idea was, it would surely guarantee it. Talk about irony, he was doing exactly what Vanessa had done. Then a thought struck him. Was she setting him up?

"Thank you, Mathew. You don't know how much this means to me."

"Let's get started then." An hour later, he glanced at her and asked. "Why do you have so many?"

"I was afraid to sign anything else."

"How did you know something was wrong?"

"I thank James for that. He suggested I try learning something from those endless manuals. If I hadn't I wouldn't have been suspicious. These people come into my office, tell me how wonderful, what great deals we are about to strike, heaven knows what else, and point to the dotted line, which is what Clive Richmond did. Made himself a neat bundle and is long gone. And I wasn't the least bit surprised to discover that he was Lawrence's friend. Did you know my brother stole from Stevens?"

"I heard rumours but wasn't sure."

"It's true. Daddy confronted him the day he died." Her mind went into the world of memories. How many lies she told. She didn't blame him if he never forgave her. "He gambled his fortune away. Grandma always said he carried a giant chip on his shoulder. How's that for a pun?"

"Remarkable." He glanced at a contract in his hand and turned the page. "Do you know a man called Booysen? He's representing…" He flicked through a few pages. "Ink Processors Inc. Do you print a paper or newsletter on the premises?"

And she heard how far her incompetence stretched. Feeling the blood drain from her face, she listened to Mathew tell her that someone was trying to embezzle two hundred thousand Rand, that it was even possible that Clive Richmond had left a partner in his stead. He suggested she hand him over to the police.

"I intend to, as soon as my police friend returns."

"You have a friend in the police?"

"Don't look surprised, I do know other people apart from our families."

"Naturally." What she didn't know was that he was jealous. "What division?"

She couldn't jeopardise Bruce's efforts, so she lied. "Murder and robbery."

"I suppose you met him after your dad… How is the investigation going?"

"The culprit is apparently dead, but the police are still trying to get some of his pals."

"And I hope they catch them." He had nightmares when listening to the stories people told. If someone was intent on wiping out Stevens Textiles, did he mean her harm too?

"What else is going on in there?"

"Everything looks fine." He pushed his fingers through his hair. "This one," he pointed to a blue folder. "It's a good deal. I know these people and they are tough. So," he smiled. "They either like you or you have a good man working for you. But this one," he searched for another folder. "They are ripping you off. Call them Monday and tell them you are going over to Barrett Mills. They will either drop their price by at least twenty percent or you cancel. Stand your ground, Jessie, don't let them do this to you."

"If I knew what I'm supposed to be doing then there wouldn't be a problem, would there? But I don't. The advice I get is for their benefit, not Stevens." She got to her feet.

"Get someone you trust."

"The only person I trust is James but he's on his way to a new life, and I'm very glad for him. There is my secretary, but her knowledge is also limited. Thank you, Mathew." Leaning over, she dropped a feather-light kiss on his brow.

"It sure was odd."

She went to glance out the window. "Who knows, you might just save Stevens." Then taking a deep breath, she turned, smiled, and let herself out of his room.

He put a hand to his head. "What the blazes am I doing?"

Later, he found her in the pool. Diving effortlessly, he swam towards her. "Where's John?"

"Somewhere, do you need him?"

"No. Doesn't this almost constant absence bother you?"

"He has a right to a private life."

"Without you and the kids," his brows lifted. "But even they aren't fazed. Have you always lived like this?"

"We just have different interests."

"Everyone does but yours seem to be more pronounced than most."

"It suits us. Want to race?"

"I'll beat you this time."

"Don't be too sure. Ready, go."

As predicted, he won.

She merely laughed, punched his arm, said well done, and then asked. "So, what is your prize?"

He wondered if she knew what a glance from her did. *"I'm losing my mind."* She was sending him on an emotional rollercoaster and he doubted he'd survive the ride, as a derailing was already eminent. He stared at the scar on her shoulder. How could this be the most intense aphrodisiac he had ever experienced? If he leaned just so… *"Get a grip!"*

"No prizes today, see you later." He told her and walked out of the water.

"Miss Fischer," she said Monday morning. "These contracts can be returned, these I want to study, and this one… I won't say it. Now, I must go. Anyone asks where I am, tell them…" she looked at the plants in the corner. "Tell them I'm at the hair salon, tomorrow, a facial, and so on. Give them any excuse you wish."

"Yes, ma'am."

The truth began to emerge in bits and pieces, and she seethed with anger at her lack of business sense. They had known she was a greenhorn and taken her for the ride she deserved. No more. As Mathew suggested, she did. True, if any of the family members became reluctant to vote with her, she would lose it all anyway, but at least she could say that she had tried and gone down fighting.

She went out on daily excursions and met as many of their suppliers and clients as she could in the Johannesburg area, hardly spending an hour every morning in the office. She wondered what Miss Fischer told them. When she returned in the afternoons, she collected the post, documents, and new contracts. At first, nothing much took place, but then the interesting messages arrived, written ones, on the answering machine, and two more resignations.

Jessie paced to the window then glanced at her watch. Four hours since John had left with Mark and the boys for hamburgers. Where had they gone, Pretoria? She couldn't concentrate on anything Mathew said.

This had become a regular get-together; she brought files, he looked them over, and gave his opinion. Decisions were up to her.

He rubbed her shoulders. "Relax woman, you are like a tightly wound up clock. Anyway, I still have reservations about paying this much for wool."

"I'll check it out. Thanks." Turning, she left his room.

Something about her anxiety unnerved him and standing on the balcony, he watched her walk down the driveway. Her phone rang, she answered it, and the next minute she was running towards the house.

"What happened?" He asked, meeting her halfway down the stairs.

"Huh, John… they've been in an accident."

Things became a blur, and she was certain Mathew broke a few speed limits, but somehow, they reached the hospital.

"This way." A nurse guided.

She followed blindly, barely aware that Mathew held her hand. There lay John, deathly white, one arm and a leg bandaged. Mark, on the other bed, had two nasty stitched cuts on his brow and dark bruises to his face. "What have you done to yourselves? Where are my sons?"

"One is fine and will just stay overnight for observation." The doctor said. "It's the other one we are concerned about."

"What's wrong?"

"He needs a transfusion and both your husband and brother-in-law are unsuitable due to shock." The doctor looked from John to Mark.

"Use Mathew," John told him.

"What happened?" Jessie asked anxiously as she picked little John into her arms, cradling him lovingly. But Jeremy was as white as a bright summer moon. "Oh, God, his head."

"It's not serious, we've already x-rayed him, just a bump, and a scratch. But he received a gash on his arm and lost blood very quickly. Mr Barrymore, when you're ready."

She cried every time she looked at them. Unknowingly, he was saving his son's life and she deserved to be locked up because she was certifiable.

CHAPTER NINETEEN

It felt as if a cyclone hit her head on, one that twisted in a hundred directions, pulling, and tearing her apart. Going to work was akin to going to practice trapeze at the circus—without nets. Only Miss Fischer and Mathew kept her sane.

She glanced at a pile of posters on the back seat of her car. The chain-store people were coming Monday, what could she promise?

"Come in." Mathew invited as she stood in the hallway outside his apartment. "What brings you here?"

"All I want today is someone to talk to. Oh, you might be going out… Sometimes, I don't think."

"No. Have you eaten?"

"My appetite is disappearing fast. Just like my mind."

"You work too hard. I need to check dinner." Seeing she was about to offer help, he told her. "I've got this, sit and unwind."

"Thank you." Flopping onto the sofa, she kicked her shoes off and noticed that hardly anything had changed. Smiling sadly, she realised Maria Mena played softly in the background; an artist she had discovered while in London.

He shook her lightly. "Jessie, come eat."

They spoke mostly about the children and she felt the cruel daggers lodge themselves in her wretched heart.

Returning to the lounge, he asked. "Is there anything you would like me to see?"

"It sounds as if you look forward to my intrusions. But no work, except, there is a presentation. I could have hired an agency, and I'm sure they would do a better job, but it's creative, so I got an idea. I want our customers to understand that I do have a brain."

"Let's hear it."

"One of the chain-stores wants to produce good quality linens and needs to know if Stevens is able to handle the task," she reached into the folder.

He grabbed a colourful poster. "These are great."

She gave him a quick version of her idea. "…what do you think?"

"Wish you worked for me. What made you think of this?" He pointed to the pictures.

"I was driving on the highway and it just hit me."

"It's wonderful, they'll be hooked."

She placed a hand on her neck. "Thanks, I appreciate your encouragement."

"Sit, I'll rub those tight muscles."

She wanted to protest; instead, she did as he bade, closing her eyes as he massaged where it hurt. After a few minutes, she turned to him. "I know that things between us are just about beyond repair and I wouldn't presume to solve everything with a mere conversation, because that is simply impossible. But we are speaking to each other, when I thought we never would. It's years late but I apologise for causing you so much pain." She touched his face gently. "What I'm really saying is that if you forgive me, I might have this burden lifted from my heart for being so mean to you. I'm sorry for lying, ruining what we had, and however far off it may be, I do look forward to the day when you and I might be friends again."

"We should have talked then, but I was beyond upset. All I kept thinking was how deceitful you were, and what you were after. Of course, it wasn't like that, but I didn't understand. I too am sorry for the way I treated you. I let you down when you deserved so much better from me."

Oh goodness, no, not that song; the one she had cried thousands of tears to. Scrambling to her feet, unsteady hands threw all papers together. To her horror, her eyes filled to brimming. Avoiding looking at him, she turned to leave. "Huh… I'll see you tomorrow."

He too got to his feet. "What's wrong?"

"Nothing,"

Reaching her, he turned her around. "Did I say something?"

She shook her head, feeling the tears roll down her face. She had to say something if she wanted to get out of here. "Huh… the song."

"You know it?"

She nodded. "I hate it."

"And you cry?"

"I have to go." She gulped as the stupid chorus travelled around the apartment, reviving the time when she needed his comfort and love.

After closing the door, he went to the hi-fi to restart the song and looped it, while staring at the car keys she had forgotten on the coffee table. He wondered between here and the ground floor where she would realise she didn't have them. But what if she called a taxi? No, she was coming back; he knew she was.

Okay, they had finally apologised to each other. When she returned, things would be different.

The knock was soft, hesitant, and afraid.

With purposeful steps, he went to the door and swung it open.

"I… I forgot my keys."

"You can't go anywhere like this." Pulling her inside, he closed the door behind them again.

Finding herself in the circle of his arms was more than she could endure, and damn Maria Mena, why was she still playing her daft song?

"Jessie," he murmured. "I do forgive you, anything, everything, always." Then he chose not to kiss her; instead, he picked her up into his arms and took her to the bedroom.

They stood silently for a moment then began undressing each other. When their mouths met, and their bodies touched, neither needed words. Eyes bright with desire, their arms wrapped and entwined, wanting the elixir of the other. There were no protestations of love that night, merely the flow of physical need between two bodies that had missed each other. Then they slept in each other's arms, just as they had done so many times before.

"What an eternity," she thought. But where did they go from here now that they had been satiated? Was this all he had been after? Turning on her side, she studied him in the soft light, and caressed his cheek.

"Jessie," he called sleepily.

She kissed his brow, then getting out of bed, dressed, and left.

Waking slowly, he reached for her; the bed was empty. Snapping his eyes open, he stared at the indentation left on the pillow. He rolled over and laid his head on it, becoming intoxicated with its scent.

On his way to the estate, his brother's face made some appearances, which he instantly pushed aside. "Where's John?" Was his first question to Grace.

"You should know by now that they hardly ever come together. I don't know if I should worry but neither seems disturbed by the arrangement. Does he talk to you?"

"Sometimes." He passed a hand over his hair. "Is Jessie around?"

"Upstairs."

He saw her before she saw him, and he thought no woman could be more beautiful. "Hello," he grinned, took a quick look around, pecked her lips, and disappeared into his room.

Over lunch, Mark remarked. "This is a welcome change. I thought you would never smile again and I didn't see Carol's departure as particularly traumatic."

"Saw her the other day, she's moving somewhere."

"That's you all right big brother, breaking women's hearts constantly. They have no idea what they're up against when they meet you, do they?"

"What do you mean?"

"You ask that a lot, sure you want an answer?"

"Here we go again. I never understand the innuendoes."

"That's because you don't really pay attention. Know what grandma said about people who don't pay attention?"

"I didn't get her either. Just use plain language with me, I hate riddles."

"I'll remember that. Now, please excuse me, I have someone to visit." Mark announced.

Grace had given Jessie carte blanche to explore the house to her heart's desire, so every evening she was over and Mark was out, she explored one room, enjoying connecting with the beautiful furnishings. She was in a magnificent dining room when she got a call. James was in Paris.

He and Miss Vidal had been to see two specialists and a glimmer of hope was starting to shine. He was walking better every day, would regain potency, but the ability to produce children, most likely, never.

She felt like crying as she listened to him but chose to control herself, so he wouldn't become despondent. And to divert his mind, she asked about Miss Vidal again.

"Toni is a truly amazing woman; knowledgeable, never boring, and so very kind. I'm glad she's the one keeping me company. But so damn proper... the stubborn female won't let me buy her expensive gifts."

Jessie smiled, first name basis had to be a good sign. And he was trying to buy her gifts?

"What?" She asked in confusion, as both Grace and Mathew stared at her when she entered the salon.

"That expression on your face." Mathew explained.

"Oh, I was talking to a friend."

"That's nice." Grace said. "Jessie, why isn't John here? If I didn't go to Barrymores occasionally, I would never see him. Put your foot down and say enough or he will become a stranger to the boys."

"They understand he's busy."

"They are little and need a father."

Jessie looked away. "Where did Mark go?" She hated talking about anything remotely personal when Mathew watched her that way.

"He didn't say but he goes out a lot nowadays. Perhaps there's a girl."

"I should be so lucky." "I'll go for a swim and then to bed. Goodnight."

Shivers ran up her spine as she saw him at the water's edge.

Diving into the pool, his head surfaced inches from hers, and reaching out, his mouth travelled over the wet skin and the small scar on her shoulder. "Why did I let you go?" He moaned. "How I regret letting Vanessa come between us and igniting our festering hate. Don't you see, when you left, you took my very soul with you."

CHAPTER TWENTY

Now that all schemes were revealed, removed, and handed over to the police, work was accomplished, and as a bonus, no nasty surprises lurked on her desk. But as that part of her life improved, another deteriorated. She was feeling sick again.

"Are you okay?" John stared at the pale face one morning.

"Not particularly. I feel positively drenched."

"You don't look capable of handling anything."

She sipped her tea. "I'd much rather stay."

"Then do and call the doctor. What did you eat yesterday?"

"A tuna sandwich. It wouldn't surprise me if they were going for poison now."

He chuckled. "You do dramatize. And I'm sure they are not all bad. That guy you've been seeing seems to give you good advice."

"Which I doubted in the beginning. Aren't you going to work?"

He gave her a crooked smile. "Secrets again. Please be careful."

Days later, she knew there was one certainty; she was a master at complicating her life. That evening, John found her sitting quietly in their private garden.

"It wasn't food poisoning," she told him as she poured two glasses of juice. "I'm pregnant."

He was visibly shocked. "How the... I mean... The guy you've been seeing? Crap, Jessie, why didn't you take precautions?"

"Because I'm an idiot, and he obviously assumed I was."

"Are you in love? What about Mathew? I know he is with you."

"It is Mathew."

He choked and spurted the drink all over the ground.

"I needed help after James left. True, he didn't do much, but he steered me in the right direction. The fool that I am, signed everything that landed on my desk and we know what that caused. I was desperate, so I begged Mathew for help, not even caring if he took advantage. Better him than those piranhas. He thought I was setting him up—told me the other day—and went along. Then one day... He's guilt-ridden, going through hell, but I'm such a horrible person that I can't bring myself to tell the truth."

"Half-free is also half-dead. Tell him nothing, unless you absolutely must. In the meantime, I'm moving back to the townhouse."

"What do I tell everyone?"

"That I'm designing something top secret."

"The boys will miss you."

"I'll see them Sundays, I'll come over for lunch." He reached for her hand on the table. "How will you cope, it's hard enough as is. Please admit that you are not superwoman and go slow, even at work. And have a bed put in."

"Imagine what they'll say about that."

"But you won't care. I'm serious, Jessie, take it easy. You are always worked up and it can't be good for the baby. Now, go sleep and I will make sure you get breakfast in bed from tomorrow. No more coffee and easy on the ice cream."

"That's funny," she grinned. "I can't even smell it without wanting to puke my guts out."

Jessie studied the report. Whether Mathew knew it or not, he was running Stevens Textiles. Years ago, the mere concept would have been inconceivable. Picking up the phone, she dialled her sister and made a lunch appointment.

"How's Bruce?" She asked as soon as they sat down.

"Still away, do you need him?"

"No, and I'm glad to report there are no problems. Mom and grandma should be pleased, they must have thought this was the end."

"I can't say I'd feel sorry about it. And there's something I need to tell you about that."

"But… why?" Jessie asked ten minutes later.

"Because I want no fifteen, no one, no half a percent of anything, so you will be getting papers from the lawyers. That place scares me and look how much heartache it has already caused…" Beverley stopped and fixed her gaze somewhere above Jessie's head. "You won't believe who just walked in."

"Vanessa?" Jessie made a face. "Ugh."

The shameless female stopped by their table and traded something disguised as pleasantries, which were anything but, because some barbs just stuck their ugly heads out, and both Jessie and Beverley felt like decking her.

Then, as they were leaving, they ran into Mathew. It had to be a coincidence, but it also made Jessie feel apprehensive and jealous.

"Taking a break?" She asked.

He smiled. "Meeting my cousin Dennis."

Jessie nodded, recalling having seen the man in James' hospital room a few times, and John had also met with him on occasion. Still, Vanessa was here and no one knew how to benefit from a coincidence as well as she, or twist and concoct stories.

For the next two weeks, John took the boys to the estate, as she tried to catch up on much needed rest and battled waves of nausea and fainting spells, and in all that time, she neither saw nor called Mathew, the daggers of jealousy tearing at her heart and the morning sickness the rest.

"Mrs Barrymore," Miss Fischer's voice came over the intercom. "Mr Mathew Barrymore is here to see you."

"What?" She jumped startled. "Huh, let him in."

He closed and locked the door behind him. "Why haven't I seen you in weeks?"

"What... I mean... why are you here?"

He reached her quickly.

"Mathew," she whispered as they fell onto the sofa in a frantic rush.

"Why haven't you been to the house or the apartment?"

"I was going tomorrow."

"That's tomorrow. What about all these days, not even a call."

"Did you call?" She asked curiously.

"A dozen times, but you were never here or couldn't be disturbed. I called the house twice, but Samuel said you had already retired. Do you even look at your cell phone?"

"I'm exhausted. That's why I had this brought in." She explained. "Please get dressed before one of my executives wants to see me."

"Are you doing this on purpose, to see how much I want you?" Getting to his feet, he slipped his pants on. "Okay, here it is. I want you so much I'm losing my mind. I'm tired of waiting for the bits you can spare because I want you always. John is my brother, but I loved you first and I want you back. Do you understand? I want you forever. I want you, Jessie, like we should have been."

"What if one day I'm kicked out of your parents' house? Will you still want me then? I never want to make you choose."

"It will never happen."

"You don't know that, and I don't want to put it to the test."

"Sshh," he said softly. "I didn't mean I might never have to choose, I meant they will never separate us. I love you too much to let anyone break my heart that way again."

"Once, you also promised to love me forever."

"Once, I made a dreadful mistake and paid dearly for it. If you want John, I'll leave, but no woman ever got inside me as you have, and it has become my reason for living."

She caressed his face. "Do you realise that everyone in this building already knows that the wrong Mr Barrymore is in my office?"

"Perhaps I should come around more often."

"Imagine you appearing at one of our meetings."

"Do you want me to?" He walked to the window. "I like it here, probably because I know it so well. I'm just not sure how father would react."

"Are you afraid of him?"

"Not anymore. He needs me more than I do him and perhaps that's what finally gave me the courage to let go. If I found myself without a job, would you give me one?"

"Are you serious?" Her blue eyes watched him with amazing intensity.

"Absolutely,"

Straightening his tie, she smiled and pressed her lips against his. "I'll see you tomorrow."

"Mommy,"

"Sweetheart," she answered weakly, as she leaned against the car. "Get daddy. Huh… Uncle Mathew."

Both stormed into the house. "Uncle Mathew."

"Boys, boys, why are you running?" Mark asked as he reached the entrance hall.

"Uncle Mathew." Jeremy told him breathlessly and carried on up the stairs.

"Mommy fell." John panted.

"Where?"

"In the garage."

Finding her unconscious, Mark picked her up, delighting in the feeling for a moment. "John, run upstairs and open the bedroom door." As the boy disappeared, he pressed her closer, leaned forward, and took in her scent. It was the very idea of heaven, to have her against his body without a struggle.

"W-what happened?" Jessie moved on the bed.

"You are the one who passed out. Why?" Mark queried.

"I never had breakfast."

"You had anaemia before, what are you aiming for now?" Mathew asked crossly.

"Sorry I frightened you," she reached for the boys' hands. "Go find grandpa." She turned to Mark. "Thank you for your concern, but I'm fine now."

"It doesn't look like it." He watched the pale face. "How about some food?"

"Just toast and tea,"

"Okay, and don't move until they bring it up."

"Jessie," Mathew began anxiously as soon as they were alone. "Have you been ill?" He sat down on the bed and placed a hand on her hair.

"I'm not really sick, just tired."

"Then please rest and eat because I can't see you like this. Do you have a lot of work?"

"Two contracts I must go over."

"I'll do it." He grinned and got up. "In the meantime, deal with that."

Grace walked into the room. "How can you be so careless when you have such a hectic life? It's all bad habits. I must call your mother, so she can keep an eye on your eating."

"Not today," Jessie gave her a faint smile, feeling like a teenager. "She and grandma are planning a trip overseas, so they are visiting friends."

"Then why don't you come stay here?"

"It's too far from work."

"That's true." Grace looked pensive for a second. "If they are going away, who will look after the boys?"

"Beverley offered already, but I don't think it's fair. She's busy herself."

"That's settled then. As soon as they leave, the boys come here. And every Friday afternoon, I want to see you drive up that road. I suppose it's too much to ask what John will be doing." Grace glanced at the maid in the doorway and waved her in. "Toast and tea? Is this what you eat every morning?"

"Mostly,"

"Please look after yourself, honey, those little boys need you. Let's be realistic, John isn't much in the parent department."

"That's not true, he loves them very much." Jessie defended hotly.

"He does, but… I don't even know how to put it into words. It must just be his way."

Mathew was becoming progressively curious because anyone who had eyes could plainly see that she and John were not a couple but two people who cared about each other and flitted in and out of each other's lives. He was also becoming wise, the boys loved and trusted him, so they often told him things they shouldn't.

"So, it's just the two of you again?" he asked one evening as she visited at the apartment and told him Juliet and Serena had left. "I'm jealous."

"Please don't do this to yourself."

"I almost forgot," he announced. "I have a surprise. Close your eyes."

Laughing, she did.

"I asked a friend to bring it from London, your favourite."

Opening her eyes, she gave the ice cream a cursory glance. "Thank you, but I pass." Then pushing past him, she rushed to the bathroom.

"Jessie?" He stared in horror as she threw up dinner.

She sat on the edge of the bath. "Sorry, I should have mentioned…"

"What's wrong, sweetheart?" He knelt beside her.

"I can't eat or smell ice cream."

"But you love it."

She wobbled to her feet. "I need to lie down."

"Jessie," following her, he watched as she sank weakly onto the bed. "You are ill." Lying next to her, he smoothed the hair away from her face. "Please tell me."

She looked straight into his eyes. "I'm pregnant."

"Wh… are you sure?"

She nodded. "Do you mind very much?"

He stared at the ceiling. "How can you possibly know whose baby it is?"

"I do, I have slept with only one man in the past six months."

He sat up in bed, absorbing her words. "This is my baby?"

Her eyes filled with tears as she saw his. "Yours."

"God, Jessie, you have a lot of explaining to do if you haven't shared a bed. I'm sorry, but no husband tolerates this."

She shook her head and took his hand. "John knows."

"Seriously?"

"His one wish is for us to be happy."

"I don't understand, how does he simply accept it? He's so strange." Dropping his head on her stomach, he told her. "I'm so happy I want to cry. But work is too much, you get so sick."

"It's getting better."

Jumping off the bed, he rummaged in a drawer. "Close your eyes."

"No ice cream."

"In the drawer?" He laughed then took her hand and pointed to the wedding band. "How are we going to do this? I want to marry you."

"Are you sure?"

"Everyone was right. I don't want anyone but you."

She wiped her overflowing eyes. "I accept your ring but won't wear it, yet. It would be a bit of a thing if I appeared at the estate with it on my finger."

He sobered up somewhat. "You have always liked mysteries and it seems there is nothing I can do about it."

"The gentleman is displeased?"

"He merely gets confused but no longer cares. But I admit, life with you will never be boring."

"About the boys—"

"I promise I won't interfere and John can come and go as he pleases. And I'll do all the things he can't with them. It will be wonderful."

"Yes." A smile crossed her lips. She would tell him about the boys another time; there were enough surprises for today.

TO BE CONTINUED

Athina Paris lives in South Africa but spent her formative years in Mozambique, where she was born. Years in convents and boarding schools prompted a deep curiosity, which quickly developed into an avid interest in reading and storytelling and led to a lifelong obsession with the written word and books. By fifteen, she had discovered ancient civilizations and became fascinated with various mythologies; a love she has kept to this day.

She studied Interior Design then turned to Creative Writing and followed that with Scriptwriting.

She became a spectator of human nature, quiet and shy, she preferred recording conduct and so built a treasure-trove of observations from which she drew the plots and settings for her romantic novels.

Set in faraway and exotic places, Athina's romantic works take her characters on voyages of self-discovery while dealing with catastrophic love lives in an imperfect world.

A stint as a high school English teacher polished her skills, a position she has vacated to concentrate on her professional goals of writing, editing, and proofreading.

If you enjoyed reading this book, please leave a review and let Athina know.

Here are more titles by Athina:

 Love & Madness

 When Dani Smiled

 Knight Kisses

RockHill Publishing LLC

There are some lessons that only time can teach, but you do not learn talent, you only perfect it over time.

www.rockhillpublishing.com

www.ingramcontent.com/pod-product-compliance
Lightning Source LLC
Chambersburg PA
CBHW070740190726
48292CB00002B/356